CITY OF DARKNESS

CONTACT
THE
AUTHOR

TWITTER
@DPWright79

WEBSITE
www.dpwrightauthor.co.uk

EMAIL
dpwright.ni@gmail.com

FACEBOOK
www.facebook.com/DPWright79

CITY OF DARKNESS

D. P. WRIGHT

Matador
9 Priory Business Park
Kibworth Beauchamp
Leicestershire LE8 0RX, UK
Tel: (+44) 116 279 2299
Fax: (+44) 116 279 2277
Email: books@troubador.co.uk
Web: www.troubador.co.uk/matador

ISBN 978 1784622 534

British Library Cataloguing in Publication Data.
A catalogue record for this book is available from the British Library.

Typeset in Minion Pro by Troubador Publishing Ltd
Printed and bound in the UK by TJ International, Padstow, Cornwall

Matador is an imprint of Troubador Publishing Ltd

To Mum, Dad and Lilly –
my anchor when the clouds set in.

·CONTENTS·

·PROLOGUE·

He knew the shame would end within minutes. Deal with it. The sight of the needle, preparing its seductive payload over the flickering flame of his near empty lighter, holding it in place with a crumpled scrap of foil, the image had not lost its bite over the years.

He tried not to look at his surroundings and think about what he was doing, what he had become, but despite years of practice he still had not mastered that art. His sparse environment made haunting shapes as it danced in the flickering candlelight. The shadow's menacing macabre jig daring him, mocking him, laughing at him. Trying to force the decaying images of his current state out of his mind, the lonesome figure just tried to focus on what was soon to come. Escape.

The rec vent gave out a constant, deep monotonous hum in the background as it battled unsuccessfully to purify the stagnant air. However, for once, the thick pollution that ate away at his lungs, laden with its heavy acidic, metallic taste that always stuck at the back of the throat, was not on his mind.

The liquid bubbled. The sweet aroma crept through the room seeming to cling onto every surface. Watching the seductive smoke skip elegantly through the air, dipping under a chair and prancing over the couch, everything in slow motion, proved extremely hypnotic. Time had left this place, leaving the nervous man in the presence of this beautiful and deadly dance, caught completely in its graceful raptures.

The colour of the murky-brown sludge began to take on a reddish hue. Finally ready. Feeding it into the syringe he waved the needle over the candle. His hands were clammy and felt heavy, encumbered with fevered expectation, so he had to take extra care not to lose a drop of the precious liquid in his fumbling grasp. It was cold, although that was not why he was shaking. He could feel the hairs standing up on the exposed skin of his left arm. A sharp draft blew into the room from an old window behind him that had been cracked for as long as he could remember. He had gotten used to its methodical clatter as it rocked in its crumbling frame, the constant clank was reassuringly always there, reliable. It never went away. Someone was shouting something inaudible in the street outside and he could hear the intermittent frazzled buzzing of Hector's neon sign. Through the rush of the rain the sound of a girl crying crept into the room, although he could not be certain, his mind had been playing tricks on him of late and he had learnt not to trust his senses.

The slight prick of pain as the needle pierced his skin shocked him from his thoughts. Blood began to well out of the wound and a small streak of red formed down the length of his arm. With a discarded towel this was soon mopped up. The needle's bite was a reminder of what was to come. Forgetfulness. Happiness.

There it was…

'…missed you…'

The electric rush of numbness.

White light drenched his drab surroundings and waves of joy shot through his being, exploding from every pore, all building to a crescendo of complete…

…utter ecstasy.

Everything seemed so good…

…bright

…easy…

·THE BEGINNING·

The low, dim murmurings from whispered prayers were almost hypnotic. The few lonely souls that remained inside the chapel were knelt sparsely throughout the nave lost in their own prayers. Looking at their faces in the dim light, Father Jacob found the usual assortment of expressions. You could tell a lot about a person from looking at their face while they prayed. Some looked relaxed, with a slight smile breaking out in the corner of their mouths lost in the warm protection of the Lord, far away from the many troubles waiting outside these walls. Others had faces that twitched full of nervous energy unable, or not wanting to, leave their worries outside. Instead they carried their burdens with them and prayed to God to rid them of their misery. Finally, there were those that had faces which were easy to read, those whose souls were naked and vulnerable to the dangers that lurked in the dark. Weeping throughout their communion, sadness and agony etched across their faces, these poor souls looked to the heavens for some sort of relief from the agony of life, an agony that was quickly consuming them. Unfortunately these most agonised faces were the souls that most often graced St John's these days. It seemed happiness and joy were in short supply in these troubled times. Although he did feel pangs of guilt watching his parishioners so closely, intimately invading these peoples' lives during what was such a personal moment, this brief incursion afforded him some company in his otherwise very lonely existence.

The tired Father enjoyed the peacefulness of the church at night but he so despised the moment before the chapel doors had to be closed to the public. Those who remained at this late hour, lost in their thoughts for whatever reason, never wanted to leave. Having to cast them out, back into the world they feared where so many dangers and temptations lurked, brought a sadness to him that he found difficult to bear at times. God's protection had its limits it seemed. The diocese had now ordered the closing of all church property during the hours of night. The streets of Downtown were alive with sin of every kind but at night the Devil seemed more determined to make his mark. The darkness of the later hours, when the pitiful amount of light was switched off, when what meagre power the Council drip fed the lower districts ceased, seemed to bring about the worst in humanity. Father Jacob despaired. He had often petitioned the local governor asking why this was happening and he had always received the same response, 'saving energy for the good of the city'. Much more important than saving souls the priest thought bleakly. He very much doubted the likes of Hightown had such restrictions imposed on them.

It was a sign of the times. Dis, this city, was not what it once was, so hostile and resistant to anything good, like a ravaged body, disease ridden, rejecting the medicine, the hope, needed to cure it. With eyes closed and a sullen shake of the head, dark thoughts, which seemed to cling and infest every memory during these sombre times, plagued the priest. Father Jacob, as he often did at this time, thought of the many good souls amongst his congregation who had disappeared lately never to be seen again. Men, women and children just seemingly lifted off the street, ripping the heart and soul out of the community. The church's clergy were not immune to the tragedy either. Sister Davies, a relatively new recruit at the time, could not bear to watch the suffering of those around her while she was safely housed within these holy grounds. Straying out into the darkness, what did she think was going to happen to her? She was such a beautiful child. Another good soul gone and with it the loss of hope for the future. The priest's thoughts darkened further. In a place so in need of the love of God and the hope His grace brings, the church was hated by so many. The diocese does not now look favourably on her clergy venturing outside the church walls at night, the sickness of the city limiting God's work to a strict timetable.

The last of the lost souls were now being ushered out the door. Peering into the darkness, Father Jacob could not resist flinching at the wretched tempest beyond the church doors. He looked up despairingly towards the heavens which, of course, he could not see. God's blue sky and bright warming sun which he had read about in his ancient books had not bathed this part of the city in its light in many centuries. Eternal darkness prevailed. The heavens were left to his dreams and now, awake to this city, he could only look upon the dreary metallic chaos of the sprawl as it twisted its way upwards.

He coughed, his tired old lungs struggling to take in the wretched Downtown air. Not having a respirator with him, he could only shield his mouth from the elements, he could never stand long outside without it before collapsing with a hacking cough. Flinching at this intrusion, he could not hide his embarrassment as the last to leave, a man wrapped in a tattered green tunic and grubby, ripped trousers turned to look at the holy man with lifeless grey eyes sunk deep into a gaunt, yellowed face. He coughed and shuddered as the dead air took hold of his body. Respirators were expensive equipment and most of the inhabitants of Downtown did not have one. His expression was not one of anger or desperation but of bleak, grim acceptance. Father Jacob had seen this look far too many times over the years. The faces of people who knew they had no hope, believed

God had abandoned them and there was nothing they could do but accept their grim fate. He paused for just a second, holding the Father's stare, before nodding good night. With his arms wrapped around his shaking body, putting up some meagre resistance to the driving rain, he turned and disappeared into the dark innards of Dis. Father Jacob shouted after him, "See you tomorrow, friend!" If he heard he did not respond. The priest winced at the sound of his hollow, meaningless voice; the lost soul's silence was much louder than anything the old man could muster.

The large, ancient bronze doors were heavy to close. Broken and in worsening ill health, the burden of absolute faith in God's love weighed down on him more heavily as each day passed. Long ago he had run out of answers and only now had his faith to turn to. He grabbed hold of that belief, a small silver cross, and rubbed the worn metal, as he often did, and took comfort in the faded inscription, which he could still, just about, feel under his thumb and forefinger. His last and only comfort. Raising a slight smile and ruffling his nose so his spectacles slipped down, Father Jacob stared at it and whispered those familiar words, 'in te, domine, speravi'. A small piece of warmth in a cold world. He pushed his spectacles back into place and shook his head, as if coming out of a trance, and slammed the doors shut with a loud thud that thundered through the now empty church as it did through his empty soul.

Standing in the doorway, leaning against the old doors, he closed his tired eyes. Silence had returned to St John's. All Father Jacob could hear was the flicker of the burning candles which were fixed throughout the walls of the nave. That, combined with the calming aroma of incense and the varnish of the ancient oak beams, reminded him that sleep was needed.

It took a while to secure the doors with their many locks and bars, a telling sign that God's house was not immune from the dangers of the city. St John's had been robbed and vandalised numerous times over the years, greater security was needed in these uncertain times. Another coughing fit took hold of his body.

"Are you ok, Father?"

Brother Rothery stood in the centre of the nave, a look of concern across his chubby face, the few hairs left on his balding scalp falling down across his forehead. "Yes, yes, I'm coming." Another spasm gripped him.

"I'll send someone out to get the apothecary, that cough is getting worse. You take too much on, Father. Allow me to attend to some of your…"

Father Jacob waved the approaching priest away with his hand and through hacking coughs interrupted him, "Thank you, Brother, but that is not necessary. I assure you that I am of sound health, it will pass." Despite the priest's assertions he leaned shakily on Brother Rothery's shoulder for support as he prepared himself to inspect the church, just as they did every night at this late hour, making sure that all doors and windows were secured and the many precious possessions held within were accounted for. He always looked forward to this time. This chapel had been a part of his life since he was a boy and he knew every room, corner, carving and statue as he would any beloved member of his family. Every part of the old building had history and a tale to tell and the priest felt with some comfort that he was part of that story.

"The old girl still looks as beautiful as she ever did." Brother Rothery had walked these floors with Father Jacob on countless evenings and he always took great pleasure at seeing the weight of the world briefly lifted off his mentor's shoulders. He looked up at the large vaulted ceiling and the many beautifully carved stone guardians that stood perched along its perimeter. All gazed down towards them in various poses, some dancing, some playing musical instruments and some praying, all were smiling, dimples softly pressed into plump cheeks, curls falling across wide, excited eyes. The sound of the driving rain could be heard outside, battering against windows and the slate of the roof. The building creaked and groaned against the onslaught. "It makes my heart warm to know that they look over us."

"Yes, despite all they have been through." He looked at Brother Rothery's concerned face and immediately scolded himself. He should know better than to be down of heart in front of his clergy. Hope is what they needed and only the confidence of their faith would see them through the darkness. He composed himself and rested a hand on the worn bronze of the church's entrance, "She will be beautiful for many more years to come." He smiled but despite his intentions, was still unable to hide his many worries.

"You bear the weight of too many souls," the young priest spoke with a creased brow. "Come to me, all who labour and are heavy laden, and I will give you rest. Take my yoke upon you, and learn from me, for I am gentle and lowly in heart, and you will find rest for your souls. For my yoke is easy, and my burden is light." His voice became almost musical as he spoke, each word dancing from his tongue and seeming to bring him more warmth and happiness, ridding the worry from his face.

"Matthew 11:28." Father Jacob smiled, "Very good, wise words indeed." He turned to glance at the doors which he was still leaning on and rubbed the cool metal lovingly with his gnarled hands. Despite having lived with them for many years their beauty was not lost on him. In the dancing light of the candles he could still make out some of the faded images. The life of St John the Baptist had once been depicted so beautifully on the bronze panels but most had been worn away over the centuries by many a parishioner's loving touch. Only a few could still be clearly seen. The old priest's eyes rested on the image of Hope, a young robed girl holding aloft a candle, and closed his eyes briefly in a silent prayer. "Come Brother, it is late and we still have much to do."

With one hand leaning heavily on Brother Rothery's shoulder, Father Jacob, with his back stooped, walked through the nave extinguishing candles as he went. "How goes the restoration work?"

"Well," the priest scowled and tapped his chubby finger against his lip, "although we have encountered a particularly resilient type of critter that rather enjoys eating its way through some of our more ancient pieces. It's quite fascinating, it seems to derive from…"

"And are steps being put in place to eradicate it?" Father Jacob greatly appreciated Brother Rothery's love for his role as custodian restorer of the church and all its ancient contents. His skill and patience were the reason why so many treasures remained beautiful to this day however, in his enthusiasm, he would often ramble on about his obsessions and he was too tired this evening to listen.

"Oh yes. Rather ingenious really. Our ale, they hate it, finishes them off very quickly. So, if you don't mind, I procured myself a couple of bottles from the cellars, strictly for the Lord's work of course, and have rigorously been applying it to great effect." A broad smile creased his face and his cheeks reddened as he spoke of his success.

"Excellent." The old priest chuckled to himself. He enjoyed these late, peaceful walks, they distracted him from more weightier problems which seemed to bear down on him on a daily basis. "I hear that Brother Zachery has managed to bring us another load of relics from down below."

"Yes." Brother Rothery's eyes lit up at the mention of the recent delivery, he could not hold back his excitement. "I thought we had seen the last of those but, praise be to God, he has managed to get some more of the Lord's work up to us. I don't know how he does it, I really don't."

"It is fantastic news. God wants us to hear his voice. Truly wonderful. Have you had a chance to examine any of the items?"

"Yes. I couldn't wait I'm afraid." His cheeks reddened an even deeper hue, "I am sorry Father, it is so rare that anything new arrives these days and I couldn't wait to hear his words."

"That is ok, Brother." There were more important things in this world to get angry about than Brother Rothery's enthusiasm to read the word of God and, besides, he welcomed the warmth of his excited devotion. "What did you find?"

"A number of tomes relating to our own patron saint," he looked very proud to bring such news to his mentor. "There are some exciting references to St John's imprisonment, however the books that contain these words are in a very poor condition."

"Will you be able to recover the knowledge?"

"Yes, for the most part. It will be difficult though, the Purging and the centuries since have not been kind to the artefacts." He began to wring his hands, and mutter to himself in worry.

"Proverbs 13:4, the soul of the sluggard craves and gets nothing, while the soul of the diligent is richly supplied."

"I understand but if only we had a digital reconstructor. I hear those machines are truly wonderful. We could possibly save some of the words that lie within those relics that are in a very poor state indeed."

Despite his pleading looks, Father Jacob gave a sharp reply to the request, "Now Brother, if our good Lord wants us to hear his words we need to labour diligently to reap the rewards. Machinery only serves to corrupt the soul, distract us from God's work."

"Yes, Father." He bowed but could not hide his disappointment.

He rubbed his heavy eyes, "I have some pressing business that I must conclude tonight. Could you finish the inspection whilst I retire to my study? I must catch the courier going up to the Bishop before I sleep and I am so very tired."

Brothey Rothery smiled back, "Of course, Father." He turned, extinguished another candle, and continue the evening's inspection alone.

Opening the door to his private study, Father Jacob sat down at his desk, leafed through some paper and wearily picked up a pen. He had not been writing long when he heard a faint knock. "Yes?" He sighed at the intrusion.

The door slowly creaked open and from behind it emerged a hooded head. A small, sharp face with squinting eyes and thin lips entered the light of the room. "Sorry for missing the service tonight, Father. I had a little trouble with the broken window in the Jerusalem Chapel. No worries though, it's all secure." His soft voice was broken by a stammer that clung to every consonant.

"This is getting somewhat of a habit of late, Brother Glaxon. Punctuality is of great importance in the service of our Lord. If you are not here to spread the word of God the people will not hear it."

"Yes, Father. I understand." He bowed his head in obedience.

"No. I do not think you do. The Devil's work is all around us. You must always remain vigilant and focused on the light for disaster awaits us in the darkness. Do not neglect your duties again, Brother." He frowned at the young priest from behind his desk. "I hear that you have been spending time outside again. You know how I feel about that, the Bishop himself has said for us not to leave these walls at night."

"Yes, but there is so much suffering all around us, I cannot help but reach out and offer what aid I can." From the long sleeves of his robes thin hands were held palm to palm as if in prayer.

"You will not be much help to anyone if you add yourself to the long list of those lost. If another member of the clergy were to vanish or come to harm I believe the Bishop will insist on us all leaving this place for the safer heights and only God knows what would happen to our community if they were left all alone. It is here," Father Jacob tapped the desk with his fist to emphasise his point, "that God's word can be heard and his warmth spread, not out in the slums where you are so fond of going lately. There, temptation and sin lie in every corner. Remember what the scriptures say, 'on this rock I will build my church, and the gates of hell shall not prevail against it.' The fight against the darkness starts here." The old priest dropped his pen, leant back on his chair and stared at Brother Glaxon, "You look tired and you are losing weight."

"I am having trouble sleeping."

"The Devil is in your head. Fill your mind with prayer and forgiveness and God will grant you peaceful slumber."

"Yes, peace. It's all I want. An escape from this turmoil." Brother Glaxon talked slowly as if a thousand thoughts weighed down each and every word.

Father Jacob leaned forward, his brow furrowed, "God grants those eternal peace who absolve themselves of sin and accept his forgiveness." He sighed, tired of teaching his young priest the same basic lesson time and time again, "Actions, Brother Glaxon, not just words. Show our Lord that you are a true Christian soul through how you act on this earthly plane and he will grant you the keys to the gates of paradise."

With his head bowed and swaying a little, Brother Glaxon spoke, "That is all I want," he repeated.

Father Jacob shook his head and sighed. His old bones ached, "I am tired, Brother. Sleep draws me towards her and I still have much to do tonight."

A wave of his hand signified that the meeting had finished and Brother Glaxon bowed even lower than he already had been, "As you wish, Father." The young priest disappeared into the darkness outside the study, closing the heavy wooden door as he went.

He took off his spectacles and again rubbed his eyes. Taking hold of his cross he mouthed a prayer and sat in silence staring at the flickering flame of a candle, its weak light holding back the shadows around his desk. Father Jacob let out a long and weary sigh and returned to his work.

·A RUDE AWAKENING·

A cough, somewhere in the distant reality, wrenched him from his stupor. In this vegetated state, his first and only instinct that remained within his wasted mind was one of self preservation. Practice had taught him how to survive the brutal, harsh reality of a chemical comedown but it did not make it any easier.

Not wanting, or perhaps unable, to open his eyes, Kessler began to listen. Hearing was always the first sense to return from the numbness. There was a persistent, piercing ring that attacked his bruised and burned-out mind. Beyond that, a tapping could be heard broken intermittently by a muffled voice. What was being said could not be understood but it was definitely a woman. Words did not register but the thick Midtown brogue with which they were said sparked a flicker of recognition which ignited a small, blurred memory. Cogs began to slowly turn, images in his addled mind began to take focus.

He only knew one woman who could carry such a thick mid-city accent which carried an attitude that made each harsh syllable hit like the hammering of a piston. Macy Duzekus. He swore to himself, unsure whether he spoke out loud or whether he was still lost in the depths of his scattered mind. That could only mean one thing, he was in his office. A hoarse moan escaped his dry, cracked lips as the disgust began to seep in. Still laden and burdened with the heavy haze, he began to painfully construct simple thoughts. First came abhorrence at the state he found himself in, then self-loathing, pity, hatred and finally anger. The cycle of emotions usually repeated itself until finally the body was ready to accept more poison, then the debauched routine began its merry dance all over again.

Kessler, still with eyes closed, not yet ready to admit the outside world, continued to search for answers as to his current situation. He could now smell a viscous odour that could be only one thing. Himself. Stale tobacco, the sickly sweet smell of cheap bourbon and the musky scent of a man who had not had a wash in days, hung in the air around him. The usual collage of aromas born from days of reckless abandon.

A click of a latch, a door screeching on its hinges and the 'clak-clak' sound of footsteps coming closer put in jeopardy the safety of Kessler's prone state, threatening the very thing which was keeping him sane. Complete denial. He was not yet ready to deal with reality and accept what was to come.

The strong smell of Macy's coffee now invaded Kessler's senses. He was yet to find a drink so vile as to compare to the bubbling chemical sludge that made up that lethal concoction. Another feral sigh escaped from his lungs.

"Drink it."

His head was lifted and the thick, hot liquid brought to his lips. He gagged as the syrup-like substance made its way down his throat. "Enough!" The overpowering taste forced coherent words. His head hit the floor with a thud.

"You know the routine, Kes. It's the only thing that gets you going."

"I can't stand that tar you call coffee."

"Well, if you want to pay the cred for the real stuff then I would be happy to make you some."

She was right, it did its job. Without having to taste the evil brew, the smell alone began to bring feeling back to Kessler's broken body, forcing full consciousness upon him. Opening his eyes brought a shock of light painfully to bear on his fragile psyche. They stung raw, as if claws had raked their surface. Squinting and trying to focus, his blurred vision began to clear. His head was resting on the hard floor. He continued to lay prone, not wanting to try and engage his aching joints and muscles. From this position he could see, beyond the dirt and rubble that caked the floor of his office, a door was slightly ajar and through it he could make out the edge of a desk on top of which was a computer and a large red plastic flower. He took a couple of deep breaths. His eyes moved across to the right. Shiny, black stilettos gleamed in the low electric light that came in through the window from the city outside. Long, slender, tattooed legs towered above him. One of the stilettos began to tap the ground noisily.

"Emm, Kes? Hello? I was wondering, do you want me to cancel all your appointments today? It's just that if you do, that's fine, but you know what that Mrs Grubaker is like, she will be calling the office all day. She never takes a hint. Too much time on her hands if you ask me. I remember the time she needed…"

"Ugh." Kessler grimaced as reality took hold. His mouth felt as if it was filled with dust, his tongue swollen, and his throat was as dry as sandpaper. All he could muster was a primitive growl. Still, it had the desired effect of stopping Macy's constant chatter.

Trying to move proved difficult. Kessler seemed to have been prone, crumpled on the floor, for quite some time by the feeling, or lack of it, in his right arm. With his left, he waved half heartedly in the direction of his desk trying, without much success, to turn off an alarm that had begun to buzz continuously. After a few failed attempts, which only succeeded in knocking it further away from him, Macy grabbed the alarm and switched it off.

"Kes." Macy sighed, "I don't know why you insist on getting so wasted, and at work too…"

"Not now, Macy." Kessler's voice rasped and cracked as it tried to form words. He had no time for one of Macy's lectures. Grappling onto the edge of the desk he raised himself, somewhat unsteadily, off the floor before falling heavily back to his original position. His head spun, the strength within his large frame gone, he found it impossible to get up.

Macy sighed, stooped down and, struggling to take some of the large bulk of her employer in one arm, she helped him up to his feet and onto a red plastic chair by his desk. It creaked as it strained to take his weight.

He could smell the sharp aroma of Macy's perfume. A quick glance out of the corner of his bloodshot eyes revealed the immaculate image of his secretary. Her short, spiked blond hair, typical Midtown fashion, full rouged lips and tight-fitting red and black body suit making the most of her slender figure, all made Kessler more aware of the filthy state he currently was in. He pushed her away and turned his head from her stare. He knew what lay waiting for him in those watery blue eyes of hers and was not in the mood to face that just yet, he would be reminded about it enough in the future he was in no doubt.

Macy shrugged and turned to leave. Kessler, looking out of the window trying to avoid any eye contact, mumbled, "Macy, ugh, thanks." Stopping in the doorway, she turned her head slightly and, with pursed lips, nodded before leaving.

Reaching down to an already-open drawer, Kessler fumbled through papers and an assortment of discarded ration packs and Nutri Bar wrappers before finding what he was looking for. A half empty bottle of Piper's bourbon. Unscrewing the cap and taking a violent swig of the noxious liquid, he jerked his head back in one quick movement and screwed his face up as the strong, cheap whiskey burnt its way down his throat. He swung his arm across the desk, sending the alarm clock and Macy's still-steaming coffee clattering onto the floor.

The intercom began to buzz.

Slapping the button hard, Kessler growled into the com, "What is it?"

"Kes, it's Mrs Grubaker on the line for you, I told her that you were in a meeting but she insists on speaking to you, she says it's a matter of life or death." Kessler stared at the panel, the light on the receiver flashing crimson, waiting for his answer. The thought of dealing with Mrs Grubaker's menial jobs disgusted him. Life or death, he thought cynically to himself, she didn't know the meaning of the words. However she was a regular client that provided good money, something that, especially after the last few days, Kessler was aware that he needed.

"Put her through."

"So Mr Kessler, how did it go?" Mrs Grubaker's Hightown shrill screeched down the line.

"How did what go?"

"Your meeting, Mr Kessler. I've been trying to get through to you all day and your incompetent secretary has been telling me that you have been attending some meeting of Dis-shattering importance. So how did it go?"

"Erm..."

"What I would like to know is, have you saved the city yet? Because that is the only outcome I would expect from a problem that would distract you from something that, right as we speak, is destroying my life. And I like my life, Mr Kessler." The nasal quality of Mrs Grubaker's Hightown voice reverberated around Kessler's head, like a hammer pounding away at his skull. Fighting the urge to tell her exactly what she could go and do with her life, he forced himself to remember how much he needed her right now, or rather her credits. He always found it difficult to deal with her. She represented everything that had gone wrong with his life and everything he hated about it, it was just never meant to be this way. How had it come to this? A thought that Kessler often found himself pondering these days.

15

"Sorry ma'am, it's been a long night. You know how it is, with the city the way it's going. I'm very busy at the minute, always problems to… solve," he lied. Above the constant low hum of the rec vent, Kessler could hear the city's cry clawing at his window, threatening to pull him and his crumbling life down into the maelstrom. Dark thoughts, mixed with the last remaining traces of chem, swirled around his mind.

He did not know how long he was staring at the flashing red light of the com before he realised that her voice was barking at him, "Hello? Are you still there, Mr Kessler? I have no time for your daydreaming. Now, will you or won't you?"

"Erm, will I or won't I what, Mrs Grubaker?"

"Go straight over to that little hussy's house and catch that rat of a husband of mine right in the act."

Fantastic, thought Kessler, another fine day ahead for him. "What's the address and I'll get right on it," he sighed.

"District 5, Hightown, 66 Keblako Drive, Duma Sector. I'll expect a full report first thing tomorrow morning." With that the intercom went dead, static from the empty line filling Kessler's ears and irritating his already growing headache.

Taking another couple of long gulps from the bottle of bourbon, he rubbed his forehead before getting up from his desk and stumbling towards a grimy basin that clung to a wall in his office. Damp clothes lay rolled up in a ball in sickly green and brown stagnant water. Throwing its contents to the floor and, with his fingers, removing whatever sludge was blocking the plug hole, Kessler filled the basin with water and submerged his head into the dark cloudy liquid, letting out a howl as the biting cold reminded his nerves how to feel again. After what felt like an age, he raised his head out of the sink and looked at his reflection in the small, cracked mirror which was balanced precariously on the side against the wall. What stared back at him was what Kessler had come to expect. He was used to the ravaged image which now greeted him. Greasy black locks, shoulder length and now flecked with grey, shallow, red raw eyes that contained, somewhere beyond the bloodshot, piercing light blue pools now dulled with experience. The chemical coma from which he had just woken from was the closest thing to sleep he had had in what felt like weeks, however he did not feel any benefit from it. He pulled the skin down from under both eyes to reveal more of his shattered pupils. He looked particularly rough today. His square jaw was hidden behind days of stubble, his scar, a jagged memory across his right cheek, as always, seemed to angrily glare at him. No amount of stubble could hide that dark blemish.

Grabbing his black plastichem coat from the back of the chair, he ran his hand through his hair and pulled down his large hood to just above his eyes. Kessler began to move towards the door when he stopped just as he was about to punch the switch. He turned, walked back to his desk, opened another drawer and from it pulled out his plasma carbine, its metal gleaming silver and its power cells pulsing a faint blue glow. He paused for a brief moment looking down at the weapon in his large, grubby gloved hands, before holstering it. He pulled his coat around him and exited the room.

In the small corridor outside, Macy was chatting on the com, filing her nails and taking long draws from a nic stick which was balanced between bright red lips, "Cancel everything for today Macy, I'll be out dealing with Grubaker all day." He doubted he had any appointments but it kept up the pretence.

"Ok Kes, will do." Macy said, squeezing in the reply amidst her various activities.

Kessler slammed the door behind him, nearly shattering the frosted glass as he did so. He paused, standing in the hallway and, before continuing out of the building, looked back at his office door.

'Mr S. Kessler. Private Investigator.'

He was feeling particularly annoyed today.

·DOMESTIC BLISS·

The plastisteel door gave way to a cacophony of noise making Kessler stagger back. The hordes pulled, crawled, pushed and crowded the streets. Thousands of hands clawed, fists punched and feet kicked their way through the mass of bodies as citizens went about their daily business of survival. From above, the upper districts of Midtown and, eventually, Hightown towered and below, Downtown and the lower depths festered. The city encased everyone in a toxic urban sprawl. In all directions it spewed out a carbonised iron and plastisteel nightmare all dressed up in the reds, yellows, greens and blues of garish neon lights. This urban tomb pressed hard against Kessler's senses, his comedown raging with more and more ferocity with every second he stood in amongst the chaos of Dis.

From the shelter of the doorway he peered out into the rain. The city bled it's filth from above, a constant chemical torrent poured from the factories, houses and sewers in the upper districts, covering everything in a thick layer of sludge. He checked his hood, tightly secured his coat and peered into the eternal gloom as the hooded cowl of the Grand Director peered down on his subjects from a vast glimmer board which hovered above the sector, his booming voice drowning the citizens of Midtown with his mantra, "Ox, light, life. The Council provides all to its citizens." From an inside pocket he produced a pair of optics and placed them over his eyes and immediately the weak, dull light from the city was replaced with sharp, more vibrant colours. He coughed as the dense foul air lay thick in his lungs and quickly took a hit of Ox from his inhaler before heading out into the turmoil.

Kessler pulled up his sleeve to reveal his inked bioware panel, pressed down hard with his thumb and immediately flashing yellow lights and a blaring alarm joined the surrounding commotion. The masses shifted in a sudden wave as a small section of the pavement began to rise from beneath their feet to reveal a battered blue junker which Kessler quickly entered. The driver's door only half closed to a series of groans and creaks from its motor and, to a series of rants and curses, he pulled it closed with some difficulty. Eventually it was locked in place allowing the blue light of the body scan to pass over him. The dashboard came alive with a series of green and red lights. Once the coordinates of his destination had been entered, the thrusters, with a violent shudder, ignited in a cloud of thick smoke.

As Kessler's altitude increased, above him the underside of Midtown's District 4 came into view. Thousands of communication aerials, antennas and webs of cabling swung in the wind and rain together with the vast arrays of network hubs flashing and crackling with energy, all reaching out towards him from the darkness and, amongst it all, the gates to the Skyway emerged.

Kessler joined the large queue of traffic and was immediately greeted with the usual stares of citizens glaring at his battered junker through their canopies wondering how anybody who owned such a wreck could afford to travel the Skyway. He tapped the dashboard affectionately, it was a piece of scrap, Kessler admitted to himself, but it was his piece of scrap.

Hovering in place, waiting for his turn to move through the hypertube, Kessler listened to the impatient roars of engines and thrusters as citizens jostled for position. The Skyway was always busy and travelling up city always felt manic and aggressive. Those citizens who had the permits to live higher up never liked spending too long in the lower parts and were always desperate to get back up top. Too much time in bad air and filthy rain did not agree with their delicate constitutions.

Peering out of his canopy, he could see the cluttered skies over his district. The huge letters and logos of the many corporations hung in the air reminding those below who exactly was in charge. Those who had a seat on the Council such as Dai Lung Technologies, Federated Arms and Cycorps, as well as the many smaller outfits such as Draxton Berry and Red Line, all dominated the skyline. Hundreds of infobots, holo boards and audio drones swarmed above each district and were a constant reminder as to the corporation's grip on the city.

Kessler's headache thundered and his heavy eyes itched as the last remnants of the poison ebbed out of his body. He reached over to the passenger side, opened a compartment and, from in amongst the rubbish, took out a half-empty tube of pills and threw them down his throat with a large gulp of Piper's. He threw the empty bottle onto the passenger seat just as a drone whizzed by and glared its spotlight right at him, illuminating his cabin in bright green light. Within moments the brightness turned into a projection as Kessler's retinas were scanned. He groaned as the image of a happy uptown family smiled back at him. Kessler had seen this one many times before and batted his hand through the holographic image in frustration.

To the sound of birds singing and a dulcet slow electric melody, mum, dad, son and daughter all waved at the detective. The young daughter laughed, turned and looked up admiringly at her mother. Each member of the family recalled what they liked about living in Hightown where you 'can leave all your troubles behind', or rather 'below you', Kessler thought cynically. He always winced when it came to the son's turn to speak, he could not have been more than eight years old. "I like it here because the corporations look after all our needs. I am safe to breathe the air, play in the park without worry and eat delicious health rations without the fear of contamination. All provided by the Council."

"Great," Kessler muttered under his breath, "get them while they're young." The infomercial ended with the boy playing with a pet dog, another reminder of the wealth and lifestyle of Hightown. Kessler had seen a real dog once, when he was young. It was old and the Midtown air soon finished it off. In a flash, the projection vanished and the bot flew on to its next target. Kessler rubbed his eyes as the low hum of his engines and the dull light from the canopy returned.

The peace, however, was short lived as another image, this time from a huge glimmer board that hovered just above his vehicle, showed a newsreel of one of the many riots near the Rim. Rank upon rank of the Dis Police Department, with gleaming black armour, pristine white cloaks, towering shields and glowing blue spark flails, marched forward fighting back the ragged masses of angry Dregs. The impoverished denizens of Downtown threw themselves fanatically at the DPD wielding an assortment of primitive and makeshift weapons as rain cascaded down over a hooded reporter who appeared on screen wearing a DPD armoured vest, "More violence reigns down on the Dis Police Department as Humanity First radicals take out their frustrations. Power shortages, lack of clean water and bad air top their list of complaints. However, the Council tell all citizens not to worry as these terrorists will soon be dealt with quickly and effectively. Live productively citizens." With that the reporter waved goodbye, a large smile appearing from behind her respirator.

The traffic began to move and Kessler was soon at the gates of the Skyway. To enable access to Hightown, Mrs Grubaker had given him a permit which the hypergate now scanned, acknowledged and billed her for the toll. Once the payment was processed, the gravity drive took control of his vehicle and he entered the tunnel which was lit up in an electric-blue glow. As he waited for the vehicle to be placed into the correct position, another scan penetrated his cabin and, to images of a golden sun he had never felt and beautiful pale blue skies he had never stood under, the soothing female tones of the Dis City Lottery girl sang about dreams and the chances of winning settlement permits up city. "Waste of creds," Kessler sighed aloud. Eventually the console came to life as the drive powered up and everything outside became a blue blur as the mag rails took control and Kessler's junker picked up speed.

As he travelled higher and higher up city, Kessler passed through the districts of Midtown and at each border the canopy again filled with light as his clearance to travel was verified. The low hum of the gravity drive and soft light from the console made him feel drowsy. The pills he took were finally beginning to dampen the pain in his head, sooth the aches in his joints and numb the fire in his eyes. He began to drift into unconsciousness when a blaring alarm sounded. The holo display appeared before him and a voice indicated that he had arrived at the border to Hightown 5. DPD officers lined the route from the hypertube and the border control point bristled with cameras and an array of heavy weaponry. Kessler's vehicle came to a stop as two stood stiff to attention with assault rifles at the ready as another, with a more delicate frame and brimming with self importance, stepped up towards the detective and signalled for him to open the canopy. "Damn Venters," Kessler sighed.

"Identification citizen." He flicked his white cloak behind his shoulder to reveal his shining black plate armour with the gold cog, the Council's seal, gleaming on his breastplate. He held out a black gloved hand and waited.

Kessler looked at his reflection in the officer's black optics which confirmed how out of place he looked. Not only was his car an ancient wreck but so was he. Taking the permit out of the console, Kessler handed it over, his mood growing darker by the second.

"You are a long way from Midtown 5, citizen. State your business." His voice came from lips that sneered out each syllable.

"Private Investigator. I'm on business for Citizen Grubaker. It's all in the permit." Kessler had expected this.

"You have a plasma carbine in your possession, I need to see your ownership certificate and right to carry documents."

His head began to throb again, despite the pills, "Of course, officer." Kessler handed over the correct documents and they were immediately scanned.

"Exit the vehicle. Now." The other two Venters stepped forward and powered up their rifles. The power cells emitting a high pitch squeal as they charged with energy.

"Oh c'mon." Kessler sighed and pointed to the Venter still holding his permits, "I have the right docs, I have a right to be here." He knew his words were meaningless, they did what they wanted, interpreted the Council's laws in their own unique manner. They levelled their weapons at him and he immediately released the canopy and exited the vehicle, "Ok, ok. No need for that." As soon as he had climbed out the two officers slung their rifles and pinned him against the cracked blue panels of his vehicle, "Mind the body work," Kessler mumbled.

"We do not appreciate trouble here in Hightown. Your Midtown ways have no place here." The officer holding his documents threw them onto the empty passenger seat and began to search him by roughly patting him down.

Kessler started to turn around to face him but was immediately slammed hard back against his junker, "I'm just a good citizen trying to earn a living. Nothing more, nothing less." He stared out at all the vehicles, all expensive shiny fiberplas and chrome plate, being waved past undisturbed by the police. Each driver slowed to stare at him. He gripped the edge of the junker's roof hard, trying to control his temper as his face was forced against the cold plastisteel bodywork. He shook with rage.

The officer finally finished searching him, "Move along citizen." His two goons released him, giving him one final shove in the back, and returned to standing to attention in their original positions.

Kessler turned to stare at them, burning with anger. He briefly thought about his weapon which was still holstered by his side but quickly dismissed such thoughts. He had enough problems in his life to deal with.

The drive system in his vehicle was initiated and Kessler quickly left the DPD behind and sped down the highway that would lead him directly to Duma and, eventually, Keblako Drive. He gripped the controls tightly, resentment still pulsing through his veins. "Focus, Kes," he muttered to himself before punching the junker's console in frustration, "damn Vents," he cursed again and lowered the canopy to take a couple of deep breaths of the clean, rainless air and slowly began to calm down.

Even in this low district of Hightown life was better. The darkness of Dis remained and still, above Kessler's head, people lived and worked in the city above, however the garish neon signs and manic masses were gone instead replaced by static street lighting and a dead calm. No stalls littered the sidewalks, no vendors begged citizens to part with their credits. Hightown 5 was mostly a residential hub for low-level corporates who worked higher up city and as a result an empty silence shrieked from every street and vacant building. However, as he drove into Keblako Drive, he immediately noticed one resident who was not at work today.

Parking at the entrance to the street, Kessler picked up his viewfinder from the floor and exited the vehicle. Elbows resting on the roof, he peered through the lenses at the familiar image of Mr Grubaker's bright yellow chopper parked outside number 66. Its fiberplas body shone under the light of the street lamp and the chrome plate detail sparkled. Beyond it, a small, square, plastic green lawn was neatly laid out and from it a small tree was placed. Kessler paused at the sight of this mock vegetation, briefly zooming in his viewfinder to focus on the dark green leaves stiff in the breeze and the small pink shiny buds. He always wondered what use plants had in life, imitation or otherwise. What function did they play? He had heard stories as a child of a place right at the top of Dis where hundreds of miles of lush vegetation flourished under a burning sun and blue sky. He looked up at the blanket of darkness he knew was hiding the underbelly of Hightown 4 and thought of how unbelievable such tales were.

66 Keblako Drive was like most apartments in Hightown 5, white plastisteel cubes with large windows allowing the occupants a view of their pristine streets and expensive vehicles. The cramped, shabby blocks of lower Midtown seemed a far distant memory. A couple, the man with fine delicate features, pale skin and clean-shaven face with sleek black hair wearing a sharp corps suit and the woman, with a long flowing purple glimmer dress and face sculpted to perfection, walked past Kessler and immediately raised gloved hands to their mouths with an audible gasp. He took off his optics and looked at them straight in their eyes, reached into his inside coat pocket and rummaged around for a cigar that had already been half smoked. Taking it between his fingers he dusted off whatever debris it had collected and lit the end with his lighter and took a long drag, exhaling the thick dark smoke into the air.

"Filthy Getta!" The man's pinched words were spoken quickly before he grabbed the arm of the woman and they hurried past.

Kessler finished smoking and threw the butt onto a nearby lawn and got back in his junker. He briefly smiled, irritating stiffs was one of the few delights of his job but even this pleasure was short lived. His head pounded and even this fine air could not stop him hacking up from his lungs the bile of the past few days' debauchery. He pulled the seat back and rummaged around the floor to see if he had another bottle of Piper's with him. He quickly realised he did not.

He took another disinterested look at 66 Keblako Drive and prepared himself for a long day.

·AN UNWELCOME DISTURBANCE·

Sleep. Such a simple word and a straightforward act. Billions of people did it every day. He closed his eyes, steadied his breathing and leant back on his chair and allowed the warmth of unconsciousness to take him…

Kessler jumped up with a start and slammed his fist into the desk in frustration. He was so close but every time, just as sleep began to draw him towards her, he was wrenched back to the waking world. He rubbed his eyes. They hurt. Throwing back more pills, he washed them down with some Piper's and belched loudly. "Who needs sleep anyway?" He barked.

With stinging, heavy eyes, Kessler focused on the light of the com which buzzed constantly, forcing an oppressive reddish hue throughout the room. He sat with his head in his hands silently staring at this constant irritation, unable to rest his thoughts away from what his life had become. He knew why the com was flashing. Every biting buzz was another smack in the face, each one harder than the last. It had been trying to get his attention the moment he had returned from the Heights. Mrs Grubaker seemed to have this innate ability to know when and where, down to the exact second, he was at any moment in time. He could not get rid of her, she seemed to be a better detective than he could ever be. Their lives were forever shackled together. He was an errand boy for a paranoid battleaxe that seemed to take pleasure in ordering him around like some servant, on call twenty-four hours a day to do her every bidding. Who was he kidding anyway? She was his only client and had been for longer than he cared to remember. He took another swig of Piper's and slammed the bottle down hard on his desk spilling some of the brown liquid over papers scattered across its surface. She was wealthy and always willing to throw business his way. He knew he could not, should not, complain. Life had no room for principles and standards, just cold hard creds and survival, every minute of every day. That was what existence had become. Survival.

Kessler snapped out of his self-reflecting trance by jabbing the receive button and was instantly greeted with the familiar tones of his receptionist.

"Kes," Macy exhaled air violently, as if it was a lot of effort speaking to him, "Mrs Grubaker has…"

"I know Macy," he spoke quietly into the receiver with a hoarse whisper, his headache thundered with a vengeance and even the slightest noise brought agony. He began to rub his temples to little effect, "Tell her I'm out following a lead on her husband, or some damn thing, that should keep her satisfied." He pleaded. Hoped.

"Ok, I'll tell her that you are out for the rest of the day and unavailable but you know what she's like…" Words were sandwiched between hits of nicotine as she sucked loudly on her nic stick.

"Just tell her Macy!" Kessler yelled and the com was cut-off by his fist, sending the receiver crashing off his desk to the floor.

The trip to Hightown still left a bad taste in his mouth. A journey to the Heights was always a quick reminder that his life was on a downward cycle. Looking round at the mess which was his office, he began to take in what he had become. He lived and worked in a busted tin hovel in Midtown 5, an old red plastic chair, a yellow shredded sofa to match and a desk more full of empty bottles of bourbon than anything else. The detective's eyes rested on a picture that stared at him from the floor where it had been thrown. Young, happy faces with mocking eyes glared back at him. The image reminded Kessler of what once was and could have been. "Who am I kidding," he mumbled, "I was always going to end up this way, wasn't I?" Without turning his stare away from the picture he took another long drink.

Kessler reached for the bottom drawer of his desk and from it took out his gun. Resting his hand on the weapon's handle, he continued to stare at the image of him with an old friend, smiling and dressed in a smart blue uniform. His steely blue eyes seemed bright, filled with hope and the energy of youth. That wouldn't last long, he thought as his hand twitched and his grip began to tighten around the gleaming fibreplas handle. He could feel the coolness of its metal press against his fingers and could hear the static begin to build as the plasma charged in its energy cell. All thoughts but the present fell away to nothing, no past, no future, only this exact moment lay before him. Everything stood still. Nothing mattered, only his pain…

The heavy silence within the room was broken by the wailing of the com. Kessler shook his head and finally wrenched his eyes away from what was tormenting him to the piece of dented metal which now lay on the floor in the centre of the room. He growled, his boiling rage only matched by his thundering headache. Standing up abruptly from his desk and bounding over towards the com, Kessler grabbed hold of it, "Do you ever listen to anything I say? I told you to tell Grubaker that I'm unavailable!" He bellowed so much that the very act made him out of breath. He fumbled around for an inhaler, dropping the receiver and letting it crash back to the floor as he grabbed a cylinder from the depths of the sofa and breathed in its contents.

"Mr Kessler," a forced formal tone clung to Macy's Midtown brogue, "a Miss Turner is here to see you, she apologises for not having made an appointment but says she would be very grateful if you would have the time to see her at such short notice? Should I send her in?" Macy paused waiting for a response before adding with a hint of sarcasm, "Unless you're too busy?"

Kessler fumbled for words and stuttered, "I'm just finishing some important er... work... send her in five minutes." Kessler lied.

"I will do, Mr Kessler."

"And... thanks Macy..."

"Always a pleasure, Mr Kessler." She over pronounced his name in mock formality and with that the com went dead returning a quiet to Kessler's office, if not his head.

His thoughts began to pick up speed and awake from their drudgery. He had to catch his breath, straighten himself out, make himself look presentable. The sheer scale of that task however was not lost on him. Kessler placed the dented com back on the desk and, after taking another quick gulp of Piper's, placed the bottle back with the others. His stare turned and rested briefly on his gun which still lay on his desk and, after a moment's pause, he powered it down and returned it to its drawer.

Turning to stand in front of the tarnished, broken mirror, he attempted unsuccessfully to pat down the creases in his soiled shirt. He wet his hands under the tap and greased back his hair before sighing and shaking his head, "Ok Miss Duzekus, tell the lady to come on through."

The office door gently creaked open and in shuffled the most crumpled bag of nerves Kessler had seen in a long time. She looked like the city had gobbled her up and spat her right back out again. Her head was bowed, her face covered by soaking wet jet black hair. Two pale, delicate, nervous hands emerged from a plain brown heavy set dress that hung from her thin frame. She stood in the centre of the office in silence as water flowed down from her sodden clothes and began to form a puddle on the floor.

Kessler scratched his head. He did not have time for charity cases. The city was full of them. His first thought was to throw her out but her trembling form made him hesitate, "You shouldn't go out in the rain without cover, it's not good for your health. Don't you own a coat or rain protector?" She shivered but remained standing in silence. "Here let me get you something." He looked around the room but could not see anything fit for purpose. He pressed the com, "Macy, could you bring, er, Miss, er," he struggled to remember her name...

"Miss Turner?"

"Yea, Miss Turner. Could you bring Miss Turner a clean blanket. One of yours."

After a couple of seconds, Macy let out a short sigh, "Of course, Mr Kessler."

Kessler strained to smile back at the girl who remained standing in silence until eventually Macy walked in with a bright pink blanket and gave it to her. With a quick movement of her hands, she took it and pulled it round her. Scowling at Kessler, Macy quickly left.

"So how can I help you?" Her right hand nervously rubbed the thick material of her dress and her left wrapped around her stomach, clutching the blanket as if her life depended on it. More seconds passed without a word from her. The nervous energy was beginning to become infectious and Kessler began to get impatient. "Look lady, is there anything I can help you with?" The bourbon he had taken a few moments earlier had given him a taste for the strong liquor and he found himself fingering the handle to the drawer. "If it's food and clean water you are looking for I'm afraid you have come to the wrong place. As you can see, I don't have much myself."

"Thank you for seeing me sir, I, well I... you see I need..." A muffled, stammering voice emerged from somewhere behind the thick, matted strands of black hair.

"What do you need?" Kessler sighed, "Listen, I'm a very

busy citizen and have a lot of important work to be getting on with at the moment." He had gripped the handle of the drawer and, without realising it, had jerked it open causing the bottles to rattle audibly.

"I'm sorry for disturbing you sir but I need your help." She began to whimper.

Kessler looked around the room uncomfortably and thought about calling Macy into his office to deal with this. She certainly did not look like anyone who had any credits to her name. "Sorry, I don't do free." His hand hovered above the com.

"I have credits." Her hands disappeared into the folds of brown cloth and emerged holding a bundle of shiny silver bars. A few fell to the floor with a clatter as she struggled to hold them all. She looked up at Kessler for the first time revealing her face. The detective could not make out if it was from tears or the rain but tracks of dirt ran down her cheeks and underneath all the knotted hair and city grime, he could just make out pale, almost ghost white, skin. Two large, shimmering emerald pools sparkled in the pale electric light. He stared back, lost in the vivid colour of her eyes and eventually took a breath and moved his hand away from the com.

"Ok. Let me get you a drink and let's talk about how we can sort out your problem." From the drawer he pulled out the bottle of bourbon, dusted off a couple of paper cups that lay on the floor by his desk and poured a large drink for himself and a smaller dram for Miss Turner. He took a large gulp. "So Miss, what would you like me to do?"

Miss Turner took the cup and played with it nervously for a few moments before setting it back down on the desk, "My uncle...was murdered. He was all I had in this world, he was everything to me." A sharp cry tried to escape from her trembling lips but was partially stifled with her hand.

Kessler went to offer her a handkerchief but quickly refrained after realising how dirty it was. "Ok, I'm sorry to hear that." He knew his attempt at comfort sounded hollow but it was the only thing he could think of saying. Everyone knew the streets of Dis were mean, often brutal. Citizens died all the time. "So what would you like me to do?"

Taking a deep breath she seemed to compose herself, suddenly gaining strength from some unknown source. Looking Kessler straight in the eyes she stated clearly, with a new found firmness. "I would like you to find out who did this and bring them to justice."

"I'm sure the police are looking into it as we speak. Save your money, go to your local station and they'll be able to provide you with all the details you need." Kessler lied. The DPD had better things to do than help some city urchin.

"They don't want to know. I have been trying to get information from them for weeks, the last time I tried they…" Her hand brushed against a bruised cheekbone. "I think they were sick of seeing me."

The detective could not make out her accent. She spoke with an educated clarity that suggested privilege but her words had the harsh deep tones of the lower city. He poured himself another drink and her eyes darted between the bottle and Kessler's cup. "Ok. Tell me about your uncle."

"He is…I mean was…the priest at St John's. A Christian church in Downtown 2. His church was everything to him, he spent his entire life helping those in need and, Mr Kessler, there are so many in need. Without St John's so many lives will be without hope," her voice cracked with emotion.

Already Kessler did not like the story. He hated Downtown. Filth always flowed downhill and Downtown was so deep in the city that all the muck in Dis seemed to end up there eventually. He also had no time for the many cults that popped up throughout the city promising a better life, a better world. Despite being illegal they were just like everything else, all out for a quick cred. "Miss Turner, no offence but I don't need to hear what good religion does for people. You are looking at a non-believer. This world is all we got, people should put their energies into worrying about this life, not the next. Besides, if the Council heard you talking about that type of stuff you might end up meeting your god quicker than you think."

Anger briefly shot across her face, "Well if you don't care about the soul, Mr Kessler maybe you care about justice, about doing what is right? About three weeks ago it seems someone, or some people, broke into the church and killed him. Police say it was a robbery but I don't believe them."

"Maybe they're right. Downtown is a dangerous place, Miss Turner. Unfortunately tragedies like this happen every day and could be committed by any one of the billions living down there."

The lights flickered and, to the sound of static, went out allowing pitch blackness to envelope everything. The rumble of the city outside seemed to intensify as a panic set in.

Kessler could barely make out the form of Miss Turner, "Don't worry. It's just a power shortage, it will pass soon."

"They happen all the time in Downtown. I'm not afraid of the dark."

After a few moments the power returned and the city outside settled down to its usual grind. With the return of the light, Miss Turner seemed to have composed herself. She moved to sit on Kessler's sofa, after giving it a wipe with Macy's blanket.

"The police are lying. I know that community, it was my home. My whole life my uncle and I lived and breathed that sector, everyone knew us and we knew them." She shook her head from side to side, her eyes closed, trying to suppress the raw emotion that was desperate to escape, "We knew everyone through St John's, they depended on us not only for the hope we gave them but for shelter, food and what Ox we could spare. There is no way they would harm him or desecrate the church. I tried everything I could to get anymore information." She leaned forward, resting her head in her delicate hands, "The night it happened I was awoken by the police and taken from my bed without being able to see him, to say one final goodbye. They have had the church boarded up and guarded ever since, letting no one in to worship. Not allowing me back into my own home." Her voice wavered as she wiped a stray tear.

It did prick his interest as to why they were devoting so much of their time to a simple murder in a run-down church inside the slums. The Venters rarely travelled below the Rim, certainly not as deep as D2, that far down the Council preferred to let the various gangs and district governors sort out their problems between themselves. "Had your uncle experienced much history with the DPD, been involved in anything he shouldn't have been?"

"No. He was a good man." She looked disgusted by the idea. "The Council's hatred of any form of religious expression outside their own devotion made them portray him as some heretic. They spread lies about him to try and shut us down. Over the past few months there has been vandalism, just pro-Council trash, the usual stuff. It's easy to know where it came from, there are not many people living in Downtown that would support the Council." The timid girl that walked into the room a few minutes ago had gone. In her place was an angry woman, with a desperate confidence. Her green eyes seemed to flash and pulse in rhythm with her rage, "He was just a quiet man that cared greatly for the people of Downtown. He was loved by all. Why would anyone want to kill such a person?"

Faith, religion were dangerous business on Dis. How many wasted hours had she spent putting her faith in her god before trying him? Praying for an answer that would never come. Kessler knew the type. He knew that there was no place for it in this city. He had known a few men and women who had found a god and each one had suffered greatly for it. Looking at this distressed women, Kessler felt sorry for her. If she had counted on any god protecting her from the evil that lurked round every corner in this wretched place she would be disappointed. She must have noticed him staring as she began to look uncomfortable and started to fidget nervously again. The fleeting flash of anger she had shown a moment before was gone replaced again by the fragile expression of complete and utter desperation. Her mouth began to move forming silent words, her full red lips a shock of colour in an otherwise pale face.

He wondered how many had turned her down before her desperations brought her to his sorry place. Not many P.I.s he knew would want to work down that way, certainly not the cheap ones. He must have been way down the pecking order. "Ok, I may be able to help you. First of all we should talk about payment. My rate is one hundred credits a day and there's no budging on that lady, for that you get years of expert experience at your disposal." He could not turn down the chance at quick money, he certainly needed it.

"I have not got much." She closed her eyes before speaking again, "That is quite a lot, but I should be able to get you the credits. She counted out a number of silver bars and placed them on his desk with small, delicate fingers, "That is enough for the first day, Mr Kessler."

"If I do find out who killed your uncle, what then?" Easy credits. He imagined spending a couple of days rummaging around the slums. That should satisfy her that her uncle was gone for good.

"Justice, Mr Kessler. They will be brought to the police to face their punishment."

Kessler was sceptical, "And if they don't want to admit to their crimes and come willingly?"

Miss Turner looked down at the floor as she spoke, "I am sure you can be very persuasive."

Kessler stared at her for a few seconds, letting the words hang in the air. "That type of job will cost extra. A dangerous business getting justice these days. Say two thousand credits, on top of my daily rate, upon delivery of whoever killed him?" Kessler nodded silently to himself, no way was he heading down city for anything less, "Listen if you don't have it we can work out another, cheaper package…"

"I can get it." Bethany wiped away rainwater from her eyes.

"Ok. You're lucky that I have had a cancellation today, means that I can get right on this," he lied. "First port of call will be finding out where they sent your uncle's body, I know a few good citizens that work in the hospitals I can get in touch with."

"He wasn't sent to any hospital. They left him at one of the local skin labs in Downtown 1. There are so many I couldn't find out which one it was."

"A skin lab?" This was curious. The usual procedure was to take bodies involved in violent crime to Corps hospitals for incineration. "Ok, I can find out which one. I'll call you after I've been to check on the lab and the church."

"No. I want to go with you. It's important I say my goodbyes to him, I must get his body back to have a proper funeral, we, I mean myself and the parish, need to say our goodbyes and we need to celebrate his passing to heaven."

"Listen to me. I don't mean to upset you further but it's been three weeks since your uncle died, they will have disposed of the corpse by now."

Miss Turner flinched at the word 'corpse'. Kessler continued, "I work alone. It's a dangerous place down there and I wouldn't want you to get hurt."

"No. There are things in that church that I must get back. Not just mere trinkets that are precious to me but particular items that are of great importance to my religion. They are priceless and I must retrieve them. I'm coming with you and there's no budging on that Mr Kessler."

"Look lady…"

"I insist."

He stared at her and took another shot of bourbon. "Fine. But I guarantee you that anything of value in that church will be long gone, if the DPD have anything to do with it." She stared at the detective with the set look of determination. "I'll meet you at the church." He looked at the clock on his desk, "It's 08:34 now, I'll meet you there at 13:00. There is no way you're coming with me to the skin lab though, that's no place for a young citizen like you. I've some business to take care of down there anyway." A slight smile edged its way on to his face as he stared at the neat pile of shining credits on his desk. He poured himself another drink. She got up to leave but Kessler continued to speak, "And, Miss Turner, I'm not much for formality," he coughed as another cup of Piper's hit the back of his throat, "call me Kes."

Reaching into her pockets she produced a card and gave it to the detective, "St John's address," and as she turned to leave spoke, "and you can call me Bethany, Mr Kessler."

·THE SKIN LAB·

Traffic was a screaming brawl in a thick fog of toxic fumes. Hundreds of machines roaring and snarling at one another, jostling for position before entering the Pipe. This huge plastisteel encased tube wound its way through most parts of Midtown, through the Rim and deep into the depths of Downtown. Travelling through it was, like most things in Dis, a constant battle with a citizen's sanity. There was always a hint of panic as adrenaline and fear mixed with the staleness of the Midtown air and the thick poisonous soup being churned out by the chaos produced a heady, often violent, cocktail that clutched at your lungs.

Everything was at a standstill. The city's arteries clogged with plagues of commuters. Kessler peered out of his junker with gritted teeth at the daily grind that played out around him. A jakker leaned out of his techbucket window and was snarling, his head, with its wires and implants, jittering violently. His mohican, a bright shock of pink and sickly yellow, stood out in sharp contrast to his blacked out optics and inked skin as he howled at the vehicle in front to do the impossible and move out of his way. An old woman sat in the back of a droshky with lips pursed and eyes narrowed as she did all she could to ignore the chaos around her. The driver, in the usual drab grey uniform of a droshky chauffeur, nodded slowly to himself in a daze of boredom, a nic stick hanging out from under his low brimmed hat. Up ahead, a baby cried from the arms of a pale, greasy girl, her deep red, bloodshot eyes seeming to pierce through the brown smog that seemed to be enveloping her vehicle. Towering above this snapshot of Dis life where two huge armoured wagons bearing the Council's golden cog. This frenzied play was acted out time and again in the drab, relentless rain of Dis.

Kessler gripped the steering wheel tightly. He could see the Pipe's entrance in the distance and he focused on it. It was not the usual turmoil of the Midtown streets that troubled the detective. He needed a reprieve from the pain of what he had done to himself. His body craved what was given to it the night before and Kessler was in no mood to deny it any longer. With that bit of business coming his way this morning he had some credits at last and with credits came the possibility of an escape. He knew how hopeless it would be trying to find anyone amidst the chaos of Downtown, especially about a murder that happened more than three weeks ago. They could be anywhere by now. The next couple of days would be spent hanging around looking busy. Easy credits. His console flashed red and the noise jabbed through his musings. Kessler took a hit of Ox and in a cracked voice he grunted, "What is it?"

"Hi, Kes," Macy spoke quickly as if out of breath, "those men were here to see you again and left you a package. They got heavy."

"Did you tell them what I told you to?"

"Yea the usual, that you're out working a case and will com them when you get back. I don't think they're buying it anymore, though. They got rougher than usual and made a complete mess of my office. We need a new water filter now, by the way." Her voice was reassuring in its familiarity, one of the few things that had stuck around for any length of time in Kessler's life. He could tell she was angry.

"Well, don't worry about them. I'll sort it." At this moment in time Kessler did not have the brain function or energy to dedicate any of his thinking capacity to this particular problem.

"I know." She had heard that reply too many times and Kessler knew it but he said it anyway. "See you when you get back to the office."

Kessler sighed, "Yea, catch you later." He never knew why Macy Duzekus still hung around him. He could offer her only minimal pay and a leaky roof over her head in a low Midtown slum and he was convinced that she could easily get work in one of the higher districts where the pay was like the air. Better. Still, he was glad she was there. Kessler promised himself that he would get her a new water filter, once he closed this case, one of those new kits with the rad screening he had seen advertised on the glimmer boards. She would like that, he hoped.

The Pipe offered a reprieve from the chaos of the Midtown streets. Gone was the oppressive, violent noise and incessant rain and instead, a blanket of silence encased Kessler with only the low humming of the mag rails for company as he shot at speed down the transtube. Outside, the vehicle was surrounded by a cluster of colours that streaked across the dark, lighting up the junker's canopy.

It would be easy to get hypnotised by the blues, reds and greens as they danced past and the quiet rhythmic whisper of the Pipe. The mobocracy of the city seemed far away as Kessler delved deeper into Dis. However, this serenity was short lived as the destination alarm lit up the canopy with a green glow, the light flickering every few seconds. "Destination: Downtown District 1." A voice spoke from the vehicle's console and it came to a halt as he entered the queue of traffic exiting the transtube.

The vehicle eventually began to lurch forward and the sight of the heavily guarded border loomed ahead. Two huge towers soared above Kessler, covered in the flags and banners of the thirteen Corporations who had a seat on the Council. All hung lifelessly in the stagnant air. Venters stood to attention in ranks alongside huge turret cannons. Angry corps officials, all sucking desperately on ventilators, looked uncomfortable in their suits as their junkies stood next to them holding aloft huge rain protectors in a vain attempt to keep them dry.

An alarm flashed red signalling his arrival in Downtown where the Council's dampening fields prohibited non-licensed vehicles from flight mode and immediately locked them down to manual drive the moment they arrived. Another method used by the Council to ensure those citizens unfortunate enough to be stuck in Downtown stayed in Downtown.

Kessler peered through the exhaust fumes and, as the smoke cleared, he could see the chaotic, frantic throng of those trying to get above the Rim. Local merchants, their caravans brimming with their wares, desperate to get to the Midtown markets in time to stake their claim and thousands of migrants, a never-ending stream trying to get higher up the city, waving their permits or pleading with what meagre credits they had. Amidst the screams, cries and yells the sound of violence was never far. Two Venters were hard at work on some poor Dreg, standing over his prone body as they hammered down the butts of their rifles. Kessler could see what he assumed were his family, looking on in complete distress from their cramped junker. Amongst bags and boxes, a young girl with a pink ribbon in her hair wailed and clutched a screaming mother. Kessler wondered what crime he had committed.

"I.D. Citizen." A metallic voice crackled through his ventilator as red eyes stared back at Kessler through the driver's window. He tapped the plastiglass canopy with the nozzle of his assault rifle, "Quickly."

Kessler reached into the inside pocket of his coat and produced his I.D. card, lowered the window and reached out to hand it over. The Venter scrutinized his details and had already begun walking to the next vehicle when he spoke, "Move along."

Kessler's junker rolled onto the worn carbonised iron of Downtown's District 1. He quickly adjusted his optics to try and compensate for the lack of light. With power in scarce supply this far down light was at a premium even during designated daylight hours, as a result the dilapidated buildings, buckled roads and the burnt out vehicles appeared as distant shadows in the gloom. This was not helped by the oppressive rain which crashed down in an endless torrent but what made everything even more grim was the stench that clawed its way from the depths of the city through the drains and sewers. It made it difficult to breath the tainted, dense air. All this; the darkness, the air, the filth, the stench and the poisonous rain, gave Downtown a claustrophobic hysteria. However, as Kessler drove through the streets he did not notice the impoverished surroundings or the horrid fumes rising from below, at least not as much as he used to. He had other things on his mind.

Through his canopy, the detective could see the inhabitants of Downtown at work, Dregs, Mutes and those citizens unlucky enough to be stuck this far down, all scurried about in the murk. The darkness and lawlessness promoted a feverish black market which seemed to appear in every shadowed corner, fuelled by the exotic items from below that were difficult or impossible to procure in the city above. Nowhere else on Dis could high born Corps mingle with lower Dregs, would Venters allow Wasters and Mutes to freely sell their wares. Only here could chemheads pick up simpacks on the side without any heat and jakkers could hook up in illegal burn rooms free from Council eyes.

Kessler passed a sign that was lit with a flickering light 'Boundary Town', the lettering was faded and barely legible. He immediately turned down a side alley where a couple of ramshackle noodle bars spilled out onto the street, their vicious cocktail of spices adding to the Downtown stench. Steam spewed from vats of some unknown delicacy and the quick, guttural Downtown chatter could be heard above the clatter of pots and pans. This was mixed with the call of gaudily dressed whores, grubby, soaking bodies covered in a gross collage of muck and running make-up which was smeared across gaunt faces. They smiled at would be customers with a macabre, artificial grin, aided by whatever sim or krag was running through their veins.

The Skin Lab itself was just a door in the dark. Its buckled, thick metal was covered with graffiti; tags and names of local punks were scrawled alongside the names of anti-corporate groups and pro-Council gangs. Kessler knocked three times, the noise being lost in the humdrum of life and the clatter of the rain. There was a single fluorescent pale light that threw a dull glow over the doorway revealing the gruesome paraphernalia of the trade. Needles and used caps lay in piles at either side, as if someone had swept them to clear the path.

Waiting by the entrance, lit up in the low light, Kessler kicked away a rat that had crawled onto his boot. He drew up the collar on his coat and pulled down his hood further to ward off the deluge. Despite the ghastly surroundings, he felt a calm seep through his body. He welcomed it. For the first time today he felt more his usual self. His body knew what this place was all about and relaxed at thoughts of what was to come. He smiled, adrenalin filling him with relief and the thought that things just might be ok. A manic cackle pulled him back to reality and he realised that he had been staring at a Dreg huddled amongst the waste. He was lying in the foetal position, his face covered in obscene sores and welts. One eye was scabbed shut, the other grey and lifeless. He was violently shaking with laughter, his open mouth revealing blackened gums bereft of teeth. Thick gobs of spittle ran freely over his matted beard. The dead eye suddenly seemed to come alive as it returned his stare, "There is another way, you know," he spluttered between coughs.

With a clunk, a panel opened revealing steel bars and two eyes which darted quickly from side to side. The heavy, battered, misshapen door that was the entrance to the lab scraped along the ground as a huge orderly in plastic gloves heaved it open with a grunt, his huge biceps appearing from under a blood-stained surgical gown.

Strip lighting, giving out a sickly yellow glow, buzzed loudly and every few minutes would violently flicker. The waiting room contained the usual tragic cases. Dregs from the lower city and chem heads looking for their daily fix. The skin labs catered for all these wretches, giving health, or its version of health, to the hopeless. However on this particular occasion something was different. The waiting room was barely half full. Usually there was standing room only and now Kessler could make out the grubby tiled floor.

The familiar face of Nurse Stacey Steckles nodded towards Kessler as she sucked on a nic stick from across the room behind a clear plastiglass barrier. He moved to join her. Stacey's skin was pale and greasy and her dark purple hair had fallen below her soiled white nurse's cap. Large purple lips sucked hard on the burnt-out stub. She cursed, throwing the butt on the floor, stood on the dying embers and looked up at the ceiling blowing dark smoke which seemed to hang still in the airless room. Her face was round and slightly chubby, not beautiful, but cute. The nurse's hazel eyes seemed sunken into her skull.

"What do you want Kes, I'm busy." She was nervous, eyes darting quickly around the room.

Kessler's coat was still wrapped tightly around him as he dripped water on the floor. "Mind if we have a quick chat?"

An alarm briefly blurted out a high pitched groan and Stacey rolled her eyes as she bent her head towards the com. Her voice crackled across the waiting room, "Number three hundred and seventy four make your way to surgery two." A balding, quite stocky man rose up with one hand dragging a large ox cylinder behind him and the other carrying a young girl of about six or seven. Her skin was a sickly yellow colour and every few seconds her body would strain, retch, then go limp. He was struggling to carry both the girl and the canister and stumbled more than once on his way past. His face was one of forlorn resignation. The man's difficulties went unnoticed. In the toxic air of lower Dis the breathing disease was a common sight, people were so used to seeing it that it did not warrant them taking time away from their own worries. "This way, Kes." Stacey had leaned across her desk towards him, her face just a few inches away from the barrier that separated them, her breath briefly misting up the plastiglass as she whispered, trying to be discrete.

Straightening her uniform, she stood up and, looking behind her, shouted, "Marge, cover me, I need to get something from the store." Her eyes motioned to the left for the detective to follow.

Kessler knew exactly where to go and very quickly left the reception area trying not to run and let his childish excitement overcome him. Stacey was fumbling around outside the store room looking for her key card which lay somewhere in her deep pockets. Standing in the corridor, impatience threatening to overcome him, Kessler could hear the usual muffled screams and moans of the skin lab all wrapped up in the smell of cheap disinfectant. Today, however, there was the added acrid aroma of smoke.

The door opened into a narrow space packed with a jumble of medicines and chemicals. "So what is it this time Kes? You must be quick, I'm really busy." She took out another nic stick and began fumbling around in her pockets for her lighter.

"Things to do? Usually you have the Dregs packed in solid but it's like a mortuary in there, excuse the pun." Kicking over a jar of some unsightly green liquid, Kessler tried to make space. He pulled down his sodden hood and sat on a ledge that was covered in paper bearing the familiar mark of Merryll Laboratories.

"Dregs and those unable to find the cred for Corporate Medicare are still coming in for their cheap fix but most of 'em are now coming in dead. Do you know how much paperwork you have to fill to get rid of a body? Even this far down the Council are all over us. The logistics would blow your mind." The nic stick was lit and the small space was quickly filling with smoke.

Kessler could not wait any longer, "Listen, I need some sim, to see me through the downtime. How much you have?"

"Only have three caps, wasn't expecting a call from anybody today."

"Fine. I'll take them, usual rate?"

"Yea, plus the ten creds you owe me from last time." She was perspiring and stared over Kessler's shoulder at the door, as if she expected company at any moment.

"Yea that's fine, I've come into a bit of luck recently and have the cred." Again Stacey reached into her pockets but this time very delicately took out three tiny caps of clear liquid and handed them to Kessler. In a flash, she quickly grabbed the credits from him.

He took the vials and brought one up to the light, flicking it with a finger. "Clear eh? Looks good." He brought the shot of sim up to his eye and, with a squeeze and a familiar hiss, delivered the precious payload into his body. He sighed happily as a wave of chemicals swept through him.

"Yea they're the last of the clear. I only have brown left back at my place once that goes."

The chem haze began to rise. His headache disappeared and his muscles relaxed. He could feel his heart begin to pound in his chest and the familiar metallic taste of the chem in the back of his mouth. His mind was clear now. His eyes twitched with energy, the dry rawness now a distant memory. He could now focus on the world around him and everything had a more defined, sharper edge.

"So what type of luck have you come into then? How much ya making?" One thing about Stacey Steckles, Kessler thought to himself with his eyes closed enjoying the hit, she had a nose for money and the means, or merchandise, to tempt it from anyone.

Kessler, focused on the warm wave taking hold of his body, spoke, ignoring Stacey's question, "So where are all these bodies coming from?"

"We're not sure exactly but we think it's some new chem running the streets. They call it Lux. It's something else, completely out there, brings you right to the edge." She reached down into her blouse and pulled out a necklace, a piece of string with an ornate pendant showing a child kneeling and praying, wings folded down its back. She unscrewed its head and took a sniff of whatever lay within. Immediately her head jerked back and her lips pursed as the sting ran through her sinuses. She looked up at Kessler, her pupils now filling the whites of her eyes and her head swaying slightly from side to side.

"Sounds interesting."

"Stay away from it," her lips gripped the nic stick and sucked, "it's no good. You should see how it leaves people… I've never seen anything like it… no good. The bodies have come in looking bad." She spoke quickly.

"Bad?"

"Yea, bad. Even for down here. Emaciated, covered in red sores and their eyes," her hand shook as it held the nick stick close to her mouth, "they're always completely black. I hear that the pleasure is so great it burns you out quickly, doesn't leave much behind." She paused for a while lost in thought before eventually coming back to reality. "We've had to hire people in to handle the disposal of all the bodies." Her hands were claws, tense, against the ecstasy.

So that was the smell Kessler had noticed in the corridor. "Damn, what's in it?"

"No one knows. We've tested it but," she shrugged, "nothing unusual." She was sitting on the floor now, legs pulled up to her chest and arms wrapped around her. She looked almost innocent, child-like. Kessler found his eyes drifting towards Stacey's pendant. The child kneeling, praying, reminded him of the reason he came down this way in the first place. "Listen Stacey, have you heard any biz on a dead Christian priest that passed through here a couple of weeks ago? I checked and I heard he was sent here, no questions asked like, hushed up." Stacey seemed to regain some focus and stared at Kessler. She stood up and leaned slightly precariously on a shelf. "I was wondering if you could give me some info, I heard the Vents brought him here from D2."

"Shut up!" Stacey whispered abruptly, pushing her hand over Kessler's mouth. "What do you think you're doing?" She pushed the detective to the side and put her ear to the door.

"Hey, what's the problem?" Kessler was used to Stacey's paranoia, she was wired most of the time to some chem, powder or sim. All that uptime would make most brains go to mush but Stacey was tough, had been through a lot and survived some hard times. She could handle herself.

She knelt down, with her back leaning against the store room door and brought a painted finger to her lips signalling Kessler to be quiet. "Kes, I can't talk about it."

The detective helped her to her feet and drew her close, "It's ok, you know me, this won't go any further than these four walls." He tried to speak in a calming tone but found it difficult as the chems fired through him. He took hold of her cold, clammy hands. He could not tell if they were shaking due to the chems or from what she was being asked, "What's got you all worked up?"

She leaned forward and put her mouth just inches from his ear and whispered, "A few weeks ago the priest's body arrived, surrounded by Councilmen."

"Councilmen?" Kessler interrupted.

"Shhhh!!"

He continued, speaking quietly, "What do they want with

49

some religious freak?" The Councilmen were employed directly by the Council. Officially they were part of the DPD but everyone knew they were corporate. They rarely made a show of themselves in public and when they did rumours had it that you did not live long enough to tell the tale. "You must be mistaken. Taking too many chems. Hallucinating."

"No." She closed her eyes and whispered.

"You need sleep."

"I can't sleep."

"Yea, I know the feeling." Kessler's mind was stirring. What would a priest wasting away in Downtown have to do to get the attention of those evil goons? "Councilmen? Below the Rim? Why?"

"They closed the lab down and carried out tests. Made it very clear we were not to mention any of it…or else."

"How did he die? Anything unusual?"

"Well that's just it. We knew straight away how he'd died. He looked like all the rest. Eyes as black as tar, his body sucked dry of life. That's how they look you know, after taking too much of it."

"Hold on a minute, are you telling me the priest overdosed on sim? Now, I know nothing about religion but isn't one of their beliefs to never get completely burned up on chem?"

"Such a shame. He was a nice old man, tried to help the Dregs but you know, what's the point, most don't want to be helped."

"You knew him?"

"He came up this way once in a while, trying to help some kick their habit. There were a few who would hang around and talk to him."

A door slammed from somewhere outside the store room. Stacey jumped up with a start, took one long drag from her nic stick and, just before opening the door and darting back into the corridor, took a brief moment to look up at the detective with pleading, bloodshot eyes, "Don't tell anyone, Kes."

Kessler waited a couple of seconds before following, thinking it might look slightly suspicious if anyone seen him emerge from a store room with the nurse.

Stepping out into the corridor with smoke wafting from the confines of the store room, he blinked his eyes repeatedly, attempting to adjust them to the intensity of the strip lighting that buzzed overhead. His mind raced. Why would Councilmen care about a priest? It was true religion was illegal but the Council rarely took any notice of the hundreds of cults which sprung up every week in Downtown. As long as they did not appear above the Rim they were usually happy to leave them to the local governors. He had also never heard of holy men getting smacked out on sim. The questions whirled and spun around in Kessler's head. He gave himself a shake and took a hit of Ox.

Brushing his hand through his greasy hair, he let out a sigh. He definitely did not need any heat from the Council, his life was rough enough as it was without attracting that type of attention. A com cackled into life, "Dr Skreegal please report to theatre two. Immediately." The nasal voice was immediately followed by screams and wails of some poor patient before the com abruptly cut off.

Putting on his optics, he quickened his pace and, walking with determination through the waiting room, made for the exit. Kessler had spent longer with Stacey than he had intended, time had escaped him. It usually did when he met her. He would have to travel fast or he would be late for his meeting with Bethany at the church.

·ST. JOHN'S·

The junker landed in a cloud of exhaust fumes on an old, worn cobbled square. It had been a long time since Kessler had been this far down and, looking outside the canopy into the darkness, he hoped it would be his last. Downtown 2 was the beginnings of the old parts of the city, gone were the carbonised iron highways and the towering plastisteel buildings now replaced by ancient crumbling stone and rotting brick. Even during daylight hours darkness had its impenetrable grip over the entire district. The odd neon sign and flash of a torch far in the distance penetrated through the murk but, other than that, light was in scarce supply. Kessler was thankful for the chems still running through his system, it would make this experience a lot easier. He reached over to the passenger side and from a compartment took his torch and a spare canister of Ox.

The canopy opened and Kessler jumped out onto the street and immediately was drenched in the deluge. He bent over to shield his mouth away from the filth and tried to take a breath. He gripped the sides of the vehicle as his body shuddered in protest until, after a couple of hits of Ox, he began to breathe easier. Raising the collar of his coat up and tying a cloth round his mouth and nose, he tried in vain to protect himself against the foul torrent.

Even through the augmented sight of his optics, Kessler

struggled to see more than fifty feet ahead of him. Not far from where he had parked his junker, a neon sign flashed a rare hazy light across the far side of the square. From it, he could see the dark, shadowed forms of a couple of Dregs stumbling through the gloom. Everything was wet. This rain was a torrent of foul-smelling sludge and it coated everything. He could feel it under his boots. He could even taste it. The cramped, claustrophobic conditions of Downtown only served to make matters worse. Ancient buildings towered over small, crooked, crumbling streets, trapping the stench of decay at ground level. There was no breeze to rid the senses of this odour, only a stifling heat. Kessler let out another sigh and tried to shrug such thoughts from his mind, "Think of the credits, Kes," he spoke aloud but his voice was drowned out by the crashing rain.

Soon he turned a corner and St John's came into view. It was lit up by a number of piercing white beams and the red flashing lights of the DPD Interceptors. Kessler could make out the silhouettes of four Venters guarding the entrance to the church. He whistled to himself in amazement at the site of Vents this far down. What made this church so damn special?

Over the constant drone of the deluge, he could hear the brief flash of a raised voice and the mechanical tones of the Venters barking orders. It was only when the columns of light turned towards an angry voice that it revealed, out of the darkness, the figure of Bethany Turner. Now wearing a transparent rain protector over her dress, she was shouting and waving her arms, furiously remonstrating with the police. He had to admit that she certainly had some guts to be giving it to the Vents like that. He sighed, if he did not do something soon she would end up dead before he could get anymore credits out of her. Closing his eyes and cursing to himself, he left the protection of the darkness and walked towards the Vent's dancing beams of light.

As he approached, the Venter's huge forms came into view.

Their black plate armour glistened and their sodden white robes lay limp, stained brown in the rain. It was obvious that the situation was escalating quickly. A Venter had taken hold of Bethany's neck while another was waving his assault rifle in the air, gesturing towards her. He adjusted the cloth around his mouth so that he could speak. "Damn the light," Kessler mumbled, "what have you got yourself into?" His mind raced as he raised his voice to speak aloud, "Hey, there you are! I've been looking all over for you." Raising his arms in mock relief, he smiled at the officers and at the furious Bethany. This close to the Venters he could now hear the mechanical breathing of their respirators hiss and wheeze. He turned towards all four who were all now staring at him. He squinted his eyes and lowered his head as beams of light from their shoulder mounted torches blinded him. "Thanks for finding her, she's gone completely nuts, absolutely crazy." He twirled his finger round his ear and pointed at Bethany, "Completely insane. It's the breathing sickness, it's gone to her head. I'm taking her straight to a skin lab for treatment." The blaring light was momentarily averted from his eyes as the Venters turned towards her. The detective took the opportunity to peer over the Vent's right shoulder at the church entrance. Nothing seemed to be out of place, if anything the crumbling stone tower and walls had a somewhat peaceful air about them. Two figures, beautifully carved out of stone so rarely seen in the city above, depicted two young children standing either side of a large metal gate. Their chubby faces creased in an innocent smile.

The officer holding Bethany looked around at each of his colleagues and after a few moments let go of her rain protector and shoved her towards Kessler, "Tell her to keep out of Council business." He emphasised his point by powering up his rifle.

"Of course, I wouldn't even dream of interfering with your very important work." Kessler backed away, head lowered in mock respect.

"Wait, what do you think you're doing I…" Bethany's furious rant was quickly cut short by Kessler's hand over her mouth. He lifted her over his shoulder and walked away from St John's carrying her squirming form back to where his vehicle was parked.

Dropping the irate girl next to his junker, out of sight of any hostile eyes, Kessler spoke, "Quiet. Now I'm taking my hand away and you will be silent." He held her roughly, one of his large hands firmly over her mouth and the other held tight around her waist. After a few seconds she stopped trying to force herself free and ceased her muffled cries. Now silent and still, she glowered at the detective, "Ok. Now if we are to get anything productive out of this investigation you can't be going up to the Vents ranting and raging. It will get us nowhere and you, and me, will be thrown in Council cells or worse." He released her from his grip.

She adjust her dishevelled clothes and spoke in a desperate, urgent tone, "Well what are your plans?"

"The DPD seem to have the building in complete lock down." He wiped the rainwater from his brow. "I don't need this trouble. The Venters are not people you want to mess with, they will not hesitate to end both of us. I have seen it done many times before." Kessler looked down at her. She turned her back to him, put her head in her hands and began to sob.

The detective turned to leave but hesitated and, with a heavy sigh, leaned on the bonnet of his vehicle. Lowering his head and sheltering it under his hood, he lit a cigar and turned back to look at Bethany. Her cheap rain protector had not prevented her clothes becoming soaked and through the clear plastic Kessler could see them clinging to her body revealing a curvy, slender form. Her wet hair was pulled back revealing an attractive face and of course there were those green eyes. Kessler knew straight away that this girl was going to be nothing but trouble. She had a vulnerability that told him she would not last long in this city alone, but deep in those emerald eyes of hers, the way the light caught them to reveal a flash of reckless yellow, there hid a determination to see this through to whatever lay waiting at its end. Not many people would stand up to the Vents like she had done. Stupid and reckless, but she was brave, all qualities that got citizens killed fast. Sure, Kessler had known those types of women before, known them all too well, and it had never ended pretty.

"Please help me." With wide eyes she pleaded.

Kessler knew this was coming. He opened the junker's canopy as Bethany grabbed hold of him and tried feebly to pull him towards the direction of the church. He could not help but let out a laugh. "I admire your determination but look, whatever the DPD want with your place they're going to get it." He pulled his hood further down over his head and shrugged off the water that was freely flowing over him and nodded towards the faint glow of the Venter's spotlights that could just about be seen from around the corner.

"I've hired you to do a job." Her face was creased in desperation. "I can't do this by myself."

Kessler cleared his throat, "Look, nothing is worth getting tangled up with Council business. Get in the vehicle, I'll drop you off anywhere you want. Somewhere dry."

She reached into a bag that she had slung over her shoulder and threw a small pouch at Kessler who fumbled to catch it. "There you go Mr Kessler, an added incentive for your troubles."

Looking at the small pouch, Kessler untied the string to reveal the familiar glint of chrome bars, "The church pays well it seems." He looked at Bethany, her arms folded and returning his stare with a blank expression as she waited for an answer. Kessler toyed with the bag of creds, jostling them in his hand, listening to the sound of them clinking between his fingers. There was no denying that he needed the cash but one look towards the church and the Vents quickly convinced him. "Look lady, there is no way I'm going in that building. Like I said, those that mess with the Vents have a tendency to disappear, if you know what I mean, especially this far down." He stepped closer to her and took a long draw on his cigar, eventually exhaling the smoke, "They can do what they like down here, no one cares." He shook his head, exasperated at her persistence.

Kessler turned to get into his vehicle and Bethany again tried to pull him back, shouting, "You're afraid, aren't you?"

He closed his eyes and half turned his head away from her, "No. I'm surviving."

"Wait," she pleaded, "remember, I grew up here. This church is all I've ever known. I know every single nook and cranny. If we could just make it over the wall, I know of a way in and there is no way the police will have found it. As a child I used to love exploring every inch of the old building and would hide for hours trying to avoid the many chores my uncle made me do every day. There is no way the police would know about it. No way."

"Listen, I have enough headaches in my life as it is and that doesn't include the pounding one you're giving me right now." The sim he had taken earlier was beginning to wear off. He rubbed his brow and winced at the thought of the little sleep he had the previous night. He knew, with disgust at himself, what was in store for him once the chems left his system.

"Mr Kessler, please. The night my uncle's life was taken everything I'd ever known disappeared. I'm all alone in this world and only have the next to look forward to. The only thing left for me in this life is justice." She drew close to him, both of her delicate gloved hands holding tightly onto the lapels of his coat, her bottom lip trembling as she tried to desperately hold back her fear.

He stood looking at the young girl. The city had a tendency to destroy any good in its citizens sooner or later and, if they lived long enough, replace it with the hate, anger and the fear needed to survive. He did not know what it was about this particular sob story, there were millions of sob stories in Dis, many more tragic than this, but the thought of this city getting its claws into this trembling, innocent kid did not sit right with him. Perhaps it was her eyes, shimmering green pools all alone in this world, maybe her jet black hair that fell across her face when she shook her head or perhaps the old detective was just tired of being miserable, but whatever the reason, he felt sorry for her. So here it was, Kessler thought ruefully, more bad decisions. "For the light's sake! Ok. I could do with the cred and anything to get out of this damn rain."

Bethany led him around the church to a gap in the now disintegrating perimeter wall. The Vents were easily avoidable, their powerful torches giving them plenty of warning as to their presence. Most of them seemed to be hanging around the main entrance, completely focused on looking menacing to every Dreg who happened to stumble near them and completely oblivious to anything else.

Peering through a hole in the crumbling wall, Kessler could make out the rubble which lay strewn throughout the church grounds. Bethany spoke in a low whisper, "The gravestones of people long dead. They have been here for centuries, you can even still read words on some of them, messages to people lost in time. I didn't have much company growing up here, Uncle didn't like me mixing with people within the parish, always telling me that he knew their sins and didn't want me part of them. Many children have imaginary friends, Mr Kessler, mine just happen to come from the very real people that are buried here." Bethany smiled at the memory.

He never understood the old ways of burying the dead in the ground. Solid ground, that of the ancient world, was so rare on Dis. Why waste the space on the dead? Looking out into what was left of the church grounds Kessler could see that the incessant rain had washed away the old earth long ago revealing its grisly contents. In amongst the piles of stone, skeletal features gawked back at them. The dull, low light of Downtown half hiding the horrors giving the skulls and bones an even more sinister quality.

Both crouching down close to the ground, they made their way across the church yard, obscured under the cloak of darkness and by the dense rainfall. Bethany led Kessler by the hand, nimbly navigating her way through the many obstacles that lay on their path, however Kessler still managed to trip over and knock into gravestones and statues at any given opportunity. She must have spent many a childhood day playing here, he thought, and could easily imagine her running around in her younger years, her uncle calling after her, unable to catch or find her.

Eventually they came to a stone structure with four steps which led down to another crumbling wall. Kessler looked up from underneath his hood, water cascading down over his coat, and immediately fell back in horror as a monstrous face appeared out of the dark. He gasped and half yelled over the noise of the rain, "What type of place is this?" Two stone carvings stood either side of the structure. One held a knife aloft, its open maw revealing long fangs, the other sat with wings spread wide, ready for flight, a huge mischievous grin on a hideous face.

Bethany smiled, "Don't worry. They're only gargoyles. In the past people used them to ward off evil spirits." Kessler looked out into the gloom, nodded in understanding and joined Bethany huddled at the base of the steps, a small stone overhang giving them some reprieve from the torrent.

"I thought you were going to get us into the church?" Kessler was confused, they were still some distance away from the main building and he could not see anything resembling an entrance that would get them inside.

"Below us are the old crypts where people used to keep their dead. I spent many hours down there as a kid. It's quite beautiful."

"Sounds great." Kessler said sarcastically. "You spent your childhood hanging around dead people, rather you than me."

"I can assure you that I had a very well rounded and fulfilling upbringing."

"So how are we going to get in then?" Kessler was getting impatient. The faint glow of the Venter's lights could just be made out over the wall on the far side of the church.

"I was getting to that." Bethany placed her hand into the open mouth of the gargoyle holding the knife and grabbed hold of its tongue. With a slight twist of her hand the wall began to open with a deep rumble. She looked up at the detective smugly, "I told you, I know this place."

"Let's get in quickly before the Venters catch sight of us. If that happens I guarantee you that we will both be joining your dead friends sooner rather than later." Kessler could not help but raise a slight smile under his hood, he was impressed by the girl's resourcefulness.

"This crypt was used by some wealthy family back in the days before the Purging. The family crypts are down here, come see." Being inside the church seemed to have an almost instantaneous effect on her as she excitedly darted around the familiar surroundings of her childhood.

Bethany climbed down into the darkness with the same dexterity she had shown in the graveyard. Kessler stumbled down the steep, well worn ancient stairs and immediately struggled for grip as rainwater flowed over the smooth stone. He felt awkward, hands either side of him braced against the walls keeping his large bulk upright as he fumbled in the dark. His clothes were heavy, soaked through, and now that he was sheltered from the elements he could smell the rot of the rain which mingled with the damp odour of the crypt itself. He sneezed and with a quick, panicked curse tumbled down the final few stairs with a crash. Hard plastic crates broke his fall, and their contents, thousands of sheets of paper, now lay scattered everywhere some still fluttering gracefully through the air. The detective lay on the ground, cursing to himself and rubbing the back of his head.

He came round to see Bethany standing above him. She had her hand outstretched, offering to help lift him from the mess in which he now found himself entangled. Feeling like a naughty child he swore again, "I can't see a damn thing in here," he mumbled under his breath, feeling awkward at his sudden show of vulnerability. He took off his optics and put it in his coat pocket and gave his eyes a rub, they itched like hell. He could feel the chem leaving his body and his strength going with it.

"Mr Kessler, you must be quiet if we are to avoid the attention of our friends outside." Despite the gloom, Kessler was sure he could see a smile on her face. She had a candle in her hand, lit it and again offered her hand out to him, "Let me help."

Kessler batted her away, "I can manage." He was too old for all this, out of shape and he knew it. But what he also knew was that there was no way that he was going to let Bethany Turner discover this. Not a chance.

Untangling himself from the mess, Kessler straightened himself out, pulled back his hood and surveyed the scene around him. The pale light of the candle revealed thousands of sheets of paper strewn everywhere. He could just make out at the edge of the light a stone column that reached up to a large vaulted ceiling about twenty feet above their heads. "Is this real paper? It looks old." Kessler picked up one of the many yellowed crisp sheets that littered floor. "I remember seeing some in the markets but it was only a small torn piece. It didn't have any writing on it." He fingered the paper in his hands, the writing was a language he did not understand however he gazed in wonder at the beautiful long elegant strokes that made up the lettering. He could not help but think that something so delicate belonged to a very different time.

Bethany picked up a pile of paper and neatly stacked it

inside an empty container, "Old manuscripts, letters, books. Anything that mentions God or his teachings we find and try and retrieve the knowledge, learn from it. All are from the old world before the Purge."

"I didn't think much survived."

"You'd be surprised. Some have travelled deep down into the lowest parts of Dis and returned with fantastic treasures. I've seen them." Bethany waved the candle slowly around the room to get her bearings, revealing more of the crypt. Many sarcophagi came into view, ghostly faces of long past carved into the stone, the dancing light throwing shadows across them giving each of their expressions a more menacing look. It was beyond Kessler the reasons why people wanted their dead hanging around, it gave him the creeps.

The ceiling was supported by cylindrical columns each bearing intricate designs that Kessler could just make out to be lost scenes from a different time. Trees and flowers, myths from a lost age, were carved into the stone, images now only found in children's stories, corporate ads and infogrammes.

Walking slowly through the crypt, carefully watching each step for fear of falling flat on his face, Kessler followed Bethany and her candlelight. He passed many boxes which, on closer inspection, contained bottles, hundreds of them full of a brown liquid all labelled 'Holy Ale.' "What is this place used for these days?"

"For storage mostly." Bethany turned to see Kessler closely inspecting one of the many bottles. "My uncle also brewed some alcohol down here to pay for the upkeep of the parish."

He looked at her and smiled, "Your uncle brewed ale?"

"Yes, in the past the priests at St. John's used the hidden rooms below the church to brew ale and make wine." She put her hands to her hips and shook her head, "It's not what you think. They sold it to make the credits needed to maintain the church and its grounds."

"Some operation he had going on down here." He looked around the room, the light now revealing boxes, hundreds of containers, glasses, jars, jugs and, up against the wall just ahead of them, barrels.

"It was for the community." She stated flatly.

The thought of drink made Kessler feel edgy. His mouth became dry like sandpaper, images of that half-full bottle of Piper's back in his junker came to mind. He cursed himself for not bringing it with him.

Despite having spent years enduring the pain of a chemical comedown it had not got any easier for Kessler. His skin felt clammy and was beginning to itch. The familiar tremor had also begun in his left hand, it always started there, a warning of future troubles. He shook his head, he had to focus on the job, be professional. Blinking his eyes he focused on what lay ahead, wiped his brow with his sleeve and he gritted his teeth. He noticed Bethany staring at him, hands on hips, biting her bottom lip. Kessler took a breath of Ox and spoke, "That's a very lucky community, must have been shifting some cred looking at this lot stored down here. The Council, however, mustn't have appreciated the competition. Might explain the Venters taking an interest in this little operation, people disappear to the Undercells for much less." Like many things on Dis, the production of booze was strictly prohibited and heavily regulated by the Council. Only approved corporations were allowed to produce and sell it throughout the city, and would make a fortune doing so. With a quick sharp burst of gas that seemed to reverberate around the crypt, he popped the top on an ale and glugged its entire contents down his throat. Placing the empty bottle back on top of the box he belched and wiped his mouth on his sleeve. "Mmm, not bad." He closed his eyes, appreciating the fine beverage. "Your uncle knew what he was doing. It has quite a kick, what's his secret?" A quick scan around the crypt answered his question for him. Barrels marked with the familiar winged and haloed 'M' and 'L' logo of Merryll Laboratories lined the far wall. He smiled at the irony of highly dangerous, illegal chemicals being stored right beneath the feet of citizens seeking forgiveness from their sins.

"It was a tradition passed down over the centuries. The clergy believed in the words of St Benedict who wanted all those in the service of God to live by the labours of their own hands, Mr Kessler. The community in Downtown have very little credits and the church is not going to ask them for charity."

"No, but you would sell them booze for profit?" Kessler had already grabbed hold of another bottle. "Must have been difficult getting chems from Merryll all the way down here passed the Vents guarding the Rim."

Bethany ignored Kessler's comment and continued, "Now, if you don't mind we have to be getting on."

He stared at the bottle, probably for longer than he would have liked, before setting it down carefully. It was good ale, he mused before turning to Bethany, "Yes ma'am, you're the boss." Kessler chuckled and felt somewhat secure in the grim knowledge that everything and everyone was tainted on Dis, no exceptions. At least life in this damned city was consistent.

"There is a stairwell that leads from here all the way up to the nave. A trap door opens right by the north transept which is just across the way from my uncle's study," Bethany stammered, "where the police found him."

Kessler followed Bethany to the base of the stairwell. He could hear the dripping of water from somewhere in the darkness, beyond the candlelight, reminding him of the harsh conditions outside. With every movement came the creak of sodden material and the squelch of waterlogged boots. Puddles of water pooled around his feet as they made their way up the stairs which consisted of narrow steps, well worn by the feet of the many clergymen who had lived and worked at St John's over the years.

The steep stairs ended abruptly at an old wooden hatch which Bethany immediately began to open. Kessler quickly grabbed hold of her arm and pulled her back, "Careful. Let me go first." He whispered to her with short, abrupt urgency. "We've come this far. It'd be a shame to get caught by the Vents and not find out what's so damn special about this place." Kessler had to admit to himself that he was curious. "Anyway," Kessler drew himself closer towards Bethany to emphasise the importance of what he was about to say. She winced and turned her head at the smell of his stale breath as he continued, "Our day would not end well if they found out we had sneaked in here."

Bethany looked up at the trapdoor for a few moments then down at Kessler who still held her arm in a tight grip. "Of course." As she nodded in agreement she audibly exhaled as if she had been holding her breath all this time in anticipation of what was to be discovered above their heads.

Leaning against the rough stone wall to the left of her he squeezed past. The soaking wet cloth of her dress clung tight to her body and Kessler could not avoid noticing Bethany's cleavage which, the candlelight revealed, grew with every excited intake of breath. Realising he was staring he looked away, blushing, and carefully pushed the hatch open just a few inches. Despite his caution, the old rusted metal hinges creaked loudly.

Peering out of the small opening, Kessler found himself looking across the nave to the other side of the church. The walls consisted of beautifully carved stone and highly polished dark golden wooden beams which arced gracefully far above the church floor. Columns, much like those found in the crypt but on a larger scale, elegantly rose from the floor to hold another beautifully grand vaulted ceiling. A silence seemed to caress everything within the church and calmed Kessler's nerves. He listened to the rain hammer against huge windows which had long ago been robbed of light by centuries of muck and grime and shivered in his wet clothes.

A sudden clatter shattered the calm. Kessler watched as a man stormed inside slamming shut the church's large front doors, the force of which reverberated throughout the building. He was dressed in a long grey military great coat with gleaming gold buttons and black shoulder boards embossed with the golden cog of the Council. Kessler knew that he was a Vent and an important one at that. Instead of the full plate helmet and respirator worn by those guarding the church outside, he wore the grey cap and gold trim of an officer. He had the look of disgust about him as he stood at the end of the nave patting the rainwater from his iron grey uniform. His frame did not have the bulk of the grunts outside, he was of a slight build, his face grey and gaunt with pallid skin which seemed to be stretched almost to breaking across his high cheekbones. His features were further twisted by an ugly scar that cut into the left side of his face at jagged angles giving him a ghoulish, sinister look. The shadows cast over his deep sunken eyes seemed to add to his menace. He ruefully looked at the state of his bare hands. The thick greasy rain had covered them in its brown soup, which he tried to rub off without much success. It brought a smile to Kessler's face at the officer's discomfort, he obviously had not been this far down before or he would have worn gloves.

The officer looked up from his sodden uniform to convey the innards of the church with an aloof-like nausea and began to walk through the rows of ancient wooden benches. He lashed out and threw to the floor books that were laid out ready for service, each one crashing with a thud that echoed throughout the building. The Vent did not show any care for the rarity of the paper just hatred for what lay within.

Soon, with the books now haphazardly piled high in the centre of the room, the officer stood just feet from where Kessler hid, smirking up at something obscured behind a pillar to Kessler's left. Close up, candlelight revealed that where his eyes should be now glowed red cyberware implants. Purple veins mixed garishly with wires under his sickly pale, taught skin and from this close, Kessler could hear the gyros hiss and whirl as they tried to focus. In the warmth of the church and the candlelight, the dank wet from outside seeped from the officer, encasing him in swirling smoky, toxic tendrils. The distinct smell of burnt flesh and chemicals oozed off of him making Kessler turn away back under the trapdoor, trying not to gag. Bethany looked up at him from the stairs, the flickering light shadowing her creased brow, "What's going on? Are you ok?"

The detective batted away her concern as he composed himself, "Quiet," and returned his attention to the Venter just in time to see him spit on the floor, adjust his coat, turn and march out of the church, his heavy set boots clattering the worn stone floor as he went. Once gone, silence returned. Kessler ducked back under the hatch and spoke to Bethany, "Ok, we're going to make our way quietly to the opposite side where the far aisle is shrouded in shadow. It will give us good cover." Bethany nodded her understanding.

Crouching low to the ground, Kessler, with one hand round Bethany and the other resting on his holstered carbine, cautiously climbed up into the nave and they began to make their way to the other side. Halfway across, Bethany released his hand and stopped, frozen to the ground, colour drained from her cheeks. "Bethany?" Kessler whispered, trying his very best not to attract any unwanted attention but failing miserably as his voice echoed throughout the large empty expanse of St John's. "Quickly, before they come back!"

Bethany dipped her fingers in a bowl of water that lay to the side of the altar. With eyes fixed in front of her she knelt and crossed her body, "By this Holy Water and by your Precious Blood, wash away all my sins O Lord."

Kessler's eyes darted between the kneeling Bethany and the large doors of St John's where, he was sure, just outside a whole lot of trouble was getting ready to join them. He knew this would happen. What was he thinking of agreeing to this insanity? He cursed himself. He was getting soft in his old age. "Bethany!" The detective barked and pulled her towards him when the focus of her attention came into view.

Beyond the pulpit was the large, beautifully carved stone figure of a man nailed, hands and feet, to a cross wearing a barbed crown. His head was bowed, eyes closed bearing a terrible pain. A dark substance, which appeared to be blood, had been sprayed over the sculpture and five rats, some of the largest rats he had ever seen, lay dead at its feet. Kessler had heard of this Christ figure, the man who called himself the son of God. He had seen his Christians on the newsreels which always depicted them, and the hundreds of other cults which sprung up on Dis every week, as illegal and troublesome, a breach of Council Protocols, all promoting lazy and unproductive behaviour. Citizen's energies, the Council preached, should be focused on the advancement of commerce and the city, not wasted on false idols. It was a mantra bored into the mind of all the children of Dis from a young age. Kessler could never work out why they risked and endured persecution just to look up to a man bearing so much agony, who endured so much suffering when all around them their own lives were nothing but pain and misery. Surely they would want something that allowed them to forget this sorry existence?

Kessler tugged at her coat, trying to urge her to move into the cover of the shadows but instead she knelt down and stared at a jumble of pictures and an assortment of items which lay spread out at the base of the altar. "What're you doing?" His voice was sharp with agitation.

"These are the lost. Those that have vanished from our community."

"Vanished?"

"Yes, it started happening a few months ago. A child here, a husband there. Soon every day people were just disappearing off the streets. We are all very close here at St John's and knew everyone of the lost, knew everyone of the heartbroken wives, husbands and children that they left behind."

"I didn't know. The newsreels have not reported it."

"No. We tend to fend for ourselves down here, nobody takes much notice of us. The congregation leave pictures of those missing with items that were important to them in life by the altar. It helps them pray to God for their safe return. Gives them hope."

False hope, Kessler thought cynically. "Does anyone know where they were taken? What happened to them?"

"No. My uncle was looking into it but…" Bethany tailed off, lost in thought. She picked up a small dirty doll that had been splattered in dark red and tried unsuccessfully to brush off the blood before taking a picture from her pocket and placing it in the centre of the pile. Three priests, one of whom looked very serious and the other two, much younger, smiled broadly.

Kessler assumed the old priest to be Father Jacob, "Who are the other two priests with your uncle?"

"Brothers Glaxon and Rothery. They lived here with us and helped my uncle run St John's. They went missing the night he died. I have not seen them since."

Kessler shook his head, aware that time was not on their side and eventually managed to drag Bethany away from the altar. Holding her firmly behind a column, he looked into her eyes and barked, "Get a hold of yourself, we don't have the time for this. Now snap out of it and show me where he was found."

"His study." Her eyes brimmed with tears as she stifled a sob. Her bottom lip quivered, "Over there, beyond the chancel." She pointed to the east end of the church.

Father Jacob's study was in complete darkness. Kessler turned on his torch which immediately revealed evidence from the priest's violent demise strewn throughout the room. The ancient wooden door lay in splintered pieces on the stone floor, part of the frame and the hinges still hanging from the wall. Bookshelves, which must have lined the study, were overturned with all their contents scattered everywhere. An old wooden desk with the delicate carvings of flowers and winged children similar to those seen in the nave lay at an angle in the centre of the room. Large gouges and deep, jagged scratches defaced the once beautiful golden wood which now lay cracked and broken. It was as if some savage animal had been let loose. Examining the scene further, Kessler noticed no computer or machinery of any kind, no plastisteel or network jacks existed in this world. He knew of a few antique dealers up in Hightown that would kill to get their hands on the precious wood, stone and paper that lay within these walls.

Kessler's attention focused on an area that was clear of clutter, the floor covered by a grey rug which was matted with a dark substance. He knelt down and dabbed the area with his fingers. More blood. "He must have died here. Whoever it was certainly made a fine mess." Empty vials, similar to the sim Kessler purchased back at the skin lab, lay everywhere. He picked one up and smelt the spent capsule revealing a sickly, sweet aroma. It was definitely some sort of chem but none he had ever smelt before. All the caps were marked with the same image – a bright yellow sphere, burning like a sun. It was common for different types of sim to be branded and Kessler knew most of them but he had never seen this on the streets before. He put a couple of empty caps in his coat pocket and, still kneeling close to the floor, looked up at Bethany who was staring at the chaotic scene, wringing her hands nervously. "Did your uncle ever indulge in chem?" Bethany turned and stared at Kessler blankly, "Just to take the edge off?"

"No, of course not. Why do you ask?" She spoke quietly, her eyes fixed on the empty vial which Kessler was holding up to the torch light before her.

"It's a tough city, Bethany, especially living this far down. Many citizens do it." He looked away from her, the innocent shock in her eyes making him feel embarrassed at suggesting such a thing.

"No. Never. He spent time helping chem addicts at the local skin labs, he was always very clear that it was the Devil's scourge. A blight on our community." She spoke in a whisper, her stare unmoving from the cap which Kessler still held between his fingers. "Why would people want to hurt a man who had spent his entire life helping others?" She wiped away a stray tear and cleared her throat. "All these beautiful things," she said glancing at a pile of overturned books and torn paper as she walked over to the desk. Taking a small metal key from a chain that hung around her neck, she opened a drawer amongst all the carnage of splintered wood, and took the contents from within. "Got it." She stood by the desk, arm in the air holding a silver ring dangling by a piece of string. Kessler leaned closer and took it in his hands to examine it. The ring bore the symbol of a black book with a sparkling cross filled with diamonds and it was immediately obvious to him that it was as beautiful as it was rare. He had never seen anything like it before.

"This place is full of treasures, that's for sure. This ring would fetch a small fortune in Hightown. More than enough creds to live comfortably."

"The knowledge within these books, the history behind all these items from the past, is the real treasure, Mr Kessler. Rediscovering our soul is far more valuable than any credit or Hightown residence permit."

Kessler doubted that. "When the air has poisoned your lungs or the filth of the city has infested your body, all these books, this learning, means nothing. Credits can buy you a better life, not knowledge, not a soul."

Bethany continued, ignoring him, "As for the ring, I don't intend to sell it. It belonged to my mother, the only thing I have

71

in this world that used to be hers. Uncle was keeping it safe for me until, as he always used to tell me, I was responsible enough to wear it." Her voice trailed off in thought then all of a sudden burst into anger, "I want the people that did this to me, to this church," she waved a clenched fist across the room, "to burn in hell." After shaking for a few moments in silence she placed the ring around her neck, underneath her rain protector and dress.

Kessler looked upon the girl who had lost all those that had loved her, a girl who was now all alone and only had one thing left in this world, hatred for those that had done this to her. She gripped tightly to the hatred, its fuel giving her the energy to continue. Where was her God now? "Don't worry they will," he said reassuringly. "First we need to find a reason why this happened. Has anything been stolen?" Kessler needed a motive. His thoughts kept returning to the empty vials of sim. He had seen chemheads lose it many times before and if the priest was messed up with that business then it could be connected. Theft came to mind but sitting in this room amongst ancient items that would fetch a small fortune up town, he doubted that was the case. Looking at the state of the study and the defaced altar, a violence had been unleashed onto this place that suggested more than just a simple robbery.

"I can't tell in all this mess," Bethany's eyes darted throughout the room finding it difficult to focus on any one thing that may have been taken. "I don't think so."

"Maybe it was the ring they were looking for? I know many that would kill for something that rare." Silver and especially diamonds were almost unheard of on Dis, only the very wealthy Hightowners may ever have hoped to own such wealth.

"I don't think anyone would have known about it, my uncle always kept it in this drawer, for safe keeping."

"Not that safe. In fact, that drawer would be the first place that I'd look for valuables and they didn't even try to jimmy the lock." Kessler looked around for a console to access the church security and personnel files. "Did your uncle not use any tech whatsoever? How did he survive? How did he run this church without access to the Mainframe? I need anything that reveals something about the time leading up to his death? His records, accounts, journals? Anything?"

"Books, he believed in books." Bethany trembled in shock as she fought hard to get the words out of her throat.

A muffled noise from outside the room made them both freeze in their place. "What was that?" Bethany placed her hand over her mouth and stared at the flickering shadows outside the doorway.

Out of habit, Kessler's hand went straight for his weapon, "Sounded like a door. We best be quick."

"That shelf over in the far corner is where he kept his journals." She pointed to an overturned bookshelf under which were a pile of beautifully-bound black synthleather books, each had the date written in gold leaf on the front and spine. Kessler immediately started to rummage through them.

"All these books are from years ago." Kessler spoke out of breath as he slowly made his way through the huge pile.

"His current diary would be in his desk," Bethany said in a matter of fact tone.

Kessler stopped his search and looked up at her, "Thank you for the information," he sighed sarcastically as he got to his feet.

Bethany continued unaware of Kessler's annoyance, "I remember as a kid thinking he was funny, the only person I ever knew who refused to use computers. Stuck in the old ways. He was always at his desk, scribbling his thoughts down in that journal, eyes squinting close to read the text over his glasses which always were slipping down his nose. His eyesight was awful and of course getting a bioware implant or cyber fix was not an option." She laughed at some memory. "He would always scold me for talking about any type of tech, and would tell me in a stern tone, 'The cold metal of machinery had taken us a long way from the warmth of God.'" She mimicked her uncle's deep voice and smiled before emerging from her memories and sadness returning to her face.

Kessler put his torch in his mouth and using both hands frantically continued his search. Books were thrown either side of him, discarding a wide range of texts, all depicting words and scenes alien to him. "Are you just going to stand there or you going to be of any help?" Bethany was still in the middle of the room staring into space.

"Of course." She took a deep breath, "Sorry." Reaching down to the base of the desk she immediately picked up a black-covered book similar to the hundreds Kessler was searching through. "Here it is."

Holding a bundle of diaries and sweating profusely, he looked flustered and glanced up at his expressionless companion, "Thank you," Kessler repeated with a mixture of annoyance and more sarcasm as he wiped the sweat from his brow. He was not sure that Bethany Turner knew how precarious their situation was.

"You know Mr Kessler, I always thought the exciting life of a detective would keep a person fit but I think I am doing you a favour hiring you. You obviously could do with the exercise."

He did not register Bethany's jibe, but was staring down at the surface of the desk which was now clear of the books that had cluttered it. Words appeared in the shaking torchlight, again in a tongue not of the detective's understanding, crudely hacked onto the desk's surface.

"What are you staring at?"

"Take a look at this." Kessler spoke as he produced a viewfinder from his pocket and scanned the surface of the desk.

Bethany walked over to where the detective was standing.

"Oh my." Bethany's words caught in her throat.

"Do you understand it?"

"'Lux Ferre', I know what it says but I do not understand its meaning. It doesn't make sense…"

"I recognize the word 'Lux', it's a new chem that has been doing the rounds all over Downtown."

"I was only a young girl when my uncle took me in and he was an old man even then. He was always concerned that there were not any kids for me to hang around with and worried that he wasn't much fun and didn't know how to raise a girl. To keep me amused he spent his free time educating me. He taught me an old language that only him and I knew how to speak. It was like our secret club. We used to leave each other messages that only we could understand."

"Ok, so what does it mean?" Kessler was getting impatient with Bethany's reminiscing.

"Yes, of course, it means Light Bringer."

A few moments passed in silence as they contemplated the words before Kessler moved from the desk and took hold of Bethany's arm. "Let's get out of here." He moved for the door, taking the diary from Bethany and placing it in his pocket.

"Ok, I just want to take some of uncle's stuff with me. I…"

"We don't have the time," Kessler interrupted her, all he could think about was leaving. Fast. "We need to… what's that smell?"

Bethany had not noticed the distinct bitter acrid smell of smoke. He grabbed her hand and pulled her out of the study when immediately they were confronted by a barrage of heat, a wall of flames cracking and roaring. The large pile of books that had been thrown to the floor by the Venter had been set alight, the old paper quickly turning into a maelstrom of fire and smoke. Large flames coiled and danced their way throughout the church, the nave was a shower of embers as the ancient wooden beams embraced the inferno.

Bethany threw herself towards the blaze and screamed, "No! We can't lose them!" Her desperate wail was cut short by the big arm of the detective as he wrapped it around her midriff and drew her protesting form close to him. She was writhing in his arms in a panicked frenzy. "Let me go, let me go you fool, you don't know what we're losing."

"The whole place is going to come down!" Kessler shouted over the chaos.

Suddenly, as he was holding her tightly in his grasp, trying to shield her from the overpowering heat, there was an explosive grown as the statue of Christ came crashing down around them. Bethany let out a terrified shriek then went limp in Kessler's arms. Flames began to flow up her leg and the detective frantically smothered them using his coat. He looked at Bethany's tear and soot-stained face to make sure she was ok, amongst all the chaos she looked so innocent, almost at peace.

The detective surveyed the diabolical scene that was playing out before him. Fire performed its demonic dance over all that was precious to the poor girl. The statue of Christ was bathed in flame, its face half black, cracked and broken, making part of its mouth misshapen into a bestial grin. Towering flames were spread across the centre of the nave between Kessler and St John's large front doors. "Think, damn you, think." He bellowed as the blaze took hold, "You may be a Midtown bum not worth a damn," he took another look at Bethany's unconscious face, "but this girl's got some good in her, she doesn't deserve this!" The din of the inferno drowned out his frantic cries.

The intense heat backed him and his unconscious companion onto the altar. He turned to shield his face from the inevitable as the flames began to lick his legs and arms when he saw, in amongst the raging fire and thick black smoke, the gleaming white stone head of a child, his wing tips just visible through the thick haze, holding the bowl of water Bethany had used for prayer moments before. Rising up off his knees, he found a new energy and vigour and powered through the fire to reach the statue. Pain and the weight of Bethany strained every sinew and muscle.

The child looked up at the detective with an innocent face.

Time seemed to slow as the fire closed in. Kessler focused on the kid's virtuous features, everything else seemed insignificant. His delicate hands were raised, offering Kessler the bowl of water. He took off his coat, drenched it in the precious liquid and wrapped it around Bethany. Setting himself against the flames, he charged forward carrying her limp form in his arms, shielding her from harm. He only had one thought in his mind and that was the trapdoor which led to the crypt and, hopefully, to safety.

Within moments, a blackened mass of smoke and fire burst through the hatch, shattering the old wood, and tumbling down the steps. Kessler was just able to smother the flames that had latched onto him, check Bethany was still breathing, before collapsing onto the cool stone floor at the base of the stairs.

The crypt brought with it a brief respite from the raging torrent above. The roar of the flames were replaced by the staggered breathing of the unconscious Bethany and Kessler's rasping coughs. He lay flat on his back, an arm still protectively wrapped around his charge who remained covered in his soaked coat. He could smell scorched skin and singed hair. His knee ached and his right arm, which had borne the brunt of the fire, felt tight, the burnt skin crackled and blood wept through his shirt.

The pain was getting worse, every slight movement brought agony. Kessler was tired, his eyes were heavy and were stinging from the thick smoke of the blaze. He just wanted to close his eyes for a moment. Find peace and quiet. He thought of sleep and how much he needed it. All the chaos of the fire was beginning to slip away, become a distant, blurred memory, replaced by an overwhelming desire to rest, allow sleep to carry him away from all this harm. He had earned a rest, what would it hurt just to close his eyes for a while? He began a dazed dream.

He imagined thousands of stars across a clear night sky. The space to take a breath…

A brief spike of reality suddenly penetrated Kessler's consciousness. The air had that thick damp quality and he could smell the heady fumes of chemicals. He opened his eyes wide. Downtown. The crypt.

Black smoke was beginning to fill the room. The stars Kessler had seen in his dream were now thousands of burning embers raining down around him. Above, the church floor, which had stood firm since ancient times screeched, groaned, blistered and buckled under the blazing chaos. He lifted his head to his right and looked at the prone Bethany and back to the stairs leading out of the church to the graveyard. The floor above had already given way and a column of flames now barred his way out.

He raised himself up, leaning on his one good arm, as the flames closed in around them. A sound, like a gush of wind, drew his attention back to the many barrels of chemicals stacked up against the far wall. The air seemed to be sucked from his lungs and he struggled for breath as a blanket of liquid fire reached out to cover them. He fumbled with his shaking, uninjured arm, to his coat pocket and grabbed his canister of Ox and placed it over Bethany's mouth and gave her, and then himself, a couple of hits. Desperation and sheer terror overcame him. With a feral shriek he found reserves of energy he didn't know he had and stood up with gritted teeth and flung Bethany, like a rag doll, over his shoulder.

His situation was desperate. "Think Kessler, think!" He shouted but the cacophony of the flames roared louder. He could not see the barrels now as they were obscured behind fire and smoke which had taken on a dark green hue, the stench of the potent chemicals catching Kessler's lungs and raked his body in hacking coughing fits. He knew it was now or never. Instinct took over and he leapt, still holding Bethany, to the nearest sarcophagus. He heaved with all his might and slid the heavy stone lid to one side, threw in Bethany before tumbling in himself. With the last ounces of energy he pulled the lid shut just as an almighty explosion rocked his senses throwing the pitch black world within the tomb into a maelstrom, spinning and churning into nothingness...

·OFFICE TIMES·

A grating cough in the darkness roused Kessler into consciousness. He could not breathe and something heavy lay across his chest. Every intake of breath brought about an agony, his throat was red raw and his mouth cracked and dry. He tried to call out for someone, something, but only a wheezing hiss creaked from his scorched innards. Trying to move brought a flash of white pain to the darkness, he struggled to raise his left arm and his head pounded, a constant high-pitched whining noise rung in his ears. The caustic, acrid smell of burning filled his lungs combined with the thick smell of decay. He began to retch but the pain was too much for his broken body to bear.

The detective tried to focus on something to get his bearings, piece together fractured images and memories to give himself a hint as to where he was. A shaft of white light pierced through the dark and he watched as millions of dust particles danced through it. He wondered where it came from. Something moved on top of him and let out a weak sigh, hair flicked over his face and he remembered. Bethany. He reached out into the black and felt the smooth stone of the tomb. With a roar he heaved it to the side and immediately he was showered in light. The cool sludge of rainwater pattered over him.

An alarm blared from somewhere up above and through the murk three powerful search lights scanned over what was now an apocalyptic scene of utter devastation. Kessler pulled up his hood and shielded his eyes from the glare of the lights. Surrounding the now overturned sarcophagus, which had protected him from the inferno, were the smouldering remains of the church. He peered up from what was the crypt but now just resembled a charred crater in the ground. St John's ancient wooden beams had disappeared leaving only a burnt, splintered frame around the building's edge, its precious stone columns and their carvings now rubble. Jutting out from the debris, the remains of the walls lay broken and blackened. A sweep of the light revealed that the windows were now gone, as was a large portion of the vaulted ceiling. Throughout the destruction lay globules of white 'safe foam' which the fire drone had sprayed to smother the blaze. The large underbelly of the bot flew slowly past him and he shook his head in utter disbelief that he had survived such destruction.

Looking down at the tomb, he could see the unconscious Bethany lying entangled in the bones and rags of its original occupant. As another search light swept over them from above, something sparkled just to the left of her head, in amongst the grim rubble of the sarcophagus. Kessler bent down, wincing as his muscles and skin creaked and cracked from the fire's touch, and lifted from the debris Bethany's silver ring. Holding it in front of him by the frayed piece of string, he stared at the spinning jewels as they glistened. Even in the low light of Downtown the diamonds sparkled with a dazzling intensity that almost hypnotised him. "This would sure pick up a fair amount of cred uptown." He mumbled to himself through his pain, "Make a lot of problems go away." He looked down at Bethany, her dress was hitched up to her waist revealing ugly, blackened skin that went all the way up her leg. Her white undergarments were also torn and charred by the fire and streaks of blood were splattered across her pale white skin. Kessler, still with the ring dangling from his clenched fist, looked around him and took in the wreckage that was Bethany's life. He sighed, placed the ring in his pocket and pulled her dress down to cover her bare legs.

Bending low to pick her up, he looked into the eyeless sockets of the skull which lay by Bethany's head, almost resting against her, and said dryly, "Thanks for looking after us, chief." He flung the girl over his shoulder with the thought of telling her that one of her imaginary friends had saved them from the fire amusing him and served to distract him a little from the discomfort of his injuries. However, if Bethany was to live long enough to hear that story he had better get back to his office quickly. She was deathly pale and her breathing was laboured.

The Venters were nowhere to be seen as he quickly returned to his vehicle. He placed Bethany in the passenger side where she slumped, head resting against the canopy. She coughed and spluttered then was silent. Kessler reached over and took out his spare respirator, placed it over her mouth and started feeding her much needed Ox then grabbed hold of the com. "Macy, damn the light, where are you?" He kicked the console and swore to himself, "This cheap tech…"

"Hey Kes? I've a message for you." Her usual bored, Midtown tone with a hint of attitude greeted him.

"Don't worry about that right now. Call Doc Galloway and tell him to meet me in the office. It's an emergency. I should be back in two hours." If the traffic was light, he thought to himself.

"He's quite a busy man, but I'll try. You ok? You sound terrible."

"Just tell him, if he knows what's good for him he'll be there. Tell him I have a girl suffering from smoke inhalation, burns and…" Kessler looked over at Bethany, "just tell him she's in a bad way."

"Will do."

"Just make sure Doc is there." He jammed down the receiver button and started the engines. He didn't have time for talking. He made quickly for the Pipe.

The journey took longer than expected. Kessler rummaged around Bethany's coat and found her I.D. but despite both having visas to travel up through the Rim to M5 the Vents at border control could see he was desperate. The red of their cold mechanical eyes stared back at him through the canopy as Bethany bled out on the passenger seat. What would they care if another low dweller died? Just one less statistic amongst the billions trying to crawl their way higher up city, one less problem they would have to deal with. It took a whole bunch of credits for them to take an interest and get them waved through, most of what Bethany had already paid him. Kessler cursed under his breath at the Venter as the mag rails took hold of his junker and sped them up the city to Midtown 5.

*

The hours of night were approaching, street lamps dimmed and the garish neon jungle faded as Kessler eventually arrived at his building with the unconsciousness Bethany in his arms. He kicked his door open and strode in passed the open-mouthed Macy straight to his office where the tall, gangly figure of Doctor Galloway stood, tapping his feet impatiently in his long white synthleather coat holding his large black medical bag. The two men exchanged a brief glance before Kessler, quickly kicking away old food cartons and empty bottles, lay Bethany down gently on his sofa.

The doctor barged past him and began examining her. After unwrapping Bethany from Kessler's coat, he checked her pulse, her breathing and immediately gave her more Ox. Turning to open his case, he spoke between sighs, "So what happened this time or should I not ask?" He looked up at the detective through his yellow spectacles, his voice carried the educated and refined tones of Hightown.

"Don't ask." He doubled over in a coughing fit and hacked at his lungs to release whatever poisons he had breathed. With shaking hands he took a hit from his inhaler, wincing in pain and cradling his arm as he did so. With the race back here now over, the adrenalin that was holding him together began to ebb away leaving a shattered body behind.

"You're injured, I'll have to take a look."

"Just worry about the girl," words were spat out between spasms of coughing.

"Anything that I can do Kes?" Macy stood in the doorway looking at him. As usual she was immaculately presented, wearing a short red body suit that seemed to flow over her slim frame. She looked down at Kessler shaking her head with concern and held out a hydration pouch. "Drink some of this."

"There's only one drink I need." He batted away the water, stumbled over to his desk drawer and pulled out a bottle of Piper's, wincing from another shock of pain from his arm and shoulder. He quickly glugged half its contents down his throat in one swift movement.

Macy walked over to his desk and put down the water. She had seen Kessler in far worse states than this and was used to his ways. "He never drinks enough fluids." She spoke to the doctor as she left the room.

"You're lucky to have her, Kes."

"I don't need any mothering, I can look after myself."

"Obviously." He looked up, frowning at Kessler from where he was kneeling over his patient.

"How's the girl doing?"

"She has inhaled a lot of smoke and has severe burns down her left side and leg. I'm going to give her something to sleep and, hopefully, prevent infection. We will have to see how well she responds. The next twenty-four hours are vital."

"She wants to live, Doc. She's strong" Even if that strength was born of a desperate need for revenge, she wanted to live to see it done.

The doctor took a large syringe out of his case, flicked it with his finger and watched the dark liquid bubble and fizz before taking her arm and delivering the medicine into her blood stream. "You don't have to watch me you know."

"I wasn't watching." Kessler cleared his throat again. "Just hope she pulls through."

"Sit down, I'll be with you in a second." He began applying a salve to Bethany's wound and wrapping them in bandages.

Kessler sat down on the chair by his desk and watched Doc work. He was young, no more than thirty years of age but wore a constant frown and the wrinkled face of someone way beyond those years. His delicately manicured hands worked quickly, unbuttoning the top of his white shirt and rolling up his expensive polyfibre sleeves. As he worked, he talked repeatedly under his breath. Kessler had known Doc Galloway for years, first meeting him at a time when both their luck was down. He had worked for Merryll and had permits to live quite a few districts up city from here. The world was at his feet, a young doctor looking forward to a prosperous career within the corps and all the perks that ran with it. The only one small flaw to this plan was that he had quite a severe taste for Methrogen, a particularly nasty painkiller. Getting the job at Merryll was like handing him the keys to the cookie jar. It didn't take long for him to lose everything, Meth addiction is a nasty business and it was particularly cruel to the doctor. After losing his job, and his free access to the Meth, he was soon living rough in Lower Midtown, his Hightown life a distant memory. With an expensive addiction to feed he soon lost everything. That was when Kessler ran into him.

"She's got a fever, we need to wait for it to break. Her burns have been treated and should mend." He looked away from Kessler who sat hunched over his desk, holding his stomach, wheezing for breath, and back over to the unconscious Bethany, "Her lungs are damaged, that is the major concern. She has breathed in some toxic fumes which have scorched her insides.

If she lives she will have a very nasty scar down her left side. It could be fixed with some delicate bioware and…"

"She would never want it done. She doesn't care about such things."

Doc nodded, took off his latex gloves and threw them into a bin. He fetched a clean pair from his bag. "Now let me take a look at you."

"I'm ok," he lied.

"Let me be the judge of that." Doc took hold of Kessler's face with both hands and roughly turned it from side to side. "You were never the prettiest creature before. This scar will sure not improve that."

"Humph. Adds to my charm."

"Yes, well you certainly have buckets of that." The serious face nearly cracked a tiny smile. He gave him some meds to numb the pain and bandaged his shoulder, the frown becoming more stern at the sight of the injury to his arm. "You should rest."

"Don't have the time. Just patch me up."

Doc shook his head and looked at Kessler over his glasses, "You will need to keep this dry, if the rain gets into the wound then you could lose the arm, if you are lucky."

"That filthy rain keeps you in business." He tried to laugh but hacked a cough instead.

Ignoring Kessler, Doc continued, "Take this medivent and wear it at all times, especially while you are outside. It's a mix of oxygen and one of my cocktails to keep infection away." Kessler took the respirator and immediately fitted it over his face and took a couple of long, deep breaths. The effects were immediate and he felt more relaxed, his injuries less sore as the vapours carried their payload into his body.

"I was busy at work when you called, I had to leave patients waiting." Doc sat by Bethany's unconscious body, watching Kessler breathe in the medivent's healing air.

"You're lucky to be at work at all." The detective's short statement came between deep gasps of breath.

The doc rubbed his eyes, "I'm straight now, things are going well."

"I'm glad." Kessler didn't have to say anything else, Doc owed him and he knew it. He had come a long way since Kessler first met him in that stinking cell nearly ten years ago. He would never have lasted. No educated kid from Hightown could make it in that hell hole. He looked at him in his smart poly-fibre shirt, white synth leather trousers, delicate spectacles and shook his head. He had done well to rise up from the filth of the Council cells and turn his life around. "Owes me, big time." Kessler muttered under his breath.

"You risked her life taking her through the Pipe, she lost a lot of blood."

"I wasn't going to take her to some Downtown Stitch Doc to hack her to pieces. No way." Doc nodded and adjusted his spectacles. "Listen, I need some information on a new chem that's running the streets."

"Kes, I want nothing to do with your chem use. I told you before, patching citizens up is one thing," he gave a quick sideways glance at the unconscious Bethany, "but I'm not helping you waste away on chem."

"Yea, whatever. Save your preaching for someone who gives a damn. I'm not talking about me, it's this case I'm involved in. I hear this chem is particularly nasty, been burning a lot of wasters in Downtown." He fished around in his pockets and took out the priest's diary and one of the empty caps found in his study. "It may be running in vials with this symbol. Heard anything about it?"

Doc Galloway took the cap and held it up to the light before bringing it to his nose for a quick, sharp sniff. "A burning sun. Haven't heard of it but there are so many different sims out there and my knowledge is not current anymore." Doc stared at the vial, lost in his thoughts. "Smells a bit off though. What is in it?" He took his spectacles off and gave his eyes another rub.

"I was hoping you could tell me."

He took another sniff, "It has a sweet smell, like child's candy."

"From what I've heard it's not quite so sweet to whomever takes it. It's a killer."

"I'll take it back to the lab and test it."

"Thanks."

Packing his bags he stood up to leave. "Has she got anyone to look after her over the next few days?"

"No family, she's got no one. She'll have to stay here, I'll get Macy to look after her." Having a client stay in his office was the last thing he needed but what was he supposed to do? He could not throw her out onto the streets. He needed her credits.

The doctor stood in the doorway putting his coat on, "I've left some extra canisters for the medivent, replace them when needed. Call me if she takes a turn for the worse. I'll be in touch when I have run those tests for you." He turned towards where Macy was sitting behind her desk, "Make sure he takes his meds."

Kessler leaned back in his chair and put his feet up on his desk. He was tired and his eyes were heavy. He stared at the sleeping Bethany Turner and was jealous of her slumber. She looked at peace. The meds were drawing him towards his own rest but he knew there was no time, there were questions that needed answering if he was to discover who killed the priest and why. The presence of the Venters and their interest in the church suggested Council involvement. However it did not seem their style. If they wanted its expensive contents they sure went about it the wrong way. Now all that was left was rubble and ash. The splattered blood over the altar and the mess of the priest's study, as if some sort of animal had torn it apart, all were images that flashed through Kessler's mind, together with the ominous words, 'Lux Ferre'. Why would someone spend the time to write that message and who did they expect to read it? Light Bringer? What could it mean? The more he thought of it the less it looked like any robbery he had ever heard of. Finally, of course, there were the empty caps and the manner of the priest's death. Kessler's head began to spin and before he knew it he was staring at the capsule of chem he had bought off Stacey Steckles. He took off his medivent and shot it through his eye.

"Yes," he sighed. "Just what I need." He smiled to himself as the thick fog of reality lifted ever so slightly. His mind was clear now, not burdened by tiredness nor distracted by pain. He reached for the priest's diary that lay on his desk. As soon as the book was opened, a piece of synthpaper fell out and landed on the floor. He bent down to pick it up. It was a short letter written in the now familiar hand of Father Jacob, seen many times by Kessler in his journals back in his study. It appeared to the detective to be an unfinished draft as many words were neatly crossed out and their replacement written above. It was dated a few weeks back to a Bishop Sansom, Eden Inc. Grey Abbey Sector, Midtown 5 and was a request for a meeting of 'utmost urgency'. It voiced his concern about increasing dangers to the church and stated options about getting Bethany safely out of Downtown. Kessler's thoughts began to turn sombre. He looked over again at Bethany and thought of her life living with her uncle. Growing up in most parts of Dis was never easy but in Downtown it must have been a very lonely life, locked away in St John's, an uncle's vain attempt to shelter her from the filth that surrounded them on all sides.

The diary itself was a beautiful piece of art, like many of the treasures within the now destroyed church. The priest must have spent many hours carefully writing and reading from this book. It contained the usual daily comments on the ordinary goings on of life within St John's: brief notes on sermons, comments on various repairs throughout the building, daily running costs, remarks on the quality of the ale being produced and ideas on how to expand the business. There were a couple of entries about a series of threats from a local gang of Corps Boys whose business interests seemed to conflict with the priest's Holy Ale enterprise. Father Jacob noted many times Bishop Sansom's concern at this unwanted attention.

In the last few weeks leading up to his death, the name Judecca Glaxon appeared often, alongside the details of numerous trips Father Jacob was taking to the slums. An address was written in the margins of the diary '407 Nimrod Heights, Morbus Sector, D2'. He remembered Bethany mentioning a brother Glaxon had worked alongside her uncle at the church but what were they doing in the slums? Kessler had heard of Nimrod Heights, often mentioned in the newsreels as being a particularly nasty area full of Dregs, Mutes and chemheads. Why would Father Jacob, obviously well aware of the dangers of Downtown, want to go down there? Stacey Steckles had mentioned that he visited skin labs, maybe he was out trying to convert the local Dregs? If he was, he was brave. Or perhaps he was going to get fixed up on sim? Questions without answers crashed around Kessler's chem-addled brain. He shook his head and rubbed his eyes, a dead priest, a church burned to the ground, Bethany's life as she knew it destroyed, and then there was the new chem causing havoc amongst the Dregs that somehow ended up in her uncle's body. Dark thoughts made his head spin.

He broke into a sweat as the chems took hold and dropped the diary onto his desk. Images flashed through his mind in a range of gaudy colours. Monstrous faces with glowing red optics were feeding off of the church, taking large handfuls of the building and gorging on it. Men dressed in black with large luminous yellow cogs on their uniforms laughed hysterically as green flames burned their flesh. Citizens prayed before an altar looking at pictures of missing loved ones before taking huge syringes out of their robes and injecting their eyes. 'Lux Ferre.' The words swilled around and around in his head. What could it all mean? The sim talked to him and danced its magic through his body. He could feel its delightful tendrils flow in waves, lapping over him and pulling him into the sea of unconsciousness.

·EDEN INCORPORATED·

omplete, utter darkness. He searched his pockets for some form of light but found nothing. Arms outstretched, he began fumbling forward. Whispers emerged from somewhere, "Hello?" He shouted louder, "Is anybody there?"

Strange, guttural sounds surrounded him. Murmurs from the dark.

"What? I don't understand. I can't see." He turned, round and round, frantically moving towards voices which now snapped and barked from every direction. He spun around blind, feral noises closing in, getting louder and louder, "Please, I can't see you. Who's there?" Something cold took hold of him. Shadows encircled him.

The darkness disappeared in an almighty flash as it was replaced by a bright, burning sun. "Come to the light."

"Lux Ferre."

Kessler woke up with a start, nearly falling off his chair. Sweat pounded out of every pore as he wheezed heavily, desperate to get air into his corrupted lungs. Rubbing his face, he tried to focus and get his bearings. With his damp, soiled sleeve he wiped saliva from his mouth and through blurred, heavy eyes stared at the clock on his desk which told him he had been out for three hours. His body ached for sleep but like a scratch he could not itch, he had to deal with it. He knew the routine.

As the foggy haze and shards of shattered images faded from memory the nightmare was replaced by thoughts of burning buildings and painful injuries. He gingerly touched his heavily strapped left arm and was greeted immediately by an arc of pain. He reached for the medivent and sucked heavily on its mouthpiece. The empty canister rattled back at him and he threw it to the side and reached into his drawer for some of his own painkillers.

Across the room, Bethany lay asleep on the sofa, her injuries covered by Macy's large pink blanket. Her face had been cleaned of the soot and grime, her hair brushed, the stress of the last few days and the terror of the fire now gone. If it was not for the medivent that was feeding her medication, helping her breathe, anyone would think she was in a contented, deep sleep. Macy's head rested on the sleeping patient's shoulder. With her carefully spiked blond hair, face studs and red plastichem bodysuit that ended just above the knee revealing long, slender tattooed legs, Macy was a girl that followed the fashions of the city. The closest thing he had to a family, a daughter, she made this place look good, Kessler thought as she began to stir from her sleep.

Propping herself up on her elbows, Macy squinted at the detective in the low light until eventually his bulk came into focus. "Kes," she let out a large yawn, "you have messages."

"You should have gone to bed, you didn't need to stay up with us."

She laughed, "Bed? I was getting ready for a night out with Deaks when you called. Besides, I told Doc I would keep an eye on you two."

"Humph." Always mothering him, he thought.

"She doesn't look too good." She looked down at the prone Bethany still holding her hand.

"So tell me about these messages." His head began to swirl back and forth at the effort of trying to talk. He looked around for those spare medivent canisters that Doc had left.

"Kes, I know you have a lot on your mind right now," Macy looked away, took a couple of breaths before returning her attention to him, "the Le Morte brothers called again to say they're done with running after you and…" She trailed off with a sigh.

"Yea, go on."

"Ok. They were done talking with you and would let their knives speak for them from now on. They left one as a reminder."

"Nice."

"No more jokes, Kes. It's getting serious. They trashed all my stuff. I thought they were going to kick off and I nearly reached for my pistol."

"Never do that." It was serious, there would be no doubt of the outcome if Macy had confronted the Le Morte brothers, they would not hesitate to slice her to shreds with their beloved blades. "Not with those guys, anyway."

"I know it's just I get so pissed at…"

"I'll take care of it, I promise." He interrupted her and stood up, wincing as his body protested. He reached over for a clean shirt which had appeared, draped over his desk. He nodded a thank you to Macy as he discarded the bloodied rag which he was wearing and, tentatively, over bandaged arm and shoulder, pulled it over his head. "Anything else while I was away?"

"Mrs Grubaker has called four or five times."

"And what did the old lady want this time?"

"She wants you to go and pick up something from her husband's house. Wouldn't give anymore details. She was her usual self and refused to speak to the help."

Mrs Grubaker's Hightown ways were difficult to take but her Hightown creds were not. "Macy, you know the score with Grubaker, she's harmless. She also pays for your wages."

"Ha! Wages? I thought I volunteered for this outfit."

"Yea, well, I understand I owe you some cred…" Kessler mumbled his reply and rubbed the stubble on his chin sheepishly.

"Just make sure you com her, Kes, otherwise I'll say something I might regret."

"Will do but it'll have to wait. Macy, I know it's a lot to ask, but could you look after Bethany while I go back out to check on something?" Kessler glanced at the fragile-looking girl on his sofa and wondered if she was going to pull through.

"You're not seriously thinking of going anywhere in your state?" Her voice was raised as she shook her head.

"You know how it goes, time is money." He unstrapped the medivent and lit a cigar. "I'll have Doc come by later on and check up on her."

"He wouldn't approve of you smoking that thing. Here, have this instead." Macy had that look which Kessler had seen many times before, lips pursed and frowning, the look of disapproval. Her hand was held out and holding a canister of medicine. He stared at her as she leaned forward and with her free hand took the cigar from his mouth and stubbed it out in the over-flowing ash tray. "This place is disgusting, I honestly don't know how you find anything." That disapproving look slowly scanned the room.

Kessler was sitting in his chair, canister in hand and mouth open. "I like this place as it is, and I don't want you messing with it. I have everything right where I want it." He picked up the empty medivent, fitted the canister and took a long, deep breath.

*

Kessler sat outside his office in his junker eating the carton of noodles which Macy had given him. He did not realise how hungry he was and could not remember the last time he had eaten. Now that the final embers of the sim were slowly ebbing away, the detective felt ravenous. He wolfed down the whole container in seconds and sat for a couple of moments in silence, savouring the flavours of his favourite food. Macy always knew how to make him feel better.

Looking outside the canopy into the urban sprawl, he began to form a plan. Who killed Father Jacob and why? Ignoring the possibility that the old guy had gone crazy in a chem-induced frenzy and desecrated his own church before overdosing on this new gear, who else could have killed him? "Anyone could have," Kessler mumbled aloud, answering his own question. The city was full of sick people, especially Downtown.

He forced his thoughts back over the events of the previous day. The DPD were obvious culprits. It was common knowledge that any form of religion was illegal giving the police a good reason to burn the church down. All the way below in Downtown, far from Council Protocols and prying eyes, they could easily get away with pretty much anything. However, Kessler had never heard of them enforcing law so far down city where the district governors governed, especially for a small operation like St John's. All the Council cared about was business and profit. What benefit would they get for sending their goons down that far below the Rim? It was a costly exercise. Perhaps they wanted to put a stop to the booze the priest was selling? Maybe one of the corporate-backed Corps Boys complained, did not like the competition. Stacey's sighting of Councilmen seemed to confirm that something serious was going on. Kessler's thoughts turned to the priest's activities in the last few weeks before his death. He needed to pay a visit to Nimrod Heights and find out what Father Jacob found so interesting about the place. Much to Kessler's disgust, another visit to Downtown seemed unavoidable but first, taking the priest's note from his pocket and scanning over it, Kessler hoped Bishop Sansom at Eden Inc would be able to shed some light onto events surrounding the death.

His head began to hurt thinking through all the possibilities, "For light's sake," he cursed frustratingly, "maybe he was just a chemhead who burned bad on this new stuff." Kessler shook his head and reached down to ignite the junker's thrusters when a sharp clinking noise to his left froze him in place.

Pascal Le Morte was tapping the driver's side window with a knife, its blade glistened in the yellow light of a neon sign that flashed nearby. He stood smirking at the detective with long, straight, pale blond hair and pointed sharp face, the black gloss of his cyber shades reflecting back the detective's haggard looks. "Hey mon frère, you are not looking too good these days, is that belle fille not looking after you?" He brought the knife up to his mouth and, with his obscenely long tongue, slowly licked the blade.

"Hey," Kessler forced a smile, "I've been looking all over for you I…"

"Non, non, non, mon frère, you have been a naughty boy, me thinks." Pascal opened the door and with one hand started juggling the blade, the other waved for Kessler to get out.

The detective put the empty carton of noodles on the passenger seat and looked around to see the other Le Morte twin. Wherever one was the other was always close behind and always playing with their knives. Each was a disease on society, but together they were an epidemic. Killers to the bone. He was grinning and waving at Kessler, leaning against their distinctive, bright yellow roadster. Such a beautiful vehicle, he thought to himself, shame he could not look at one without being reminded of these two poisonous wretches. He turned and smiled at Pascal and got out of his junker.

Pascal stood a full six inches above the detective. Slender and tall and dressed completely in white synthwear, his long white flash jacket gleamed with distinctive gold thread. "You see Mr Kessler, your long absence from our lives has upset my brother," he looked over his shoulder at the other twin who was now making his way slowly towards them, "and you know how angry he gets when he is disappointed, and he is very disappointed, yes he is." Pascal smiled as he spoke. "Edouard, I was just telling our friend how angry you are."

"Merci beaucoup brother, but that is an understatement." Edouard, looking identical to his twin apart from the blue trim lining of his coat, grabbed Kessler by his collar and lifted him up to his eye level, his strength belying his slender frame.

"Easy there Edouard, easy, it's cool, I have everything under control." Pascal placed the back of his hand on his brother's chest and Edouard backed slowly away.

"You see mon petit ami? Little Chi needs that cred or else he will let us off the leash, comme ça?"

"I have it, or I will have it very soon. I'm working on a big case at the minute, c'mon guys you know me."

"Ah oui, we know you Mr Kessler all too well." Edouard had his knife drawn to Kessler's throat and was moving it slowly down his body. "If Little Chi don't get his five thousand creds in two days then we will have to get very intimate." He pressed his knife hard against the detective's groin.

"Ok, ok, easy. No problem." Kessler's back was against a wall as he tried to pull away from the blade.

Pascal started laughing, "It better be no problem or that fine secretary of yours will experience an entirely different intimacy." Both brothers walked back to their roadster, laughing hysterically. They strutted away slowly, swaying their hips as if to some silent music. Kessler got back into his junker and, with his coat sleeve, wiped the sweat from his brow. He had to think clearly, he had to get somewhere with this case, it was his only chance to clear this debt with Little Chi. He looked around to check for the Le Morte brothers and could not see them. Things had gone too far, no one messed with those two parasites without coming to a painful end.

Five thousand creds was a lot of cash. He only had two clients, Grubaker provided a steady stream of cred but that was small time, he needed far more and fast however his only other client was unconscious up in his office. Bethany was the answer though, he was sure of that. If he could just find out who killed her uncle he was sure that she would pay whatever it took to satisfy her need for revenge. She could do whatever she wanted with them, Kessler did not care, as long as he got paid for his work. Morals took a back seat when your balls were on the line.

He typed the name 'Eden Inc.' into the naviscreen and immediately the computer took control of the vehicle. Kessler hoped that the intended recipient of the unfinished letter had the answers he needed.

The old junker drove through the streets of District 5. Morning was fast approaching and with the life blood of Council power flowing more freely through her arteries, she began to come alive. Tower blocks were lighting up as citizens stirred from their slumber, the gaudy colours of flashing neon began to dominate the sprawl as businesses opened and began to ply their trade and the frazzle and buzz of thousands of lights began their daily fight with the eternal darkness of Dis. Soon Kessler came to a stop at the side of a road and exited the vehicle. Using his bioware, the vehicle was lowered into a parking bay.

In amongst the sludge, smoke and blackened plastisteel of the city the polished white marble and chrome plate building of Eden Incorporated majestically stood far above the clawing Midtown sprawl. Kessler stood outside as the rain hammered down around him looking up at the impressive building. Walking up the steps to the entrance, Kessler was greeted by huge doors of thick reinforced plastiglass which instantly opened allowing him to walk into a large lobby of glistening chrome and polished white plastic. The doors closed behind him and immediately the noise from the busy Midtown streets ceased, replaced by the gentle, flowing tones of some upper city orchestra.

The receptionist stood behind her desk below the gigantic golden letters of 'Eden Inc' wearing a flowing white gown with black rimmed glasses and blond hair tied back into a tight bun. She was surrounded by the glowing green light of multiple holoscreens and was waving her hands over them quickly, her pale blue eyes completely focused on the banks of flickering text in front of her. Kessler cleared his throat and tried to get her attention. Small groups of citizens were dispersed throughout the lobby, some sitting down reading, others in discussion or watching one of the many monitors built into the curved wall that wrapped around the room. Some wore the white robes of the receptionist but most tended to wear the fashions of Hightown, gaudy coloured circlets wrapped around their ankles, sleeves and head. Kessler wondered what important errand would bring them so far from the safe heights of their home. He began to feel awkward as he stood waiting to be acknowledged by the girl. His grubby Midtown rags had no place amongst the expensive clothes and crisp robes found within this building and all of a sudden he was aware he had not washed in days. "Hey lady, am I invisible or something?" Kessler waved his hand in her direction. A sharp pain down his left side reminded him that he had left his medivent in the junker.

With a wave of her hand and a low hum, the holographics disappeared in a flash and she turned towards him, "How can I help you, citizen?" Her eyes quickly glance over his attire.

"I need to speak to Bishop Sansom."

The woman's blue eyes again moved, glancing quickly around the room, "There is no one of that name here." She turned away from him to speak to a couple who had just come in from the rain and were deactivating their expensive red and blue rain shields and unwrapping scented cloth masks from their faces, their delicate Hightown nostrils not appreciating the colourful odours this part of the city had to offer. The pair both pressed their hands together and bowed in greeting. The receptionist replied in a similar fashion and immediately the familiar sparkle of light drew Kessler's attention to a ring worn by the otherwise plainly-dressed citizen. After a moment's talk they walked through an opening that appeared from the slick white gloss wall and the receptionist returned back to her work. He had to suppress the urge to grab the lady from behind her desk and teach her some manners.

The detective's attention went from the receptionist's jewelled finger to the large gold lettering mounted behind her desk, above which the Eden Inc symbol of the book and cross could be seen, a symbol he had seen before on Bethany's ring. His hand went to his pocket as he remembered that he had picked it from the wreckage of the tomb. Taking it between his thumb and forefinger, he played with the ring as his thoughts strayed to its sparkling diamonds and how much cred he could get, easily enough to cover his debt to Little Chi and set him and Macy up in better air further up town. He knew of a couple of fences in this part of the city who could access that amount of cred quickly, no questions asked, especially for something so rare as diamonds.

A very tall, slender Hightowner nudged passed him, followed by her entourage of four servants who, with bowed, hooded heads, carried various assortments of baggage. She turned and looked haughtily down at the detective from behind her scented cloth mask which she held to her nose with a wiry, gloved hand. Taking the ring from his pocket, Kessler took off his gloves, and placed it on his finger. It was a large ring for a girl and fitted perfectly on Kessler's middle digit. He clenched his fist in determination. He hated Hightowners. They looked down at everyone from their lofty perches up above, believing them better than everyone else. 'I may be a down and out Midtowner,' he thought to himself, 'but I'm no Dreg.'

Approaching the receptionist with a new-found determination and mimicking the greeting he had seen moments before, he pressed his hands together, "Salutations citizen," he spoke clearly, trying to clean each syllable of his slurred Midtown brogue, "apologies for my abruptness before, I have had a very difficult past couple of days but I bring urgent news from St John's for the Bishop." He opened Father Jacob's unfinished letter and let her glance over its contents, making sure to flash the ring. He carefully measured his breathing, trying to remain calm and polite. He was tired, his arm hurt and with the image of the Le Morte brothers fresh in his mind he was all too aware that time was not on his side.

She stared at the ring and cleared her throat, "This way." The shiny white of the wall disappeared to reveal a darkened entrance leading into the cool, dry air of a huge vault. The receptionist moved fast and, with his injuries blazing with every move, he struggled to keep up. Squinting his way through the low light of the room, he could see on either side of him row upon row of towering shelves that reached up to a distant ceiling. Each shelf was filled with boxes brimming with all manner of old items from books, statues and ornaments to dust-covered pictures. It reminded Kessler of St John's. Reaching the other side of the large room, the woman placed her hand up against a scanner and, after a few seconds, the locking mechanism of a huge, heavy carbonised iron door turned revealing a tunnel lit by a series of dimly glowing panels.

After a few moments walking steadily downwards, the plastisteel tunnel levelled off into a large, rocky open space. He had never seen natural rock this far up city. Huge banners were draped across the walls on either side of the cave and both had the symbol first seen on Bethany's ring, the book and cross. Throughout the room were desks covered in paper and along the walls large shelves towered up towards the cavern ceiling. Men and women, all dressed in the white robes of the receptionist, were all feverishly at work, some reading, writing, some in heated debate and others hanging from long ladders searching through the many hundreds of books that lined the shelves. At the centre, suspended from the ceiling far above their heads, hung a large wooden cross with the same image of Christ Kessler had seen at St John's. On the cave's irregular, jagged walls hung a series of torches, their large flames throwing a mass of shadows across the rough, uneven rocky surface. The smoke from the fires filled the open space with a musky, acrid smell which mingled with the same perfumed scent Kessler had smelt back at the church. He held his injured arm through his thick plastichem coat as he remembered the fire.

"What is this place?" He mumbled but the receptionist ignored him and kept walking through the cave as Kessler drew glances from the robed workers who took time to stop whatever they were doing to stare at him.

They eventually reached the far end where, cut into the rock, stairs rose up into darkness. "Wait here." She pointed to a well-worn stone bench that lay to the side and quickly walked up the steps.

Kessler welcomed the time to rest, the woman had led him down from the lobby above at a quick pace making his injuries come alive under their bandages. He could feel his tight, toasted skin crack and weep with every move. The smoke-filled air made his already laboured breathing even more difficult and he doubled over as a raking cough took hold of him.

"Can I be of any assistance, friend?" An old man croaked from behind a desk close to where the detective was sitting. He had risen with difficulty, and approached swaying precariously on an old, crooked wooden staff. His face was a mass of wrinkles and his skin so pale it was nearly translucent.

Kessler spoke between fits of coughing, "No thanks old man, I just need a second."

"Yes, I am old," he nodded to himself, "but God has granted me many years filled with wonderful experience." He crossed himself and mouthed a prayer. Kessler nodded at the man as he stood, hunched over his wavering stick, staring at him with his faded watery hazel eyes. After a moment's silence he spoke again, "In another life I was a doctor. A long time ago but, I assure you, I remember." He began chuckling to himself.

Taking a deep breath, Kessler smiled back and watched him totter over to his desk and rummage around in one of his drawers. He was mumbling to himself as he brought out a number of items, each time shaking his head dramatically in frustration at not finding what he was looking for. The detective put his head in his hands and began to despair at the thought that he was wasting his time here. He cursed himself for not going straight back to Downtown. He really did not have the time to be delivering half-written letters and talking to crazy old men.

"A-ha!" He waved his stick in the air and nearly fell over. One of his much younger colleagues, who was working nearby, ran to his aid and helped him back onto his feet before being batted away with the staff. "Get off me, I'm not an invalid." He found his balance and approached Kessler, "Here. This should do the trick," he said, with a big grin etched across his creased face. "Rub that on your chest twice a day and it will keep the doctor away." Kessler took the jar of ointment off the old man who was now laughing uncontrollably, his free hand now mimicking rubbing the salve onto his own chest. His hands were almost bone with blue veins trying to burst through thin layers of pasty-white skin. Kessler noted his gold ring which looked gigantic on the tiny frail hands of the elderly man, his bony fingers struggling to lift its weight.

"Erm – thank you." Kessler just wanted to be left alone. His antics had drawn the attention of a number of people who now all stared at him.

"It is my pleasure. God has blessed me with skills for a reason although, unfortunately, I do not have the opportunity to practise them enough, for my sins." He again made the sign of the cross and mumbled to himself. "One question if I may? It has been so long since I have been outside and was hoping you could provide me with information on the state of the hospitals here in Midtown? Has the Council begun to distribute vaccines for…"

"Father Benjamin," the shrill voice of the receptionist emerged from the darkness of the stairs, "I am sure you have work to be doing, I know we have." He looked up towards her and dithered, seemingly lost between thoughts. "The Devil makes work for idle hands," she continued.

Father Benjamin looked dejected as his gaze went from the detective and back to the stern-looking woman, "Ah, yes. Of course," he brought a hand to his lips, as if about to say something, then shook his head. "My apologies." He slowly slumped back to his seat, head bowed, and opened the large book that he had been studying previously. Kessler felt sorry for him and guilty for not paying him more attention. He looked up at the receptionist who stood, arms crossed, shaking her head at her ancient colleague. Kessler did not like this citizen one bit.

"Bishop Sansom will see you now."

The Bishop's office was cut into the rock itself at the top of the stairs. Under the flickering light of the torches Kessler could see the straight patterned lines of the gouge marks left by the machines used to hollow out the room. The study itself was spacious, one side consisting of a very large transparent plastiglass wall which commanded an uninterrupted view over the entire room below. Monitors and hardware cluttered the opposite wall, buzzing and whirling with data. A com system flashed in the corner. Sat behind a huge white plastic desk, the Bishop stared at a holopad, his huge frame threatening to burst out of his dark grey suit. One large, bulbous hand played with a small statue that lay on his desk, the now familiar image of Christ appeared between heavily-jewelled fingers. Again a ring similar to Bethany's could be seen. His other hand cycled through various holographic images. The bishop's large, bald head seemed loosely wrapped in layers of excess fat which wobbled ever so slightly as he repeatedly nodded to himself. Large gold, looped earrings dangled from his small pinhole ears.

The receptionist stood in the room beside the detective with her head bowed awaiting a response from Bishop Sansom. Long seconds passed. Kessler watched the obscenely obese man who sat squashed into his chair, enveloping it in his large rolls of fat. He was chewing noisily on an assortment of sugar-coated candy as a fan on his desk squealed and droned as it attempted to try and cool his vast sweating frame. Finally, he spoke in a lazy manner, "Sister Katelyn tells me that you have come from St John's." His voice was pinched and he laboured over each word, over pronouncing each syllable.

"That's right, I barely escaped with my life. I have questions that need answered."

"How dare you talk to his Grace in such a manner, we do not ask questions of the Bishop!" Sister Katelyn had a look of thunder and her face reddened with rage.

Bishop Sansom sighed, "That's ok Sister, this good citizen…"

"The name is Kessler," he interrupted.

"Mr Kessler," the Bishop looked up from his perch at the detective, "does not know our ways, I think. I can spare five minutes. Leave us please." Kessler could not help notice the numerous sweat patches that seemed to seep through the Bishop's shirt and trousers, up from every crevasse of his vast bulk.

Sister Katelyn glared at him with a look of complete disgust. "Very well your Grace. I will be waiting downstairs if you need me." She left the room, closing the door very firmly behind her.

"Ignore the good Sister," the Bishop continued to stuff his face with candy while he talked, some missing his mouth and falling to the floor, "she is wary of strangers. Our faith is not, eh, let us just say, appreciated by the Council. These are dangerous times Mr Kessler, one cannot be too careful." His languid manner made him hard to follow.

"What exactly is this place?"

The Bishop smiled revealing yellowed teeth, "As I suspected. The ring you wear is not yours." He licked his fingers, "Before I answer your questions, please, let me ask two of mine."

"Ok."

106

"Are you happy with," he waved a fat hand in Kessler's direction, "with your life? This city?"

"Sure I am. Life's just great." Kessler humoured him.

"This city consumes us in darkness."

Kessler nodded, "The Council does not provide us with much light, even during daylight hours." The detective looked through the clear plastiglass at the cave below, "You would need to move your little operation further up city if you wanted more light."

The Bishop was shaking his head slowly from side to side with his eyes closed. Both hands were clasped, touching his chin "Ah but the light is here, you just need to open your eyes to see another world beyond this one, beyond the darkness, an escape from all the pain and suffering of the city. A place full of love and open to all those who want it. You just have to know how to ask." He spoke in a flat tone.

"Yea, sorry chief, I'm all for wanting to escape this cess-pit existence but I'm a non-believer."

The Bishop continued, ignoring Kessler's reply. "God guides us in many ways towards the light. The signs are all around us." He feebly waved a hand from right to left to emphasise his point and swivelled, with some difficulty, in his chair to face him.

"Like I said, each to their own but not for me."

"Of course." He laughed and wiped his brow of sweat. "Which brings me to my second question. That ring that you are wearing is very interesting, where did you get it from?"

"It belongs to Bethany Turner, Father Jacob's niece."

"You see Mr Kessler, those who possess a ring like the one currently in your possession are true believers in Christ and will always be granted access to our centres throughout Dis to worship in peace, away from the dangers of those who would very much want to shut us down. It is a very valuable, extremely old item, property of the church and we would very much like it back." His hawkish stare remained fixed on the ring still on Kessler's finger. The detective put his hand in his pocket, hiding it from view.

"No chance. This belongs to Miss Turner who, unlike me, is a true believer."

"So be it." He dismissed Kessler's statement with another wave of his hand and returned to his candy and holopad.

"So all this serves as a place for people to worship your god in peace?"

"Exactly. A haven where good Christians can talk to God, improve their knowledge of the old ways, all without the danger of Council interference. Of course, officially we are a registered corporation with the Council. Eden Incorporated makes its way in this world selling and buying antiquities and items exotica from ancient times. We are very famous you know, citizens come from all across Dis to purchase our wares."

"Yea, I seen them up in the lobby."

"The old world, the time before Dis, has left us traces of the past, markers if you will that give us the chance to glance into the workings of that forgotten time. These are signs from God, Mr Kessler. They give us a chance to learn from an age when Christians walked the earth freely and God's work could be seen living and breathing from the earth and the seas to the sky above. Here we collect these items and try and gather as much knowledge as possible." Bishop Sansom leaned forward, stopped chewing on his candy and pointed a finger at the detective, "Many people would like to know about this operation, Mr Kessler, many people would go to great lengths to shut us down. I would appreciate your discretion."

"Listen, I'm no lover of the Council either so they won't be hearing anything from me about your little get-togethers."

"Thank you." He very slightly bowed his head in appreciation. "Now I am anxious to hear of what happened at St John's. It had stood for over a thousand years, its contents were priceless, precious beyond belief."

"Yes I saw it."

"You were in the church? Fantastic news! I believed that the

DPD were not allowing anyone into the building. I thought it gone for good."

"Books, stone carvings, ancient wood. Many an expensive item."

The Bishop's eyes widened at what Kessler was describing, "Yes it is our way. Man has left his mark as a black stain on this plastisteel and carbonised iron world. We seek comfort in what nature, God, has given us. So you must understand the importance such items are to our faith." He shook his head from side to side, "Many times I had pleaded with Father Jacob to send the church's relics to Eden to preserve, study and protect them. I am eager to learn Mr Kessler, what has become of all the ancient lore?"

"Gone. The DPD burned the church, and its contents, to the ground. Myself and Miss Turner were lucky to avoid the same fate."

The Bishop looked aghast, his huge bulbous head taking on a grey hue. He clutched at his medallion which rested on his belly and tried to find his breath. "That is dreadful news, so much lost. So much. A tragedy. I had heard rumours of mounting trouble coming from the depths, our churches in the lower parts are under increasing pressure to move uptown to safety. The Devil tests us always." After a long pause, the Bishop, sitting motionless with his head bowed as he contemplated Kessler's news, suddenly turned away from him and back to his holopad. He snapped, "Now, how can I help you Mr Kessler, I am a busy man."

Kessler passed Father Jacob's unfinished letter to Bishop Sansom, "I am working for Bethany Turner, helping her find out who was behind her uncle's death. I thought you may be able to shed some light on the matter. In his letter to you he seems worried, he requests a meeting with yourself to speak to you about getting Bethany safely out of Downtown. Tell me, what danger was he referring to?"

"Mr Kessler," the Bishop sighed and spoke in a dismissive

tone, "if you want to discover who was behind Father Jacob's unfortunate demise all you have to do is look all around you. Try switching on one of the many infogrammes, listen to the broadcasts, the Devil's voice is everywhere and he makes no apologies for his hatred of the human soul." The bishop spoke as he examined another piece of candy.

"You mean the Council?"

"Of course. You said yourself that they burnt St John's down and all its treasures within. They look down on us from above so naturally they think they are our god." The bishop looked up from his holopad to stare directly at the detective, his lazy, whimsical look replaced now with a cold, steely stare, "But, Mr Kessler, Hightown may be above us but it is no heaven. The Council are just men, sinners like us all." He crunched down hard on another candy, "As for his niece, well, Downtown is a dangerous place, especially for children. I had been suggesting to him for years to allow her to stay with us, above the Rim."

"Well it makes sense that's for sure." Kessler rubbed the bristles on his chin in thought, "In the weeks and months leading up to his death he mentioned in his writing numerous incidents from vandalism to violent acts against the church."

The bishop nodded, "St John's, like much of the community in Downtown, has been constantly harassed by the Council through their gangs of Corps Boys. The Devil's children, I tell you. The few God-fearing citizens left down there do not have a moment's peace. The Council's influence grows within the Corps Boys with every passing day bringing with it more confidence. Their acts of violence are becoming more brutal of late and district governors have their heads turned by Council credits. I told Father Jacob this. Many times. He was a stubborn old fool."

"Their attention seemed to be more concerned with the creds the church was making as opposed to what it was preaching. You Christians seem to have a knack of making cash," Kessler stared at the gold jewellery which the Bishop was laden with.

"Times are hard. Our parishes must find the means to sustain themselves to be able to spread the word of God."

Kessler continued, "You don't seem to be doing too badly." It was hard not to notice the many glistening jewels that seemed to weigh down his plump fingers and the large gold medallion which rested on his belly, its thick chain becoming lost amongst the excess skin on the back of his sweaty neck.

"Mere bobbles," he gave Kessler a toothy grin while nervously playing with a ring, its large red stone glistening in the pale electric light of the room, "the real treasures are found within."

"Before the church was burned to the ground there was a DPD patrol outside guarding the gates and there have been rumours of Councilmen in Downtown. Strange to see the Council take any notice of the lower city."

"Yes, Jacob mentioned he had seen police in and around District 2. Hotel Sunset, that's where you'll find them, by the way. Conniving with their Corps Boys. Not that you will want to go there, Hell itself, I have been told."

"Again, strange to see DPD so openly supporting lawless gangs." Kessler did not know what to believe.

"Evil attracts evil, Mr Kessler." The Bishop had turned away from him and now seemed fully focused on eating his candy.

"In the days leading up to his death, Father Jacob was making numerous visits to Morbus Sector, a particularly nasty area in the slums of D2. Any idea why?"

Bishop Sanson looked irritated, "We have many clergy spread throughout the city, how am I to know what Jacob went there for? I am a very busy man with a lot to do."

"One more thing before I go."

"Be quick then. I have other, more pressing matters to attend to." He sighed between words.

"Do you understand what this says?" Kessler took out his view finder and showed him the holo projection of the words 'Lux Ferre.'"

"Where did you see this?"

"These words were hacked onto the priest's desk, a calling card left by whoever killed him, I guess. Miss Turner said that it was written in an old language used by you guys."

"Yes, in centuries long past. It reads 'Light Bringer.'"

"It certainly doesn't sound like anything the Council would do."

His eyes still stared at the image, "They claim to provide light to the citizens of Dis but there is only one true bringer of light and that is Christ."

Kessler lit a cigar, "Thanks for your time."

"God be with you." Kessler had already left the room before the Bishop could finish his sentence. He did not care to hear anymore of his god's words.

·SUNSET IN DOWNTOWN·

Midtown's District 5 buzzed with activity. Citizens from across the city packed the streets, shoving, pushing, all bustling past, eager to get to the Midtown markets. Dotted throughout the throng, the yellow, blue and red rain shields and expensive fashions of Hightown mixed shoulder to shoulder with the black garb of techpunks with flash jackets, the synthwear of jakkers and the many Midtowners who sheltered under thick, gaudy coloured plastichem. In amongst this melting pot, Council Adepts, draped in their thick, black synthleather robes, chanted praise to the rulers of Dis and the ever present Venters menacingly trained their assault rifles on anyone who dared to glance in their direction.

The familiar sight of merchants from Downtown could be seen emerging from below, desperate to get their exotic goods to market, trying not to miss the early busy buzz and lose out on any opportunities to make a quick cred. Their long train of Dregs in the drab, grey rags from below struggled with huge packs strapped to their backs. The load, which towered over them, swayed precariously in the rain and every few steps they would stumble under the strain. The warder was sitting atop a carriage strapped primitively together with an assortment of scavenged carbonised iron and plastisteel tied together with rubber tubing, cables and wiring and was being carried by four grim-faced men who struggled to support their master's weight.

Every so often he would stand up wielding his huge spark whip and lash out at his servants barking, "Quick, quick," in a thick Downtown accent that seemed to gurgle from the depths of his throat, his flailing whip forcing the throng to part in his wake causing the more high-living citizens to shout and curse.

Kessler could feel the heat of Downtown seep through the carbonised iron that lay beneath the hordes of feet as he walked through the lively streets of M5 and he could not help but think of what dangers lay waiting for him down below. The Bishop's hatred for the Council was not to be unexpected but for them to be so active in Downtown and so openly in support of the Corps Boys? Kessler thought it was unlikely. Not even the Council could explain that move to the citizens of Dis whose attention was always glued to the many infogrammes reporting the news and gossip throughout the city. It would be very difficult for them to keep their squeaky-clean reputation intact.

He stood still and tried to gather his thoughts while the jostling crowd forced its way passed him. He was tired and his shoulder and arm were aching. He now had his medivent with him but was wary of using it too quickly as he did not know when he would be able to meet up with Doc for a refill. Kessler was angry at himself. Forgetting to take his meds while enduring the Bishop's company had resulted in his entire body raging in protest with every movement and, to add to the pain of his injuries, he cursed himself for doing that sim back in the office. He should have known better but now the last traces of the chem still left in his body dulled the effect his meds were having and his eyes itched as its claws left their mark. He took a hit of Ox from his inhaler which seemed to momentarily ease the throbbing.

Kessler did not like where this investigation was going. If the Corps Boys and the Council had a hand in the priest's death then, "Light help me," Kessler sighed. How would he get his creds from Bethany if they were involved? No one interfered with Council business and ended up smiling. What justice could she expect to get? Besides, the last thing his broken body needed was a trip down to Hotel Sunset. The fat Bishop Sansom had got one thing right, Sunset was a place you did not want to be.

Kessler knew that there was one person who could provide the answer to his questions and he happened to be resident a few streets from the Pipe here in M5. Jimmy Six always had answers, just not always the right answers.

With a plan set out in his head, Kessler strode with purpose through the crowd down a side alley where, amongst the rubbish and refuse of Midtown, he grabbed hold of a heavy manhole cover and heaved it to one side. Adjusting his gloves, hood and securing his medivent, he climbed down a ladder, making sure to stop to seal himself inside, leaving the detective in complete darkness.

Kessler hated this place. The sewers below the streets of M5 were a boiling haze of putrid fumes. He stood, back against the slime-covered wall, and made sure not to fall into the torrent of filth which thundered down the tunnel to eventually be ejected out over the streets of Downtown. The city and its millions of citizens pumped out a never-ending deluge of waste from above and it all ended up here. He cursed his old friend for choosing to live right in the middle of it.

Kessler had known Jimmy Six for many years. Always the expert with any tech around, he also had an eye for forging documents and gathering information. These particular skills had gotten them out of a fair few scrapes in their younger days but in more recent times had helped Kessler solve what few cases came his way. Lately, Jimmy had disappeared off the streets, sought refuge under the ground of M5 and rarely, if ever, emerged. Alone and undisturbed by prying eyes, Jimmy kept his optics on the city through his own network and his permanent jack to the Mainframe. If anyone knew anything about this bad sim running around Downtown or the Corps Boys business then it was Jimmy.

After walking down a narrow ledge, guided by his torchlight, making sure not to slip on the rubbery, green mould that grew out from every surface, Kessler reached a doorway. Its shiny metallic finish stood out from its grim surroundings and a camera, which moved noisily back and forth, tracking Kessler's every move, gave it away as being the entrance to Jimmy's place. The detective looked up, pulled down his hood, took off his optics and waved. After a few moments there was a loud 'clunk' that echoed down the tunnel and the door slid effortlessly open.

Walking through the entrance into a small room, Kessler was greeted by a large screen on the wall which flickered into a fuzzy picture. Large goggles, flashing with yellow and red circuitry, rested on a small, round nose. A large, toothy grin stared out at Kessler, "Hey Jimmy, long time no see."

"Kes! Great to see ya. Where you been all this time? Why you not come to visit your old friend?" His voice switched from a low, deep Midtown brogue to the fluctuating mechanical pitch of his voice box. One of the many permanent reminders of the six times Jimmy had been blasted and somehow lived to tell the tale.

The door behind him closed and the floor began to descend with a low hum. "No offence Jimmy but your place isn't exactly welcoming, could do with some brightening up, a clean here and there maybe?" Kessler looked in disgust at his coat and gloves which were now covered in the same green slime that caked the sewer walls. He took off his medivent and breathed in, with great relief, Jimmy's clean, filtered air.

"Nonsense, you complain too much! What's that I see on your face? You hurt?"

"I had some trouble in Downtown, got caught up in a fire. I'll be alright." The floor came to a juddering halt and the door opened to the buzz, whirl and hum of machinery.

"Always the adventurer Kes, always in trouble. Take a seat my friend and tell me all about it. You want something to eat, drink? I have the best as always?"

Along the left wall a bank of monitors lit up the space with various images throughout Dis and a very large screen played an Endelian Enterprise infommercial, the familiar sultry tones of the Endelian girl filling the room with her catchy jingle. The far wall consisted of a large, curved glass window that revealed, to Kessler's uneasiness, the dark abyss that looked over Downtown's upper level. Various lights lit up the 'sky' above the lower city, corps drones and various media satellites zipped by, their green, red and yellow flickering lights competing with the white glare of the consoles which illuminated Jimmy's room. Far down below, through the haze of rain, lay Downtown 1. Kessler took a step back. "I never get used to that view."

Jimmy sat in the centre of the room on a huge chair that bristled with tech. His slight frame was covered by the thick black rubber of his synthwear which pulsed electric blue with energy and linked him, quite literally, into the Mainframe. He was immersed in a tangle of tubes and wires which grew from the suit and into the chair. A large pump, which hissed and wheezed, was connected to Jimmy via a large red cylinder that was attached to his chest.

"You're looking ill." Jimmy pointed a mechanical finger at Kessler.

"I'm ok."

"Rubbish. You look terrible. Take this, it will ease your pain, give you energy."

"I need a clear head, I'm on a case at the minute."

"It's good to hear you're working." He paused and stared intently at Kessler, "I can see from your eyes that you're still partaking in sim? Well, this will take the edge of the comedown, brother."

"Thanks." He grabbed the tablets from Jimmy's hand, which had extended across the room, and quickly threw them down his mouth.

"And eat this." He handed Kessler a Nutri Bar. "Go on, I insist."

Kessler took the silver foil off the Nutri Bar and stared at the dry, grey husk that made up the staple diet the Council tried to force onto its citizens. He turned it over in his hand thinking of how much he hated this tasteless, bland food before stuffing it into his mouth.

"Good. Wash it down with this and then we talk." His chair moved along a rail to the back of the room where he grabbed a can of soda from a fridge that appeared from the wall at a push of a button. Jimmy threw the drink at the detective and Kessler caught it.

As he drank down the cold, fizzy liquid he watched one of the many small bots that were littered throughout the room. It stared at him and followed his every movement. "I don't know how you can stand living down here all day every day."

"I like my privacy and this place gives me it. Residing under Midtown has its benefits. It takes me off the grid and out of the way of any Council meddling and besides, here I have got direct access to the Frame, I'm permanently jacked into the network through the Council's own telemasts," Jimmy chuckled to himself, "and they have no idea."

Kessler glanced outside through the thick reinforced glass to see the black silhouettes of the hundreds of masts and cables that reached out from the underbelly of Midtown. It was through these that the Council could keep a check on its citizens, watch what they were doing, listen to what they were saying. A large drone suddenly swept past obscuring his view, its huge spotlight slowly passing over the room.

"Nothing to worry about Kes, the glass is blacked out from the outside, and I have scrambled their sensors. It can't detect us."

Kessler put down the empty soda can and the robot mimicked his movement. "I still think you should get out of here sometime, it's not healthy being cooped up in this tin can all day."

Jimmy continued to laugh, looking pleased with himself at getting one over on the Council. "What would I want to go outside for? Everything I need is right here," he clutched his neck and visibly winced as he spoke. "The Council aren't going to control my life, no filthy rain or bad air is going to get me, and besides I have my bots for company and, of course, my monitors keep me up to date with the outside world. I can access everything at the touch of a button, no need to worry about me, Kes." He cleared his throat and looked Kessler up and down, "I am, however, worried about you."

"I told you, I'm fine. Surviving."

He nodded slowly, still examining his old friend, "Well then, let's get down to business. What brings you down to my delightful abode?"

"There's a new sim running the streets in Downtown, pretty nasty stuff, burning a lot of Dregs. Do you know of it? The vials I found are marked with a burning sun." Kessler reached into his pocket and gave it to Jimmy. "I haven't heard of it making an appearance here or further up city."

He examined the empty vial, his goggles extending close to magnify the image, "Yea, I've heard of it. The Frame's alive with chatter, mostly chemheads wanting to get their hands on some. This Lux, as they call it, is the next best thing, I hear." Jimmy threw the cap back to Kessler, "You know how chems work, Kes. There is always some new next best thing doing the rounds."

"Where did it come from? Who's making the stuff?"

"Not sure. It surfaced in D2 a few months back and has been steadily making its way up through the city. Sorry friend, that's all I know. You give me a couple of days and I'll find out though."

Kessler nodded, his thoughts turning to the Le Morte twins and how little time he had to pay his debt, "I was in D2 earlier on and saw the strangest thing, a squad of Venters."

Jimmy turned to his monitors, "The city is talking of something big happening below us. The Council seem worried.

It's all over their dispatches. More and more Vents are being sent down for some reason or another."

"I hear that they are now openly supporting the Corps Boys."

"Yea. The Boys have been holed up in Hotel Sunset making their booze and dealing their chem ever since the Council had taken them under their wing. With Council credits they are running riot down there."

"And the district governors are allowing this? Council have no authority below the Rim."

"Please, those governors are all handpicked by the Council, they'll do whatever they're told."

Kessler rubbed his eyes, "Yea, but to openly support a bunch of crazies like the Corp Boys? Even that far down, they'll not be able to keep that quiet. Citizens will not want to spend their credits so freely with corporations supporting lawless gangs."

"The Council seem to put up with their drug use and their indiscretions with the law as long as it doesn't make its way above the Rim to Midtown. They need them. They're using Sunset as their base of operations, preparing for some big show down below." He typed a command into the console, "About a week ago a whole detachment of Vents were sent down to Sunset, and let me tell you these guys aren't messing around, they are packing some heavy heat. They mean business." Jimmy turned back to Kes, "Tell me, brother, why so interested in Council business anyway? What you messed up in?"

"The Corps Boys or the Council may have something to do with a death I am investigating. I need to find out for sure so I can get paid."

"I would skip this one, brother. Like I say, these guys mean business and you don't need to be on the end of it." Jimmy stared at Kessler who looked forlornly out the window and towards the city far below, lost in thought, "You need the cred that bad?"

A few moments passed with only the glare of the monitors

and the constant buzz of the machinery for company. Still looking out of the window and into the darkness, Kessler eventually spoke, "What I do need, old friend, is a way into Sunset." Jimmy shook his head in disbelief, his synthwear now glowing a bright pink. Kessler continued, "Like I said, I just need to find out who killed my client's uncle, then I get paid."

"How long have we been friends for?" Jimmy's seat moved across the room towards Kessler.

"A long time."

"Tell me, who do you owe the creds to?"

"Little Chi."

Jimmy whistled, "How much? Big?"

"Let's just say it's big enough and I don't have it."

"Little Chi is not someone to be messed with. Only a few weeks ago he got poor Hector diced up real good. He won't be jacking into anymore burn rooms now, that's for sure. Real shame."

"Yea, I heard." Kessler rubbed his eyes and noted Jimmy's pills had yet to work, "Can you get me what I need?"

"Of course, but these things don't come cheap, as you know."

"Yea yea, I know. I have some cred. I need it sorted straight away."

"Ok, so let's see what would be best." Jimmy cracked the metal knuckles in his right hand and grinned with glee as he poured over his keyboard, "Something creative, something that you can pass off with your erm, particular charms."

"Don't be too creative, I need to blend in, don't want to draw attention to myself." Kessler knew Jimmy all too well. He was in his element and took to his trade with a youthful passion and delight that belied his fifty-plus years. He may have changed physically, the machines that he relied on for his trade he also relied on to keep him alive, however he had always retained a child-like excitement in what he did, an innocent enthusiasm that was so rare on Dis. It reminded him of when they were younger. So long ago now. He looked at the flurry of activity that was Jimmy Six at work and wished he had more of the qualities he had as a youth. He at last was beginning to feel the warming caress of Jimmy's pills eventually beginning to take hold and his burning retinas and arm ached less.

"Most of Council communication is heavily encoded and impossible to access but the traffic between the more junior officers is less secure. In their arrogance they just love to hear their own voices and they get careless, believe that they are untouchable, that no one would dare monitor Council communiqués."

"You mean they don't count on someone as nosy as you spending hours snooping through their mundane meaningless personal affairs in the hope of finding any juicy info that can make you a quick cred?" The robot again copied Kessler's movements and gave a high pitch 'bleep' as it attempted to mimic his voice. He knocked it over with his hand, "You definitely need to get out more."

"Well, what I found out was that the officers sent down to Sunset don't know why they are being posted below the Rim. Apparently they are as in the dark as we are. However, what I do know is that they are not impressed, the network is filled with their whining. Seems they are as surprised as us as to why the Council is bothering with the lower parts."

"So how are you going to get me in?"

"I'm getting to that part." Jimmy gave Kessler a sideways glance, feeling slightly hurt. "With all these Venters going down the Council have also commissioned a couple of bounty hunters to join the party," Jimmy started to giggle again, "the officers don't like that either, think they are proper gutter trash."

"Ok. What does the Council want with bounty hunters? They usually keep all their dealings in-house." Bounty hunters were a tough breed. They had come from all over the city, from the slums and gangs of Downtown to the wealthy families of Hightown. Whatever their background they had come together for reasons only they knew. Their guild was much feared and not much was known about them, some say even the Council were afraid of them.

"Strange times indeed. I don't think one more bounty hunter in amongst all this activity will be noticed."

"You want me to be a bounty hunter?"

"Yes, you could have been, once."

"That was a long time ago." Kessler turned away and closed his eyes, not wanting to dredge up old, long-forgotten memories.

Jimmy, ignoring his friend's discomfort, continued. He held up a small capsule that pulsed with light, "This is a holo suit, you attach it to your parietal lobe via your ear. You will be able to activate it through your bioware and there you have it, a bounty hunter, with the correct docs of course."

"And this will allow me to walk right in, no problems?"

"Of course. You will however have to do whatever business needs doing fast, say within three hours before the power cells run dry."

"Sounds expensive. How much is this all going to cost me then?"

"You will just pay for the holo suit, I'll throw the docs in for free seeing that we go way back – one hundred creds all in."

"One hundred creds, that's steep." Jimmy never surprised Kessler, always the businessman. "Eighty and we're done."

"Ok, ok. You're killing me. Do you know how much this stuff costs?"

"Jimmy, remember who you are talking to, I know you. You spend all your time cooped up in here making this tech from scratch, at a fraction of market price. You make a killing." Kessler took out what remained of the creds Bethany had given him and realised there would be very little left after this expense. He weighed the bag in his hands as his thoughts returned to the Le Morte twins and Little Chi and reminded himself to com Macy and tell her to lock up the office and make herself scarce for a while. He did not want those ghouls anywhere near her. He threw the cash over to Jimmy who immediately inspected the cred with feverish intensity. "Don't worry, it's all there." Kessler sneered and he made a note to himself to ask Bethany for expenses.

"Business, you understand, old friend."

"Yea, whatever." He never changed.

"So what do you want to look like? Long or short hair? Moustache or beard? I haven't kept up to date with the current fashion."

"Whatever, just make it convincing." Kessler stared again into the vast expanse of Downtown which lay sprawled out below Jimmy's hideaway and wondered just what was happening down there that would get the Council so spooked?

Jimmy continued, completely focused on his task, "We have to make you look the part, a face that has seen many a battle. Then of course your District tattoo, say Downtown slums." He looked pleased with himself. "I think the black and grey garb of the lower city will suit you. And there we have it. So what do you think?"

"Looks fine." Jimmy's monitor revealed a large face with square jaw and a nose that had been broken more than once. A couple of scars ran across the face just below dark brown eyes. A rough black beard and thick, spiked hair completed the grizzled look.

"I tried my best to make him look meaner and uglier than you, it was difficult but I think I've succeeded." He threw the holo suit at Kessler. "And these are your docs, your average contract detailing your terms of service as a bounty hunter working for the Council." Jimmy held up a shimmering disc which was about two inches in diameter. "It should hold up to a reasonable amount of scrutiny but I wouldn't hang around for too long."

"I don't intend to."

*

His journey back to Downtown was never going to be easy. Whatever pills Jimmy had given him to ease his pain had only offered a brief respite. They hardly scratched the surface. The pain in his life had built up over the years, layer upon layer, compacting into a hard crust that would take a lot more than the weak rubbish Jimmy had given him to break through and make a difference. He had rubbed his eyes raw and so viewed the world through blurred vision even his optics could not fix. Vehicles were a haze of yellows and reds as they streaked past his slow, overly-cautious drive. There were deaths in the Pipe every day, it was a fight for survival as citizens entered a zone not monitored by Council eyes. The mag rails latched onto the power cells on the junker's undercarriage and turned it into a blazing missile making its way through Dis in a blur of light and to the sound of crackling electrical discharge. Power surges or cuts, which were a common occurrence on the ageing network, regularly pulled cars off course and only the most vigilant driver avoided disaster. Kessler sweated as he tried to keep his burned out retinas focused, the low rhythmic, hypnotic hum of the transtube reminding him of the sleep he very much needed.

Forcing his mind away from the hurt, Kessler concentrated on the task at hand and found himself thinking of the unconscious Bethany. Life was tough on Dis, tragedy had its needle in everyone, he had it in bucket loads, but, despite this, he found himself looking down at the com on his dashboard, dreading the call from Macy or Doc telling him she had not made it. Was it that he was desperate for her credits or that a thread of humanity was trying to break through to the surface? Hopefully he would finally get some answers from the Corps Boys and shed some light onto who killed her uncle.

Hotel Sunset lay in Kalaupapa sector of D2. The whole area had been abandoned by its inhabitants at some stage in the far distant past. Whatever it was, rad leak or some epidemic, it did not surprise Kessler. These parts of the city had many such tragedies, almost on a daily basis. The citizens in the upper levels would gorge over the infogrammes which reported on these catastrophes, the hardship of those Dregs struggling below the Rim all dressed up in the red glossy lips and bio enhanced bodies of reporters on the newsreels. Citizens would feed off the misery of these lower parts, give them something to talk about over their hydration pouches and ration packs, and who could blame them? The warm glow that others were having a rougher time than you always made your day that bit easier.

Kessler drove through desolate streets, the only sound coming from the hammering rain and the hot gusts of wind which howled and whistled through the empty shells of buildings that towered forlornly either side of the road. The low light restricted visibility and this, combined with the lack of traffic, made the sector feel isolated from the rest of Dis. The only sign that the area had any inhabitants whatsoever was the frequent appearance of graffiti on crumbling stone walls, most of which depicted pro-Council doctrines, and the various tags of Mutes and Dregs. All to be expected from an area controlled by the Corps Boys.

A quick look on the navi-com told Kessler he was coming up to Hotel Sunset and he parked the junker in some unnamed, darkened alleyway a couple of blocks away. He took a few long breaths of the meds to ease his pain slightly and turned it off to save what was left. He lay back and closed his eyes, enjoying the warmth of the medicine as it tingled through his body. He did not look forward to venturing out into the thick Downtown air without it. Not wearing it up in Midtown whilst visiting the Bishop was difficult enough but this far down it was only going to get worse. His breathing was still laboured from the fire and every few breaths his chest still wheezed and spluttered. Rummaging around inside the junker, he took out his last Ox and placed it in one of his pockets. Jimmy had told him that his disguise would only last about three hours but he had no intention of being around anywhere near as long as that.

Following his instructions he placed the device in his right ear and pressed down on the inked bioware panel on his wrist. Kessler looked down at his hands, arms and legs and they began to flicker as his disguise took hold. A low hum vibrated slightly in his ear. The face that stared back at him from his reflection in the canopy took Kessler by surprise. He had to give it to Jimmy, he had certainly done a good job. The square jaws of a grizzled bounty hunter with long, shoulder length black hair and thick stubble with dark brown eyes filled the mirror. A series of violent, jagged scars arced across a heavily tattooed face to complete the disguise. Kessler immediately started the timer on his optics, the display flickered – 03:00:00 – before his eyes, and began its count.

It was easy finding the hotel. As Kessler left his junker, he soon began to hear a low hum penetrate the crashing silence of the rain and then, quickly, this developed into a feral cacophony which guided him through the sodden darkness towards his destination.

From his raised position, Kessler could see that the repetitive grid-like pattern of the streets gave way to a vast empty space at the centre of which lay Sunset. Bright spotlights surrounded the building, mounted on a high perimeter wall and scaffolding towers which reached high up into the murk. The light cut into the thick darkness, its shiny tendrils reaching out into the surrounding space revealing large mounds of rubbish, barbed wire and burnt out vehicles littering the area.

Kessler checked the display on his optics which told him he had two hours and fifty minutes until the batteries went dead. Taking a swift breath from his inhaler, he continued to walk. Through a series of large speakers that hung from the scaffolding towers, loud music, piercing and screeching like metal grinding against metal, battered his senses. Kessler began to feel very self-conscious. Any waster standing along the perimeter wall or manning the large towers would have seen him approaching from a long way off. He looked down at his hands, hoping that the holo suit was doing its job and cursed the fact that he had not turned off his torch light that hung from the lapels of his plastichem coat, its light reaching out into the darkness, swaying and bobbing with every step.

As he approached the building, a tall rusted metal doorway, sprayed from top to bottom in garish graffiti, like that seen everywhere in this sector, came into view. Two kids guarded the entrance, one holding a large spear-like weapon that appeared to be a rusted pipe which had been sharpened at one end, the other an old looking servo-wrench. Both tapped their weapons in time to the drone of the music. They were dressed in a ramshackle assortment of clothes and makeshift armour. One wore the bug-like mask of a rad suit, a battered and tarnished marine breastplate and torn pink trousers while the other proudly displayed the shredded uniform of a Venter officer with two hubcaps strapped to each shoulder.

As Kessler approached they stopped swaying to the noise and the boy holding the servo-wrench slammed his fist against a console. A shock of silence washed over them as the grinding assault of sound disappeared. They both pointed their weapons at the detective who now stood on the edge of the light.

"Halt!" The high pitched voice of the boy with the spear seemed to echo in the quiet.

"Name your business with the Corps Boys?" A muffled voice came from underneath the ridiculously large radiation helmet.

"You best answer carefully citizen." The words could have come from the venter officer that had once worn the kid's uniform but seemed to lose their menace in the thick accented squawk of this Dreg youngster.

Kessler paused for a second and took a couple of breaths. He had to remember that he was not the broken, down and out from Midtown but a hardened, bounty hunter, seasoned from years of violence. He reached down to the depths of his tired, drug-addled brain to a time before everything, when he had meant something, when violence was part of his life too. He walked with purpose towards the gate and went to brush past the guards when they moved to block his way, "Out of my way, boy." Kessler's deep voice sneered.

The guards looked at one another, "Who do you think you're talking too? This is da Corps boys' house. You gotta be stupid to talk like that round here." He prodded Kessler's chest with his sharpened pole and the other started laughing hysterically.

Kessler grunted in annoyance, batted away the primitive weapon and reached into his inside coat pocket. At this sudden movement he was met with raised weapons, "Easy!" He growled, "Here are my docs, now let me past, it's been a long journey down city and my throat is dry, I have drinking to do."

From the small disc in Kessler's hand, the holographic projection of a contract between him and the Council appeared before the pair of Corps Boys. They looked intently at the wall of text before them, appearing to think long and hard about its contents. Kessler doubted either could read but what they definitely did notice was the official Council stamp together with the eye and dagger symbol of the bounty hunters. They immediately stepped aside and, without speaking a word to each other both heaved at the heavy metal door which opened to an angry screeching from its rusty hinges. Kessler sighed to himself in relief, his holo suit seemed to be working. The Corps Boys may be made up of a bunch of kids but he knew not to let that lull him into a false sense of security. He had heard stories of the terror they caused throughout this area. They assumed what little wealth there was this far down was theirs for the taking and did so by controlling much of the lower city through fear and brutal acts of violence and destruction.

Kessler stepped through the gateway into an empty large inner courtyard where the constant rain had mixed with the piles of rubbish to make rivers of waste that flowed freely across the ground and over Kessler's feet. A door burst open from across the yard and a Corps Boy stumbled out past the detective cursing and shouting, slurring his words in a state of complete drunkenness. The opening revealed the raucous sounds of loud voices, laughter and the clinking of glasses but this was soon drowned out by a blaring, grating noise as the music by the gate started again. Above the door was the battered picture of a dark orange sun with the name Sunset in a blaze of red neon. Kessler looked up at the darkness above then quickly readjusted his hood against the rain. The irony of the name was not lost on him, the sun had set on this place a very long time ago.

Laughing drew his attention to his right where a lone boy was slumped up against a wall sheltering from the rain underneath a tattered cloth overhang. Kessler took another glance at the doorway and back to the laughing boy and decided to try and avoid contact with the mob that lay within the hotel.

He slumped down by the kid who sat smiling with his knees drawn up close to his chest. He wore a tattered flash jacket that had long ago lost its glow and baggy plastichem trousers with scuffed, heavy boots. His damp hair was thick and wild and had been sleeked back to reveal a chubby, freckled face which smiled back at Kessler, dimples denting his red cheeks. The boy could have been any mother's cute kid in another life but, in this one, his bloodshot eyes bulged from their sockets and his tongue hung between rotten teeth as the chems had their way with him. Kessler lit a cigar from his pocket and took a long draw before speaking, "Good chem, kid?"

The boy's head rolled around to look at Kessler and he giggled, "Best." The word sloshed out of his wide open mouth.

Kessler nodded, "Listen, I need some info and have cred to pay for it. Buy all the sim you want?" The boy stared at him, his body shaking and eyes twitching, still with that permanent grin strained across his face. A tear fell from a red eye. Kessler reached into his coat and from it grabbed a couple of creds before returning to face the kid, "Have you heard of St John's church? A Christian joint run by a Father Jacob, close to this sector? He…" Kessler stopped talking. The boy's head had slumped to rest on his shoulder. He grabbed hold of a tuft of hair and stared into the now lifeless eyes. A quick check of the boy's pulse confirmed that he was dead. Taking another long puff from his cigar he stumped out the end on the wall and put what was left back into his pocket before getting up and making for the door into the hotel itself. As he got up the boy's body fell to the floor with a dull thud.

Complete chaos reigned inside the building. The old hotel would have been a grand sight back in its day judging by the impressive chandelier which hung in the centre of the room and the huge spiral staircase that swept up to the floors above. However, these details were all that was left of its once fancy past. The expansive lobby had been converted into a saloon, the reception, which formed a large circle around its centre, was now the bar where a horde of boys now queued to get served by a harassed-looking barman. Music, which could just barely be heard above the cacophony of screams, curses and laughter, was emanating from the far side of the room. An old man, whose rags hung from his gaunt frame, was chained to a large instrument of some kind. Every so often he would stumble in his playing only to be struck by an assortment of objects from the crowd. The ground by his feet was littered with the many different missiles used previously to keep him playing. A group of Corps Boys were having an argument over a game of dice, a table had been overturned and it was getting physical. One kid was sprawled across the bottom of the stairs shooting up sim and as the drug entered his system he began to writhe in ecstasy, his little legs kicking out in all directions. A large group were crowded round a table cheering and shouting, watching two huge rats claw and bite each other. Creds were being thrown onto the ground by boys hoping that the vermin would make them a quick fortune. Across the room, on the far side of the reception, a group of men sat silently around a table in the black gloss uniform and white capes of the DPD and next to them, sitting by himself smoking a long, thin nic stick, was a face that Kessler recognised. The Venter officer from St John's, who had so unhappily stood just feet away from him before the church's altar, sat staring into space, lost in his thoughts. His sinister, ghoulish features and cyber-optic implant, which glowed red in the low light of the saloon, were hard to forget.

So the rumours were true, Kessler stared, shocked by what he was seeing. The Council were openly allying themselves with the Corps Boys. It must have been of great importance for them to risk tarnishing their clean image which they spent so much time, cred and energy trying to maintain. Kessler wiped his brow and steadied his breathing. Whatever it was it must be something big and he was just about to walk right in on it. He cleared his thoughts and reminded himself of the reason he was here. He needed to find out if the Corps Boys had any involvement in the death of Father Jacob and time was not on his side. He walked through the bar towards where the DPD were sitting and nervously touched his ear where the capsule was still generating his disguise and sat down on a stool. This part of the bar was half empty and, unlike the Corps Boys, most of the Venters sat in ordered silence, looking down at their drinks and mumbling under their breath. Both groups seemed to be keeping their distance from one another.

Kessler looked around for a barman to get himself a drink. His new look, which stared back at him from a mirror behind the bar, had got him this far and had not drawn the attention of any of the Venters from their drinks or their hushed conversations. He ordered a whiskey and made sure the barman left the bottle. He stared down at the brown, cloudy liquid swirling around in his glass. Finally he was beginning to feel at ease. He lifted the drink up to his mouth and let the burning liquid slowly spread its warmth through his body. It was not Piper's but it would do. Downtown whiskey had a gritty, grubby texture to it and to begin with always felt as if it was burning a hole through your insides. It was nothing compared to the more gentle caress of the Midtown standard Kessler was used to, but he drank it anyway, enjoying every drop, every kick.

A Vent was sitting on a barstool next to him shouting for the barman's attention. The flustered man appeared from around the corner, wiping his hands on a soiled apron. "You don't take no notice of those kids, the law needs serving over here, if you know what's good for ya." Unlike his colleagues, his voice was loud, words emerging between drunken slurs.

"Of course sir, what can I get you?" The barkeep kept shooting worried glances over at the other side of the bar, towards the horde of drunken boys demanding his services.

"Ale. Make it quick!" He started laughing into his empty glass as the man scurried away to get his order then he turned towards Kessler, "I don't know how you can stand drinking that lower-city muck, however, their beer is just about bearable."

"I've had worse." Kessler growled. Like most people on Dis, bounty hunters had no love of the law and he did not want to sound too eager in his attempts to garner information.

"Yes, I expect you have." He thumped down hard his empty glass and took hold of the new bottle that had just been put in from of him. "You lot are used to the lower districts," he sneered.

Kessler ignored the insult, "I did once taste a fine ale down these parts, a Christian church close to this sector, St John's I think it was called, made quite a drink. Shame, heard it burnt down recently."

"No place on Dis for preachers and cults. That's the law."

"True." Kessler mused, "but shame the priest died taking his recipe with him. Now we're stuck with this piss water."

The Vent doubled over with laughter slamming his hand against the bar drawing glances from some of his colleagues, "He got what was coming to him."

Kessler felt adrenalin pump through his system and mix with the warmth of the whiskey. He could sense he was close to an answer. He remained calm by pouring himself another drink and gulping down the entire contents of the glass. "Preaching under the nose of the Council, it was inevitable he would come to bother." Kessler lied in mock agreement.

"Trying to brainwash citizens into wasting their time with his god. That old man should have known there is no place for preaching in these parts when you have this filth." He held up his bottle of beer and took a long drink, "Now I'm in heaven!" Another burst of laughter followed, drawing a stern look from the Venter officer, his face a disgusted sneer.

Kessler waved over the barman and ordered another bottle for his new found friend who grinned back at him. "Probably good you got rid of him, less competition for Council booze. Although, like I say, that Holy Ale was damn fine."

"Yea someone got him real good, saved us the bother."

"You're telling me you didn't end him? C'mon I know you lot all too well."

The Venter quietened down and through his drunken haze whispered slurred words. "His business was finished. His secret," he looked around him as if worried others may be listening, "was chems from Meryll but we soon put a stop to his supply. All that was left to do was take him in but," he burst into wild laughter, holding onto the bar to prevent himself falling off his stool, "like I say, someone else got to him before us. Very nasty end I hear. Serves him right, he was a chem head.

"What about these kids in Sunset? They seem to do what they want."

134

"Not without our say so. No. It was probably some pissed chem dealer, anyway, we do not have time for Dreg priests with what is happening down below." He hit the bar with his fist toppling his drink to the floor with a loud crash. "Now look what you made me do!" He paused and while swaying slightly from side to side squinted at Kessler, "Wait a minute, do you have a serious twitch or something? Your face, is like all flickering."

Kessler quickly looked in the mirror. His face blinked slightly and the buzzing in his ear was becoming erratic. A quick look at the time told him he still had over an hour left. "Damn that Jimmy and his dodgy tech," Kessler mumbled under his breath ruefully.

"Wait a minute, were you wearing a different coat a second ago? You're all fuzzy."

Kessler looked down at his chest. The holo suit was obviously failing. He had to get out of there fast. Turning back to his drunken companion, Kessler was greeted by the sight of the officer grabbing his colleague.

"Lieutenant Bane, I…"

"Get a hold of yourself Constable Illder." Bane stuck him hard with his gloved hand and the man shrieked, "Get out of my sight." His red optics turned towards Kessler who sat nervously on the stool, his hand moving quickly towards his carbine.

The detective got up to leave, everything around him was spinning as panic began to take hold of him. Looking around he could see the chaotic clamouring hordes of boys pushing to get served across the bar, the whimpering drunken Vent who was now holding his swollen face in pain, stumbling up the stairs and the officer standing before him, in his immaculate grey great coat and brimmed cap, despite the heat of the saloon. He raised a long thin hand to Kessler's chest, "Going so soon? You have not finished your drink." His mouth opened to reveal sharp, yellow teeth. Kessler could hear the whirling of gyros and cogs as his implants focused on him.

"Out of my way, Vent." Kessler told himself to calm down,

his only way out of this place was to keep faith in the dodgy tech and the docs Jimmy had given him.

"This place," he looked Kessler up and down, his long spindly finger trailing slowly from his stomach to his chest, "is covered in filth. It disgusts me." His head turned towards his departing subordinate, "It needs to be purged before it infects us all." Kessler moved again to escape when the officer stepped close to him, barring his way. "Your face paint tells me, bounty hunter, that you are from the refined air of Hightown 3 but your accent, I just can't seem to place it."

Kessler cursed Jimmy again, he had told him his district tattoos placed him from Downtown. He looked around him, trying to buy time to think of a response. Most of the Venters sitting quietly at their tables were all staring at him. "Listen," Kessler tried his best to put on the high nasal quality of Hightown, "this accent has been all over just like I'm going to be on you if you don't get out of my way."

"Yes, I suppose it has," he began to chuckle to himself, a wheezing and rasping sound from the depths of his throat gurgled his pleasure. Suddenly, he stopped laughing and stood completely still and silent as he looked into the detective's eyes. "That weapon you are carrying, it has been a long time since I have seen a Luther. Very rare indeed. Only awarded to those who have committed the finest of deeds." He peered into Kessler's eyes and nodded his head slowly, "It must have been a very difficult kill to take such a weapon as your own."

Kessler looked down to see the chrome plate and glowing power cell of his carbine, still holstered by his waist, as his disguise flickered violently. He began to sweat. He stared at the gaunt face of Lieutenant Bane, his grey lifeless skin seemed stretched tight over his implants, dark purple veins pulsing just beneath the frayed surface. Moments passed. All Kessler could think about was the holo suit capsule that was stuttering for life in his ear. He had to get out of Hotel Sunset. Fast.

The detective made for the entrance hoping that the officer would not be quick to act on his suspicions. As he waded his way through the crowd he could hear his suit crack and fizzle as its power cell began to run dry. Kessler could feel the officer's eyes boring holes into his back as he slowly barged his way through a wall of drunken Corps Boys. He could see the door to the outside world on the other side of the saloon, beyond the hundreds of shouting, brawling, wasted bodies. Looking behind him, the officer still stood by the bar staring at him, his fellow Venters now risen from their seats all stood around him. One of them turned and pointed towards the detective. Kessler wiped his brow, all around him faces, glazed drunken eyes, toothless grins, hooked noses and tattooed bodies all turned to stare at him. He began to feel claustrophobic. All seemed lost, his hand went to his ear and touched the power cell, hoping it would last. The Venters strode towards him and began to work their way through the crowd, catching up with him quickly as the mob parted more easily for them.

Suddenly the crowd lurched forward carrying Kessler with it towards the exit in a surge of bodies. He felt the holo suit fail with a loud pop followed by a burning sensation which made him clutch his ear in agony. He looked around the bar, desperate that no one noticed his changed appearance. The officers were in the centre of the melee, their barked orders at the hordes of boys who barred their way now lost in the din of the saloon. Still, despite the chaotic scene, the ghoulish red glow of Bane's cyber optics were on him at all times. His face had a grim determined look, his jaw set. Kessler couldn't help but nod his head towards the furious officer before donning his hood, stepping over a prone body which lay sprawled across the entrance, and making his escape.

Walking past the two guards, he exited the compound and quickly made for the safety of his junker. He continued to curse himself for using Jimmy's second-rate tech and promised that he would think twice before trusting him again. Kessler looked back at the darkness behind him, checking for anybody following him. He was in no doubt that Bane would quickly send out a patrol after him. He grabbed the capsule from his ear and smashed it on the ground before jumping in his vehicle and making for Nimrod Heights.

·NIMROD HEIGHTS·

Kessler gripped the junker's controls tight as he strained to concentrate, blinking repeatedly and wiping the sweat from his brow, trying to focus on the road. Every so often he looked behind, waiting to see the Venter's Interceptors emerging from the darkness, sirens blaring, engines roaring. He could feel the clawing need for a hit of sim begin to bite at the back of his throat, the voice in his head trying to reassure him that it was the only way to clear his mind, think straight, defend his body against the blind panic that was beginning to take hold. Questions crashed around his mind. Had the Vents seen through his disguise? Had the holo suit failed and revealed his face? Kessler was sure that it had. He cursed himself for his stupidity and smashed the console with his fist in anger, "Great Kes, just walk right into Sunset and ask a couple of questions, get some answers and stroll straight back out. Fantastic plan!" He shook his head, now that they had seen his face it would only be a matter of time before the DPD or, even worse, Councilmen picked him up off the streets. Using illegal tech, forging Council docs and gate crashing the Vents' love-in with the Corps Boys, Kessler laughed at himself, he was done for, there was no escape, they had eyes everywhere. His thoughts went to Macy and he wondered if she could fend for herself, all alone in this city, if he was rotting in some Council cell. A fit of coughing interrupted his thoughts and the vehicle swerved suddenly as he reached for the medivent which was lying on the passenger seat. The canister's rattle told him that it was nearly empty but he did not care. Long gulps from the medicated oxygen soon slowed his breathing, numbed his pain. After a few measured breaths he took hold of his Luther and laid it beside him, at the ready, just in case bad company was close by.

Nimrod Heights was a huge crumbling, decrepit tower block in Downtown 2, one of the many thousands which festered throughout a district where millions of Dregs lived out a meagre existence, left to rot by those living in the city above. The whole of Downtown was decaying under the feet of those citizens living above the Rim who were too focused on their own survival to care for those rotting in the depths below them.

Kessler was determined to get some answers. If the DPD or Corps Boys did not kill the priest then who did? He did not have much to go on and felt the steely, clammy grip of desperation begin to tense his body. His life began to close in around him. Little Chi and the Le Morte twins, the Council pulling him from the streets never to be seen again and then this danger from below that had got even the Council spooked, all these thoughts swirled around in his head. A sense of foreboding took hold of him and all he wanted to do was curl up into a ball. His mind again strayed onto thoughts of taking a hit and allow all his problems to leave him in an instant, allow him to escape. He realised, as his thoughts played out in his head, that he had stopped the junker by the side of the road and his left hand was fingering his coat pocket where the last of Stacey's sim lay waiting. Sweat poured down his face and he shivered as a chill took him. Shaking, he pulled his glove off his right hand and reached around to take the vial of chem. He looked out of the canopy into the gloom and the rain and then back to the sim which he held between his thumb and forefinger.

A quick, well practised, flash of movement and the chem powered its way through his system. Immediately all was better, immediately the darkness surrounding Kessler did not seem quite so dark. The junker's engine came alive and he continued on his way.

It was not long before Nimrod Heights came into view. Pulling his hood over his head, Kessler got out of his vehicle and looked up at the tower block which soared up into the gloom above him. A sign hung precariously above the slum's entrance and sporadically flashed red neon through the relentless downpour. He recognised the building from the newsreels. A few weeks back it had been a chaotic scene as a couple of Dreg gangs had come to blows. Many district governors had little or no control over some of the more powerful groups of Dregs and without the DPD breathing down everyone's necks, the gangs were left to their own violent devices. The only reason Kessler remembered this scuffle in particular was because the reporter, an attractive midcity girl with purple hair and large augmented breasts, famous on the infogrammes around M5, was killed by some Mute live on air. Her head came clean off. Kessler chuckled, not even the Council could censor that one. It was the talk of the district for months.

Kessler turned on his torch, adjusted his optics, and made for the entrance. Moving was difficult because of the heavy bandaging across his chest and his sodden plastichem coat felt heavy in the bad air. However, with the chem firing through his veins he did not care about the pain.

The door to the tower block was buckled and wedged against its frame between crumbling brick walls. Pushing it to the side, Kessler was immediately hit with the pungent smell of human waste. Ahead of him, through the faint frazzled buzz of the strip lighting he could just make out a stairwell.

Standing within the half-light of the lobby, out of the driving rain, an eerie silence greeted the detective, broken only by a low skittering sound coming from whatever infested this ancient, dilapidated building. He adjusted his hood, tightened his medivent and pulled the collars up on his coat in an attempt to keep out the filth and depravity that he was sure lurked in every corner. He knew that all manner of diseases were rife within the slums and the thought of having any one of them creeping inside his already battered body made him retch. He felt light-headed and had to steady himself, taking long slow breaths through his vent.

Looking around, Kessler could just make out the remnants of what used to be the lift. Splattered in graffiti, the door was open and revealed creaking cables and chains which descended down below to the darkness of the basement. The whistle and high pitch howl of a haunting wind echoed down the shaft from far above. With a sigh, he turned his attention to the stairs and readied himself for the climb.

The metal grating let out a resounding 'clunk' as Kessler stomped his way up towards the twelfth floor where, according to the faded display on the lobby wall, apartment 407 awaited him. He could not believe the priest would have anything to do with a place such as this and journey so far from the safety of his church. From his writing and from what Bethany had told him he knew of the dangers the slums contained.

Every few steps his boot made contact with something soft underfoot and Kessler reminded himself to scrub down his clothes next time he was back at the office. As he rose up through the floors he came across a couple of Dregs kissing and groping each other across the stairs blocking his way. The man was a typical low dweller, pale skin and large bulbous yellow eyes, from years of too much bad air and low light. He wore a sleeveless black top, revealing chalky white skinny tattooed arms which were currently making their way over the curves of the girl who, wearing nothing but grubby pink boots and tight, worn plastichem shorts, glared at the detective. Her unblinking, unrelenting stare revealed the severely bloodshot eyes of someone completely burned on sim.

Kessler tried to get his large frame past them, "Move," he said with disgust. The girl's vacant eyes followed him, open mouthed, lipstick smeared across her greasy face, as the man continued to grope and fondle her small, ghostly white breasts. Kessler shoved them to the side and continued his climb. "Dregs…" He sighed to himself.

As he continued upwards, more haunting noises began to greet Kessler from somewhere in the floors above. Hysterical laughter, manic cries, animal-like grunting and howling, all brief snatches of sound, whispered out from the darkness around him. The climb left him gasping for air as the stagnant heat within the tower weighed down on him. He paused unable to breathe, his chest ached and his lungs, still scorched from the fire, begged for good air. Finally, his rapid gasps of air were quickly followed by the rattle of the empty medivent. "For light's sake!" He snatched it from his face, gave it a shake before throwing it down the stairs. He reached into his pocket for his Ox inhaler and took a long, deep breath and steadied his breathing. Resting himself against the wall for a moment, he tightly fastened his cloth mask across his face and climbed to the twelfth floor.

Opening the heavy metal door from the stairwell into a long corridor, the thick smell of waste became suddenly stronger. Doors leading to apartments lay either side of the hallway, some open and others closed shut, all caked in the same grime and graffiti found throughout the sector. In amongst the rubbish and human waste which littered the floor were Dregs, some lying prone, others standing with their back to the wall with their heads rolling back and forth and some hunched over their gear, burning up chem or sniffing some kreg. Loud, heavy electro music drowned out the senses. Two Dregs were sluggishly swaying from side to side, seemingly trying to dance to the barrage of grinding sound. Kessler retightened his cloth mask in a vain attempt to prevent him breathing in this decay.

143

Stepping over a prone body, Kessler finally found apartment 407. Like everything in this monstrous place the door was caked in the phrases and symbols of the local gangs but in amongst the garish pink and yellow graffiti the words 'Lux Ferre' were carved, again as if by some feral beast, into the cracked metal panelling. He scratched his head and his thoughts went back to the priest's study in St John's and the chilling message on his desk. "Light Bringer," Kessler whispered to himself as his gloved hand traced the shape of the letters.

A Dreg lay by the door looking up at him, his bald head half pale, sallow skin, the other half completely covered in tattoos. He ginned at the detective as the same question reverberated around Kessler's head again and again. What would a priest, especially one as devout as Father Jacob supposedly was, have anything to do with this cess pit? He shook his head in exasperation before knocking loudly on the door.

After a few minutes of waiting the door to number 407 edged open an inch and a single, black veined eye, peered out of the darkness. "What do you want?" A low, gravelled voice hissed from beyond the doorway. The old Dreg on the floor started laughing until a hacking cough made him double over in pain.

"I have some questions that need answering. I can pay."

"Who's asking?" The voice was low and Kessler struggled to hear it. The eye darted erratically about, trying to see everything at once.

"I'm asking. Just want the answer to a couple of questions, no trouble."

"Go away."

Kessler's boot prevented the door from slamming shut, "Mind if I come inside?" The clock was ticking, clues as to why the priest died were few and far between and this was his final throw of the dice. Kessler did not have time to mess around. He pushed open the door, easily overcoming the strength of the Dreg and walked inside as the creature scurried to the far corner.

"What do you want of me?" It spoke in a panic, the low hiss of speech now becoming a squeal.

The room was in complete darkness bar a small red light that glowed from the com system on a nearby desk and, adding to the thick, filthy air, the room was filled with a sickly sweet stench. Kessler raised his hand across his masked face and tried to resist the urge to gag.

He threw light onto the cowering creature who immediately turned its face away from the glare. It wore a black hood and from it emerged a skeletal, emaciated fetid grey face. White reflected torch light shone back at Kessler from black, deeply sunken eyes. Its skin had a clammy sheen and was covered in putrid, red bulbous sores. Kessler staggered back at the sight and again covered his face with his good arm. "For light's sake, what sickness is this?"

"Stay away!" The creature pleaded.

Kessler dimmed his torch but kept it trained on the creature. With the glow of the light dulled, it raised itself, stopped shaking and seemed to grow in confidence, "You will not take them. They are mine!"

Kessler ignored it, "The priest, Father Jacob," the creature let out a howl and visibly winced at the name, "he came here, often, in the weeks and days leading up to his death. Why would such a citizen visit this," Kessler looked around the apartment, "nightmare?"

It stood up straight, its full height making it nearly as tall as Kessler, and took a step towards the detective. Bending forward, the creature tried to get a look at his face, "Who are you? What do you want?" The words hissed from the gloom.

The detective took another step back and immediately reached for his Luther, "Get back, sit down." Something crunched beneath his boot. Lowering his light to the floor revealed hundreds of cockroaches that skittered over a grey sludge of festering waste on the apartment's floor. In amongst the foul-smelling decay was the now familiar image of the burning sun which stared up at Kessler from the many empty caps littering the ground. He felt light-headed and with his free hand took a hit of Ox before repeating, "Why would a priest visit this place?"

"Yess, yess. Ok, ok." The Dreg's words were now measured and he took his time to pronounce each syllable. Walking back slowly, it bowed its head close to the ground, before sitting down on a chair. Spindly arms emerged from the flowing black robes to play with a long chained necklace which hung low from its neck. Its eyes rested on Kessler's Luther which remained pointed straight at it, "No, no, no. I cannot do that. We agreed. I am finished with that nasty business." It shook its head and spoke in pleading tones, appearing to be having a conversation with itself, "I am so close, so near. I can see the light, almost touch it. Leave me be. We had a deal." It raised a pointed finger to thin lips in thought, "Yes. I know he wants it. Ok. Ok." It suddenly finished speaking with an angry growl and turned back to smile at Kessler. With its constant, nervous mumbling now ceased, only the skittering sound of the critters crawling underfoot and the low, muffled beat of the music out in the hall, filled the room.

Moments passed without a word before Kessler spoke, "Enough of this." He powered up the cells of his carbine, "You have one more chance, nut job, before I end you. Tell me why was Father Jacob visiting you?"

Looking away from Kessler to the other side of the room the Dreg chuckled, its laughter bubbling up through its throat in a painful wheeze. "He thought he had all the answers. Don't do this. Do that. Then you will hear him. His light, his warmth is everywhere, you just have to look. That is all he would ever say."

"Father Jacob told you this?"

The creature continued, ignoring Kessler's interruption, "All this to hear God's words, to feel his light, to know that something, someone, is looking over us. I just wanted to be told that everything was going to be ok." It wiped its teary eyes with its sleeve before creasing up its face and speaking through gritted teeth in fury, "He lied! All lies!"

The Dreg held its necklace in a tight grip and shook it, catching the light from Kessler's torch and drawing the detective's attention. Kessler had seen that symbol before. A cross shone back at him, similar to that seen at the church and up in Eden Inc. "You know, that necklace you're wearing looks expensive. What is it? Silver? Pretty hard for a Dreg of your means to come by." The creature seemed not to hear Kessler, its stare still focused away from him. "You Dregs disgust me. What did you do? Steal it from the priest's corpse?"

"What if I told you that there was another answer? That the Ox, and the warmth of light that we all seek, can be got. We just need to grab it."

"The Council are..."

"No!" It interrupted, "No. Not the Council. Just take a hit and you will be given what you want. That's what they said."

"Who said?" Kessler struggled to understand.

The Dreg continued, "He wouldn't listen, wanted to take the voices away from me. I told him, I hear the words now but old Jacob would not understand. Told poor Judecca to pray more, stay locked up in that old church and never go out, stay and listen to everyone's sob stories like a good priest. He was jealous that I could speak to the Light Bringer and he could not hear his voice!"

Kessler took a step forward as he heard the familiar phrase, "Light Bringer. I have heard those words before." He focused on the creature, "Those words are on your door, were on Father Jacob's desk." The detective's hand shook as he kept his weapon trained on the creature. At last shattered images, unanswered questions all came crashing together and he began to feel he was close to getting the answers he needed. The creature's name sparked a memory. Bethany mentioned a Judecca working with her uncle back at St John's. "Did you kill Father Jacob?"

"They told me the only way I could hear his voice, feel his light and breathe his air, was to help them talk to Jacob. So I did."

"You mean take more sim. That is how you hear the voices? I see empty caps of Lux all over this place, you have certainly been busy."

Judecca jolted upright with a start, "I knew it," anger returning to his voice. "He told me you came to steal my beautifuls. I said no, no but he said yes."

Kessler, still keeping his Luther pointed at Judecca, moved to the other side of the room where he had been staring so intently. Waving his torch across the area revealed a sink covered in a dark substance that had congealed over piles of dirty plates and rotting rations. "Quite a lot of blood around here, you must have cut yourself badly, eh?"

"Poor Judecca just wants to be left alone!" He sobbed into his cloak.

Kneeling down, the detective opened the drawer beneath the sink to reveal a large box bearing the image of the burning sun. "And what's this Judecca, have you been a naughty boy?"

"No. Leave my beautifuls!" He lunged forward, squealing but his sickly, feeble body moved slow enough for Kessler, despite the pain in his arm, to adjust his weight from his crouched position and bring down the butt of his Luther hard onto the back of Judecca's head. He hit the floor with a thud.

Inside the box was a large stash of Lux. He whistled and shook his head, he had never seen so much sim in one place before. He grabbed a fistful. Pain returned to him and he struggled to breathe as the thought of sim entered his mind and he shuddered at the possibility of its gentle, warm wave taking hold of him. His grip tightened on the vials and he threw some into his pocket.

Kneeling over Judecca's body, Kessler slapped him across the face. "Come on, wake up, I don't have all day." Something wasn't quite right. Judecca's insanity was obvious but somebody had brought him all this chem and that did not come cheap.

Judecca opened his eyes and groaned. Kessler held one of the many caps of Lux up to his eyes with one hand, the other had his Luther at the ready. "Who brought you this chem? This much sim could fetch a lot of cred."

"I earned it. It's mine." His eyes remained closed as he spoke, "He wanted to stop my beauties. Take them away from me." Judecca's voice was almost a whisper. Kessler had to kneel close to hear him.

"You mean Father Jacob wanted to help you ditch the sim?"

"I told you, he wanted to stop me from hearing, wanted to stop others from hearing. I tried to tell him prayers don't hear, the church hears nothing from Him anymore. Now I hear everything. I see the light."

"Who gave you all this chem?" Kessler repeated.

"You know. You've seen it."

"I've seen nothing, Mute."

"Acheron. They came from Acheron, deep down below to answer our prayers." He laughed, a sharp gurgle frothed around in the back of his throat. "They opened my eyes and now I know what awaits us. Soon everyone will see, everyone will bathe in the light, have their prayers answered."

Kessler stared at the whimpering mess as it lay crouched in the shadows before him. He had seen many times before the creatures that dwelt in the lower parts of the city. Years drenched in the polluted rain, living off the tainted Downtown land and grinding what was left of their brains through the chem blender. He remembered back to the picture of the three priests at the church, the old, stern looking face of Father Jacob and the youthful, smiling faces of the youngsters, arm in arm. That happy image was a far cry from the chem-addled wreck who lay quivering on the filthy floor of this Downtown slum. Judecca's mind was clearly broken and his addiction had consumed him quickly. Kessler understood now the fear in Stacey Steckles's eyes when she spoke of the dangers of this new chem. He paused for a minute, again thinking of the photo of the three priests. Judecca spoke in low soft whimpers, "He was my friend. I would never hurt him, never. He wanted to help poor Judecca. But he didn't understand. They just wanted to give him their warmth, show him their light. Go on they said, leave the window open at night, after service. We only want to talk to him, tell him to stop being so mean to poor Judecca. Tell him to stop telling people not to listen. They wanted to make him understand."

It all began to make sense to Kessler, "So because Father Jacob was telling Dregs not to take Lux your friends wanted to teach him a lesson. I understand. And Brother Rothery? No one has seen him since."

Judecca's face curled up in disgust and he spat, "That idiot. Seeking answers in tattered old rubbish when all he had to do was look at what was here. He wouldn't listen so they took him. They need people to help make enough to allow the rest of us to see the light."

"So you let them into the church and they took Brother Rothery and killed Father Jacob, bashed his head in and filled him with sim. Gave him some of the very stuff he was trying to stop you taking. And all so you could get more of this." Kessler still held up the vial of Lux.

Judecca stopped his sobbing and pushed the box towards Kessler, "Go on, I know you want some. Even through your shades, I can see it in your eyes. You cannot hide it from me. You and me are the same, me thinks," his voice rattled with a sudden rush of excitement. "I can spare one if you leave Judecca to his business." His voice hissed and wheezed as he stared at Kessler. He scratched at a couple of sores on his arm leaving a large angry red welt.

"We are nothing alike." Kessler threw a cap against the wall where its dull thud was greeted with a manic howling from

Judecca. He lifted his leg and brought it down hard on the box, bursting hundreds of vials which leaked their poison onto the floor...

"No!" Judecca's voice changed to a growl. He lunged for the detective and sunk his teeth into his arm. Kessler spun around, wildly flailing but the Dreg's bite held fast.

A sudden flash of torch light on metal was followed by an explosion of agony as Judecca, with unnatural speed and viciousness, brought a large jagged blade from under his robes and stabbed Kessler through to his stomach. In a rush of frantic movement and through a heavy shock of pain, the detective brought his Luther to bear on Judecca's snarling, frothing maw and he squeezed the trigger releasing a flash of white searing hot plasma, causing the creature's head to instantly explode.

Crouching over the now lifeless body, Kessler breathed heavily with the noise of the blast still ringing in his ears. Parts of skull and brain matter lay sprayed across the floor and the familiar burnt smell of plasma filled the room, wafting up from the nozzle of his Luther. He turned to stare at the door to the apartment. He had to get out of there fast and make his way back to Midtown with the news that this new sim and the priest's death were fatally connected. Stacey Steckles had mentioned seeing the priest around the skin labs helping Dregs kick the habit and this was confirmed by Bethany back in the priest's study. Judecca said that his new-found friends had been angered at the priest sticking his nose into their business, it seemed they didn't much like what he had to say about their product. Kessler stared at the many broken caps of Lux throughout the room. It appeared that whichever gang, chemheads or whomever was making this sim were the ones responsible for killing him.

Sighing to himself, Kessler surveyed the grim scene. Lux took a hold of the body more quickly than anything he had ever seen before. In a matter of months, Judecca had been turned from a man of faith to a monster willing to betray his friends and family all for a hit of this chem. Kessler was not looking forward to telling Bethany the grim reasons behind her uncle's death. The answers to her questions were never going to stop her anger or rid her of grief but this was what she wanted and what he was paid to do. He slumped back to the floor as a flash of pain took his strength and reminded him of his wound. Wincing, he examined the weeping cut. The Dreg had managed to penetrate the plastichem of Kessler's coat, right through his shirt and into the side of his stomach, he had to give that wretched creature some credit, he didn't think he had the strength in him for such a move.

Kessler pulled his arm from his coat, tore the sleeve off of his shirt and wrapped it tightly around the wound to try to staunch the bleeding and gingerly got to his feet. Another spasm took what little breath he had in his lungs and he doubled over in agony. He knew he was not going to make it far and had to get to help. Fast.

Reaching down into the bloody remains, Kessler retrieved Judecca's silver cross and placed it in his pocket. Proof for Bethany just in case she required it. Adjusting his coat and holstering his weapon, he staggered back out into the corridor making sure to close the door firmly behind him concealing the bloody scene from the Dregs who still loitered in the corridor. With the deafening grind of electro music still ringing in his ears, he adjusted the cloth to cover his nose and mouth as the heavy, putrid air began to catch the back of his throat. The old Dreg, with his bald head and wrinkled face glistening with sweat, still sat on the floor by the door, eyes wide in the red chemical haze, mouth sucking feverishly on his bottom lip as whatever chem he was on took hold of him. His twitching eyes stared at Kessler.

"Hey Just Come, did ya find what ya lookin fo?" His head tapped the wall repeatedly to the beat of the music.

Kessler reached into his pocket and took out one of the vials of Lux taken from Judecca's stash. "Do you know where I can find more of this?"

He stopped chewing on his lip to howl with laughter. "That is so fine that juice ya be carryin JC but you won't av it for long time if ya flash it round down dis part of town."

Kessler knelt down and grabbed his ancient face, bringing it close to his own. "Listen Dreg, I don't have time for games." He grinned revealing blackened, toothless gums and stuck his tongue out. The stench of death crept out of his mouth and his eyes began to roll back in their sockets. Holding up the cap of Lux, Kessler continued, "You can have this if you tell me where I can find those who make it."

The Dreg stopped banging his head against the wall and briefly focused on the vial. For once his body was still, the manic energy of before seeming to quickly disappear. "Why, it no secret where da light come from, JC. You just need to look into your dreams."

Nothing made sense anymore. He went to put the chem back into his pocket and began to leave when the Dreg, whose focus had never left the cap of Lux spoke, "Men came from down dere all flash like a couple of months ago, came from nowhere with all dis tools."

"And these men, do they make Lux?

"Yes." He seemed to catch his breath and pulled the detective even closer to him, their noses nearly touching, "They make the light down below where da fire is. You find dem in Acheron way deep in Down 5. Far, far below. That's what da voices say. Tell us to come visit. Can't you hear dem?" He reached for the cap in Kessler's hands, long, grubby, yellow fingernails curling themselves around the sim which Kessler batted away.

He shook his head as broken images from his dreams flashed through his mind. "Humph," Kessler laughed at himself and cursed the sim still running through his system. "Nice try. No one goes down there."

"Some do. They do."

"The Council would never allow it. "

The Dreg burst into laughing. "Council! There is no Council where the light shines brightest."

Kessler let the cap of Lux drop to the ground and made his way down the hallway as the old Dreg frantically scrambled around the floor looking for what he had earned. The detective could feel his skin begin to itch and bile build up in the back of his throat. He felt unclean. "Be careful now JC, dancing in the light can be a dangerous business." The Dreg's voice, and the preceding cackle, echoed down the corridor, following Kessler out into the stairwell.

Kessler welcomed the relative quiet as he descended the stairs, the drone of the music and the manic voices of the tower's inhabitants now only a dull hum in the background. He was sweating, his chest ached and he could feel the bite from his stomach wound. He leaned against the wall for support as his head began to swirl. "C'mon Kes," he told himself, " just make it to the junker and you're home. Easy." He fumbled in his pocket for his Ox inhaler and took one final hit before throwing the empty canister to one side and steadied himself. Rubbing his eyes, he prepared himself for the remainder of the descent when something caught his eye. Peering over the edge of the stairs through the half-light down towards the lobby, Kessler could see the faint glow of red and blue lights which flashed intermittently through the tower's entrance. He sighed and powered up his Luther.

Turning off his torch, he made his way down the stairs cautiously clinging to the wall not wanting to be seen by whomever was down below. As he approached the lobby he began to make out the unmistakable barks of a Venter, interrogating someone in the entranceway of the tower. "Tell me where he went." The metallic clunk of the officer's breathing apparatus only served to remind Kessler of his own breathing difficulty. He quickly managed to stifle a cough and cursed at his worn out lungs. He looked outside careful to not be seen.

The Dreg from the stairwell was standing, shoulders slumped, head bowed, before a DPD officer. The girl he was with lay prone on the ground at his feet, her pale skin glowing in the blaze from the Venter's powerful torches. Through the crashing rain which glistened in the bright light, he could see the other officer standing by his junker, bending over and peering through the canopy.

Kessler cursed himself. They must have followed him from Hotel Sunset, he had been naive to think that he could escape the DPD so easily.

"Who ya talking about? My head is sore pig." The unmistakable slur of a Downtowner was answered with a dull thud. The Dreg squealed in pain. "Why ya do dat?"

"Answer my question. Did you see an uptowner enter this building?"

"Ya people tink ya can come down here an tell us wat to do. It ain't right. Sure I seen him, not many citz from above come by this way. He went up da stairs, tenth, maybe twelfth floor. I dunno, I was busy with ma business."

The Venter turned to his partner. Alarm bells started ringing in Kessler's head. The thought of his imminent discovery spurred him into action. He quickly looked around in the low light of the lobby for somewhere to hide. He couldn't run up the stairs, in his condition the Vents would soon catch up to him. Another look outside saw the two officers beginning to march towards him. Kessler's attention quickly returned back to the lobby. The lift was his only option. He made a leap across the entranceway, praying that the dull light would hide his bulk. Quickly pulling across the rusted metal cage that barred his way, he threw himself over the edge of the lift shaft and clung to an old ladder on the far side. It swayed precariously, producing a painful screech each time the detective put his full weight onto the flimsy rungs. The stale, hot air howled through the empty shaft making the chains and cables that dangled from above sway

155

noisily from side to side. Rain had found its way into the shaft covering every surface in the greasy slime making it difficult to keep a grip of the ladder. Kessler pulled his hood up as his blood mixed with the rain and ran down his side.

Holding his breath, ignoring the cries from his body and the raging fire in his stomach, Kessler gasped for good air that was not there and waited to hear the heavy armoured footfalls stomp by. Judecca's bloodied body was lying upstairs in his apartment with all the chem lying around, the DPD were bound to discover it and they would quite easily link his demise to him.

Within moments the two passed, the brief, high pitch whine from the assault rifles indicating that they meant business. They marched quickly up the stairs, the hissing and wheezing of their respirators disappearing up into the tower above.

Kessler reached over across the elevator shaft to the opposite side and balanced on the ledge below the opening. He tried to pull himself up but the pain was too much and unconsciousness threatened to overcome him. He fell back but, just before he was going to plummet down into the darkness below, he gathered what little strength he had left and grabbed hold of one of the chains dangling from above and pulled himself to the lobby floor, his body straining as it fought the agony, trying not to make a sound for fear of discovery, finding the energy he needed to escape.

Staggering outside into the rain, the detective stumbled past the Dregs who sat on the ground staring up at him vacantly and, once at his junker, fumbled for the latch on the vehicle's canopy. Kessler slumped into the driver's seat and quickly fired up the com, praying for a signal this far down. "Hey Ke... I can't... screen. Bad signal..." The crackling and rasping of interference interrupting Macy's Midtown tones.

"Get the Doc down here quick, I can't make it back." A wave of pain gripped his chest, he bit down hard waiting for the agony to pass, "Follow my tracer and get Galloway here I..." The com cut off, the signal lost.

To the sound of empty static, Kessler reached over and flicked on the beacon. He could feel himself begin to slip into unconsciousness, a mixture of tiredness and pain wearing him down. He powered up the vehicle crashing into the side of a building as the junker lurched forward. His vision was going and he struggled to see in the dim light and heavy rain. His faltering mind now solely focused on finding a place to hide from the Venters.

He threw the junker to the left and turned down an alleyway and, struggling for control, he smashed the vehicle against a wall. Sparks lit up his vision as metal ground against metal until Kessler released the accelerator and slumped across the passenger seat. He was tired of fighting, always trying to survive. He had no energy, no air, no chance…

·THE MORAL COMPASS·

*D*ark shapes crowded around him and cold, clammy hands pulled and pushed him down. He tried to resist, tried to stay on his feet but there were too many. Everywhere they chanted the same word, a low deep mantra that increased in speed as did the frantic flurry of the poking, prodding and clawing fingers. The dark was alive and slowly swallowing, asphyxiating him in a thick sea of complete blackness. He raised himself up in a desperate attempt to break free and breathe one final gasp of air as from all around him, just as the darkness spilled into his mouth, lungs and body, voices screamed from the dark.

"Lux Ferre."

He woke with a start. An electronic, repetitive squeal blared somewhere in the far distance. What was it? An alarm? Sirens? A rapid patter could be heard from somewhere up above. Rats? Maybe the rain? He felt wet and pain prevented him from moving. He was cold, his back hurt. He was lying on a hard surface. Not a bed. No, the floor perhaps. A muffled sound began to grow in volume. Words. Someone was speaking. There was the sharp rush of gas, the quick intake of breath as someone used an inhaler. He began to remember not being able to breathe. His body jerked aggressively as it tried to take in air but instead the stale, stagnant taste of Downtown clutched at his insides and with it the realisation of where he was. He let out a groan and tried to get up but as he opened his eyes the world began to spin and he slumped back to the ground.

"So the patient has returned to the land of the living?" He recognised the refined Hightown voice and managed to open his eyes enough to see the disapproving bespectacled face of Doc Galloway approach, roughly take hold of him and place a medivent over his mouth, peer into his eyes and checked his pulse. "We thought we had lost you. Here, take this, it will make you feel better." Doc handed Kessler a plastic beaker, "It is just water with some painkillers and antibiotics."

Kessler cleared his throat, "You can't get rid of me that easily." He sat up with some difficulty and took a long drink of the cloudy liquid.

"I may not be able to get rid of you, but your heart may be able to. It's about done Kes, and this place, this air, is not doing it any favours. We have to get you back up to Midtown where the air, although still awful, is better than this soup we are breathing. If you were one of my patients I would recommend getting a rebreather installed but I understand bioware is expensive."

"Well, thanks for your help but I'll be fine."

"I can't take all the credit, as much as I would like to. You would not have made it if it wasn't for the jar of Prinax I found in your coat pocket. That stab wound," Doc shook his head, "I don't know who you pissed off this time but whoever it was missed all your major organs. It did, however, pick up a nasty infection, would have poisoned your blood and, if you lasted long enough, would have eventually made it to your heart and..." Doc waved his hand across his face and pushed his spectacles back up his long pinched nose, "The Prinax instantly cleared it up. Amazing really. I know that you can get your hands on a variety of pharmaceuticals but I didn't realise your contacts stretched to high-grade medi-chems. Quite rare, I myself have never seen it before now, only heard about its properties on the Mainframe blogs. Merryll Laboratories are very selective on who they give it to." The Doc held up the now half empty jar, "May I ask the name of your contact? I would very much like to get hold of some."

Kessler thought for moment, clearing the cloud of confusion in his fractured mind. 'Yes, that's right,' he searched his thoughts, "An old man gave it to me."

"Well, you owe him your life."

"God protects those who fight for him." Bethany Turner stepped into the light. She wore one of Macy's tight fitted, lightly padded plastichem coats and her long black hair was tied back revealing a couple of cuts on the side of her face. She smiled revealing bright white teeth and dimples that brought a beautiful innocence to her good looks. Kessler smiled back, he had to admit it was good to see that she was ok.

"Well, well," Kessler's voice was hoarse and cracked as it emerged from his dry throat, "I see that I'm not the only one who has pulled through. Good to see you Miss Turner."

She continued smiling, knelt down beside where Kessler was slumped and placed a hand on his bandaged arm, "Like I said, God watches over those who fight for him."

"Humph," Kessler sighed. He opened and closed his eyes as he tried to clear his blurred vision. Looking down at his chest he could see that his shirt was soaked in blood.

"You were lucky that Macy got enough from your com. Any later and we would not be having this conversation. Your wounds from the fire had opened up." Doc looked down at his white synthleather longcoat and with his gloved hands tried to brush away the brown sludge, "This damn rain is even filthier than usual this far down," Doc took a long, deep breath from his inhaler and closed his eyes as he enjoyed the hit, "it is quite simply lethal."

"I ran out of Ox, I thought I had enough," he patted down the pockets in his coat, looking for his cigar. Once lit, he drew long puffs, savouring every minute of the delightfully heady smoke.

"And that is certainly not going to do you any good."

Ignoring the doctor, Kessler continued, "Where are we?" He looked around. A lamp sat on Doc's bag provided light revealing a large, dusty space with a high ceiling.

"You happened to crash your car into the wall of this warehouse, or whatever this place was. Doesn't seem to have been used in some time"

"Damn. Will she drive again?"

"That old rust bucket of yours looks in bad shape, worse than you."

"Hey careful what you're calling a rust bucket, we have been through a lot together." He put his head in his hands thinking about his loss, "She is a classic."

Bethany again placed her hand on his arm, "Tell us what happened." Her touch was gentle, her face creased with concern.

Kessler looked away from Bethany's comforting stare. This close to her he could smell the fragrant scent of Macy's soap on her skin, its strong floral tones cutting through the chemical odour of the rain. It reminded him of home. He took a couple of puffs on his cigar before speaking, "To begin with I thought your uncle was killed by the Council. It's common knowledge that they hate any religion other than their own and then there was the trouble he was having with the local group of Corps Boys…"

"Yes. Before service they would surround the church and taunt people as they came to commune with God. Pushing, shoving and cursing at us. Sometimes windows were broken but nothing like this. Did they kill him?" Her nails dug into Kessler urging him to continue.

Kessler prised her grip from his arm as he thought carefully on his next few words. It would be easy to tell her they did it. He could take her credits and try to piece together his life. The lantern flickered and the light danced around them as he stared into her green eyes. Moments passed in silence. She bit her bottom lip, like she always did when she was nervous, and waited. Kessler shook his head slowly, "Anybody messing with Council profits is looking for trouble and your uncle's booze business would have certainly got their attention. The Corps Boys are the only ones allowed by the Council to push their booze down these parts, nobody else, and looking at your uncle's records he was doing pretty well, raking in a fine amount of credits."

"All for the upkeep of the church."

Kessler continued, "Then there was the presence of the DPD at St John's and the fire. All seemed to point to Council involvement."

"Yes, go on." Bethany leaned forward, waving away the cigar smoke.

"I spoke to Bishop Sansom," Bethany nodded in recognition of the name, "and he certainly believed they were to blame. But he was wrong, it was something much bigger than that." He took another draw from his cigar and after a few moments released long tendrils of smoke that he watched swirl into the ether. He raised his arm, testing the state of his injury, "Doc, you have done wonders, you really have."

"Really it's the Prinax. It's truly remarkable." Doc spoke in hushed tones, his long spindly fingers stroking his small, neat beard, deep in thought.

"Mr Kessler, please, I beg you, continue." Bethany urged him on.

"I've just been chatting with a friend of yours, from St John's. Judecca was his name."

"Brother Glaxon? Here? He's alive?" Bethany's face lit up at the thought.

"Your uncle, in his work with the local skin labs and his attempts to get the chem heads off their gear, came across a new sim and those that made it did not appreciate his snooping around. They used the young priest, Judecca, to get to him." Bethany took a sharp intake of breath and Kessler continued,

162

"The usual story, combine a weak will with a grudge to bear and they had an addict who would do anything they asked if it meant getting more chem. In this case it's a particularly nasty one called Lux." Kessler looked away from Beth's trembling form and paused before continuing, "I found empty caps of the stuff all over your uncle's study and the skin lab, where he was taken, told me that he was full of it when he died." Bethany let out a stifled cry and shook her head as Doc prepared a syringe. "He wasn't using the stuff, if that's what you're thinking, it was some sick message left by whomever is pushing the chem," he paused as images from his nightmare returned to haunt him, "as were the words 'Lux Ferre' on his desk. I also found it hacked into Judecca's door." Kessler rummaged around his coat pocket for his view finder and switched it on to reveal the flickering image of the phrase. Doc dropped the syringe he was filling as he jumped up with a start and cursed to himself. Kessler looked away from the green holographics and rubbed his eyes, "Some type of calling card, or whatever, I guess."

"I don't understand. Judecca was using this chem? I don't believe you. He was a good priest. Sure, he struggled with the strict rules my uncle expected him to obey, but he was a caring man of God."

"Chems do not discriminate, Miss Turner. Everyone is vulnerable to their lure." Kessler's eyes briefly met Doc's before returning to Bethany. "They convinced him to let them into the church where they killed your uncle. All it took was the promise of more sim."

"I can't believe it. I have to speak to him." She got up from where she was knelt beside Kessler, raised her hood over her head and pulled her coat tightly around her, ready to leave.

"He's dead. I told you Miss Turner, he was a chem head. This new stuff kills those that use it. He was not the priest you used to know, his mind was completely gone, a complete whack job. He stuck me with a blade for destroying his substantial stash. I must be getting old to have not seen that coming. Anyway, I blasted him. He was lucky it was a quick death because that Lux he was taking kills you from the inside, it's not pretty. I did him a favour." Kessler winced in pain as he reached down into his coat pocket and gave Bethany Judecca's blood-stained silver cross.

Bethany's eyes widened as she took the cross in her hands, "This was my uncle's." She sobbed loudly as she continued to speak, "And poor, good natured Brother Rothery? Did he say what happened to him?"

"Yes. He was taken, I don't know where." Bethany, head in hands, wailed as she took in the information. Kessler returned his attention to the doctor, "Doc, did you get anything back on that sample?"

"Nothing I could trace. It had the usual concoction of carthadric chemicals to pump the heart faster, to get the stuff into the blood as quickly as possible. Nothing out of the ordinary."

"Nothing at all? I've seen first-hand what this filth does to people, there must be something in it?"

"No, well there was something strange but it has no relation to the chem's effects."

"What?"

"From the residue left in the cap my findings told me that the constituent ingredients weighed twice as much as they should. It was strange but there must be some explanation, I accounted for each ingredient. Perhaps my equipment was not aligned properly, I don't know."

"You look tired." Kessler noticed that Doc had deep shadows under his bespectacled eyes.

"I am not sleeping well of late. Work, you know how it is?"

"Yea. This lack of sleep seems to be catching. Does anybody ever sleep in this damned city?"

Bethany took a breath from her Ox inhaler. "So it's confirmed then. I've lost everyone I've ever loved, my family gone." A coldness hung on each word as she continued, "Brother Glaxon left God's House for that of the Devil's. God's justice, Mr Kessler."

Doc Galloway approached the detective, the syringe now loaded with medicine, "A cocktail of my own making, Kes, just to help you recover and give you some energy."

"I like your cocktails, Doc. Work away." He rolled up his sleeve and the medicine was quickly administered.

"I have been told those who killed your uncle can be found in a place called Acheron, below us, all the way down in Downtown 5." The medicine coursed up his veins like fire, delivering energy and vitality to his broken body. He breathed quickly as he braced himself against the chem as it took hold of him, "I don't know what you will do with that information but what I do know is that there's nothing left for me to do. I've concluded our contract Miss Turner, I've found out who killed your uncle and why." Kessler looked away from her expectant eyes and stared down at his feet. He did not know why but despite the success of his investigation he felt the pang of guilt deep down. "So we now need to talk about my fee."

"Of course," she reached into a bag that was by her feet and took from it a large purse that clinked with the sound of creds. She stared silently at the bag for a fleeting moment then threw it at Kessler.

The detective looked at the silver purse. The light from the lamp made its delicate cloth glisten and he could clearly make out the bars of credits through the thin material. Everyone was silent as Kessler stared at it, his thoughts dark with concern. He was sure that Bethany did not have much more to live on, if any at all. How was she going to survive in this city by herself? He shook such thoughts from his mind. He needed the creds to pay off Little Chi and he had Macy to look after. It was not enough but maybe he could cut a deal. Maybe. He noticed that his hands were playing with the caps of Lux he still had in his pocket. When did he pick those up? Why did he have them? He shook his head again, he had his own demons to battle. Life on Dis was tough, everyone had their problems. He leant forward and peered inside the bag. "Seems a little light."

"One thousand two hundred credits. You've done well, Mr Kessler, but have yet to bring my uncle's killers to justice. I felt half is a fair price for the service given so far."

"Judecca is lying in his apartment with his head splattered all over the floor. Like you said, your god's justice."

"Yes but he did not kill my uncle."

"It ends here. There is no way of finding those Dregs or chemheads, whoever they are."

"You said those that make this poison come from Downtown 5."

Kessler laughed, "It's impossible. Even if you could make it down that far, I have heard stories the air is so bad, so toxic, that even to move around in it is death. Only corporates are allowed that deep." Kessler pulled himself up, wincing as his injuries protested and spoke to Doc, "How did you get from Midtown to here?"

"My vehicle." Doc Galloway was packed and ready to go. "You will have to take it easy Kes but you should be fine if you apply the Prinax cream once every day. Remember to be frugal with the amount, it should last you a couple of days but once it's done there's no more."

Kessler's attention returned to Bethany, "We can drop you off in Midtown, I would recommend Eden Inc. I'm sure the Bishop would be happy to help you." His mind was racing. Without the cred to pay off Little Chi he needed to get Macy and hide somewhere safe. Fast."

"Forget it. God's work has not been finished. I intend to make my way to Downtown 5 and administer our Lord's justice myself."

"Listen, you won't stand a chance. If you think this deep is bad then D5 will be a whole lot worse. I hear that strange dangers lurk down there and if the air doesn't kill you then the Councilmen surely will."

"Then come with me, my uncle's work remains unfinished. That chem still eats away at the city."

"Well I don't owe Dis anything. It has given me nothing but misery."

"Then what of the good souls living within it?" Bethany stepped closer to the detective, "There are still good people living here."

"I have my own problems and I don't need to add to them. I already have the Council breathing down my neck, for light's sake, I nearly killed myself getting away from them. I've done my time in Council prisons and I don't intend to go back. My life isn't much but it is *my* life," Kessler spoke quietly. He continued to stare at his feet. "I found out who killed your uncle and where to find them. We are done here." He looked up at the doctor who met his stare only briefly before turning away and pretending to be busy adjusting the collar on his coat and slicking his long white hair back before donning his hood.

"God has brought us together for a reason. We need to continue my uncle's work and stop this evil from spreading throughout the city. I have known since we were saved back at St John's that God was keeping us alive. Kept you alive by providing ointment to heal your wounds."

"Miss Turner, God had nothing to do with saving us back at the church. A six inch thick stone coffin and a large dose of luck were the only things that kept us from being toast."

Bethany shook her head in disagreement, her fists clenched and waving passionately with each and every word. "There's a war going on throughout Dis, Mr Kessler, between good and evil and right now evil is winning. Look all around us, darkness smothers this city and the Devil lurks in every shadow. My uncle knew this was happening, knew the dangers but still fought for us, for the goodness that he believed was inside us despite the relentless sin trying to tempt us at every turn." She thumped her chest with her fist and looked at both Kessler and Doc Galloway. "We live in a world where the best lack all conviction and the worst are full of a passionate intensity. Humanity is falling apart and someone needs to do something about it."

"You have the wrong guy, you don't know me. I'm no hero." Kessler glanced up at the doctor, "I've," he paused in brief thought, "I've seen things, done things that are questionable, that no man can come back from." He closed his eyes and turned his face away from the pleading, shimmering green pools that looked up at him.

"In Him we have redemption through his blood, the forgiveness of our trespasses, according to the riches of his grace."

"Save your preaching for someone who's worth it. Doc grab your bag, let's get out of here. This air stinks." He took a couple of deep breaths from his medivent, "Here take some Ox," he threw it at Bethany and stood up on his feet, taking a few moments to get his balance.

"Ok, if fighting for what's right doesn't appeal to you then how about cash. You're a businessman aren't you?" Her voice stammered and reached a high pitch that threatened to break into another sob.

"You have no money, and besides, you couldn't afford to pay what it would cost to reach that deep. It's three districts below this and then some, hardly any air."

"My mother's ring is worth more than enough."

Kessler took the ring from his pocket and looked rather sheepishly at Bethany. "Sorry, I forgot I had it. It helped me get into Eden Inc and speak to Bishop Sansom." He held the sparkling ring in his large bloody hand, his gaze fixed on the diamonds which danced in the light. "It really is beautiful. I haven't seen diamonds before." He held the ring up to the light of the lamp, his eyes wide in awe, "It really is something."

"It's yours if you take me down to Acheron, help me put a stop to this chem and to those that make it."

"You mean kill them."

"An eye for an eye, Mr Kessler."

He looked again at the jewels as they glistened in the light. His thoughts turned to the possibilities that amount of cred would bring. Little Chi would be a distant memory and he could leave his toxic low existence in M5 behind for the cleaner air further up town. "It's your mother's, all you have left of her."

"She is looking down on us from heaven willing me to complete God's work. For what other reason would the Lord have allowed me to retrieve it from my uncle's desk? It allowed you access to Eden Inc." Kessler nodded and she continued, "And now it allows our mission to continue."

Kessler looked over at the doctor who stood muttering to himself before meeting his stare, "Now Kes, I've seen that look before. You're in no condition to venture anywhere, never mind down to D5. It's ridiculous. Impossible."

"I know someone who travelled that far down city. Father Zachery went down there years ago to spread God's message and find out more about the old world, the time before the Council when the Lord's words were as free and as pure as the air from the heavens." Her eyes were closed as she pictured the impossible images of the past, and the beginnings of a smile turned the edges of her mouth. "It is possible."

Kessler took one more look at the shimmering diamonds and then back at Bethany, her eyes now filled with hope and the images of a better world. This world, this city was all about survival and this pay cheque would give him more than just the ability to endure the daily grind. There was just no way he could turn that opportunity down and he knew it. The detective sighed, "What if we travel all the way down to Acheron and can't find these guys?"

"We are in God's hands now. He will guide us. Take us there and, whatever happens, you will still keep the ring."

"Ok. It's a deal. We travel to Acheron and take a look around." He held up the ring, took one long draw from what remained of the cigar, dropped it on the floor and stamped out the dying embers.

"Well, I'm terribly sorry for interrupting this insanity but I really must be getting back to my lab. I really don't know how they're coping without me. When I left Midtown to cater to your needs we were extremely busy." He pointed a finger at Kessler, "They really were struggling. I must get back." The doctor was standing at the ready with his large bag in his hands and hood up.

"Listen Doc, I need you to stick around on this one."

"Not possible. I've a business to run and I'm in no fit state to travel that deep down city, in fact none of us are."

"You owe me."

"No. I can't. This is not my problem." His face had turned a pale grey and he began to wring his hands nervously.

"You can and it is. Listen Doc, you do this and we are done, you can walk away after this show. I need you down there with us."

The doctor stared at Kessler who walked past him towards the light of the lantern, took out his Luther and began to power it up. Doc leaned close to Kessler's ear and whispered, "I have known you for a long time Kes, and I have always accepted my debt to you, I have always been there for you but I can't go down to D5, I mean are you crazy?" He began to run his hands through his hair, adjust his hood and mumble to himself. His glasses fell off his shaking head and he fumbled to catch them. "The Council forbid it and," Doc blinked as he tried to form words, "I hear that strange creatures lurk in the deeps."

"Children's tales. You know that."

The light from the lamp threw shadows of Kessler's large burly form and the long lanky frame of the doctor across the dusty floor. Doc continued, "No I don't and neither do you. I've never heard of anyone returning from that far down."

Kessler grabbed Doc firmly by his sides and, standing nose to nose with him, spoke in a slow, steady tone, "Doc, you're just getting soft in your cosy Midtown life. I remember you when we first met, don't you forget that."

After a moment's silence Doc quietly mumbled, "D5 is no place for a young lady," however his protests had no effect on Kessler who batted the doctor away.

"Enough. Let's go." Kessler moved towards the door, the white, sparkling light of the diamonds filling his head with possibilities.

"Finally, Mr Kessler." Bethany stood at the edge of the light with her hands on her hips.

Kessler turned to Bethany, "That reminds me, before we set off there is one rule that I would like to remind you of."

"Yes?" Bethany stood in the doorway, ready to leave.

"Call me Kes, everyone else does. I insist."

"Ok," Bethany smiled, "and you can call me Beth."

"Great, one big family now," Doc fretted.

"The only one I've got," Bethany muttered under her breath.

·PROVISIONS FOR THE DEEP·

Kesssler viewed the remains of his junker. Critters, which infested the slums of Downtown, already had made their home amongst the mass of twisted metal and plastisteel and skittered around amongst the wreckage.

"Yours it is then Doc."

Doc Galloway walked past the detective in silence and stood by his vehicle, an Excalibur S3, its black gloss and chrome exterior in sharp contrast to the bleak Downtown surroundings. With a quick scan of his thumb print the doors quickly made way to reveal a plush interior filled with cushioned seats surrounded by an array of monitors showing a variety of infogrammes. One screen showed the Council's generous food aid programme, smiling officials in crisp corp suits feeding Dreg babies as a crowd looked on, another selling Hightown property, 'The gateway to a better life,' and finally a newsreel on a recent chemical spill at a Merryll Laboratories plant, the images of grateful citizens shaking hands with a corporate clean-up crew in full protective bio hazard suits suggested they were in full control of the situation.

Cool air caressed the group as they entered, reminding them how much they missed clean Ox, "You certainly have it good Doc, that air is delicious." Kessler took deep breaths and closed his eyes as the oxygen entered his system. Bethany gasped frantically and lay down on the back seat, "Easy girl, slow and steady breaths."

"This air is from heaven." Bethany snatched at the air as she filled her lungs.

"No, just from a Remmington 500 Air Reconstitutor." Doc said flatly

Sitting in the passenger seat, Kessler whistled and shook his head as he continued to enjoy the cool air circulating round him, "No expense spared." He looked over at the doctor who sat stock still with white knuckles gripping the controls hard.

"So where to then?"

Kessler ignored him, turned on the com and, presented with an array of flashing lights and displays which emerged from the sleek, black console, he gingerly attempted to dial his office, "How do you use this expensive tech?"

Doc glared at the detective from above his glasses and spoke with sarcasm, "Make yourself at home." He pressed down on a concealed lever in front of him and a blue light key pad hovered before Kessler. "Now dial."

"I need to get hold of Macy if I am to be kept busy down here." The com buzzed and, despite the interference this far down city, the powerful communication system in the Excalibur quickly got through to Midtown. The beautifully-drawn face of his secretary greeted Kessler on the monitor.

"What am I going to do with you Kes? You constantly have me worried sick."

"I'm fine, listen to me carefully."

"No, you listen to me, mister. Come home, I'm worried about you."

"I'm still on the Turner case."

"I've a bad feeling about this one Kes, come home, you'll get other work, you always do. We'll be fine."

"Just listen to me will you?" He paused for a moment as Macy composed herself. Kessler noticed that she had been crying as her thick makeup was smudged and left trails across her cheeks. She looked away from her monitor as he continued to speak, "You have to lock up the office and go and stay at a friend's or something. Get out of the sector."

"Great Kes, really great. I knew something like this would happen. Come home, please. We'll sort it, like we always do." She shook her head, "We'll be fine."

"No." Kessler repeated, "Little Chi's goons are going to be paying the office another visit in the next twenty-four hours and you need to be as far away as possible. Once I finish this case we will have no more trouble from them," he leaned forward, closer to the screen, "we'll have a little more cred to maybe move uptown, get you a nice office, get some better air."

"We don't need it, Kes. Come home and be safe. You look a mess."

"No," Kessler repeated, "I'm tired of just surviving. I can't do that anymore. If… I mean when, I finish this case we'll be set. I promise."

"Ok. Ok. If you're sure." She seemed to calm down. "Fine. I could go to Deaks's place. She was asking me to help her with the shop anyway, I suppose."

"Great. Take some cred from my desk, that should see you through. There should be some in the bottom drawer in the cigar box."

"You take care of yourself Kes, you hear me?"

"Hey, you know me, I always pull through, somehow." She kissed the tips of her fingers and pressed them against the monitor before the screen, with a sharp frazzle, went blank.

"She really loves you Kes," Bethany whispered from the back seat.

"I'm all she's got, she has no one else." Kessler continued to stare at the com's blank screen deep in thought.

"Yes, I know how she feels but the Lord will look after her."

"He'll need to," Kessler thought cynically.

The three sat in silence in Doc's car as the enormity of what they were about to try and do played out in their heads. Bethany looked at her mother's ring, Kessler still stared at the now blank coms screen, his head filled with concern for Macy, and Doc sat in the driver's seat, lips pursed, hands still tightly gripping the steering column. Bethany eventually broke the quiet, "How do we get all the way down there?"

"Well, first we'll have to get through Districts 3 and 4. I don't know much about them," Kessler rubbed his tired eyes, "I've heard the Pipe breaks down just after 2. Not much need to maintain it I suppose, waste of credits when nobody uses it. We'll have to make our own way down from there somehow. What I do know is that we need a few things before travelling that far down city. Respirators with enough Ox to last the journey and…" he took a sideways at her, "we'll have to look into getting you a weapon of some kind. You'll be needing it, that's for sure." Doc let out a long sigh.

"I've never had to use one before." Bethany spoke from the back of the car, her voice wavered nervously.

"You'll learn. It's amazing what the body allows you to do when your life depends on it. Besides, how else are you going to administer God's justice?" Kessler gave her a wry smile. "Doc, do you still have that hand cannon of yours?"

"I haven't had much use for it up in Midtown," he paused in thought for a few moments, "but yes, it's under my seat."

"Good, you haven't changed as much as you think. You always were a cautious man."

"Obviously not cautious enough judging by what we are about to do."

A low rumble from the darkness made the three duck down. Kessler looked at Bethany and brought his finger to his lips, "Quiet." He had forgotten how precarious their situation was. Doc was parked by the entrance to the alley, by the side of the main road which ran through the sector, its expensive fibreplas bodywork a shining light in the impoverished Downtown surroundings. "Power down the vehicle!" Kessler barked, realising that, against the darkness, the Excalibur's lights could be seen for some distance and it was not only the usual denizens of Downtown that they were avoiding, the DPD would be on the look-out for him as well.

A caravan slowly lurched passed carrying someone wealthy, possibly a merchant or some district governor. The lanterns that hung from the sides of the carriage bobbed back and forth throwing light over the pale, muscular skin of the Dregs who strained with every step to carry their charge along the highway. A purple curtain fluttered from a window revealing a large bulbous hand lazily waving a fan to cool a face obscured by shadow. The groans and sighs from the cavalcade came in waves, sung in time with the bobbing of the procession. The mantra was only interrupted every so often by the hard crack of a whip.

As the procession continued, lights appeared in the distance. Starting as a series of white pinpricks emerging from the black, the light gradually grew in size. "What is that?" Doc looked concerned, "Looks like some heavy traffic coming our way."

The sighs from the caravan were gradually drowned out by the roar of engines and splutter of thrusters and very soon the familiar image of the golden cog came into view emblazoned on the side of the vehicles which thundered past. The cavalcade consisted of police Interceptors and larger troop carriers which roared through the caravan scattering the slaves in every direction much to the anger of the large occupant of the carriage who now began screaming and cursing. Even the wealthy of Downtown did not get much respect from the Vents it seemed. "They're going somewhere fast." Kessler sat up and looked around him cautiously.

"Now that is a first. What are so many DPD doing this far down?" Doc raised his hand to his creased brow in thought as he stared at the strange sight.

"Something's got them spooked. I've been running into them all over Downtown the past few days."

Once the DPD had rumbled past and disappeared into the distance, Kessler returned to the com system, "We need to stock up on some supplies if we are to make it down to D5 and back. Ox, respirators, any medicine we may need and I don't know about you but I'm starving and need to get out of these bloody clothes." After a couple of taps of the dialler, Jimmy Six's face with broad, toothy grin, and huge goggles surrounded by a tangled mass of wires and flashing lights filled the screen.

"Oh no." Doc shook his head and looked away.

"Kes! How do you do old pal? I see you survived that trip to Downtown?" The mechanical oscillations of Jimmy Six's voice greeted them.

"Yea, no thanks to you. Your substandard tech nearly got me killed."

The yellow pulse of Jimmy's synthwear turned a dark blue, "Your words cut through my heart like a dagger. How can you say such things?" He leaned back with his mechanised hand thumping his chest with a severely dejected look on his face, "I try my best, times are hard."

"Well, next time I see you I'll hit you with something hard." Jimmy visibly flinched at the reproach.

"Ok, ok. I owe you." His eyes moved to Doc and, now glowing a bright pink, his arms went to embrace the screen, "And the good doctor! Well this is like old times. How are you? I haven't seen you since that awful time you had with the pleasure bot. Did you get that all cleared up?"

The doctor sighed, "It's none of your business." He spoke through gritted teeth and looked sheepishly at both Kessler and Bethany.

"Ha! Everything is my business, you know that."

"Listen Jimmy, I need some information. We are still down city, in D2…"

"What? Still down there? That would explain this dreadful reception." He gave his screen a whack and it flickered violently, "Oh Kes that air aint no good. It'll begin to mess with your insides if you breathe it too long."

"Tell me about it, that's why we need to purchase some supplies as we'll be travelling down even further. Know of anywhere round here who can provide us with provisions and a way down?

"How far down?"

"Deep. D5. A place called Acheron. Heard of it?"

Jimmy laughed, "You're joking with an old friend, for sure!" Kessler stared blankly into the monitor and eventually Jimmy stopped chuckling to himself, "You're serious? Well you are mixing in dangerous company these days that's for sure. Acheron I hear is a furnace town, it keeps this rotting city all lit up and pretty. But Kes," Jimmy waved a long robotic finger at the screen, "The Council say no, no, no to anyone other than their own corporates going anywhere near their precious power. Everyone knows that." He bent down and pressed his goggles against the sides of the screen, trying to look behind Kessler, "I tell you it is off limits. Doc, tell him he's a fool for attempting such a journey."

Doc crossed his arms, shook his head and looked to the floor as Kessler leaned forward, his face only a few inches from the monitor as he spoke quietly, "Jimmy, I need to square things with Little Chi otherwise, well, things won't be good, you know that. Now, do you know somebody, someone discreet?"

He adjusted a dial on his chest before speaking, "Of course, of course. D2 you say. Well," he shook his head and began sucking loudly on a tube that fed him blue liquid from a large thin cylinder that stood to the side of the screen, "not much call to do any dealing down there these days but there is someone I know." The flashing monitors in Jimmy's office lit up the screen as he focused on quenching his thirst, "I'll send you the coordinates."

"This guy is good, right? You know him?" Kessler knelt close to the monitor, "I don't want any nasty surprises, Jimmy."

"I can't believe these words, of course he is discreet. Sure, he has a temper and an extreme dislike for authority but we all have our interesting sides."

"Yea, I've ran into a few of those recently. Will he have what we need and take us down?"

"Yes, yes. Years back he ran some shanty up near the Fringe, 'The Crow's Nest', I think it was called. Pilgrims seeking the old world used to stop off there before going down and let me tell you, he made quite a bit of cred from it. Haven't heard from him in a long time now though. He lived in Baron's Town, just ask for Beck. If I recall, he serves very tasty Ox, something you may need down there." He chuckled as a small bot peered from behind his shoulder and waved at the screen. Jimmy batted it away, "Remember Kes, I always look out for you, just like the old days."

"Ok. I know we go back a long way."

"Now hold out your bio and I'll send you over the cordinates." Kessler placed the underside of his wrist against the console and in a flash of blue light the information was downloaded. "Oh yes! One more thing old friend."

"Yes?"

"Beck has a little genetic problem," Jimmy wrung his hands as he thought of his next words carefully, "he does not appreciate anybody, especially uptowners, mentioning it."

"Great, a Mute. Thanks Jimmy."

"Wait, wait Kes. Want me to talk to Little Chi? See if I can give you more time?"

"Thanks, but I'm all out of time."

Jimmy nodded in understanding, "There ain't much good down in Acheron from what I hear."

"There's not much good anywhere on Dis, you know that."

"This is true, very true." Jimmy paused and stared intently at

Kessler before continuing, "Make sure you tell your old friend your story when you get back and," he pointed a long mechanised finger at the screen, "you make sure to suit up! The rads down there are hot hot!"

Kessler gave Jimmy a mock salute and ended the call.

"I hate that guy." Doc continued to stare out of the canopy and into the darkness.

·JOURNEY TO THE FRINGE·

The road was silent, the dim light from the Excalibur's console and the flickering monitors in the rear lit up their small world which extended only a few yards around them before the darkness closed in. The low hum of the vehicle's engine and its rec vent, which whined loudly as it battled to keep the stifling heat and the dead air outside the cabin, were their only company as they were left alone to contemplate their own thoughts and fears. A constant weight pressed down on them, as if the city itself was resting on their shoulders. The quiet brought each of them time to come to terms with the events that were unfolding around them.

Doc focused on the road ahead, every so often releasing a hand from the controls to wipe his sweating brow. His permanent frown and constant nervous mumbling betrayed his worried thoughts.

Kessler gritted his teeth and closed his eyes. He felt burnt out and in need of rest. These quiet times were always the worst, times when he was left to his own thoughts which always seemed to want to drag him down into the darkest recesses of his mind. With nothing to distract him, his body began to remind him of the past few days and the beating it had taken. His stomach wound smouldered beneath the numbing effects of the salve the old man had given him back in Eden Inc as images of Macy, Judecca, the burning church, the Le Morte twins, the Venter officer and his own worthless life tumbled around in his tortured mind. He hoped Macy was ok and cursed himself for leaving her all alone up in Midtown but then, he thought with some disgust towards himself, at least he was being consistent. He could barely remember a time when he had not been wasted, completely burned out on some type of chem or full of enough Piper's to not give a damn. He shook his head and cursed himself. What was he thinking? Macy had been running things by herself for a long time now. Good, he thought, practice just in case he did not make it back from wherever on Dis this case was taking him. Anger clouded his mind. He was going against his gut feeling, a feeling that had served him well in the past, allowed him to survive the worst the city could throw at him. However, credits, he needed them fast and the payload from this case would turn things around for him, allow him to start again, allow him to make things better for Macy. She deserved it for putting up with him over the years. The sparkling diamonds and their possibilities began to appear in Kessler's mind, "Yes," he mumbled under his breath, "it's worth the risk."

Bethany moved in the back and let out a short sigh from her slumber and Kessler wondered what she was thinking. Surely her anger and want for revenge, or God's justice as she called it, would come to nothing? Revenge was a dangerous business. He had seen it destroy people, make citizens take bad choices. There was always going to be someone meaner, someone nastier that would always beat down on good citizens like Bethany. Dis was full of them and he was not sure that she had what it took to kill anyone, never mind those that were behind her uncle's death.

Kessler knew what he needed. Behind every thought, every action, there was always that constant weight pulling him down. There was only ever one thing that he had faith in, one thing he could always depend upon. It called out to him from somewhere in the depths of the darkness making promises that everything would be ok. It was a warm blanket which could shelter him from the choking air, the filthy rain and the clawing, desperate existence of surviving this city. The Excalibur juddered as it sped over a large part of broken road, the noise jarring Kessler from his thoughts. He looked down at his hand and noticed that he was holding one of the vials of Lux that he had taken from Judecca's room. It was soft to the touch, the malleable plastic of the capsule bending out of shape as he pressed down on it. It was such a familiar, calming feeling, toying with the supple cap, the excitement beginning to creep up his body over what lay within. He stared at the cloudy dark chemicals as they swirled around the vial. What made this chem different than any other sim on the street? Kessler's eyes followed the liquid as it danced, pirouetted and pranced before his eyes. He brought it closer, his stare intently fixed on the cap and spoke quietly to himself, "Why would anybody take such bad chem? What makes this stuff better than the rest?" Something Judecca had said stuck in his mind. He mentioned that they had taken Brother Rothery as they needed help making it but what did a priest know about making sim? One thing he was sure about, all these questions had their answers deep down in the depths of the city, somewhere out there in the darkness. He closed his fist over the cap and brought his hand to his mouth and took a deep breath, "Just a couple of hits to clear my mind, help me think what to do next, that's all I need…"

"I do not think now is the time or the place for you to indulge in your chem habit," Doc spoke flatly.

Kessler did not realise he was speaking out loud and quickly changed the subject as he peered out of the canopy and into the murk surrounding them, "Have you ever been this far out from the Core?"

"No, I hear the Fringe, the edge of the city, is a wasteland full of Mutes and Dregs who want to be left alone. Society's cast outs."

"Well at least we won't have to worry about running into any Vents this far out," Doc sighed as he spoke.

"Perhaps. A few hours ago I wouldn't have expected to see them below the Rim so who knows, besides, there are far worse dangers than the Dis Police Department to worry about where we are going."

Doc's anger clung to every word but everything he said Kessler knew to be true. He did not know much about the city's edge down in the lower districts of Dis but what he did know was not good. The Fringe of Dis lay far out from the central sectors of Downtown where millions of Dregs crowded around the city's Core, the central spine of Dis, all clambering over one another in desperate hope they could gain access to the Pipe and the city above. Far away from the chaos of these crowds, by the Fringe, the citizens of Downtown were more sparsely spread throughout the wastes. Citizens living this far out lived there for a reason. Kessler had heard stories of criminals, Mutes and even whole towns of Dregs and outcasts riddled with all kinds of plagues who had been forced away from the heavily populated areas. All just stories, Kessler hoped.

The detective rolled up his sleeve, wetted his thumb with his tongue and rubbed away a patch of dried blood that covered his bioware. They had been driving for five hours and his eyes were heavy with the need for sleep but he knew that was impossible as images from his nightmares flashed across his mind. "Hey Doc, you have been driving for awhile now, you must be tired. Want me to take over so you can get some sleep?"

"No." Doc peered out at the road through squinting, watery eyes.

"You sure?"

"I'll be fine, besides, you look shattered."

Kessler spoke quietly, "Yea. I keep having the same damn

nightmare, over and over again." Doc nodded as he spoke, his expressionless stare never losing focus on the road ahead. Kessler continued, "I can still hear the voices."

For the first time since they had left Morbus Sector Doc turned to look at Kessler and the car's speed slowed, "What were they saying?"

"'Lux Ferre'. The words which I found hacked into the priest's desk and again on Judecca's door. It means Light Bringer in some old language Beth knows. I just can't stop thinking about it." Kessler rubbed his eyes before continuing, "Strange."

"Yes. Very strange." The Excalibur's speed picked up.

A cough from the back made Kessler turn to see Bethany now awake. Her eyes, still heavy with sleep, stared into the distance. He cleared his throat and, realising he was still holding the cap of Lux, quickly put the sim back inside his coat pocket. She shakily spoke, "I hate the darkness, I always have." Bethany pulled over her coat and wrapped her arms around her and shivered slightly.

"Are you cold? I can adjust the temperature of the cabin?"

Kessler began to reach over to the console as she replied, "No. I'm fine." She rested her hand against the canopy and peered outside, her breath causing the clear plastic to mist up, "My uncle always used to tell me that the Devil hid in the shadows. When people started to disappear I thought they were being taken by him. He would make me remain always within the light of the church, never venture beyond it. Now here I am going deeper and deeper down into the city so far away, getting darker and darker and the church now gone." Her words caught the back of her throat as she spoke, "Who knows what lies out there waiting for us?"

Doc despaired, "Your uncle seems to have had some sense, something we are severely lacking."

"Now Doc, that's enough. No need to scare the girl." Kessler turned around in his seat. Bethany sat with her knees brought up to her chest making her look like a frightened child. "Listen,

185

Beth, Doc does have a point, I have to be honest this is not going to be easy. It's going to get a lot worse the deeper we go. I need to let you know what is in store for us. The darkness may be just as bad as your uncle told you."

"It's no place for a young girl. What am I talking about?" Doc began to shake his head from side to side,"It's no place for any of us. Bethany, let's turn back, from the little I know of your uncle, he spent his life protecting you from the dangers which lay all over this damned place. He would want you to be safe." Doc looked in the rear view mirror, "He would want you to come back with us now and leave this place."

"Doctor Galloway, God has not forsaken this city, at least not entirely." She leaned forward, "Don't you understand? There is no one left at St John's to continue God's work, there is only me. My uncle spent his life in God's service and he looked after me for the sole purpose that I could continue in it when he passed. He died trying to protect our community, trying to stop this chem killing people. It has taken Brother Rothery, tempted Brother Glaxon down into the depths of hell and destroyed a church that had stood as a House of God for many, many years. This Lux is the Devil. It destroys lives, threatens our very humanity and we must stop it."

The doctor glared at Kessler and with a frustrated sigh returned to concentrating on the road ahead. The detective looked up at Bethany and shook his head at the determined girl who sat with fists clenched. He was usually a good judge of character, during his time he had seen all types but he kept getting Bethany Turner wrong. Her naive and vulnerable exterior hid a strength which burned inside her and if he knew about anything it was strength and its value in surviving the city. "Ok. So the plan is that we stay at The Crow's Nest for a night, we can get some rest before our descent to Downtown 5." The prospect of getting some peace to rest his tired body and close his burned out eyes brought about a giddy excitement. "Before we leave we will purchase provisions with the cred you gave me Beth, get enough Ox for the journey, respirators too."

"That's your money. I'll pay you back."

"It's ok, the cred from that ring will be more than enough." Thoughts and plans of what he was going to do with the payout filled Kessler's head and, for a brief moment, distracted him from his wounds and the dangers that lay in the dark.

A faint haze began to grow on the horizon and then, after a short while, gradually separated into distinct, dull spheres of a sickly yellow light that very slowly began to multiply and fan out across their field of vision.

"This must be it." Doc gave Kessler a firm nudge with his elbow breaking the detective's waking trance.

Blinking his heavy eyes repeatedly, Kessler squinted into the distance, "I'm so tired." He gasped as he tried to focus his senses on what he had to do.

"I can give you something to help you sleep if you want?"

"To knock me out? No. I need to be alert for whatever awaits us in Baron's Town."

Doc nodded silently, "I can give you something for that as well."

"There's only one thing I need right now."

Doc rummaged around in a compartment under his seat and eventually pulled out a small tube of orange pills. "Here, take these. Does not exactly have the kick of sim but will take the edge off and keep the tiredness at bay."

"Thanks." Kessler knocked back the tube's entire contents.

Doc leaned forward and scrutinized a wall of glowing red text which appeared hovering above the console. He tapped a couple of buttons and squinted his eyes in concentration, "The air has high concentrations of sulphur oxides and nitrogen dioxides. It's pretty awful out there so keep your inhalers to hand. It's hot as well, ambient temperature is forty degrees, keep water bottles close by, we need to stay hydrated." With another click of a button more text appeared throwing its red light around the cabin. "The rain is heavy, keep your faces covered and hoods up." From the compartment he produced three surgical masks, "Here take these."

Kessler picked up the mask and stared at it through tired eyes, "We'll be fine." He had forgotten how paranoid the doctor could be.

"Doctor Galloway, you forget, I'm used to living in Downtown. I am aware of the dangers."

"Near the Core maybe, but the further out we go the more treacherous the conditions. With the rising heat, the bad air and the worsening rain it will get more and more hazardous. Breathing difficulties, infections, lethargy will become more and more of a problem. The rads will increase the lower we go and we'll eventually have to wear heat suits for protection."

"Jimmy's guy will have them," Kessler interrupted.

"He better, otherwise we are done for before we even begin." Doc cleared his throat before continuing, "Now, I have gloves if anyone needs? I would not recommend allowing your skin prolonged contact with this rain unless you wish to develop mutations, cancers and a long list of brain defects at some stage in the near future." Doc spoke in a cold monotone and held up a pair of latex surgical gloves.

"I have my own, thank you." Bethany quickly rummaged around in her shoulder bag for her gloves, took a deep breath of the cool air in the oxidized cabin and put on her mask.

Kessler threw Doc's surgical mask over his shoulder to the back of the car, "Thanks for the info Doc," and covered his mouth with his own. He adjusted his thick brown synth-leather gloves and securely fasten his coat when the Excalibur lurched forward suddenly throwing Kessler hard against the vehicle's console. "Doc! Watch the road!"

The Excalibur juddered to a halt. Straight ahead of them, lit up by the dim glare of the vehicle's headlights, large gates barred their way, either side of which, two Venter Interceptors could just be made out in the low light of the gloom. "Police? All the way out here?"

Kessler powered up his Luther and unlocked the canopy just as Doc leaned forward, grabbing him by the shoulder, "You can't be serious? Threatening the DPD with that carbine is only going to get us killed."

Kessler took a brief look at Doc before exiting the vehicle, "I'm just going to have a quick look, that's all," he spoke as he was drenched in the downpour and the dead air caught him in the back of the throat.

Taking a hit of Ox from his inhaler and turning on his torch, Kessler surveyed the scene. Large metal gates were sealed shut between two guard towers that disappeared into the gloom above. The town's stone perimeter wall faded from view beyond the glow of their lights. Kessler crouched by the Venter's vehicle closest to where they had stopped and found it to be abandoned some time ago. Most of its gleaming black panels had been ripped open and those that were left were dented and torn apart, its canopy was smashed allowing the rain to coat its insides in a thick toxic soup and the console had been smashed apart, spilling its guts out onto the floor. All tech of any value seemed to have been scavenged from the vehicle, leaving only its skeletal plastisteel framework behind.

A high pitch scream jolted Kessler from his investigation. He turned and peered through the murk, his optics enhancing the torchlight enough for him to just make out Doc's white coat.

Running across the road, he found a whimpering Bethany being comforted by Doc, "What happened?"

Doc's spectacles peered out at Kessler from his large hood, "Look in the Interceptor."

Pointing his torch into the smashed canopy of the second DPD vehicle quickly revealed the cause of Bethany's terror. What was left of a police officer lay slumped in the driver's seat.

Most of his plate armour was missing, revealing grey, emaciated skin riddled with red bulbous sores. The sleeve on one of his arms was rolled up to reveal more decayed skin, a syringe bearing the image of the burning sun still hung from a flap of long dead flesh. His helmet remained and through his cracked optics Kessler saw a horror that he had seen before. Eyes as black as tar stared lifelessly from a face frozen in its final, terrifying, depraved act. Kessler looked away in disgust.

Doc shouted over the din of the rain, "I recognise that symbol. It is the same as on that cap you gave me to analyse."

"Yes." Foreboding thoughts limited his response to a single word.

"And the same chem as was found in Bethany's uncle? And now in this Venter?"

"Yes."

Doc had moved away from Bethany and stood holding his long-barrelled Lazarus rifle in both hands with his bag slung over his shoulder, "What have you got me into?"

Kessler took a few minutes to calm the tempest of thoughts cascading around in his mind before walking over to the gate and staring at the obstacle before them. He pressed hard on the carbonised iron, "It won't budge."

"This trip just gets better and better." Doc had followed Kessler and stood beside him. He pointed at the wall as he spoke, "This symbol, do you recognise it?"

Two wings either side of the letters 'M' and 'L' below a halo were stamped onto the centre of the gate, "Merryll Laboratories."

"Yes, but below their logo you can see a skull." The torchlight cast shadows of concern across his features, "This is a plagued site."

Kessler wiped away the rainwater from his heavily-stubbled face before speaking, "A plagued site?"

"A site under corporation control which the Council deems too dangerous for citizens to access. They are most often set up when contagious diseases break out in an attempt to stop them spreading onto the next sector. Another reason for us not to be here."

"This way, I have found a way through." Bethany shouted over from where she was standing by the far tower, her torch frantically bobbing around in the dark as she waved for them to join her.

Kessler walked past Doc, throwing him a quick stare as he did. Doc shrugged, "Unbelievable. What about the Excalibur?"

Kessler continued walking towards Bethany and did not turn around as he spoke, "Leave it here." He did not have the time or energy to feel guilty and besides, he reminded himself, Doc owed him. Big time.

Doc took one quick look at the skeletal remains of the two DPD Interceptors and back to the gleaming fibreplas of his Excalibur. "Brilliant," he cursed through gritted teeth and rolled up his sleeve. With a quick press of a button on his inked bioware panel an armoured shell encased the vehicle and, eventually, he followed Kessler to where he was waiting with Bethany.

Inside the tower was a small square room with stairs leading to the floors above. Directly opposite the entrance, a door swung slightly on its hinges. "Good work." Kessler went to leave.

"Wait." Bethany's slim form shook as she spoke, "That policeman. He had a syringe in his arm. I have never seen eyes so black. He looked monstrous."

Kessler stopped by the doorway, "Its Lux. It does that to those who take it."

"It's terrible, just absolutely terrible." Bethany began to sob, "My uncle did he… did he look like that?"

"Don't think of that. Remember, your uncle knew what this stuff did to people, he had visited the skin labs, probably knew that it was eating away at one of his very own priests. He sacrificed his life trying to stop this chem killing, trying to help those hooked on it. He was a good man, a rarity in this city." Kessler held his Luther before him, adjusted his hood and continued out the doorway into Baron's Town.

·THE CROW'S NEST·

The three stood outside the entrance to the guard tower staring down the main road which made its crooked way through the centre of Baron's Town. The street lamps, the few that were operating, threw their anaemic glare into the dark, hardly denting the thick haze which smothered the area, resulting in the group having to rely on the weak light from their torches to navigate their way through the murk. Along either side of the road, a series of ramshackle, crumbling, two-storey stone buildings stood, nothing stirring within the black of their interiors. The only movement came from the torrents of rainwater which surged over the worn cobbled street. Kessler wiped away the brown sludge from his forearm to reveal his inked panel and accessed the coordinates which Jimmy had given him, "This way."

As they travelled through the town, in amongst the Humanity First ramblings and angry anti-Council scribbles that littered the crumbling walls and rotting buildings, were doorways covered in clear plastic sheeting all bearing the same Merryll Laboratories skull emblem which was seen on the gate outside the town. "Where is everybody?" Bethany spoke from under her hood.

"This place died a long time ago. Look at the dates on the Merryll notices," Doc said, holding his Lazarus rifle nervously before him, his torch light darting from one place to another at sounds only he could hear.

"Doc's right. This one is dated six months back." Bethany pointed her torch at one of the many doorways which had been branded with the Merryll warning.

"Looks like your good friend Jimmy Six has let us down, there is nobody who can help us here. I never trusted that guy." Doc 's muttering could be heard just above the drone of the rain.

"Well, we're about to find out, we've arrived." A small, pale light could be seen through one of the windows under a glowing blue neon sign which marked the building as 'The Crow's Nest Tavern'. Kessler pressed down on the com and Bethany took a couple of hits from her inhaler and coughed into her face mask. Doc stood tight against the building's wall trying to make use of the cover offered by a small strip of plastic which hung limply from a couple of broken pipes that protruded from the roof. His gloved hands held the collar of his longcoat tightly around his neck trying to protect himself from the downpour. He stood staring out into the gloom with his round spectacles catching the reflection of a street lamp which flickered weakly from a building across the road.

Kessler hit the com again and peered through a window thick with grime, "I think I can see something moving about in there." He banged hard on the door with thoughts of what he was going to do to Jimmy if he let him down again beginning to form in his mind.

After a few moments the door opened and from the darkness a bald head peered up at them through the black plastic of an old optic array, "Yea, what ya wan?" The low rumble of a Downtown accent emerged from between huge bulbous lips.

The dull blue light from above the door revealed the small frame of a Dreg, wrapped tightly in a purple and gold syth-cloth poncho. Through the dirt, Kessler could see that at one stage in its life it would have been an expensive piece of clothing easily found around the shoulders of many an upper Midtown citizen.

The Dreg had a long thin neck which had a series of small holes up either side that contracted and expanded with every breath. He looked thin and fragile as the rain pattered over his pale, almost translucent, face.

Kessler leaned forward close to him and shouted over the din of the deluge, "We're looking for Beck Goodfellow. We've had a long journey and been told that this is a place we can rest and resupply?"

"Then enter, you're all welcome at The Crow's Nest." He scurried away into the dark and turned on a couple of small lamps which were dotted around the room. Inside, the tavern was warm with a thick musky smell which hung heavy in the air. The low light revealed a small room within which every space was crowded with all manner of items. Along the walls, shelves were packed full of tools, machine parts and boxes, most labelled 'miscellaneous robotics'. A variety of face masks and rain protectors of different ages were packed high against the far wall and beside them a range of chem and bio hazard suits hung from hooks. Exotic items of all shapes and sizes were piled alongside the mundane and in its centre the Dreg hurriedly scampered around a small rectangular green plastic table, wiping it with a grimy rag.

The three pulled down their hoods. Kessler took off his optics and wiped the rain from his face as Doc cast a disinterested glance over everything. The Dreg approached the soaking group, bowing slightly while playing nervously with the rag in his hands, "I apologise for the abruptness when I answered the door, we do not get many travellers in these parts, at least not recently. I'm Beck Goodfellow, and this is my place, it isn't much, times are hard." The gruff manner that greeted them instantly disappeared changing to a more educated speak, although his lower city accent remained.

"We've travelled far and have still some distance to go. We'll need provisions for the journey ahead and a room," Bethany cleared her throat and Kessler continued, "two rooms for the night and a good supper if you can?" He took off his gloves and coat and looked around for somewhere to put them when Beck, pausing briefly as he glanced Kessler's bloody shirt, dashed around the table and took them from him.

Kessler spoke sheepishly and sighed, "And a new shirt if you have one."

"Of course," he smiled, "and your bags?"

"We'll keep them with us, thanks." The innkeeper bowed as he took the sodden garments and, giggling nervously as he glanced the rifle strapped to Doc's side, he waddled off into another room, trying not to drop the large bundle of clothes that precariously towered above him.

Bethany took a couple more breaths on her inhaler and, with Kessler and Doc, sat down around the table. "It's been so long since I have eaten anything but this air, it turns my stomach."

Doc took off his spectacles and began to clean them with a piece of cloth, "What little Ox that's pumped this far down is mostly centred around the Core. This close to the Fringe, the outer limits of Dis, the air's at its worst."

Bethany gave a brief smile to both of them before bowing her head holding her uncle's small silver cross from around her neck. All Kessler could think about was how tired he was. His eyes burned, felt heavy and he longed to close them.

Beck returned to the room holding a pile of plates and three large tankards. Strapped around his head was a torch that threw a beam of light everywhere he turned. "It's not often we get citizens from up city all the way down here, well, not for a long time anyway." Kessler looked at Beck as suddenly a wave of paranoia hit him and his hand quickly found his Luther holstered by his waist. Doc noticed Kessler's reaction and reached for his rifle.

A plate fell from Beck's grip and clattered against the table as the innkeeper froze, his large bulging eyes fixed on their weapons. He stuttered, "Apologies for my chatter, I don't mean to pry but it's been so long since I've had any company." He laughed and bowed again before exiting the room and quickly returning with a huge jug of ale and steaming hot pot and proceeded to fill everyone's plates and flagons.

Bethany leaned forward and spoke in a hushed, quick whisper, "I don't think I can eat." She brushed her nose and took another breath of Ox.

Kessler leaned forward, "Eat it. You'll need the energy for the journey."

"Apologies Miss, I forget my manners." Beck reached into a drawer and produced a jar, "It's been a while since we have needed this, us lower citizens are used to this bad air and the smell, well, I don't really notice it anymore I've been down here for so long."

Bethany blushed at Beck's humble manner and thanked him for the gesture. She reached into the jar and applied some of the ointment to her upper lip. The strong perfumed smell filled the room. Her breathing eased and she offered the jar to her companions but only Doc took it. She smiled, "Thank you," at Beck and began to eat.

"I'm afraid there is not much in the way of food going around at the moment, but I do my best."

"What is it exactly?" The doctor spoke as he played with the large grey lumps which floated in steaming hot brown liquid.

"Council standard rations with some special ingredients of my own, synthesised proteins, flavourings and a couple of secret additions." He smiled a toothy grin which seemed to double the size of his head as it balanced on his long thin neck. He looked very pleased with himself.

"Thank you." Kessler smiled back at Beck. Their new host's words were considered, spoken slowly and, although he continued to not speak in the usual slurred talk of Dregs this far down, every so often his wheezing breath would get caught on a word and he would hiss and splutter through it. Kessler squinted as Beck's head torch flashed over his eyes, "Can you turn that damn thing off?"

"Oh, yes of course, again my mind is not where it should be. The power to this sector is intermittent at best during daytime hours, at night it is nonexistent. We are left with using the chem lamps and torches, even in our own homes."

Kessler threw him a couple of cred which Beck caught and immediately bit down hard, testing the quality. "Excellent. Thank you, sir."

"We'll need some things," Kessler looked at the room around him, "by the looks of your place you should have no problem getting them for us. He pressed down on his bioware, activated his holopad and quickly typed out a list of what they needed and handed it to Beck.

"Of course."

"I will need some medical supplies, things that may be difficult to get." Doc's eyes still had not left the steaming grey mulch that was his meal, every syllable of his nasal Hightown accent hung heavy in the air.

"This far down it is difficult to get hold of some items you may take for granted up above but, of course, I will do my best. May I ask one question though, how did you find out about me?"

"Jimmy Six said that you were reliable and could help us." Kessler spoke between gulps of ale.

The smile that had been almost permanently etched across the innkeeper's face disappeared for a brief moment. "The rogue," he spoke through gritted teeth, "I would love to speak to him but the coms don't function this close to the Fringe and he avoids my messages."

"Jimmy seems to have that effect on people."

After taking a moment to compose himself his smile returned and, after another bow, the innkeeper spoke, "I will leave you to your supper. There's a bell, ring it if you need more food, drink, anything you want."

Beck turned to go when Kessler raised his voice, "A minute of your time before you go?" Kessler's hand still rested on his Luther and the image of the dead Venter lingered in his thoughts.

"Yes?" He smiled.

"This place, Baron's Town. Where has everyone gone?"

"Like I said, times are hard. Around six months back a terrible disease came upon us. No one knew what it was but we quickly found out what it did to us. Very nasty. Took most of the town I'm afraid, but no worries good sirs," his smile widened further and, with a long thin hand he readjusted his optical array, "it is all gone now. No need to worry, no worries at all."

"And the Vents? We saw wrecked Interceptors outside the town walls. They still around?" His mind held on tight to the image of the needle and the burning sun sticking out of dead skin.

Doc looked at Beck over the top of his spectacles while playing with his still-full plate and spoke before the innkeeper could answer, "And Merryll Laboratories? Their mark is everywhere."

Beck rubbed his neck which glistened with sweat, "Yes, they came down here with all their shiny tech and promises to find a cure. They took a great interest in the plight of our citizens, told us that they were looking for a remedy, told us that it could earn us visas up city, get us good air."

"What type of tests were they doing?" Bethany leaned towards Beck, urging him to continue.

"Anything they wanted, this far down nobody cares. They filled citizens with their cocktails, shot us up with their chem, slashed us open with their knives and shocked us with sparks."

"And people let this happen? The Protocols do not allow testing of medicines and experiments that have not had approval from the Council?" Bethany's brow creased with concern.

"There were never a shortage of volunteers, people came from all over the District. They queued up for hours at a time each with the hope of surviving, hope of a cure for their corrupted lungs and frail bones." The innkeeper looked away from the group and wiped his optics with his cloth, "Some escaped the labs, not all in one piece though." He mumbled something inaudible to himself.

Doc reached across the table and touched Bethany's hand, "I have heard of this happening Beth. The corporations do what they wish below the Rim. If they need to produce meds quickly they will always look to other means outside of the Council. There is a lot of cred to be had in medicines, a lot of citizens who need them, many willing to do and pay whatever it takes to get them."

Kessler chose his words carefully, his need for information more pressing than his distrust of their host who stood smiling and bowing throughout their conversation, "Please, if you have the time, join us, pull up a chair and have an ale." The detective reached down to the bag of cred and from it threw another bar which clattered on the table in front of Beck. He immediately swiped them up with his small bony fingers and again bit down on it with yellowed, pointed teeth.

Beck's eyes sparkled at the credits and he quickly pocketed them, "Gladly, as I said, it is not often I have company these days," he repeated. Reaching for the jug, he poured himself an ale and eagerly drank, closing his eyes and savouring every noisy gulp. "This town, if you can still call it that, has survived through the years despite Council rationing their power to a meagre trickle, hardly enough to keep the generators going to heat our homes, or cook our food."

Kessler took a mouthful of the foul broth and winced as the grainy, harsh-tasting liquid slid down his throat. He could not help but break into a smile. Doc was used to the more subtle spices from Hightown and Kessler revelled in his discomfort as he tried his best to keep his food down.

The strong alcohol was beginning to numb Kessler's senses and add further weight to his already drowsy, heavy eyes. Eventually his attention returned to their host, "So what brought you all the way out here? Surely for a Dreg in your line of work being closer to the Core, up close to the Rim, would provide more business and more cred?"

Beck laughed and, as he did, his gills on his neck flared, "We all have our reasons, all have our stories. Besides, out here nobody disturbs us, even the Council leaves us alone. Well," he shrugged, "until recently, of course."

"Tell me, Beck, are there any Vents or corps officials still in the area?"

"No. All gone. And unfortunately with it the increased power and ration allowance that came with them." Beck drank some more of his ale. "They went when there was no one left for their doctors to work on."

A silence descended on the room as Kessler and Bethany finished their food and Doc sipped delicately from his tankard. The only sounds were the flickering of the lamps, Beck's hissing and wheezing with every breath and the dull hum of the rain outside. The dancing flame of the chem burners returned Kessler's thoughts to his own tiredness and he did not want to continue the conversation further, the aches in his body reminding him that he needed rest. "Thanks Beck. I'm tired," he looked around the table, "we're all in need of rest."

Bethany looked over at Kessler, "I was enjoying hearing Beck's story. I'm not tired."

"We have a long journey ahead of us, it's time we slept."

"Your supplies will not be a problem, I'll have it all for you in the morning."

"And my additional items." The doctor handed Beck his own holopad and the innkeeper scanned the blue light with his optics, "Some of the more exotic items may be difficult."

"And one final request." Kessler spoke as he finished his ale,

"We need a guide, if there is anyone left in this town, who can take us down to D5. Jimmy said you knew a way."

Beck stared at the detective, the black gloss of his optics reflecting back the flickering light from the lamps, "Of course."

"We need to get to Acheron. Have you heard of the place?"

"Yes. The journey is not difficult." Beck leant forward, bringing a finger to his lip as if briefly lost in thought, "May I ask why you want to travel to such a place?"

Kessler reached into his trouser pocket and produced one of the caps of Lux he had picked up at Judecca's, "This stuff, marked with a burning sun. We're looking for those who make it and we hear they're based down in D5, in Acheron. Know anything about it?"

"Ah, sir. I am only a simple innkeeper who dabbles in a bit of trade here and there. I know nothing of such things."

"Fair enough." Kessler put the vial back in his pocket and took out more credits, "This should be enough."

"A thousand thanks." He walked away cradling the cred close to his chest and spoke without turning around to face them, his gurgled voice disappearing into the darkness of the adjoining room, "Just follow the stairs up to your rooms. Not much I'm afraid but they're clean."

The three climbed up the creaking steps at the back of the room, the flimsy metal frame swaying under their weight. Two doors greeted them on the first floor across a small landing. Bethany turned to look at her two companions, "I'll see you in the morning then." She stood in the open doorway, her deep green eyes now heavy with sleep and jet black hair still damp from the rain, "Thank you both for being here, helping me," she spoke softly and smiled, "St John's may have turned to rubble but its spirit lives on in us." She nodded at Doc and Kessler before turning to go into the bedroom and closing the door behind her.

"Looks like I'm sharing with you, Doc." He gave Doc a hard pat on the back.

"You like her don't you? That's why we are down here? That's why I am risking my life…"

"No." Kessler interrupted, "You know why we're here and know why I cannot go back up city empty handed."

"Well, keep your mind on the case and not her." Kessler pushed Doc out of the way and opened the door to their room.

Two roughly-made beds, their simple metal frames flaking with rust, separated by a plastic table, greeted them as they entered. A copy of the Council Protocols lay on the table's surface by a flickering chemical lamp. Doc threw his bag to the floor, rested his rifle on his bed and stood against the far wall, his hands on his hips. "Well this just will not do. Have these sheets been washed? If they have, what water have they been using? There is not even a rec vent in the place to clean the air." He sighed, "Everything is filthy."

"You've slept in worse. Don't pretend I don't know."

Doc looked down at his feet and shook his head, "Yes. Well, I'm just concerned about our health. We could catch all manner of ills from these covers. This place is infested with all kinds of bacteria. Disease and infection lurk everywhere." He stammered as he rummaged through his bag and from it took out a small canister and began to spray his bed. Once finished he held it out towards Kessler, "Disinfectant. I suggest you use it."

The detective ignored him, took off his holster and threw his Luther on his bed. There was a small washbasin just to the left of the door which he eagerly approached but, after hitting the button repeatedly, heard the disappointing loud gurgle of thick black soup struggling to escape the pipes. Leaning against the wall, he sighed, "I need a wash."

"Well after seeing how grubby the proprietor of this establishment is I wouldn't have held out much hope." Doc had taken off his shirt and, after folding it neatly and placing it on the bedside table, took out a nightshirt from his bag and pulled it over his bony frame.

"What did you think of Beck Goodfellow?" Kessler spoke as he sat down on his bed and began to take off his boots.

"I don't know. The simple innkeeper, as he calls himself, seems alright for a Mute but I don't think there is anything simple whatsoever about that creature." Doc put down a blanket that he had taken from his bag and gingerly laid it down, making sure he did not come into contact with the bed covers. He shuddered.

Kessler's sleep-deprived gaze went from the fretting doctor to the half-open door and the hallway beyond, his mind whirling, despite his tiredness, over what lay ahead. He rubbed his sore feet for a few moments before laying down on the stiff mattress. His clothes felt greasy and he could feel them rubbing against him as the rot from the rain filled the room with its thick odour. However, the discomfort of not being able to wash his clothes or bathe himself was overcome with the satisfaction of rest. "This has been a long time coming," Kessler spoke out loud. "Thanks for helping out, Doc. Listen when we get topside again we can…" the low rumbling of the doctor's snoring interrupted the detective, he turned and could see Doc lying on his back with his eyes closed. He held his spectacles in one hand and, after a few moments, they limply fell from his loose grip onto the floor. Doc slept in his delicate purple nightshirt and, as the chemical smell of his disinfectant reached him, he thought how out of place his companion was this far down city.

As Kessler drifted off to sleep he glanced Doc's Lazarus rifle with his hand still resting on the barrel. His final thoughts before unconsciousness took hold were of the doctor, he had not changed that much after all.

·A SURPRISE IN THE NIGHT·

Kessler woke with a start and immediately sat up on his elbows gasping for breath. He wiped pouring sweat from his brow and blinked through the haze of tiredness to try and get his bearings. The chemical lamp still flickered on the bedside table, throwing shadows across the small room and Doc, still in his slumber, moaned and rolled around twisted in his bed sheets as if fighting against some unknown terror. Kessler reached out for his inhaler and took a hit as Doc let out another frantic groan.

"Hey, Doc, take it easy." Kessler rolled out of bed and knelt by Doc's side and, taking hold of his shoulder, spoke again, "Hey, hey, you're going to do yourself an injury."

Doc's face turned and his eyes opened wide, twitching manically, "No!"

"Calm down. It's just a nightmare. Here," Kessler offered him his inhaler, "take a hit."

Doc stared blankly at Kessler for a few moments blinking, his eyes wide with fear, before inhaling the Ox and, eventually, steadying his breathing. "Sorry," he gasped, "I... I just... just need a drink of water."

Kessler leaned across to his bag, took out a hydration pouch and gave it to Doc who eagerly drank from it, "I'm going to see if Beck is still awake and run over a few things about our journey."

Doc reached out for his spectacles and, after a few moments of blindly flailing around, Kessler passed them to him. The doctor peered up at him through his yellow lenses, "It appears sleep is evading us all." He took another drink, a calm expression slowly returning to his face, before speaking again, "When you see Beck ask him about clean water for bathing, this place is filthy." Doc pulled the covers over him and turned onto his side, "Good night."

Outside the room, the hallway was shrouded in darkness and Kessler had to gingerly make his way down the creaking steps. Downstairs, a single lamp flickered weakly in the centre of the table where the half-empty bowls of broth and tankards still had not been cleared away. The light threw shadows across the outlandish shapes that were piled high along the sides of the room and the only sound, besides the constant dull patter of the rain outside, was a low, methodical hum of machinery which could be heard coming from somewhere down below.

Following the muffled buzz and clatter, Kessler walked down more stairs into a basement where he came across a small generator which hissed and whirled. Wires led from the machine to a closed door under which a pale light could be seen. He knocked loudly, "Hey Beck, you in there? I know it's late but I just need to go over a few things with you." Inside the room a sharp static sound was followed by cursing and a loud banging noise. Kessler opened the door to see Beck hunched over a desk, one hand smashing a receiver against a table, the other holding a small chem lamp which gave out very little light.

"Damn machine!"

"Mind if I have a word?"

The innkeeper turned around with a start and dropped the com to the floor. He held up the lamp, adjusted his optic array and stuttered, "Mr Kessler, what're you doing up? You've such a busy day ahead of you and should be resting." He mumbled to himself and rubbed his long sweaty neck.

"Having trouble with your com system?"

"Yes, it's an ancient piece of hardware and you cannot get a signal down here at the best of times." He walked towards Kessler making the detective take a step back towards the door. "Just trying to get a couple of the more outlandish items your doctor friend requested." A red light flashed in the corner. Beck again moved forward forcing Kessler back yet another step, "Apologies for the lack of light, the generator is very expensive to run, I only use it to power the coms when I need it. So, what can I do for you?"

"I just wanted to know exactly how you plan on getting us down to D5? Jimmy said you knew of a safe passage that would not attract any unwanted attention."

"Yes, yes it's all in hand. You've not to worry. Now I really must get back, it is late and I have a lot to do."

"Are you going to take us there yourself?" Kessler pressed on with his questions.

"Of course. An entrance to an old service tunnel. It's a very simple journey down from there." He juddered with a twitching energy, smiled and bowed, pointing to the door suggesting that the conversation was over.

"Beck, I didn't want to mention this in front of the others but I would like you to add something else to my list, something that I would like you to keep to yourself." Kessler looked at the innkeeper, his gloss black optics reflecting the sickly glow of the chem lamp, his damp, pale skin shimmering with sweat, "Can you get your hands on any sim? I know you said that you didn't know anything about such things but surely there is some Dreg around here who can get their hands on some? Just something light?"

"Ah Mr Kessler I certainly can, the best in the business, in fact, if you have the cred that is?" His frantic nature now completely gone replaced by a more relaxed, confident tone. His hands became steady and his muttering changed to the smile he wore so well before.

"Yes, but only something light," Kessler repeated, "and none of this Lux stuff that's going around. Just something to keep me going, to keep my edge."

"Of course." He bowed even lower than before, holding out an open hand awaiting payment. He looked up at Kessler with his broad grin.

The detective took from his pocket ten creds. "This should be enough." It was the going rate for a couple of hits of sim up town, this far down it would be more than enough for what he wanted. Beck took the cred and immediately put them in his pocket, "Aren't you going to count?"

"It's enough," Beck hissed. "Mr Kessler, from the moment I saw you I knew you were a man that appreciated the finer things in life and I have just the chem for you." He placed the lamp on the desk and rummaged around in the front of his poncho, "I must apologise for not being entirely truthful to you earlier on. Dealing sim is a dangerous business." He produced a syringe filled with a dark liquid.

"Do you not have any caps? I don't want to inject."

"I can assure you that it's perfectly safe."

"What is it? It's very dark."

"Like I said, the best." Beck smiled back.

Kessler took hold of the syringe, his hand shaking in anticipation, rolled up his sleeve and found a vein. Beck stood close, staring, both hands clasped tightly as the detective began to press the needle down hard onto his skin. The noise from Beck's ancient com and generator disappeared as Kessler focused on the shaking needle. His heart seemed to beat to the sound of the chem lamp whose flames danced casting seductive shadows making the room seem to move.

An explosive clatter from upstairs shocked Kessler from his concentration and Beck jumped back with a squeal knocking over the lamp and sending its burning liquid across the floor. Immediately, through the blaze of flames, light pierced the darkness revealing the walls of the room, every part of which was covered, hacked and slashed into the old stonework, the words that had followed him throughout this case, words that had haunted him in his sleep. 'Lux Ferre.'

Kessler stumbled back falling to the floor as Beck lunged for him, a large syringe held tightly in his grip. Another explosion thundered up above as Beck landed on the detective who just had the time to grab hold of his hand as its needle bore down on him. Beck's gills flared as he hissed, "Join us!"

With his free hand, Kessler landed a punch square to the side of Beck's head sending him flying to the floor. The innkeeper gave a squeal as he held his head in his hands. His optics lay shattered on the floor and he now looked at Kessler through eyes the detective had seen before. Pitch black, they reflected the fire which was consuming the room.

Kessler leapt up the stairs and onto the hallway just as another flash and crack thundered from his room. The heat from the rifle blast greeted him as he bounded through the door to a scene of complete chaos. Doc wrestled with two creatures, both trying to get a grip on his rifle. They had not seen Kessler yet so he leapt towards his bed and rummaged around in the low light desperately trying to find his Luther.

Doc howled, "For light's sake, get them off me!" He clattered off the bed with a hard thud in an entangled mass of bodies.

A burst of white light enveloped the room for a split second throwing vicious shadows onto the walls as Doc's rifle exploded just by Kessler's ear sending him spinning. The detective's head whirled in agony but through the pain and just as the last of the light was fading he caught sight of his carbine and grabbed it, immediately bringing it to bear on Doc and his two assailants. All three were a dark mass of fists, teeth, claws and feet. Kessler fired into the melee and an ear piercing shriek followed. One of the creatures lay lifeless on the floor, the other quickly released Doc and scampered away on all fours, howling as it went. Kessler got up and ran for Bethany's room.

An overturned lamp threw yellow light over the chaos. A table and chair were upended, the bed sheets strewn over the room and a window to the right of the doorway was broken. The smell from the rain mixed with his Luther's burnt plasma and the bitter metallic smoke discharged from Doc's rifle. There was no sign of Bethany.

Kessler, panting hard and trying to catch his breath, walked up to the broken window, leaned out and stared into the gloom of Baron's Town. From the light of a swaying street lamp all Kessler could see was the empty road and the rivers of water streaming down the huge drains on either side. After a few moments he went back inside and surveyed the chaos of the room. He cursed out loud and punched the wall. She was gone. A fit of coughing took hold of him.

Eventually the spasm eased and he opened his eyes to see a tiny glint of light catch his attention. Her uncle's cross had fallen down by the window, its silver finish now splattered red. Kessler dabbed it with his finger.

"What have you found?" Doc stood in the doorway holding his still-smoking rifle. The words battled to escape his violent gasps as he sucked down hard on an inhaler. His pale scrawny legs, underwear and dishevelled nightshirt made him look like anything but the man who had fought off two assailants moments before.

"Beth's cross covered in blood." Kessler slicked back his hair away from his eyes and held up the necklace for the doctor to inspect, "They've taken her."

Doc slumped against the door post and put his glasses on. His face was bloodied and his left eye already swelling, a deep dark purple bruise taking hold. "Then this, whatever this is, is over." He coughed and returned to their room.

Kessler took a brief look at the necklace, dropped it into his pocket and ran down the stairs to where he had left Beck. A concern briefly entered his head that he had scarpered during the fight but this worry was quickly laid to rest as, through the thick fog of black smoke, Beck, with a canister of safety foam, had just got the fire under control.

Beck immediately dropped the canister and ran at the detective, flailing manically with a large knife. Kessler easily avoided the wild lunges, stepped to the side and kicked the innkeeper hard in the stomach wrenching the knife from his grasp all in one swift movement. "You're coming with me." He picked up Beck and slung his small body over his shoulder. He screamed and Kessler smashed his face with his fist, "Shut up." The squirming stopped and Beck went limp.

Kessler arrived back at his room to see Doc leaning over the still body of one of his attackers. He threw Beck onto his bed where he landed with a squeal, hitting his head against the wall. Doc looked up at the innkeeper and then glanced at Kessler before returning to his examination.

The detective pointed his Luther at Beck, "You stay there and not a damn word or you will end up like your friend here." He kicked the corpse to emphasise his point. Beck curled up in the corner, rubbed his bloody nose and sobbed quietly to himself.

"So what have you found?" Kessler kneeled down beside Doc, still aiming his carbine menacingly at Beck.

Adjusting his specs, Doc popped a couple of pills and gingerly prodded his swollen eye before speaking, "Well I have never seen anything quite like it." A purple robe with hood lay in a pile on the floor, the material was soft, like velvet. "Look," Doc picked up the robe from a pool of thick black blood revealing a shrivelled body, "it's as if all the life had been sucked out of it. Whatever it is." Its eyes were jet black as were the shiny scales which covered its body and its teeth and claws were yellowed and razor sharp. A long thin tail protruded from the cloak, ending in a sharp point. There was an intense sickly sweet smell that seemed to stick to anything that touched the body making Kessler retch and stagger back. "Truly a monster. Some type of beast or mutant, maybe?"

Kessler coughed, "I have smelt this stench before, back in Judecca's place in Nimrod Heights. Those black eyes seem to be a side effect of doing Lux, Judecca had them as well as our friend here." Kessler waved his Luther at Beck who was still whimpering to himself. Doc looked up from his bandages to see the innkeeper's big, glistening black eyes peer out at him from a tear-stained face. "One more thing. Those words, 'Lux Ferre,' they follow me around. First in the priest's study, then Judecca's place and now downstairs. Its scrawled all over the walls." Kessler leaned closer to Doc and spoke in a low whisper, "It's in my dreams as well." Doc nodded slowly as Kessler spoke and lifted his bloodied purple nightshirt to reveal three long slash marks that flared with a deep red on his pale skin, blood slowly seeping from the wound. "Looks sore. Better clean it out and get a bandage on that, quick."

"Yes, doctor." Doc said sarcastically as he popped a couple more pills from his bag and began to wipe down the wound with antiseptic wipes. He winced at the sharp pain, "Who knows what I may have caught from these monsters." He took out a syringe and injected himself. "I'll admit though, you have got my interest, I have never seen a creature like this before. Fascinating. I would like to get this body back to my lab."

Kessler's head spun, "Give me some Ox." Doc threw over an inhaler and he took a couple of hits before his attention returned to the whimpering innkeeper, "Now I want you to listen carefully, Mute. Think before you speak because if I hear any trash talk I will end you right here." Kessler's head was ready to explode and his temper was at breaking point. "Who, or what, are they?" He held up the gore-sodden robe, "And why did they attack us?"

Beck stared at both the doctor and Kessler. Moments passed in silence before he spoke, "I am only a struggling businessman,

I don't know anything," barely audible words came babbling out of his mouth.

Images of Bethany and her blood-stained necklace flashed in the detective's head and he roared, "Wrong answer!" He pressed the trigger of his Luther, blowing a hole in the wall, just inches away from Beck's head.

Curling up into the foetal position, Beck screamed, "Please, please don't hurt me! I have creds downstairs, take what you want."

Kessler hit Beck across the face with the butt of his weapon spraying the wall with his dark blood. "That filth you were trying to feed me downstairs was Lux, wasn't it? Your eyes tell us you take it. The last person I saw with those ended up in the wrong end of this carbine. It wasn't pretty. Now, unless you tell us all you know you will suffer the same fate." Beck nodded slowly, his eyes fixed on the nozzle of Kessler's Luther. "Who are these creatures and why did they attack us?"

Beck seemed to regain some composure. His eyes darted quickly from side to side and he dabbed his sweating brow with the frayed end of his poncho, "About six months ago they came to Baron's Town from below, up through the old service tunnels." He leaned forward and spoke in a lowered voice, "Strangers began to appear all over town, not uptowners like the Merryll docs or your good selves but strange folk who kept to the shadows. Sometimes you could catch them moving in the corner of your eye, hear them whispering in the dark. People say they came from the fires deep down below. They weren't like anybody I'd ever seen." Beck nervously looked around him, his large black eyes wide with fear, his bald head shining in reflected light.

"Go on."

"They're everywhere, there is no escaping them. They'll kill me for telling you…"

"Go on." Kessler repeated, gesturing Beck with his Luther to continue.

"Soon people started disappearing. First only a couple a week began to go missing but not many noticed, in this place people disappear all the time. They wander off into the dark never to return. However, soon more began to vanish and business began to suffer so we reported it to the district governor. After that, Lux appeared on the streets and those that were left all used it. Nobody had seen anything like it. It... it's amazing, lets you forget, lets you escape the dark. It shows you the light."

Doc had finished applying his bandages and grabbed his rifle, "And then, when all those addicted to Lux started dying the Council sent in Merryll docs to try and figure out what this stuff actually was? There was no disease was there?"

"There's always disease in these parts of Dis, doctor, but," Beck tried to smile but his swollen, bloodied face stopped him, "but none that interested the good citizens from Merryll. No, they were here for their own ends until Lux caught their attention." He squealed a laugh, "And they had their hands full. Lux gives a lot but takes a lot in return. The flame that burns brightest lasts half as long."

"And did Merryll discover anything?"

"No. Soon they were either on Lux, dead or had gone missing. Nothing can stop it."

Kessler spoke with grim urgency, "Why do they take people?"

"To help them produce more of it, of course. Only the best, those with a good soul. Though," Beck shook his head with concern, "there were not many of those around here. Very hard to find, indeed."

Kessler turned to Doc, "I've heard of this happening before. Judecca spoke of them taking the other priest to help make it and Bethany spoke of people disappearing around St John's. The lost she called them. I saw their pictures, so many missing, just disappeared right off the streets. That would explain why this town is dead."

Doc raised his rifle at Beck, "He is talking nonsense, it just does not make sense. How can priests, Dregs and Mutes make sim? It is a very delicate and highly skilled process. Impossible." Doc powered up his weapon, "Let's kill him and go back home."

Beck began to babble and shake uncontrollably, "They wanted people to help make it, so they could make more, the best people, those who had a good soul. That's what they wanted. I couldn't resist their voices. No one can!" His gaze moved between Doc's rifle and Kessler's carbine and his hand began to nervously stroke his neck. "They spoke to me, wanted my help finding the right people. It was difficult at first. People's spirits are rotting away like everything else down here. I had to work hard finding them." He turned around with a sudden jerk and curled up tight into the corner, "What was that? Please, please, please don't let them near me! They mustn't know I told you, I beg you! Please help me!" He broke down violently sobbing, each cry a shriek of sheer terror.

Kessler took hold of Doc's shoulder, "Watch him." He walked out onto the landing and peered over the stairs. He could see nothing but the flickering chem light on the table below and could only hear the dull pattering of the rain outside and the whimpering of Beck back in the room.

"No one's here but us."

"You don't know them, they can disappear, come from nowhere, anywhere." He pulled the covers of the bed half over his quivering body.

With the pictures of all those lost scattered at the foot of St John's altar still fresh in his mind, Kessler spoke, "Where have they taken Beth?"

"Wait, you're not taking this Mute seriously, are you? Souls, monsters that jump out of the shadows? Ridiculous." Doc shook his head.

"Ah, yes your lovely lady friend. They've taken her to where you were headed, Acheron. Deep down by the heat of the furnaces. I don't know how they make it, those secrets they keep to themselves, but what I do know is that she has a rare gift, especially in these parts, rarer than the finest air or the clearest water. Her soul smells so sweet." The gills on his neck flared and a smile returned to make its way across his face despite his obvious pain. "The Malebranche is what they call themselves and they will so love her, such a sweet soul. That creature lying dead at your feet is one of their Seekers. They sniff out good souls from the shadows and drag them back down below. That's your Beth's fate."

Doc leaned close to Kessler, "Clearly the toxins in the rain and the poisons in the air have got to him. It is a common side effect of prolonged exposure to these conditions. C'mon, what is the matter with you? He is just a crazy Dreg." Kessler nodded and Doc continued, "His brain is soup. Lets finish him and head back up city."

Kessler's hands shook as he took aim at Beck, the high pitch squeal of the Luther's power cells lighting up ready to fire. Staring directly at the detective, the innkeeper spoke quietly, "You don't believe me but you hear the voices, don't you? You must do as the Seekers only came for Miss Turner and only those whose souls are tarnished, broken and bent, hear the voices of the Malebranche.

"Insane. Just some chem-addled low dweller." Doc shook his head and brought his rifle to bear on him.

"Have you been having trouble sleeping, doctor? Voices in the night keeping you awake, perhaps?"

Moments passed as Kessler's shaking finger hovered over the carbine's trigger, thoughts crashing around his mind as he tried to make sense of everything that had happened, try and decide what to do. Eventually he spoke, "It's all beginning to make sense now. The presence of Merryll this far down and their encounter with Lux means that the Council must have known about this for months. They must know how addictive and lethal it is, must have heard about people disappearing. A Vent back at Sunset called Father Jacob a chemhead. When they discovered the priest's body surrounded by empty caps of the stuff they had to investigate, they thought he was involved. That explains why they took such an interest in St John's, explains why we've seen so many Vents this far down. It's got them spooked. That's why Stacey saw Councilmen with Jacob's body…"

"Councilmen? What…" Doc stuttered in shocked confusion.

"You're taking us down there, get ready." Kessler interrupted Doc as he powered down his weapon, went over to his bed and took another hit of Ox.

"Wait a minute, are you crazy?" Doc took hold of him.

Kessler grabbed Doc's arm, pushed him up against the wall and leant in close to his ear, "I can't let those creds go, I need them."

"Yes you can, she is already dead. Your creds are long gone. Listen, she was just another case to you, nothing else."

"You don't understand, Little Chi will not act kindly if I can't find the creds I owe him. I can't show my face in Midtown without the cash to pay him. My life might not mean much but Macy's does." He paused, still holding Doc against the wall as the image of Beth's unconscious face, her flawless, fair skin blackened with soot from the burning church, took hold of him and an unfamiliar feeling in the pit of his stomach pulled him back into urgency. Kessler barked into Doc's ear. "We continue down to D5."

"Great." Doc slumped onto the bed and lowered his rifle.

Kessler took out a bent cigar from his trouser pocket and lit it, "We leave in one hour. Beck, Doc will go with you while you gather all we need for the trip and," he took a long draw and slowly blew the smoke into the air, "I still want that chem, Mute, and none of that Lux filth either, the usual street trash will do just fine." Doc looked up at him in disgust but the detective did not give a damn anymore. He may be burned out Midtown trash but if he could find Bethany Turner then maybe, just maybe, his existence on Dis might just begin to mean something once again. Maybe.

·MERRYLL INC·

The buzzing blue light of The Crow's Nest Tavern faded into the dark as the three ventured through the rain and into the gloom of Baron's Town. Doc Galloway led the way, his sullen face peering out from under his hood, his hunched figure bearing the weight of his pack as he walked cautiously forward holding his rifle close to him. Beck's stumbling small form followed close behind, two large, bulging bags strapped to his back. With every step he groaned as he struggled with the weight. Kessler brought up the rear and, gripping his Luther tight, he kept a close eye on the dancing light of Doc's torch up ahead and the swinging chem lamp hanging from Beck's belt.

"You take my things, force me out of my home. I can't leave The Crow. It's not safe out here," the innkeeper sobbed.

Kessler shoved him in the back with the nozzle of his carbine, "Just keep walking."

"I tell you, I'm no good, can't carry this weight. My muscles are weak, weak from years living deep. I'm quick to tire and slow too. I'll only hold you back and you'll need your speed if you're to escape the Seekers." Beck's head darted quickly from side to side as he searched the darkness for unseen dangers.

The detective ignored his protest, "You better be taking us to a way down and no tricks innkeeper, if you lead us into trouble with any of your friends, these Seekers, I'll shove my fist

219

down that Mute neck of yours and rip out your guts. Now keep walking."

Despite Kessler's insistence, Beck came to a halt and turned to face him, "Friends? The Malebranche don't react well to disappointment. I've seen first-hand what they do to those that displease them and I've so very much displeased them," Beck growled angrily between sobs. "Nothing can save me now but," his creased, bloated face relaxed suddenly and his stare fixed on Kessler's large hooded frame, "there is one way to guarantee they won't come for you. You know you want too. It's inevitable. The voices get more and more persuasive until you cannot resist. Take Lux and all your worries, all the darkness, will disappear. The Seekers won't harm you then." Beck turned his head to the side, "Maybe you could spare poor Beck a cap? I can feel the itch coming on."

Kessler went to rub his eyes at the mention of Beck's irritation before stopping himself and gave the innkeeper another shove, "Just focus on getting us down to D5, that's all you should be worrying about."

Beck cradled his swollen jaw and, after adjusting the position of the load on his back, he continued walking towards the bobbing light of Doc's torch in the distance.

After what felt like an age, Beck's gruff Downtown voice cut through the constant crash of the rain, "Here," he turned and walked over to his left where his lantern threw light onto a glossy piece of plastic sheeting which hung limply over a darkened entrance. Kessler shouted over to Doc to turn back around and join them. Beck took shelter in the doorway and slumped down to the floor with a sigh.

Doc approached them at a quick pace waving his rifle and torch erratically around him, "I don't like this, Kes." He whispered close to Kessler's ear, "I can see things waiting for us out there. That Mute freak is right, it's not safe here."

"I thought you didn't believe in monsters in the dark?"

Doc stared at Kessler for a few moments before speaking, "There are dangers lurking this far down, this close to the Fringe that I do not need to remind you about. There is no law down here, you know that. We would disappear and no citizen would know. This deep down no one would come looking for us."

"What's the matter, doctor? Beck grinned, "You shouldn't worry, Seekers don't want your soul. Not good enough for them I'm afraid but they still may pay you a visit unless, of course, you take some of their delicious chem. It's easy, your friend has some in his pocket, then you'll have nothing to worry about."

Doc wiped his brow of rainwater, "Just shut up, will you?"

"Don't let him get to you." Kessler turned to Beck, "You say this place has a route down to D5?" Kessler spoke with scepticism as he peered into the dark interior of the building.

"Oh yes. This is one of the many labs Merryll have dotted around this sector. The butchers needed more power for their experiments than what they could find around here so each has their very own direct connection to the furnaces. The Council deemed their work that important." Beck spoke with venom.

"And these connections will take us down?"

"Yes, if I remember correctly they have service tunnels. If this one is still operational an elevator will take you right down."

"Ok. Doc, I'll lead the way, you follow up behind and don't let him out of your sight." Doc stood stock still, staring into the dark as Kessler forced Beck to stand and pick up the large, heavy bags he was carrying.

Kessler's torch moved around the entrance hall, its beams revealing rows of smashed monitors and overturned tables and chairs. The doctor's light lay still on a flickering image of Dr Fredrick Merryll. The renowned mega-corps founder stood smiling above his famous words 'Life. Quality. Survival.'

"I hate that grinning face of his," Kessler spoke as he took a hit of Ox.

"He has a lot to be happy about, he's not stuck down in this hole with us for starters." Doc shoved Beck forward and they followed Kessler deeper into the building's interior.

Through an entrance in the far wall, Kessler could make out a shaft of pale light. He turned to Beck who gestured the detective forward, "The tunnel should be straight ahead through that doorway, just beyond the labs."

"If the tunnels are still operating then the building must be still connected to its supply." Kessler waved his torch around trying to find his way in the dark.

"Do you smell it?" Doc coughed between words.

"Yes."

"The same stench that spewed from that beast back at The Crow's Nest."

"I know."

The group continued to fumble around in the dark for a few moments when suddenly the room was flooded with light. Doc shouted triumphantly, "Found it! Luckily for us all Merryll labs have the same lay... out..." Doc stood by the wall, his hand still resting on the panel as he looked on, open mouthed, at what the light revealed. The only sounds that filled their ears were the static crackle of the strip lighting and the low quivering sobs of Beck. The three stood in the centre of a large room filled with devastation and horror. Amongst the saws, syringes, drills, clamps and the usual trappings the Merryll docs used to ply their trade, lay decaying bodies. Some were still strapped to the operating table, all tubes and guts, others hung from the ceiling, attached to large metal chains which creaked as they swayed. Over by the far wall, bodies were piled high in huge cages, their arms, like tiny match sticks, reaching out between bars in one last desperate attempt for freedom. The tiled floor was awash with grime and what looked like pools of blood which hundreds of foot prints had rampaged through.

Just by Kessler's feet, a corpse lay still with its lab coat on, the now familiar black eyes staring angrily back at him. Kessler turned to Beck, "Another one of your lot then. This trip just gets better and better."

"Absolutely fascinating." Doc had his back turned to the group and was staring at a large wall covered in hundreds of images of Dregs, Mutes and citizens of all ages. Some had the rags of the street, others wore District boiler and work suits and a few the more expensive clothing you would normally find above the Rim. Most had mutations of varying degrees and all were positioned, some obscenely, to give the best view possible of their abnormality. "Each image has notes on the pros and cons of each genetic anomaly." Doc's hand waved across a monitor and, from it, he began sifting through reams of text, "Amazing. Fascinating."

"Doc, we don't have time for this." Kessler looked nervously around the lab.

"Butchers. All of them." Beck's face was turned away from the wall. He slouched against a table to support the weight of his heavy load and rubbed the gills on his long neck.

"It seems as if Merryll Laboratories have brokered a pact with Dai Lung Tech. They were sharing notes on the potency of mutations they found." Doc spoke, his face lit up in the blue light of the screen.

"Dai Lung Tech? Their deal is usually high-end military-grade tools. Real nice expensive stuff. What do they want messing with Mutes this far down?"

A crash, glass shattering, metal rattling, tiles cracking, cut through the air and drew their attention to the far side of the room as a large shelving unit came clattering down. Doc pointed over the monitor and shouted, "Something's over there behind the table!"

"Doc, watch Beck and stand back." As Kessler powered up his Luther, he moved forward, his large frame using the carnage littering the room as cover. Leaning flat against an overturned surgical table, he could see that Doc had taken cover behind a bank of trashed monitors. Beck was nervously muttering to himself and, after a quick signal from Kessler, Doc gave the innkeeper a sharp blow to the head with the butt of his rifle which immediately quietened him. The detective tried to slow his heavy breathing and listen. Moments passed until a clatter from somewhere across the room broke the silence and was quickly followed by a hurried shuffle. It, whatever it was, was getting closer. His thoughts returned to the Seeker back at Beck's place, its claws, razor-sharp teeth and its monstrous strength. He readied himself.

Kessler raised his head above his cover just as a shadowed form, arms flailing wildly, emerged from a pile of boxes just a few yards away and threw itself towards him, catching the detective fully in the face and collapsing on top of him. The sudden, frenzied attack caught him by surprise and forced his Luther from his grip resulting in the weapon skidding across the floor beyond his reach. Bloodshot, blackened eyes peered down at him from a scab-ravaged face. He tried to free himself but both hands were pinned to the floor underneath the weight of his assailant. A howl emerged from a toothless mouth as the creature raised its hand, a viciously jagged blade clasped in both its hands ready to strike. Kessler braced himself as the knife plunged down towards him just as an explosive crack thundered throughout the room.

He opened his eyes, quickly wiped the thick, dark blood from his face and spat on the floor to clear his mouth. Next to him lay the emaciated body of his assailant and behind him smoke curled up into the air from Doc's Lazarus rifle. Kessler shouted over to him, "I'm glad to see you still have your aim."

"Yes, lucky for you."

"Yea, whatever," Kessler muttered as he heaved himself to his feet and went to retrieve his carbine. He took off his optics and rubbed his eyes, holstered his weapon and stood for a moment with his back to both Doc and Beck. He felt old. Past it.

His reactions were shot and his nerves at breaking point. He took another hit of Ox.

"You ok, Kes?" Doc shouted.

Kessler breathed through gritted teeth. He was too far into this to give up now. It was not just his life he was messing with, Macy was counting on him and then there was Bethany. He stared at his left hand which shook slightly before running it through his hair. "Think of the creds." He mumbled to himself as he took out a cigar from a pack he had lifted from The Crow's Nest, lit it and savoured its taste before turning to Doc, "Bring Beck over here."

Doc pulled the innkeeper's protesting form to where Kessler was kneeling over the body, "I don't want to see it. Leave me be!" Beck snarled at Doc.

"This doesn't look like one of those Seekers."

Beck's face was turned away, his eyes closed, "No. It's Chaff, or that's what the Malebranche call them."

Doc poked the body with the nozzle of his rifle and knelt down to examine it, "Chaff? Looks like a disease-ridden Dreg. Its wearing what's left of a Merryll lab coat, like his friend over by the door. And those black eyes…"

"Yes. Chaff are those addicted to Lux. This one was starved of it. Once they have danced in the light they will do anything to get back to it." Beck licked his lips as he spoke before he sneered, "Chaff are very useful to the Malebranche, we'll do anything for our next taste."

"Seems these Malebranche have thought of everything. Once you start taking their filth you dare not stop." Doc reached into his bag and produced a small empty vial and some tweezers and began picking at one of the corpse's sores.

Kessler looked across the lab and immediately saw the caged shaft below the large black printed words; 'Authorised Personnel Only'. He pointed in its direction, "That the service tunnel?"

"Yes," Beck mumbled.

The cage swung open to reveal a series of cables running down into darkness and, alongside it, a large platform. "You say the Malebranche used these tunnels to enter the district?"

"That's what I heard. What a surprise it must have been for the Merryll docs," Beck spoke with relish, "they were the first to taste the Malebranche's anger, although, as we have just seen, some chose to embrace the light." The innkeeper chuckled to himself.

"And this is where they would have taken Bethany?"

"Yes, or one like it. As I said before, there are quite a few labs in the sector."

"Ok. Doc, let's suit up."

Beck unbuckled his burden and stood up rubbing his sore shoulders, "Ok. I will be leaving you now, I've done what I said I would, guided you to the service shaft."

"Sit down, you're not going anywhere." Kessler began to take off his gloves and coat.

"You don't understand, I can't go down there with you." Both Kessler and Doc ignored Beck as they unpacked large, heavy suits from the bags the innkeeper had been carrying. Beck began to fret and mumble to himself, "You, you see that creature that just attacked you? The teeth gnashing, the claws gouging?" He closed his eyes and whimpered as he spoke, "Howling like a beast?" He walked up to Doc, "You're frightened of them aren't you, doctor? Well, that will be me in a few hours if I don't take more Lux."

"But the chem will kill you," Doc said flatly.

"I'll die anyway, the light calls to me. Wants to take me away from the darkness of Dis, but wasting away like that starving Chaff," Beck pointed to the corpse and shook his head, "will not be good for any of us."

"Not be good for you, you mean."

Beck threw himself at Doc and grabbed him by the coat, "I have seen it in others. Those starved of it. The voices become more clear, you do what they ask. Violent, horrible things."

Beck, now on top of the doctor who had stumbled to the floor, looked at the detective, "You see, Mr Kessler? If I come with you I'll be a danger to us all."

Kessler looked up from the bag he was knelt over and into the black eyes of Beck Goodfellow and paused in thought for a few seconds, images from his nightmares flashing through his mind. Eventually he reached down into his pocket and threw the innkeeper a cap of Lux. It landed just to the right of him and he pounced on it, before taking hold of the vial in his shaking hands and quickly injecting it into his eye. The rushing hiss of the chem drew Doc from his shocked silence, "What are you doing? What..." Doc grabbed hold of Beck's shaking and grinning form, "You filthy, low city Mute! Kes, what have you done?"

"Easy, Doc."

Doc dropped Beck to the floor and turned to face Kessler, "Why did you give him that? Did you not see what just attacked us? Have you not been paying attention to what has been happening these past few days?"

Kessler looked at Beck who writhed on the floor, his arms outstretched, hands tensed to claws as the chem took hold. His body danced to a tune Kessler was all too familiar with and the detective's thoughts turned to the caps of sim, ordinary street chem, white and brown, not the black of Lux, which he had made Beck source back at The Crow's Nest. Yes, he thought to himself, he understood Beck's need. The itch scratched at him too. "You stare at him. You may as well be licking your lips you chem head!" Doc knelt in front of Kessler and with his hand turned the detective's face towards him, "It's chems that have caused all of this. Made you the wreck that you are, yet you are still desperate for your next hit?" Doc shook passionately as he talked, his spectacles falling from his face to the floor.

Kessler spoke as he bent down to pick them up. "You're wrong."

"What?"

"It's not chem that's the cause. It's Dis. The city is just layer upon layer of towering filth. Look all around you, you can see it everywhere, in everyone, and we are all swimming around in it trying to survive. Chems?" Kessler looked at Doc straight in the eye and nodded, "Sure they're no good but we do what we do to survive this place."

"They have gone to your head."

Kessler nodded, "Better that than letting the city get its claws into you. Like I said, we do what we do to survive."

"And the creds you owe little Chi? Creds borrowed to pay for your chems, no doubt. Is that survival? What does Macy think of you doing what you can to survive?"

Kessler lunged for Doc, his large hands gripping the doctor's delicate neck, "Careful Doc, your words cut too close to the bone. I would do anything for that girl, you know that," he growled.

Kessler's grip tightened and Doc's face reddened. Eventually the gasping doctor raised a hand and backed away as he frantically gulped down the stale air and quickly reached for his inhaler. "Ok. Ok." He sighed as a hit of Ox filled his lungs, "That was a low blow, I'm sorry."

"The chem helps me forget, helps me get through the dark days." He cleared his throat before continuing, "But this Lux is different. It's something else, something not from here. It comes from deep down, in the fires of D5. Monsters leap at us from the shadows, good people, the few that live in this damned city, are plucked from the streets to never be seen again, voices in heads, and strange words…"

"Lux Ferre." Doc whispered.

"Yes."

Doc spoke low, almost beyond hearing, "I hear it. In my dreams. They…"

"Call to me." Kessler finished Doc's sentence and they both

looked at each other. The doctor's brow was furrowed as his nervous lips mouthed silent worries. After a quiet moment, Doc nodded and Kessler spoke, "We do what we must to survive."

"Yes, I suppose we do."

"Look Doc, you're right. I need Bethany's credits to pay off Little Chi, but I can't help thinking of her with those creatures, these Seekers and their masters, the Malebranche or whatever you call them." Kessler struggled to pronounce the unfamiliar name as Beck cackled with laughter in the background at something only he could see. Doc turned to stare at the innkeeper and Kessler continued with only the sound of his own thoughts in his ears, "She's not like us, Doc. All she has known, all that held the city back from corrupting her, has gone. She can't survive in a place like this, not by herself."

"I know." Doc adjusted his spectacles and returned to sorting through his bags.

Kessler took Bethany's cross from his pocket and held it out before him, allowing the necklace to dangle on its chain. He watched as the blood stained cross twirled and swung back and forth, the silver sparkling as it caught the light. After a moment's thought he placed it in the side pocket of his bag. He cleared his throat, "Doc, I know I forced you to stay down here, away from your lab, your business, your home. I'm sorry but I need you." Doc did not respond but continued to take what he needed from one of the large sacks. Kessler reached down into his pocket and took out a cap of sim and stared at its pure white liquid as it swirled around in its soft plastic vial and took another look at Beck's now prone, shaking body. His glance eventually returned to Doc who was muttering to himself, and, after a pause, put all the caps in his bag. "We have dawdled here too long. We must get the heat suits on, quickly." Kessler cursed himself for his time wasting and became a flurry of movement as he laid out the large bulky protective clothing, which Beck had been labouring to carry from The Crow's Nest, and began undressing.

"You think the air is bad here? Nothing like down below. Every step feels like ten, every breath weighed down by a tonne weight!" Beck rolled around laughing.

Doc stopped donning his suit and pointed at the innkeeper, "You see what you have created?"

Kessler threw a cylinder of Ox at Beck which caught him hard in the stomach, knocking the wind from his lungs. "Shut up and get changed."

·THE DESCENT·

Kessler stared at Doc as he tentatively pulled the heavy suit over his skinny body and up to just under the hairs on his chin. "I have never felt more ridiculous. How am I going to walk in this contraption?"

"Get used to it. Down in D5 the rads are so hot and the air so foul that this heat suit is all that will stand between you and toast."

Doc held his synthleather coat in his hand and began to pack it away. Kessler shook his head and sighed, "You should leave that behind."

"Behind?" Doc looked aghast.

"Unless you want to carry it? With these suits being so heavy we best carry as little weight as possible. Leave it here and put what you need into these satchels." Kessler threw a small bag over to Doc.

"Do you know how much this costs? You can only get this quality of synthleather above Hightown 3 – a merchant who lives in Celestia Sector. He would not in a million years think of setting foot in any of your markets in Midtown."

"These suits are just as expensive. I'm told the corps miners and engineers use them when they're working down deep in the furnace rooms. It was very good of Beck to give us them." Kessler chuckled and glanced at the mutant, who, still enjoying the intensity of Lux, just smiled back, his large head bobbing back and forth. "I'll replace your coat with the cash I get from Bethany once we get back."

"And my Excalibur?"

"Ok. Ok. But remember you owe me."

Doc stopped what he was doing and shook his head, "And you will never let me forget that, will you?"

"I will. Once we get back and this is done." Kessler returned his attention to packing the provisions for the trip down. He kicked the third heat suit over to Beck, "You have five minutes to get that suit on or I am carrying you down there without it."

"We don't have much water. We'll need more, we'll be perspiring a lot in these suits and once we become dehydrated we won't be up to much walking never mind rescuing a girl who is probably already dead." Doc fretted

"Yea, well, it's all we could find so we just go easy until we can get some more." Doc threw Kessler a couple of Nutri Bars and immediately he opened the foil packet, "Corps rations. I hate them." The detective bit down hard in disgust and winced as the dried husk crawled down the back of his throat.

"The amount of energy we'll be using walking about in these things you'll be glad of them, trust me." Doc spoke as he pulled on the heavily-padded gloves.

Once Beck had been forced into his suit, both Kessler and Doc picked up their helmets, dragged him into the cage and closed the metal shutter. Doc and the shaking Beck sat on the floor as Kessler pulled the lever and, after a quick lurch of the gears, the chains began to move with a series of sharp clicks. The service lift was a simple metal box which ran on tracks that disappeared down into the darkness below their feet. Beck sat in one corner, his knees drawn up to his chest, still enjoying the buzz from the Lux, Doc was next to him with his legs crossed and his arms resting on his rifle, Kessler dropped their three bulging bags in the centre of the platform and sat down opposite them.

They turned their torches off and allowed the dim red light from the elevator's console to keep the darkness at bay as the cab rocked hypnotically from side to side. Kessler knew that it would take some time for them to get all the way down to District 5 so he tried, unsuccessfully, to make himself comfortable. Silence descended on the three as their carriage took them deeper and deeper into the depths of Downtown, the mechanical hiss of Doc and Kessler's inhalers and the rhythmical clack of the track, their only company. Kessler pulled at his suit in a vain attempt to loosen it, it chafed at his skin and the heavy material grated against his injuries.

After a while, Doc leaned forward, "We will have to keep these on now for the rest of the journey, the air is too toxic down here." He tapped his breathing apparatus and showed Kessler the screen of his wrist monitor that was flashing red, "Breathe slow and steady and keep an eye on your Ox levels." Doc's muffled voice was hard to make out from behind his vent. Kessler lifted his helmet and placed it around his head and Doc kicked Beck to do the same. The detective took a couple of long, deep breaths and acknowledge he was receiving fresh Ox by giving the doctor the thumbs up.

What seemed like an age passed, time lost all meaning and Kessler began to feel lightheaded. Sometimes the rocking carriage felt as if they were travelling at a fast pace, and at other times the cab seemed to crawl down the tunnel. He was not sure if it was the last embers of sim still in his system, tiredness or the heat that threatened to suffocate him, but he began to feel lost in the dark. Through the haze, images of Bethany's broken body began to appear before his eyes together with the monsters, with their slick black scales, sharp fangs and large snouts snorting and sniffing as they searched for what they most desired, "Do you think that we really do all have a soul? That there is something more to us than all this?"

Doc's voice sounded tired, "What's wrong with you, Kes? Of

course there's not. We are just skin and bone. All we got in life is this damned city, all we have to focus on is survival, getting through the days, that is all there is to life."

"Beth believed in a better place, she was sure we all had souls."

"Even Dregs or Mutes? What about Vents?" Doc laughed, "No way. I do not believe it. Anyway, what has happened to you? I do not agree with much the Council preach but souls are not real, they're just excuses made by the lazy, the desperate, those that cannot survive without the hope of escaping somewhere else."

"Everyone needs an escape." Kessler held his head in his hands

Doc continued, "I have carved up many a citizen back at the lab and never found one. Get a grip for light's sake."

Beck laughed and cackled to himself as the platform continued its descent into the depths of Dis.

More time passed with the rocking carriage in the clutch of silence. Eventually Kessler spoke up in frustration, "How long does this damned contraption take? You said it was a quick journey." He had not spoken in a while and the words rasped out of his dry throat. In the low crimson light he was not sure if the others were asleep or awake. Moments ticked away without a word until Doc moved, adjusting the position of his rifle.

Beck finally replied, "Do not be impatient for what is to come, Mr Kessler. Enjoy the peace while it lasts." The Lux must have worn off as Beck spoke with foreboding clarity.

"Tell me what you know of where they take their victims."

"I only know from the whispers of those who stopped at The Crow and the brief glimpses I see in my dreams."

"Acheron?"

"Yes. That's name of the furnace town nearest this sector."

Doc spoke, his wavering voice barely audible, "What do you know of these furnace towns?"

"Same as you, that they fuel the city with the plasma that flows deep down beneath our feet."

"Yes I've seen the Council's infogrammes too but what else have you heard?"

"Everyone who takes Lux eventually sees it. Fire and the plasma, beautiful, beautiful light everywhere."

Doc continued pressing Beck for answers, "Why take them there? You said the disappeared helped them make this chem? How?"

"I don't know. The Council have dug deep down into the rock for the energy that Dis needs. I think, if my dreams are to be believed, that is where the Malebranche emerged."

"Why is this happening?" Doc bemoaned.

"Simple." Beck continued to speak calmly. "You don't understand do you? The Malebranche offer what the Council cannot, absolute freedom, the ultimate escape from this damned existence. Even you doctor, would not turn down the chance to transcend yourself, throw down the shackles the Council have imprisoned you with. Be truly free." Beck spoke in a low monotone, as if reciting from a script. "That's why so many have taken Lux. Look where we live, what we have to endure every day." Beck rubbed his neck through his suit as he continued to speak, "We have nothing to lose."

Kessler looked at Doc and nodded. If these Malebranche were not stopped all of Dis could soon be overcome. Baron's Town and large parts of the rest of District 2 had been taken by Lux, by the Malebranche. Dregs had been going missing in D2 around St John's for months and, up in D1, Stacey Steckles spoke about large amounts of dead chem heads coming in, all from taking this sim. Haunting premonitions appeared in Kessler's head of Seekers sniffing out the good, leaving only the bad to become the violent, frenzied Chaff. Doc's voice interrupted his thoughts, "The Council will soon get this under control. They always do."

Beck laughed, "The Council are finished. Their good citizens came through Baron's Town a while ago to stop whatever they thought was happening." The innkeeper chuckled, "I haven't seen any of them return."

"Well, luckily the Council don't consult you on their every movement, Mute." Doc sneered.

"True. When we arrive you will see."

Doc adjusted his spectacles and breathed heavily into his respirator as each person retreated back into their own thoughts and with every clack and sway of the cab each wondered if the images that haunted them lay waiting at the bottom of this shaft.

*

A sudden loud judder and a rattling of chains jarred everyone awake as the crimson light turned green, signalling their arrival in D5. Kessler held his Luther aloft as he stood before the doors, waiting for them to open. Doc struggled to rise in the cumbersome suit but eventually pulled himself to his feet and held his shaking rifle before him. Beck cowered behind them both.

"Get ready," Kessler warned as Doc braced himself and Beck's nervous ramblings became a high-pitch squeal.

With a punch of the panel, the door opened showering the occupants of the carriage in light. Doc, nearly falling over Beck who had curled up in a ball behind him, staggered back as a wall of heat overcame the group.

Kessler squinted towards the brightness and it was only after a few moments his eyes began to adjust to the light. The cab had opened up into a small room lit by a bank of bright phosphorus lights along its centre, the uneven rocky walls suggested that it had been cut straight from the rock itself. Rubble was strewn about the room; rocks, random machine parts and tools, most rusted and old, discarded packaging from ration packs and hydration pouches and to Kessler's right, a plastic table lay bent and broken against the wall. In the far corner of the room a corpse lay curled up in a bloody ball, a thin arm, blackened from exposure to the heat, stuck out clenching a rusted metal coil. Long, dirty grey locks covered an old wrinkled face. His other hand, half concealed in the folds of his soiled white robes, held tightly the frayed string from which a small wooden cross dangled. From the radiated, darkened skin of his neck, an angry gash spilled long dried blood down the side of his frail, bony frame, and onto the floor around him.

Doc moved forward already reaching into his bag for his tools, "Does not look like one of the Seekers." He lifted the old man's head up, "Doesn't have the eyes of one of those Chaff and most certainly does not look like a Vent or corporate, going by his age and attire that is. And what is this he is holding? Wood? Expensive."

"He's a Christian." Kessler reached into his pocket for Bethany's necklace, "He holds their symbol, the cross, just like this one of Bethany's."

"Well he is very much a dead Christian. Seems to have taken his own life." Doc held up the limp arm holding the bloody piece of metal, "Major trauma to his neck, he would have bleed out quickly, although he would have died eventually without a heat suit."

"A good soul." Kessler spoke after a moment's silent thought, "He must be one of the lost. It means we are on the right track."

Doc finished prodding the wound with his scalpel and pulled back his hair, "Seems to have been bound from the neck with a heavy collar of some sort, chained maybe." Doc turned to look at Kessler, "What do you make of it?"

"We need to find Bethany fast."

Doc stood up, "There are marks around his mouth that could have come from some sort of breathing device to keep him alive but only for a short while, a day, two, maybe three if he was strong willed. Eventually the rads would most certainly have got to him."

Kessler looked around the room, "Beck, what is this place?"

The innkeeper still sat huddled in the far corner of the carriage, his dark eyes sparkling with the white reflected light, peering over his knees, "Storage rooms used by Techs and corporate engineers. You need to travel through them all to find access to the cavern above. I think there you will find Acheron. But I know very little. The Council hold the secrets to the source of their energy close to their chest, they do not reveal them easily."

"Let's go. Time is wasted talking." Kessler walked back into the carriage and pulled Beck towards the open doorway leading to the tunnels beyond.

"Ok. I'll follow." Kessler released the innkeeper as he continued, "But before we venture further I have one request."

Kessler sighed, "Make it quick."

"My time here is over, I know that. I feel the Lux clawing its way through my insides slowly drawing me towards the light, I hear the voices when I close my eyes, see the Seekers that will tear me apart for helping you. I know this. There's nowhere for me to hide from them, they will find me wherever I go. All that is left is how I choose to let it end." He stepped close to Kessler and spoke slowly, "I crave Lux, Mr Kessler, and know that it will numb the pain, allow me to bathe in the warmth of light. You have enough of it with you to make that happen. Please, if I bring you to the gates of Acheron, give them to me and allow a poor Mute one final moment of happiness?" He clasped his hands together and bowed before Kessler's feet.

Kessler looked down at Beck grovelling before him and could not help feel disgust towards this wretched creature. He was everything about Dis he despised and he struggled to look at his mutated features without being overcome by an intense revulsion. However, he had to admit that Beck's presence after Acheron would not be necessary and with all the danger around them he certainly did not need the distraction of watching over him. "Ok, you get us to Acheron then you can have all the Lux I have, if that really is what you want."

"Yes." Beck smiled, bowed again and offered out his hand to shake but Kessler batted it away and shoved him out of the room. "You can trust me, Mr Kessler. If there's anything in life I take seriously it's a business deal. I live my life by it."

The doctor remained lost in his own thoughts, still kneeling over the corpse of the dead Christian. "Whatever horror made this citizen take his own life awaits us somewhere down here," he spoke aloud to himself, before picking up his bag and following Kessler and Beck out of the room and into the tunnel beyond.

·A LOYAL CITIZEN·

With light from the store room gone, their torches threw their glow six feet in front of them as the three ran through a series of tunnels, their heavy breathing and the clatter of boots on the metal grating of the tunnel floor echoing in their ears. At times they would stumble over debris which lay strewn across the ground; boxes, shattered plastic, wiring and rubble all made the going difficult. Doc let out a shriek from behind, "The walls!"

"Don't look at them." Kessler had seen what their torch light revealed and tried to ignore it but his mind kept straying to his nightmare and the words angrily scrawled across every inch of the rock face. 'Lux Ferre' jumped out at them wherever they pointed their light. "Let's up the pace. How long until we get out of these damned tunnels, Beck?" Kessler barked between gasps of breath as he quickened his stride.

Beck's voice appeared from the darkness ahead of them, "Not sure. Soon, I think. Keep a look out for a hatch above us."

Their bulky heat suits slowed their pace further. Kessler struggled to squeeze his burly figure through the smallest of gaps and Doc would fumble past, his rifle, which he carried over his shoulder, a constant delay as it snagged on jagged rocks. Beck seemed to slip through without trouble, as if fuelled by the new found energy of the dark pact he had agreed with Kessler. He would often have to slow his pace and would always frown at the high dwellers as they struggled to drag their tired bodies past large boulders or when they repeatedly paused to catch their breath.

The journey seemed to go on forever until eventually Doc caught up with Kessler and put his hand on his shoulder to get his attention, "Kes," he gasped as he tried to get oxygen into his heaving lungs, "we can't continue at this pace, the heat," he gasped, "our breathing. We are using too much Ox. It will not last the journey."

Doc was right, Kessler nodded in agreement. His legs were heavy and aching, and the urge to take off his respirator which chafed and pulled at his face was becoming impossible to ignore. His hands clawed at his helmet when Doc grabbed hold of him, "No, the air is poison." He waved a hand across his neck to emphasise the importance of keeping the vent on.

Beck approached the struggling pair, "Please sirs, don't dwell in the tunnels, it's not safe here."

"That smell, that sickly sweet stench, it's getting worse. It seems to be coming out of the very walls, I can't stand it." Doc had taken his rifle in his hands and fumbled it in his shaky grip as he stared frantically into the darkness both ahead and behind them.

Kessler gasped, "Just focus on the journey ahead, we'll be fine."

"I don't like this one bit, let's do what we have to and get out of here." Doc's voice shook with uncertainty.

"Sirs, the danger, the smell is from the Seekers, they have used this passage recently, we must…" Beck moved between them.

"Damn you, Mute, leave us be with your constant chatter! Give us time." Doc snapped. He struggled for breath, checked his Ox levels and stared at Kessler, "once we reach Acheron we will need to rest. Hopefully we can pick up more Ox."

"Only for a brief moment, every second we rest is a moment lost on Beth." Kessler took another deep breath, "Let's continue."

Travelling through the tunnel continued to be slow going. Beck would again disappear beyond their light into the darkness leaving the sluggish Kessler and Doc to stumble onwards behind him. Every time he left them, Kessler began to worry that the innkeeper would try and escape but he always returned, with his panicked look, darting face and pale oily skin which shimmered under the reflected light of the torches.

Eventually, after disappearing for a particularly long time, Beck returned, "I've found an exit hatch." He was excited but still managed to speak quietly, "A short journey from here the tunnel ends in a sealed door above which is a hatch that will lead us to the cavern above."

Just as Beck had described, the tunnel soon ended in a large metal door which they staggered up to and collapsed gasping for breath. Kessler's body ached as the scorching temperature took hold. Through clouded condensation, which lay thick on his visor, Kessler could just make out a ladder that made its way up to small hatch in the ceiling. "That hatch will lead you straight to the gates of Acheron." Beck pointed excitedly.

Kessler looked at Doc, "You stay here, I'll take a look."

Doc readied his rifle and pointed it at Beck and spoke, still breathing heavily from his exertions, "Do not think of going anywhere."

"Doctor, I have thrown my lot in with you. I have nowhere else to go and the one thing I have left in this world is the one thing that has allowed me to survive this long on Dis. Business. A constant in this world. Everyone wants something and there's always a deal to be made. We've made a bargain and I look forward to completing it."

Kessler had hoisted himself up the ladder and was trying to turn a large metal wheel which sealed the hatch shut but it was locked tight. He looked down at Beck and Doc, "It's digitally sealed and the damned thing's made of cadermite, way too strong to break through with carbine or rifle blast. Whoever put this hatch here meant business. Any ideas?" The door at the base of the ladder had a window but it was blacked out with grime and Kessler was unable to see through it.

"These tunnels run parallel to the cavern above and have a series of hatches leading up to it, we'll just have to travel to the next one," Beck spoke, the thick tone of disappointment weighing down each word.

"I'm coming down, try that door."

Beck looked at both of them before cowering against the wall. Doc pushed passed him, "Out of my way." He tried the handle but it would not budge, the opening mechanism locking with a loud clunk, "I think our luck maybe out." He paused for a second before putting his ear to the cold metal surface, "Hello?" He banged the door with his rifle butt and turned to Kessler who had just finished climbing down, "I think I heard something, someone talking."

"Careful, we don't know what may lurk behind those doors." Beck remained curled up against the wall behind both of them.

"We've no option." Kessler banged on the heavy metal, "We don't have time and cannot go back." He put his ear to the door to hear muffled words and shouted, "Hello, can you let us in? We're travelling to Acheron." Kessler turned and spoke to the doctor, "The hatch in the ceiling may be made of cadermite, but this door certainly is not. Pass me your rifle."

Kessler grabbled the weapon from Doc and with two quick blasts the handle shattered, the old, rusted metal no match for Doc's high powered Lazarus rifle. As the door buckled and crashed to the floor a shriek from within was quickly followed by beams of light which hissed passed the detective's head.

Both Kessler and Doc scrambled behind the wall, either side of the buckled door, and Beck lay flat on the rocky floor, his hands covering his head. The detective threw the rifle back to Doc as more lances of light fizzed through the air. He had already taken his Luther from its holster and heard the reassuring whine of the power cells charging, ready to be discharged at a moment's notice.

Peering into a cloud of dust and debris, the horrific stench of human waste mixed with the now familiar nauseating scent from the tunnels. Another shriek came from somewhere within, "Don't come near me, monsters, I'll blow us all up, stay away!"

Doc and Kessler glanced at each other, both alerted by the desperate squeal of the unmistakable tones of a Midtown accent. "Don't shoot, we just need passage through, we need to get to Acheron. There are no monsters here citizen," Kessler yelled from behind the mangled wreck of the door.

"Show your faces."

"Ok, ok. Now there are three of us and we are coming out slowly, let's keep that piece of yours powered down, ok?" Kessler waved for the other two to rise. As they slowly got to their feet the dust and smoke began to clear to reveal a chaotic scene. The room seemed to be a store of some kind but most of the shelves which had lined the walls had been overturned, their contents, boxes, pouches, bottles and various other containers were scattered haphazardly across the floor. However, what made all three take a step back and Beck cower behind the detective's burly frame, clutching the back of his heat suit in terror, were the four bodies, three of which were lying slumped in various poses against the wall to their left and the other lying on his front near the far exit. They all appeared to have blast injuries to various parts of their bodies and wore the uniform of the DPD, their grubby undershirts and white cloaks bore the gold cog as did their discarded black plate armour which lay strewn in amongst the rubble. All, through various states of decomposition, stared back with the black eyes of Lux. One body was more decomposed than the others and from its grey, dead skin red bulbous sores festered.

"Who are you?" A citizen, wearing the same uniform as the corpses crouched, partially obscured by an overturned table, stuttered manically. He was very thin and his tunic hung from a bony frame. He pointed a pistol at them, bringing it to bear on each one of them as if undecided on whom to focus, the other hand was outstretched above his head and held what looked like a thermabomb or grenade of some description. His thumb hovered over the trigger.

"Easy pal, we're just passing through. All we need to do is get to Acheron." Kessler repeated slowly as he holstered his side arm and, with arms outstretched and palm open, backed away, "We don't mean to disturb," Kessler looked around him at the grotesque scene, "whatever you've got going on here."

"You're not from here?" The man had a feral look about him. He breathed into his vent, his eyes wild as he stared at the group through the dirt and grime of his visor.

Doc steeped forward, "Citizen, we have travelled from Midtown. I'm a doctor, can I be of any assistance?" He gave Kessler a sideways glance.

"From above? You've come to save us? I knew they would send someone." He started waving his hands up and down with excitement, "Tell me, where are the others? What is the news from the Council?"

Doc reached out and held his arm, smiling reassuringly, "I'm afraid there are no others, we are lone travellers on urgent business to Acheron."

"Why would you want to go there?" He shoved Doc to the side and started pacing in a circle, his head in his hands despairing, "I knew it. They have abandoned us," he started to pray, "Oh machine that gives us heat, that provides sustenance for our unworthy bodies…"

Doc shook his head, looked at Kessler and muttered to himself, "No Council prayers are going to help you down here."

"And look what you've done, the door, the door, the door," he twitched and shook as he pointed to the crumpled metal, "they'll get me now, for sure!"

"What happened here?" Kessler tried not to stare at the bodies, their stench however forced his attention.

With mouth opened and twisted in a silent scream, the citizen's hands clawed at his visor, "We turned and turned, everything fell apart." He began to sob, "A wave of blood drowned us from the dark," his voice cracked and shrieked. "Keep the light on, always keep it on, that's what they told us."

Kessler tried to make sense of the citizen's ramblings. His mind had obviously been broken but he needed answers quickly if they were to get to Bethany. He looked at the chevrons on his upper arm of his soiled heat suit which gave him the rank of Corporal. One thing he knew about the DPD was that they were well trained and brainwashed with corporate doctrines, always loyal soldiers to the Council. Years of this devotion would not be quickly forgotten, "Corporal what is your name and serial number?" Kessler spoke with authority and made sure that his holstered Luther was in plain view.

The trembling officer abruptly stopped his babbling and for the first time stood stock still seemingly trying to absorb what Kessler had said, his gaze fixed on the detective's weapon. He looked up and spoke in a hushed but clear voice, "Corporal Eisen 65247M3." He limply tried to stand to attention, "Sir."

"M3," Kessler smiled, trying to calm him, "I was originally from there. A solid, hard-working district, full of loyal citizens." He paused, allowing Eisen to compose himself, "I require a report on what happened here, a brief one." His voice took on an aggressive, yet controlled air, taking time to pronounce every syllable, his common Midtown slur gone, replaced by the clear, direct tone of authority.

"We, we lost the battle sir, and my squad, we retreated and tried to escape back to the upper reaches…" he began to stutter and twitch, "they were everywhere, all over us. We managed to make it to this store and lock ourselves in, wait for help. There was nothing left to do, all was lost." He looked down at the remnants of his squad and briefly lost his composure, whimpering slightly before looking back to Kessler, "Soon they started to show signs of the plague, I did my duty, sir, as we have been told to do, stopped it taking them before it had them completely." Eisen looked down again at his dead companions and to his pistol which shook in his loose grip.

Kessler's mind was a whirl of thoughts. A battle? All the way down here? He had never heard of the Council losing anything. "Lux, it's spreading?"

Eisen ignored Kessler's question, lost in his own thoughts and words, "We had no chance, there were so many. You say you're travelling to Acheron, sir?" His twitching features stepped forward bending close to Kessler's face and he whispered quickly in a series of snatched wheezes, "That's where they make the stuff. Top secret," he winked at Kessler, "I'm sure you know, sir," He stepped back and cleared his throat as his face took on another disturbed look, "It's full of their monsters. You'll never make it."

"Brilliant," Doc despaired.

"Quiet!" Kessler barked at Doc who quickly nodded and stepped back. The detective needed to remain focused, he had to think. His eyes were dry and sore and his head hurt. He was sweating and could feel the familiar signs creep through his body. Panic. Blinking repeatedly, his hands went to his bag where the soft plastic caps of sim awaited him. He wanted to rub his aching eyes but noticed Eisen and Doc staring at him. After a few moments breathing, thinking with only the sound of Beck's whimpering and the rattle of Eisen's shaking body filling the room, Kessler drank some water from his pouch and withdrew his hands quickly from his bag. "How long have you been here, Corporal?"

"It's hard to say, a month maybe more…"

Kessler looked down at the floor of the room. Some attempt had been made to keep human waste to barrels and buckets in the far corner but the stench was overpowering. Empty food parcels, Ox canisters and dry hydration pouches lay strewn across the filthy metal mesh floor. He took another look at Eisen's dead companions and back at the Corporal who was becoming more agitated. "These are difficult times for us all." Kessler never had any sympathy for Venters or anybody associated with the Council but looking at Eisen's, grubby, gaunt features made him feel a kind of affinity with him. They were all fighting against this plague, as the Corporal had called it. This scourge that threatened Dis. He thought of Bethany and where she might be right now as panic again threatened to overcome him, 'Damn,' Kessler cursed to himself, 'don't lose it, keep yourself together.' He composed himself and spoke aloud, "We have to make it to Acheron, you are welcome to come with us?"

"I, I can't go back up there. No, sorry." He sat down and put his head in his hands.

"Ok. Do you have an access key for the hatch outside?"

"Yes, I have my keylite."

"Excellent. Ok." Kessler turned to look at Doc and Beck, "Let's go."

Kessler picked up Beck who looked at him wide eyed, "I didn't realise you were Council…"

"Shut-up." Kessler cut him off and raised his fist threateningly and the innkeeper immediately stopped talking and quickly followed Doc out of the room to the base of the ladder.

Eisen climbed up and opened the hatch. His small rectangular keylite quickly slotting into the lock and after a couple of clicks a blue flash indicated the hatch was open and, with the hiss of pistons, the young officer lifted the heavy door and motioned for Kessler to move quickly. As the detective passed the Corporal he reassuringly took hold of his shoulder, "A couple of hours travel up that passageway will lead you to a store room where a service tunnel will take you right back up to D2. I'm afraid Lux has taken hold up there as well but it's not as bad as down here. You should go, from there you'll have a chance to make your way back up beyond the Rim to Midtown. You have served the Council well."

"Sir," Eisen looked up at the detective, who paused atop the ladder, and spoke with stuttering uncertainty, "my unit, my colleagues, all kept talking of going to live in the light, that giving into this plague was the only way. They're wrong aren't they, sir? The Council are the only providers of light, providers of energy, aren't they?"

Kessler stared into the eyes of the young Corporal. An officer who had lived through the last month locked in a room filled with terror of the monsters lurking around them, faced with having to kill his own unit to survive and the only thing keeping him alive was his Council loyalties and ideals. "Of course, Corporal. The Council bring us light and warmth in the darkness." Kessler spoke the popular Council mantra and it seemed to bring some happiness back to Eisen.

"Thank you, good luck sir." Eisen disappeared quickly back into the room as Kessler, Doc and a muttering, complaining Beck rose up through the entrance into a shower of white light.

·RACE FOR ACHERON·

The sky shook. A bright, blinding light bathed the group and for a short while each one of them stood stock still allowing the brilliant glow to envelope them in its warmth. Then, eventually, as the moments passed in silence, as each stood in awe as their nerve endings tingled in the light, darkness gradually embraced them again, returning the vast expanse to an eerie twilight.

Kessler struggled to find words, "What world is this?"

Another explosion from above illuminated them in its rays, "It is so bright. Can you feel it?" Doc looked to Beck, "Is this what you see in your dreams? Is this what these Malebranche promise?"

Beck too stood open-mouthed staring up into the sky at the shimmering gaze, "Yes. Light and heat. They promised it all."

"It is wonderful. Truly wonderful. I have never seen so much light before," Doc continued in awe.

Soon however, as their vision adjusted, their zeal for the light vanished as it very quickly became apparent why Corporal Eisen had not wanted to join them. Beck knelt down and tried pulling on the hatch as Kessler and Doc sat on the cavern's rocky surface and tried to absorb the view before them. The cavern floor was made of highly polished black rock that flashed white reflected light. The whole space was magnificently illuminated by what looked like an electrical storm. Huge blue rods of energy cracked and sizzled every few minutes burning the air and causing a bitter, acrid smell which caught at the back of the throat. A static buzzing sound fizzed around them. The surface of this gigantic space was littered with corpses, most appeared to be wearing the golden cog of the Council. All these citizens of Dis seemed to have had their bodies slashed and torn apart, their skin charred and blackened. Some lay by themselves, others slumped in a grotesque pile of hands, feet and distorted faces.

The others, what few there were, appeared to be Seekers, their black gloss scales shining in the glow of the maelstrom playing up above. It was extremely hot and in the distance the heat played games with their senses as waves of vapour distorted the horizon. As the landscape smouldered in the stark yellow and blue light Kessler could see that the surface of the cavern was broken by various rocky outcrops, their silhouettes angry spikes and jagged edges that thrust out of the ground. An escarpment, about one hundred feet to the group's left, ran in a relatively straight line towards the horizon. The intense heat gave the entire area a bleak, scorched look.

Kessler checked his Ox levels, refitted a new canister to his vent and took some more water. The vast scale of the space dumbfounded him. He tried to say something to Doc but the words were lost somewhere between his dry, cracked throat and the immense cracking of the chaos which raged above them. He cleared his throat and again took more water, "Beck, come over here." The innkeeper shrugged his shoulders and continued to stare at the sky, "Where is Acheron from here?"

"The town can easily be seen." Beck pointed to the horizon which, at its centre, was dominated by a large glowing sphere of light which seemed to dance in the eddies and swirls of heat. "It's surrounded by a plasma gorge, a huge field filled with the liquid energy used to fuel the machines of Dis. I've seen it when I sleep. So much light in one place." Beck seemed lost in his thoughts for a moment before suddenly shaking his head and

251

shading his eyes with his hand, "You'll need to pay the ferryman passage to cross it safely. That's what I've heard. And within Acheron itself, who knows? The Malebranche have taken over, if you're not taking Lux you won't last long."

Doc spoke as he stared out into the distance, "I cannot believe the Council would let this happen... I..."

Kessler interrupted, "They didn't just let this happen. Look around, Doc. They threw everything they had at these creatures and still got their asses kicked."

Doc wiped his visor with his sleeve and continued, "No. They wouldn't allow it."

Kessler returned his attention to Beck, "Ok, you'll lead us up to this ferryman and then you can go and have want you want."

"How are we getting into the town, Kes?" Doc's stare was fixed on the horizon.

Kessler tried to blink away rivers of sweat which stung his aching eyes as he searched his thoughts, "It'll be difficult but..."

As he struggled to find an answer, Doc nodded, "It is ok. I now see it all laid out before us in this damned place. I understand now that there is no escaping this," he looked around him, "whatever this is. Lux will spread up the city. If the Council cannot stop it then, well, there is no stopping it, no running away from it." Doc held out his rifle, "Let's find a way in and get Bethany." Doc's calm tones had the reassuring air of acceptance and for the first time in a long while Kessler looked at Doc for who he really was, an old friend.

"Sounds good, Doc." Kessler could not help cracking a slight smile but was sure, behind the grime of his visor, that no one had seen it. He continued, "We need more water, let's see if we can find any in what's left of these Vents."

The three made their way slowly through the vast expanse towards a group of bodies that lay sprawled out in a near perfect circle around a small outcrop of rock rising a few feet above the surface. The loyal citizens of Dis lay lifeless, their uniforms and heat suits, like their flesh, torn from them. Kessler thought back to the monsters they encountered at The Crow's Nest with their razor sharp claws and their savage maws. They had made fast work of these Vents.

Doc knelt over and examined one of the few fallen Seekers while both Beck and Kessler rummaged through the bodies of the DPD. The crumpled, leathery flesh of a young cadet was frozen in a hollow stare as the detective examined what was left of his possessions. A standard issue combat knife, pouch of field rations, a small copy of Council Protocols and a plastic image of the cog, the type of cheap Council devotion that could be bought at any market stall throughout Midtown, was all Kessler could find. Half his helmet, along with half his face, had been clawed clean away, leaving the garish sight of blackened skin and bleached white skull left to rot and dry in the heat. "Find any water?" Doc shouted from where he was still kneeling over the dead Seeker.

"No, nothing."

Beck spoke, his head lost in the folds of a Vent's uniform, "I have to admit you were right, I am useful to you. One thing I know how to do, the one thing I have always been good at, is finding items that citizens need. I've the nose, or gills I should say, for such a task." Beck chuckled to himself as his hands went to touch his mutation that lay covered under the thick material of his heat suit. Kessler could not hide a smile as the innkeeper continued, "Water, power cells and doctor," Beck held up a red pouch, "a med kit." He looked pleased with himself.

Kessler barked a laugh and looked at Doc who pursed his lips in restrained acknowledgement. "We should rest here, at least for a short while, and eat some of these rations." Kessler looked at him and shook his head in concern, "Kes, we will not be fit to walk never mind rescuing Bethany from these monsters if we continue like this. Another hour or two in this heat, in these heavy suits, will finish us."

"Ok, just an hour to catch our breaths then we move."

Kessler looked at the beautiful white glow of Acheron in the distance and, for a brief moment, another wave of panic caught him. Acheron was the centre of all this trouble, of all this carnage, and they were just going to walk right up to it. The insanity of what they were doing was just taking hold of him when Beck prodded his shoulder and Kessler, with a shake, returned from his tangled thoughts to see the smiling innkeeper offering him a pouch of water. He took a second before smiling back and sucking its contents through his suit, "Thanks." His gaze returned to the furnace town, "It glows so brightly."

"The plasma, I expect." Beck mumbled as the storm flashed blue and yellow around them.

The three sat together around a pile of scavenged items. Beck sucked loudly on the liquidised corps rations while Doc spoke, "You can always rely on the Council to provide its men with the finest in combat stimulants but only the most basic medicines." He held up a small syringe, "Theocotaline, won't stop a fever, staunch bleeding or mend bones but it will force any broken body to stay and fight when all it wants to do is lay down and die, effective in the short term but usually deadly to the user." He rummaged around for a few more seconds and eventually held aloft a small pouch, "Kestamine. It will numb even the most severe pain but will certainly not mend it."

"Council chems. All sanctioned and legal from the biggest dealer in the city." Beck smiled and spoke as his fingers clawed at his visor. When Kessler noticed the innkeeper stopped suddenly, sat on his hands and cleared his throat before continuing, "Mr Kessler, if I may satisfy my curiosity by asking a personal question?"

"Humph," Kessler grunted as he examined an ornate knife with the Council cog emblazoned on a black synth-leather coated handle.

"Back down below, that rather fragile officer seemed to think you were his superior. Don't you find that rather odd?"

"Not particularly."

"And why would he think that? No offence, but you do not have the cold, clean-cut air of a council official about you."

Kessler's focus remained on the knife. After a few quiet moments he spoke. "He noticed my sidearm."

"Ah yes. It's a particularly beautiful plasma carbine if I may say. I have not seen one quite like it, the way the light sparkles off the polished chrome plate. Expensive. Very."

Kessler found a piece of cloth and began to wipe the blade, "No, you wouldn't have seen it before. They're only given to a particular type of citizen, someone who the Council entrust to..." the words caught in his mouth, "...anyway it was a long time ago."

"It certainly was," Doc sighed as he spoke.

Beck nodded, "It seems that we all have our secrets. Our darker side."

The group became lost in their thoughts as they drank water and ate rations. The electrical storm continued to rage and the white heat continued to press against them. Beck had just finished drinking from a hydration pouch when he rose suddenly to his feet and peered off into the distance. "What was that?"

Both Doc and Kessler squinted through the flash of light towards the horizon. Eventually Doc spoke, "You are seeing things. There is nothing there."

"No. There, in the distance."

Doc squinted, "No, nothing." He turned to Beck as the light faded again, "Either the heat or chems are making you see things, playing tricks with your mind."

"I didn't say that I seen anything. My eyes are not used to these flashes of light, more at home in the darkness of D2. However, the glare does not affect my hearing which is quite excellent."

Doc looked at Kessler who had now raised himself and was standing by Beck straining to see. Doc spoke, his voice wavering slightly, "What do you hear?"

"Just behind the static from the storm, I can make out..." Beck listened in silence before sitting back down. He began to mumble to himself and rub his neck nervously.

"What!" Kessler barked aloud in frustration.

"The noise that I have heard many times and dreaded so very much these past few months. The clatter of claws on the hard floor, the skittering noise from vicious maws. The Seekers are here. We're finished." Beck began to sob.

"I cannot see them. They must be some distance away, surely they have not spotted us?" Doc's voice wavered.

"You don't understand doctor. The Seekers do not see, they cannot see. All they have is their great snouts from which they can catch the scent of any soul, be it good or bad."

"Souls! I am sick of hearing this talk. Impossible." Doc shouted.

"Wait, the light has faded enough, I can see them. They are coming towards us. Fast."

Kessler climbed atop an outcrop and peered through his viewfinder at tiny black dots in the distance, "He's right. There's a group of them, maybe three or four. They seem to be moving quickly then stopping every so often."

"We should leave Mr Kessler, now. Quickly. Perhaps they have not caught our scent yet." Beck pulled at Kessler's trouser leg. "Please, sir."

"Go where? There is only a lot of empty space between here and the furnace town. We can't outrun them, certainly not in these suits, in this heat." The dots began to slowly form into the feral beast last seen at The Crow's Nest, bounding on all fours, purple cloaks billowing behind them, only pausing to plunge their snouts into one of the many piles of bodies which littered the landscape.

"Please, Mr Kessler let's hurry." Beck whimpered.

Doc jumped down from the rocks, "I agree with the Mute, we should leave."

"Ok. We'll move quickly, staying close to the escarpment for as long as we can."

Beck picked up his bag and began to run, "Move or we are doomed, for sure."

Both Doc and Kessler followed the panicked Beck, moving as fast as they could, staying close to the shimmering black escarpment, lit up intermittently by the tempest raging above. It was difficult to breathe as they tried to move quickly in their cumbersome suits. Kessler's thoughts cut through his frantic mind as images of Macy appeared before him. He hoped that she had stayed away from the office like he had told her to do and avoided Little Chi. Then there was Bethany. Kessler remembered the first time he had seen her, a trembling, timid bag of nerves wet through from the rain. Her green eyes bursting with anger and passion. He wondered if her faith and love in her god were still intact wherever she was right now, that is if she was still alive. He gritted his teeth and ignored the feeling of despair and tried to rid the images from his mind. He stumbled and had to quickly readjust his stride to prevent him from falling flat on his face. He picked up his pace, overtaking Doc, his strides re-energised by a renewed, desperate urgency.

Soon they slowed and eventually stopped altogether, both Doc and Kessler collapsing, gasping for air. It was impossible to keep up the pace. Their bodies ached and their chests heaved as they strained desperately to get oxygen into their lungs. Sweat flowed freely from Kessler's brow and his throat was cracked dry. He took a drink of water, most of it spilling down his face in his desperation to get the fluid into his body, "Careful Kes, we need to make sure it lasts." Kessler was too tired to reply and only nodded between hacking coughs.

Beck stood with his back to them, worryingly looking into the haze as Doc spoke, "Take some water, Beck."

"Sirs, they have picked up our scent. They're coming, we're

done for." The innkeeper sat down and whimpered to himself. Tears now flowing down his still swollen face.

"Then we must hurry." Doc pulled at Beck to move.

"No," Kessler's voice croaked and wheezed, "we stand and fight. We've beaten them before, we can do it again. How long before they reach us?"

"Not long," Beck whined.

Doc steadied himself atop a large rock, aimed his Lazarus rifle at them. He peered down its scope, "They are still too far out for me to hit but are catching us quickly." He twisted a dial on his sights, "They are different than the ones from before, they seem bigger."

"Fire as soon as they come into range."

Beck, slouched against the escarpment behind both Doc and Kessler, looked away from the approaching Seekers towards Acheron. He spoke slowly, "The last few months in Baron's Town were terrible, people dying, howling, screaming. Even the noise of the rain couldn't hide that wretched sound."

Kessler looked briefly back at Beck before returning his attention to the Seekers, "Don't think about it."

Beck continued, "Those that disappeared, rumour had it that it was a most terrifying death awaited them down in the furnace. I, I..." he stuttered, and began to sob, "there was nothing anyone could do. Just wait for the inevitable, all alone. We locked the doors, latched the windows but it was no good, they came and went as they pleased in amongst the shadows. After months of waiting, thinking about how it would all end, the mind does play tricks." Beck turned to look back at those chasing them, "When they eventually did come for me I quite happily offered my assistance, it is amazing what someone will do to survive."

Kessler stared at the innkeeper, "We've all had to do questionable things to survive this place. Do what we all do. Fight. Live."

"I gladly helped them find those unfortunate people, I'm sorry to say. " He sighed, "Your friend Jimmy was right, I was trustworthy once," Beck spoke forlornly, "my reputation was widely known throughout Downtown, someone whose door was always open to those needing a place to stay, to hide, or whatever. No questions asked." Beck chuckled, "Anything anyone wanted, I could get, just like that," he clicked his fingers to emphasise his point, "I truly am sorry for how I've treated your good selves, and that poor girl that you were travelling with, she seemed like a good citizen. Had a good soul, I could see it in her eyes." He put his head in his hands, "They'll appreciate that, I'm afraid." He sobbed. "Mr Kessler, in a way I'm glad your arrival disrupted proceedings, I'm so tired and so sorry for what I've done." He trembled, "They're nearly upon us. I can hear their incessant chatter."

As the beasts' howls reached Kessler's ears he powered up his Luther and Beck closed his eyes. The detective pointed towards their pursuers, "Doc, try and take out as many as you can."

Doc took aim and squeezed the trigger. The power of his rifle produced a vicious recoil but he quickly composed himself and returned to his aiming position, "The group of four is now three." He focused again, getting ready for another shot when all three remaining creatures disappeared from view. He pulled away from his scope and peered back again. Nothing. "I got one, but the rest just disappeared."

Beck whimpered, "The shadows."

As the light faded again between the storm's explosions Doc and Kessler looked at each other and shrugged their shoulders. All three Seekers appeared behind them and launched themselves at the stunned party. In a frenzied few seconds of howls, claws and bites all three were overcome by the ferocity of the attack. Kessler was immediately brought down hard to the ground as one of the beasts threw its full weight onto him. Its face was thick with scales which gleamed black as if they were born from the very

259

rock itself. Claws hacked through his suit and tore at his skin. The creature pressed its face close to his, its sickly sweet breath making him retch into his vent. Its open mouth filled with jagged, sharp fangs was just inches from his face as it snarled and snapped. Kessler tried to shift his weight onto the creature but its strength was too great and again it was able to pin him against the floor. It took a moment to sniff his torso, slowly making its way up to his neck, then his face. Its nostrils flared on its long pointed snout. Kessler tried to bring his Luther to bear but was pinned fast, his other arm flailing weakly at the beast. The Seeker stretched out atop of him, paused for a moment as its beady, lifeless eyes bore into him, before lunging for his chest. The detective's body jerked and pulled in a fit of movement as the beast's fangs ripped into him. Through his screams he desperately looked around for any hope, anything that might give him a chance. The beast jerked its bloody maw up into the air and arced its back to tower above him. It bellowed a vicious howl and just in that moment, as everything seemed to grind into slow motion, the screams, wails and roars all disappearing, Kessler, as a thunder from above brought more light, caught a flash in the corner of his eye. Through tears and the blurred vision of agony he caught a glimpse of another sparkle. Bethany's cross. It lay a couple of feet to his left, half hanging out of his bag. Sound and movement came flooding back as, in a blur, the detective's free arm grabbed hold of the bag and just as the Seeker's fangs came down on him he shoved it into its open mouth.

It tore it to shreds and howled in pain as it rolled off of him. Kessler staggered up as a scream shrieked from somewhere behind him. He raised his plasma carbine and took quick aim at the Seeker who was now on its four clawed feet, getting ready to jump back into the fray. He blasted two holes into its torso, the plasma exploding on impact, causing the creature to slump to the ground in a smoking, bloody mass.

Another scream drew Kessler's attention to Doc who was

pinned against the escarpment by a huge Seeker that swung its claws wildly. Kessler flew feet first, landing on top of it and in one swift motion pressed the still hot chrome plate of his Luther against the shiny scaled face of the monster. A quick squeeze of the trigger brought an explosion of blood, guts and a putrid stench.

Kessler struggled to get up, his head spinning. He looked down at the bloody mess that was his chest to see blood pumping out of an open, angry tear. Doc was now beside him, supporting him with his arm. The final Seeker walked towards them, breathing heavily from the exertion of its violence. It paused, its gaze fixed on the smoking barrel of Kessler's Luther. It looked up at them, blood dripping from its maw, gave a feral howl and, as the light faded again, it stepped back into the shadow and was gone.

Kessler's head spun as he fought unconsciousness but with Doc's help they staggered over to where Beck lay. He was drenched in blood which seeped uncontrollably from a gaping hole in his stomach, his small hands frantically trying to keep his guts from spilling out. His heat suit was in bloody shreds and his vent had been ripped from his face. Eyes wide with terror, and gills flaring, Beck's body jolted as it desperately gasped for oxygen that was not there. Doc ran for his medical bag as the innkeeper tried to speak but the dark, thick blood bubbling from his mouth made it difficult. Kessler knelt close as he gurgled and rasped, "I'm sorry, for letting them take the girl," his body shook in a spasm, "Mr Kessler," his eyes briefly regained their focus, "stay away from the shadows, stay in the light." He coughed and spluttered, took a half breath and was gone. With that, Kessler slumped to the ground and gave into the vast emptiness of unconsciousness.

·ACROSS THE FIRE·

"Hold on!" A voice shouted from somewhere in the distance. Something grabbed hold of Kessler's shoulders. A face came into focus. Spectacles sitting at an angle on a long, pinched nose and, behind it, a face that was bloodied and bruised. Thin lips were frantically moving, barking confused noise. An arm raised up into the air and came down quickly onto his chest, a sharp pain and a wave of chemical warmth immediately spreading over his body, numbing the agony and quickly slowing his jagged breathing.

"Can you hear me Kes? Say something!"

"Ok, ok!" Kessler groggily lifted himself up so that he leaned against the side of the escarpment, his head heavily swaying from side to side. He gasped, "I can't breathe." Words rasped and oozed uncomfortably from his mouth.

Doc continued to speak as his hands worked to clean the wound, "I've controlled the bleeding and am now sealing your suit. You haven't been exposed to the rads for too long." The Doc's familiar matter of fact tone brought a brief calm to his thoughts and allowed Kessler to focus, his memory beginning to piece together reality. Doc continued, "The last of them disappeared into the shadows. I have never seen anything quite like it, fascinating really."

"Beck," the last few seconds of memory before he blacked out came crashing back, "dead?"

"Yes, afraid so. Nasty way to go."

Kessler moved his head groggily to his right and Beck's corpse, what was left of it, came into view, "I tried to get to him but I was too late."

"You were busy saving me, besides, he got what he deserved in the end." Doc's hands worked with the rapid confidence only achieved through years of slicing and dicing his way through the profession he loved. Soon, the mess that was Kessler's chest was patched up.

"No one deserves to go like that."

"Even a Dreg like Beck Goodfellow?" Doc took Kessler by the head and pulled it closer. He peered into the detective's eyes and took his pulse, "It's not like you to be sentimental."

Pain arced through Kessler's body and his hand immediately reached for his bag within which lay escape. He tensed. Where was it? He raised himself, ignoring Doc's protests, and looked around frantically. It was then the image of the Seeker tearing through it came to him. He scrambled over to where its shredded remnants lay scattered over the cavern floor together with the burst caps of sim. He stared silently at the empty vials, despair slowly consuming him. He was tired, exhausted. His focus returned to Beck's crumpled body, then to the two creatures, their dark blood disappearing into the cracked floor of the cavern and finally resting back on the burst caps. He began to shake and his eyes itch. Tense hands went to his helmet and began to undo the seals, the only thought in his mind, through a haze of bubbling anguish, was to escape. He did not want to feel anything anymore. The final seal hissed escaping Ox as he began to lift his helmet from his shoulders.

Doc leapt at him and batted away his arms, "What do you think you are doing? This heat, the air. It will kill you."

"Good!" Kessler roared, hoarsely. "I just… just… can't stand it anymore!"

Doc resealed Kessler's suit, pressed his visor up against his own and stared into the wild, twitching blue eyes of the detective, "Listen carefully to me. I cannot get out of D5 without you. No way will I make it back alone and if it means I have to walk right up to that damned furnace town full of these beasts and get Beth back then so be it. Now pull yourself together."

"I can't…"

"Pull yourself together! If it helps just think of what Bethany is going through right now. Think of what might happen to Macy at the hands of Little Chi," Doc shook his head, "heck, if it helps think of what this Lux is doing to this damned city. There was a time when you cared about such things. Now deal with it and let's move. We do what we must to survive. Survival is all that matters. You told me that once when I needed to hear it, now I'm telling you." Doc took out a syringe, "Now, some more chem for you, completely legal and Council approved. It will keep your energy levels up, give you back some strength."

Kessler winced as the needle delivered its payload into his veins. The chem acted quickly, propping up his aching, tired muscles with a quick, forced vitality. Doc returned to gathering the spilt contents of his bag and Kessler's focus returned to look longingly at the remnants of his sim. The Council's manufactured soup was giving him the physical fortitude he needed but without the elation, it did not block out the mental images of all that had happened, did not dampen the despair of what was to come. He bent down and picked up from the cavern floor Bethany's silver cross which sparkled in amongst the shredded remnants of his bag. He stared at it for a few moments. Whatever it was that brought the creature pain in the bag, his sim, Lux, maybe even the disgusting Council rations, that Seeker would have gotten him for sure if it was not for the cross. Kessler held it in his fist as his thoughts raked over his memories from the fight.

After a long moment of silence, he looked up from his thoughts to see Doc standing over him. In his hand he held the detective's plasma carbine, "You dropped this."

Doc smiled and brought the weapon closer to Kessler who took a large breath of Ox before taking hold of it, "Thanks." Doc nodded.

"So, any ideas on how we get into Acheron?"

Kessler looked at his weapon and brushed his gloved hand across the gleaming metal casing, pausing to stare at his reflection, he smiled a toothy grin and holstered the carbine. "Ok. Let's get this done."

"Good. Glad you are back with me. Now, a plan?" Doc repeated.

Beck's final words were still branded to his thoughts, "We have to stay out of the shadows, stick to the light to avoid anymore surprises."

"Yes, it is astonishing how they just appeared. I would never have believed the Dreg's story about them appearing from the darkness, I thought he was just scared."

"Yea, he was scared," Kessler sighed and stared at the red and yellow glow on the horizon. "Keeping out of the shadows is going to be difficult. Between the bursts of light from the storm there's no escaping the darkness."

"And Acheron?"

"Beck said it was full of Seekers."

"There has to be a way."

Kessler picked up a purple cloak from one of the dead creatures, "Keep it simple. They can't see us so we'll just walk right in."

"It won't work. They may not have the use of their eyes but they have an enhanced sense of smell, they caught our scent from across the cavern, they seemed drawn towards us."

"Then we will smell like them." Kessler bent down and cloaked himself in the long purple robes and, after a brief pause as he braced himself, plunged his hand into the bloody corpse of the creature, deep into the weeping mass of torn flesh, guts and oozing blood. He took hold of the still warm gore and rubbed it all over him, gloves, cloak and helmet, all the while gagging as the intense sweetly sick fumes assaulted his senses.

The sporadic lightning storm overhead cracked again throwing a shock of blue light onto the grim scene. Standing amongst the dead bodies of the Seekers, Beck and the Venters, Doc stared in silence at Kessler who now looked like a wild, feral animal covered in the carnage of its prey. The large hood partially obscured his respirator which protruded like a snout and his heavy breathing hissed and wheezed. "Its monstrous, I cannot do it. Disgusting beyond words. Who knows what disease these creatures carry."

"I'm not asking you to drink their blood just use its scent to hide us. It's our only chance."

"I fear the deeper we get ourselves entangled in this horror the more we lose ourselves." Doc looked down at the bloody corpse and gingerly began to rub its blood over his suit.

"Well, like you said. We do what we must to survive." Kessler stooped down and picked up the other Seeker's cloak and gave it to Doc, "Take this and cover it in as much blood and gore as you can bear."

Doc doubled over in a fit of coughing as his body retched uncontrollably.

"Remember your own advice. Easy breaths."

Gasping between words, Doc composed himself, "You look ridiculous."

"You don't look too hot yourself." Kessler laughed.

Doc bent down and picked up something from the floor, "Well, well. A cap of Lux has survived the assault."

Kessler's body tensed at the thought of the chem. Lux was no good, even he knew that. Doc threw it back to the ground and stamped down hard bursting the soft plastic cap, its contents sizzling as it came into contact with the hot rock of the cavern. "Let's go," Doc said as he donned his cloak, picked up his bag and, after taking a quick moment to gaze at the horizon, began to march towards the distant glowing dome that was Acheron.

Kessler took a few moments to stare at what was left of Beck. In a city full to the brim of the worst kind, Beck, in the end was sorry for what he had done. He was just doing what he had to do to survive, like everyone else on Dis. He nodded his goodbyes to the innkeeper from Baron's Town and quickly marched up to join the doctor.

*

The journey across the cavern was uneventful. With Council chemicals coursing through his veins, Kessler walked with ease but spent most of his energy trying to wrench his thoughts from the sim he had lost. Doc kept pace beside him in silence, most of his time spent staring at the light from Acheron and, at times, looking up at the electrical maelstrom playing out overhead. The closer they got to the furnace town, the more bodies they passed. A couple of times they spotted movement in the distance and on one occasion Doc could see a group of Seekers through his scope gorging on a particularly large pile of corpses but, unlike before, they did not register their presence.

More time slipped by as they walked lethargically through the heat. With every step the air around them felt heavier as it cracked and buzzed with static and all the while the light emitting from Acheron grew in intensity. Kessler sucked down hard on his water tube and it gurgled empty. His tired hands awkwardly fumbled for a replacement hydration pouch.

They continued to stagger forward. A flashing red light on Kessler's suit drew his attention and told him that his Ox was running low when suddenly the cavern floor gave way. Doc stumbled and Kessler, with dulled reactions, just managed to grab hold of his companion's flowing cloak. The doctor's weight threatened to pull him down into the white molten plasma which churned and raged just a few feet below them. Sweat poured from Kessler's body as he strained to find the strength to pull the doctor back up to the cavern floor. The detective's legs flailed around trying desperately to find grip on the smooth stone and, just as he too was teetering on the brink, the cloak went limp in his hands. He got up to his knees and stared at the loose folds of cloth. His hands began to shake as he peered over the edge, "Doc?"

"Do I have to do everything myself?" A helmet with the strained, bespectacled face of the doctor appeared from below the ledge, "Well? Can I get some help?"

Kessler pulled him onto the cavern floor and laughed, "I thought you were gone."

"Well, I'm glad you think it's funny." Doc panted and took a drink of water.

They stood up and Kessler peered at the plasma which had so nearly taken his friend, "Raw plasma, I have never seen it before." The sheer brilliance of the glare was too much for him and he looked away.

"Yes." Doc took a step back, "It's extremely dangerous."

Churning blue and yellow flows of plasma formed a moat around Acheron. Long tendrils of light wheeled and flowed up from the main body of energy making Kessler all too aware of his vulnerability standing so close to such a destructive force. Beyond the swirling light stood the furnace town itself. Huge pistons, gigantic pipes, tubes and cables rose up from the haze and disappeared into the electrical storm and the roof of the cavern high above.

"Not a sight you see every day." Doc was staring, transfixed, at the plasma and the town beyond.

"Acheron. One of the furnace towns that drive the machines of Dis, all of the city's energy comes from towns such as these."

"Truly amazing." Doc pointed at the large metal pistons hanging over the moat, "I believe these are used to gather the plasma and pump it to the furnaces for processing."

"Yea, well they're not doing much processing now. They've all stopped, the town looks dead."

"Where's the crossing?" Doc raised his voice against the roar of the plasma below them.

"Not sure, Beck never said. I think we'll just have to make our way along the edge until we come across it." Kessler peered into the distance at Acheron's walls beyond the bright glare but his twitching, itchy eyes, a constant reminder of what he most craved, struggled to see. "I'm finding it difficult to focus with this light, can you see any sign of this ferryman up ahead?" Kessler passed Doc his view finder.

"Adjust the settings on your visor, it will filter out most of the glare."

"No. It's my eyes. They hurt."

Doc nodded knowingly, "Ok," and took the viewfinder from Kessler and peered along the edge of the moat in both directions.

"In the distance, I can just about make out what appears to be an entrance in the town walls. Perhaps the crossing is there?" They pulled the large hoods down over their helmets and walked along the moat's edge.

As the plasma crashed and churned just below their feet, Doc spoke, "What if we can't get across? I fear that any ferryman working here, with everything that has happened, may have disappeared long ago."

"Yea, we'll find out soon enough, I guess."

Before long, out of the shimmering horizon, two large poles came into view, their tattered, charred flags billowing in a hot wind which seemed to come from the very depths of the plasma field. Battling against the extreme elements they approached what appeared to be a jetty, its hardened cadermite struts extending out to hover precariously above the burning light. A large platform, wavering back and forth, hovered above the moat and was tethered to the jetty by thick, heavy wire.

Doc began to walk out onto the platform when Kessler raised an arm barring his way, "Wait, someone is over there right by the jetty's edge." Nearly completely enveloped in the plasma's swirling strands of light, a tall, hunchbacked cloaked figure could just be made out standing on the edge of the dock with its back towards them. It seemed to be unaware of the dangerous plasma which raged around it.

"A Seeker?" Doc took a step back.

"I don't think so. It's standing still, and not making a sound. Those beasts are always twitching, moving, and howling."

Kessler put one foot onto the dock and immediately the creature turned. Its face was partially obscured by a huge black hood. An eyeless socket stared back at them and rotting skin hung in grey shreds off of white bone. It carried a large staff that bore a pointed metal hook at one end. It made two large strides towards them before the creature was halted by a heavy chain clasped to a leg and tying it to the platform. It seemed to stare at Kessler and Doc for a few moments before speaking, "This way." The voice vibrated in a deep resonate tone as if carried by the waves of flowing light which danced around them. It stood to the side and pointed towards the platform.

With lowered heads, they both shuffled onto the ferry that bobbed slightly as it took their weight. Doc held onto Kessler's robe as he tried to keep his balance. The large hunchback creature followed them, one foot straining to drag the heavy chain which noisily scraped along the cadermite dock. The three figures stood silently as the plasma storm raged all around them when suddenly the ferry came to life with a pulse from its hover drive and began to very slowly make its way across the maelstrom. A beautiful collage of colours, blues, reds, yellow and greens exploded from the energy field in cracks and pops. Kessler wondered how such a magnificent spectacle could come from something so violent and dangerous. He stared at the wonderful patterns made by the churning energy and, like Doc, seemed transfixed.

"Careful. Many have lost themselves in the plasma fields never to be seen again." The ferryman spoke with slow, rasping words.

Both Kessler and Doc looked up at the creature from below their hoods, not knowing how to respond. After a moment's uncertainty Kessler spoke, "What are you, creature?"

"I am the ferryman of Acheron." It paused as if lost in thought before continuing in a ponderous tone, "All furnace towns have their ferrymen."

Doc cleared his throat and shouted through the noise of the plasma, "Are you citizen or machine? What keeps you alive?" Kessler glowered at the doctor who shrugged his shoulders.

The ferryman continued to stare out into the light, "Plasma. It binds us all."

The platform juddered from side to side as a wave of light flared from below. "You're chained to this ferry, who keeps you prisoner and forces you to perform this task?"

"If you stare at the plasma long enough it reaches out to you, becomes part of your very being. Once inside it calls to you. Most that succumb to the beauty of the fire follow it to their end, those few that survive are forever tied to the light."

"How have you survived here, amongst the Seekers?" Doc spoke in exasperated tone.

"Many travellers use my service." His voice, devoid of all emotion, hung in the air.

"Do you know of anything that has happened within Acheron? Of what is happening throughout Dis?"

The ferryman remained quiet, as if taking his time to gather his thoughts, "The plasma coils and caresses the flesh, does it not? Its fire burns ever so brightly."

Doc pulled on Kessler's robe, "He's completely gone. Just like his flesh, his mind has been warped by the plasma."

The far side of the moat eventually came into view, eventually revealing itself through the glare, "Would you like me to end your pain?" Kessler raised his sidearm, "It would be quick. No one should have to endure what you have suffered."

"I am eternally tied to the ebbs and flows of the plasma, it is a part of me. I cannot leave it." He took three large strides forward, dragging his bonds as he went and, with his staff hooked the ferry onto a tether and secured the platform to the jetty. With a skeletal hand which emerged from the folds of his robe he pointed for them to leave.

Doc leaned close to Kessler's ear, "Leave him, he is no longer one of us. No citizen could survive what he has endured. He is not of this life."

"You don't sound your usually scientific self."

"I have seen many strange things on our journey, I just cannot explain what is happening."

Kessler put his arm around the doctor's shoulders and reassuringly spoke to him, "Never worry, I generally don't understand most things in life, welcome to the club." Kessler, with feet securely back on the hard rock of the cavern floor turned and helped pull Doc up from the ferry, "We have witnessed some unusual things, old friend."

"It has been awhile since you called me that."

"This city, it gets into your very being, corrupts everything. Sometimes it makes you forget yourself."

Doc looked back at the swirling plasma, "Dis can be an awful place but if the Malebranche continue to spread Lux amongst our citizens then we truly are lost."

Kessler turned to the ferryman who stood stock still continuing his watch over the churning fire, "Thank you for the passage," Kessler rummaged to find some creds in his bag.

"I require no payment."

Kessler nodded, "Then farewell." They turned and began making their way towards Acheron's gates leaving the ferryman to his lonely vigil over the broiling light.

·AN ENGINE OF DIS·

eaving the intense heat of the plasma fields behind them, Kessler and Doc approached the towering walls of Acheron. Metal sheeting and twisted plastisteel girders were compacted together with a jumbled assortment of old bots and all manner of ancient and unrecognisable tech to create a colossal structure which stood guard around the town's perimeter.

Doc stood right up against the metal boundary, his dark purple cloak a hunchbacked silhouette against the deep orange rust which covered the ancient walls. He could not take his gaze away from the crumpled optics of some ancient droid. Shattered and smashed, it stared at them from its crushed prison of discarded plastic and metal. Its guts, a mass of blackened spindly wires, spilled out as if trying to escape.

"Come on, we don't have time to stand here and stare." Kessler put his hand on Doc's shoulder and tried to wrestle his focus away from his distraction. "Just a short distance along the wall I'm sure will bring us to the town gates."

Doc's attention remained on the old bot for a few moments, ignoring Kessler's demands to move. Eventually he turned and pulled down his hood, his heat suit still caked in the Seeker's blood and guts. He squinted through his dirty glasses and with an otherwise blank expression spoke in a quiet monotone, "The horrors of this place are indescribable and I fear that we have not seen the worst of it."

Kessler had to bend down and bring his ear close to Doc to hear his mumblings, "We keep moving, stick to the plan. I promise you, we'll be alright." He reached behind Doc's head and pulled his hood back up, "Careful, old friend. We do not know who or what is near. We must remain hidden behind this grim disguise until we're safe."

"Safe? All I want is to be back in my lab, installing re-breathers, implanting bioware, heck, I even miss treating Toxics and Mutes." Doc shrugged his shoulders and with a sigh began to walk along the wall, "I never thought I would miss it all so much."

Kessler looked around him and subconsciously felt the reassuring metal chrome of his Luther still holstered by his side hidden beneath the folds of his pungent robes. The chems Doc had given him still flowed through his system, enough for him to feel no physical pain however every step and every quick breath of Ox was taken knowing that an insatiable need simmered below the thin veil of control he managed to convey. He closed his eyes and wished he had taken some of the sim back at the Merryll lab when he had the chance. Now they were gone. The detective punched the wall in frustration and walked quickly to catch up with Doc who lumbered on ahead of him.

Eventually they came upon the entrance to Acheron. Two huge cadermite gates lay half open as if some mighty wind had blown the great doors ajar. Doc looked up at the gigantic entrance, "I have never seen so much cadermite in one place. Such a rare metal, where did they get it all from?"

"We're standing on rock, remember. They probably took it straight out of the ground." Even now, after all they had seen and been through, Kessler was still amazed at the thought of standing on ancient ground. The people of Dis were used to recycling old metals and creating synthetic materials from chemicals, the pure materials from the old world, from the ground itself, were extremely rare. "They must have access to a lot of it, this cadermite is ten inches thick." Kessler mused, "I remember the old stories. These towns were built by the original architects, built around the furnaces that tunnel deep into the ground in search of plasma to fuel the city. Who knows what dangers they have encountered, we know so little of these lower reaches."

Doc touched the intricately carved symbols that covered the entrance, "Well, it takes some skill to engrave cadermite, not many cutting tools can even make a dent." Doc bent down close to the metal door, "Look at the detail here." He pointed to a symbol showing a cog and a hammer. "The cog of the Council but I don't recognise the hammer."

Kessler was already peering through the gap in the gate, planning their next move.

"Listen, Doc, Beck said that the Malebranche take all the lost down to the furnace at the centre of the town. If they are keeping them alive for whatever reason then all those people should be easy enough to find."

"Sounds simple." Doc did not sound convinced.

Kessler continued, "Remember, the Seekers can't see us they can only smell us so no matter how close they get, stay calm, stay in the light, away from any shadows. We will do just fine and," Kessler looked through the gate again, "and keep your hood down low, we haven't encountered any of these Malebranche yet."

"Ok, let's get this over with."

After a quick check of their disguises they passed through the gates and walked at a steady pace down the wide road that disappeared off into the distance. Peering from underneath his cowl, Kessler saw the cavern floor, its rock worn smooth by the feet of townsfolk. Either side of the road were dilapidated, lifeless, single-storey hovels made from the same waste metals as the perimeter wall. There was no evidence of any activity, the street was empty and only darkness existed through windows.

275

Any sign of life, the general bustle of everyday living, was nowhere to be seen or heard. It was only until a gust of warm air brought an old Nutri Bar wrapper tumbling by Kessler's feet that suggested anyone had ever lived in the town at all.

Doc, who had been lagging behind, quickened his pace to bring him alongside Kessler. "Maybe this will be easier than we had thought." His words burst with nervous energy, "We may make it after all." He pointed to a large building in the distance from which a huge column of wires and pipes towered above them connecting Acheron with the far distant roof of the cavern, "That must be where they process the plasma and where the furnace is."

"Quiet! Keep your voice down." Kessler barked a whisper, his head still bowed under his cowl, "Steady your breathing, Doc. Calm down."

"What was that?" Doc's confidence evaporated instantly as he turned to his left, his body shaking.

Kessler put an arm on the small of Doc's back and pushed him forward. "Keep walking." They marched at a fast pace, resisting the urge to run. The detective did not admit it, did not want to unhinge Doc even further, but he had heard it too. The rapid snarling and guttural growling were unmistakable. Seekers. He gave his friend a sideways glance and saw from his nervous fumbling and muttering that he was right on the edge of sanity. He closed his eyes and focused on walking, trying to ignore thoughts of the dead Vents decaying beyond the town walls or Beck's shredded body, trying to ignore the fact that they were walking right into the centre of this nightmare. Time ticked by. The road seemed to go on forever. On and on they trod, further and further into Acheron, at all times the noises were with them, increasing with every step. Hiding under their disguises not wanting to make a sound for fear of detection, they faced their fears alone. Kessler thought back to Corporal Eisen sealed in that room with his dead men, weeks spent hiding from this horror. He closed his eyes again, trying to force the abhorrence from his mind.

The feral howls and screeches were now coming from all directions. Kessler looked up from under his hood and saw a group of four or five Seekers loitering in the street, their hunched robed figures stumbling around in random directions, their large maws chattering in clicks and clacks rapidly spewing out their foul bestial language. Claws could be seen appearing from long sleeved robes and waved around frantically in dark excitement.

"Kes, I can't take it no more. They're sure to discover us, how did I ever agree to such an idiotic plan. They're everywhere." Doc's low whispers cracked and wavered in panic. He stumbled and fell into Kessler who quickly righted the terrified doctor with a rough push in the back.

"Easy Doc. Easy. Just ignore them." Sweat streamed down Kessler's neck and he could feel the pull of the chems leaving his body, energy sapping away underneath the stench and the thick material of his suit. Movement to their left made Doc whimper aloud and stumble back just as something brushed up against Kessler's right arm. With his hand still on Doc's back, he pulled him close. "Steady," he whispered, still hiding his face beneath the large cowl of his robe. He made sure to keep his hand on his Luther, ready in case they ran out of options.

The numbers of Seekers grew rapidly. They seemed to appear, staggering almost aimlessly, trancelike, out of the shadows either side of the street. Kessler found it difficult to move amongst them as they shoved and pulled at his robes. He stumbled and realised that Doc was not beside him and cursed himself for letting go of him. He turned around, desperately looking in all directions, taking deep breaths and reminding himself again and again that these creatures could not see or smell him. He began to make his way back down the street searching for his lost friend. It was difficult to see anything through the bodies, the mob had grown and he was now having to push his way through them. A loud grunt to his left made Kessler stop in his tracks. A particularly large creature had turned and shoved it's disgusting snout up against the detective's face. Thick, dark saliva dripped from red gums and blackened fangs, its breath putrid and heavy with death. He gagged into his vent as the creature pressed tight up against him, it's sweet, sickly smell overpowering his senses. A claw pulled at his robes and, for a moment, all was quiet as he stared into the dead, black eyes of the beast. The creature ceased its constant, random twitching and seemed to stare back at him. Beck had told them that these creatures could smell your soul, tell instantly how pure it was. He wondered what this foul beast would make of his.

Kessler found the energy to resume his search pushing past the Seeker until eventually he emerged from the throng to see Doc standing in the centre of the street. He had two of the creatures pawing and sniffing over him, their scaled faces snorting his robes. He pulled his hood down and stared straight at Kessler, a manic look in his eyes. He let out a loud moan as Kessler desperately waved at him to be quiet before he vomited in his helmet, splattering the inside of his visor. To Kessler's horror, his hand went for his rifle which was still strapped to his back. The detective leapt towards him in blind panic but before he reached his friend, the doctor screamed and fired four rounds, in quick succession, into the two creatures. The force of the point blank blasts threw the Seekers backwards. Huge smoking holes now existed where their chests had been.

Kessler's body landed heavily by Doc's side and immediately he hooked an arm around his friend's trembling form. Quickly drawing his Luther, he took frantic aim at the hordes around them. The group that Kessler had pushed past were the first to react to the commotion and were beginning to make their way towards them. Glancing up the street and back down towards the town gates, he saw more emerging from doorways, appearing from every shadow, all had their twitching snouts raised to the air trying to smell their way towards their prey. Kessler's finger was pressed against the trigger, his aim moving between groups of them, not sure where to concentrate his fire. "We still have a chance, they still haven't discovered us."

"I am sorry Kes, I just could not stand it anymore," Doc sobbed.

"It's ok." Kessler lied. They were surrounded. Hordes of the beasts closing in on them from all sides. A Seeker with huge bulbous warts that clung to a black and red face appeared over his shoulder. It snorted and sniffed, burying its snout into the small of his neck, rummaging around in the folds of his cloak as it tried to breach the pungent aroma protecting him from certain death.

Both lay rooted to the ground in terror. Kessler looked around him for an escape, time was running out. The red- and black-faced Seeker raised one of its huge claws and ran it up Doc's back, catching his cloak and lifting it off of him. Grabbing his friend, Kessler slowly backed away from the advancing creatures until both their backs pressed against the crumpled metal wall of one of the buildings which lined the side of the street.

They glanced at each other, a look of sheer panic in Doc's bespectacled bruised face and one of grim acceptance on Kessler's. "They're onto us, Doc." Kessler whispered as the electrical storm thundered around them, its blue light revealing even more of the creature's revolting faces, claws, fangs, each one different, some with short, stunted claws, others with long barbed horns, some with grotesque snouts covered with sores, others with sleek scaled maws. All were horrifying.

Kessler desperately looked around him for a way out. The monsters were closing in and he had to do something fast. He breathed heavily into his vent, 'Think, think.' words rattled around his mind over and over again. They were surrounded and there were too many of them to blast their way out, it would not be long until they were quickly overpowered and shredded to pieces. Kessler looked at his cowering friend and then back to his Luther which shook in his outstretched hand.

A guttural snort to Kessler's right alerted him to the red, bloated sores of another Seeker who appeared from the shadows. Its wart-infested maw opened as it extended a long black tongue. He curled up into a ball, waiting for the inevitable. A crowd formed around them as the horrors closed in on their scent, obscene fangs extending out of their jaws, huge twitching snouts catching glimpses of their prey, their chatter growing to a horrific crescendo. Kessler closed his eyes and waited for the end.

The crowd lunged forward all at once. The air was knocked out of Kessler's lungs as their sheer weight of numbers crushed them against the wall. Kessler and Doc held each other waiting for the bite or gouge that would bring about their grisly end.

A door suddenly burst open, giving way to the mob's desperate force. Doc and Kessler tumbled into the building. Kessler reacted quickly and threw his weight against the door, slamming it shut. Bodies pressed against it and he struggled to keep them out, his feet frantically trying to find grip on the smooth, worn stone floor, "Doc, help! Quickly or we're finished." His friend lay sprawled on the ground, "Snap out of it Doc, for the love of the light, pull yourself together!" He screamed. "I can't hold them much longer!"

Doc lifted himself up, rubbing the top of his head and moaned, "What happened?"

"Grab that chair, quick!" Claws appeared, poking out the sides of the door as the drone of the creature's howls entered the room, springing Doc into action. He grabbed the overturned chair and flung it against the door. Kessler braced it under the handle and frantically tried to get grip as the door opened and slammed shut in a flurry of claws and growls.

A piercing howl within the darkness of the room made Doc

spin round from his frenzied attempts to hold the tide of Seekers at bay. One of the creatures had appeared in the room. With its snout twitching and snorting their scent, it flung itself, with a newfound agility and speed, towards the desperate pair. In the low light of the room, Doc frantically searched the floor for his rifle when finally he found Kessler's Luther which had fallen by the detective's feet. "Kill the damned thing!" Kessler shouted. Doc fumbled with the unfamiliar weapon .

Suddenly the Seeker was upon him. Doc screamed as Kessler shouted, "Power the cells, the switch to the left of the trigger!"

"I... I... ahh!" Doc screamed as the creature's claw raked his leg but this was soon followed with the roar of searing hot plasma and the reassuring smell of burnt flesh. The doctor gasped for breath and held his bloody leg in agony.

Kessler finally secured the door and stumbled back into the dark room, collapsing against a table

"Light, you need light." A muffled voice came from somewhere in the dark.

Doc screamed as the squeals and creaks of the Seeker's evil chatter emerged from the far darkened corner of the room. "They keep coming, Kes!" Doc shouted as he found his rifle.

Kessler retched and broke into a spasm of coughing when again a voice appeared from the dark, "I told you. You need light."

The storm cracked outside. Through a window, its blue light flashed into the room revealing the claws, spikes and fangs of Seekers. Kessler braced himself for another attack. "Here they come again!"

"No!" A panel moved in the floor and bright yellow light banished the darkness from the hovel, "Quick, inside! Come to the light before more appear!" A battered helmet with a bright shining torch on a small round head with a thick dirty grey beard appeared from the floor. "What're you waiting for, hurry, sirs!"

Both Kessler and Doc lifted their exhausted bodies and lurched forward, falling down the hole into a tangled heap. The panel was quickly pulled over, followed by a sharp hiss of air as it was sealed tight. Kessler closed his eyes and curled up as exhaustion overpowered him.

·TECH OPEK·

Kessler eventually opened his eyes to see a small face peering down at him, the light on his helmet blinding him. He shouted, "Get that damn torch out of my eyes," and pushed him away.

"Quiet, they're right above us," his high-pitched voice squeaked as he whispered, raising a finger to his mouth, urging both Doc and Kessler to be quiet. He turned to Doc, the deep wrinkles on his brow furrowed in concern, "He's a user. Has he taken it? Is he chasing the light?"

Doc, still shaking, rubbed his eyes and tried to focus, "Chasing the light? I don't understand, I…"

"Lux? Does he use it?" He stepped back and picked up a large piston wrench that was nearly the same size as him.

"No, I don't take it." Kessler coughed and his chest wheezed and rattled as he struggled for breath.

Immediately the small man's expression softened. He took off his helmet, patted his grubby brow with a piece of cloth and smiled back gesturing them forward, "Then you're welcome here. Quickly, and quietly, follow me."

With an audible heave he lifted the huge wrench onto his shoulders and scampered through what appeared to be a long tunnel. Kessler, on hands and knees, followed, stopping every so often to wait for Doc who struggled to move in the confined space, his injured leg causing him much discomfort. The passageway itself was a small tunnel packed with piping and wiring lit by hundreds of chem lamps that flickered a bright yellow light and filled the space with smoke. After crawling for some time, the compact space opened up into a large area which had many more passageways leading off of it. Two make-shift beds had been constructed from crates and rubber tubing. Boxes of food, ranging from Nutri Bars to vaced proteins, had been stacked up against a far wall. A young boy of even smaller stature than the man who rescued them sat on the floor in a cloud of smoke, a magma stick in one hand and a piece of circuit board in the other.

"What is this place?" Kessler still rubbed his eyes as they got used to the fumes from all the lamps, "Where are we?"

The small man walked into the centre of the room, turned to look at both Doc and Kessler and spoke with a rapid excitement, "Welcome to my home, well, what is now my home. Please, take off your suits, I'm sure you are tired and I know they can be very cumbersome. I assure you it's perfectly safe. These tunnels are still pressurised, the atmosphere controls still operational, thanks to my son and I." Doc and Kessler stared back at him in silence as the reality of their escape from the Seekers began to sink in. "I have to admit, with those cloaks and the smell, ugh," he pinched his nose to emphasise his point, "you sure do stink of them, I didn't know what to make of you two at first but when I heard the shrill Hightown squeal from your good self," he gestured towards Doc who had now sat down on the floor and began to attend to his wound, "disguises I guess." Silence filled the room as the three stared at each other before he continued, "Please forgive me, where are my manners! My name is Primary Engineer Opek and this is my son, Apprentice Third Class Bendle." Standing at around two feet in height, Opek smiled back at them. He wore extremely dirty red overalls and a short-sleeved shirt that at one time had probably been close to white. Long tufts of grey hair covered his wrinkled face, some spouting out of his large ears. His son had black hair with a young, child-like face. He wore the same uniform as his father, although his overalls were a couple of sizes too big for him. Big blue eyes stared back at them from under a dented hard hat.

Opek played nervously with a loose button on his shirt before continuing but this time slowed and steadied his voice, "Apologies, it has been so long since we have had company and the excitement just got to me. We have been so very lonely. Are you hungry? You look hurt, I have medical supplies and can help tend your wounds although, I admit, I'm no doctor."

Kessler looked down at his robes. In the bright light of the room the full extent of their horror could be easily seen. He pulled them over his head and threw the gut- and blood-encrusted cloth away. He looked at Doc taking his heat suit off. His small bruised and bloodied, skinny frame was lost in the thick heavy material. His manicured hands and immaculately-groomed appearance long gone. They truly had become monsters, he half sighed and half laughed to himself.

Opek stared at Kessler, examining his appearance and spoke as if reading his thoughts, "These difficult times have changed us all." He glanced at his son before clearing his throat and continuing, "But they are just clothes, they can be discarded and new ones found." He pinched his nose with a clip taken from a shirt pocket, picked up the robes and pushed them down a chute, "An incinerator. Well, it used to be one before everything happened. At least that awful smell won't be bothering us anymore, eh?" He continued to smile. "You can take off your respirators down here, these tunnels are filled with Ox.

Doc discarded his robes with similar disgust and they both sat on the floor which had been covered with a thin piece of padded plastic, "My name is Kessler and this is Doctor Galloway." He took off his near-empty respirator and took long deep breaths of the cool, oxygen rich air. "Thank you for saving us, we owe you our lives."

"You were lucky I was working the tunnel close by to hear your voices." Opek spoke while he pushed Doc's bloodied clothes down the chute, "I have spares that you can have if needed, ones that do not carry that awful stench."

"Thank you." Doc spoke between long intakes of breath.

Kessler looked over his new surroundings, "You're a Tech aren't you? I've seen your kind before working the factories and plants around Midtown."

"That's what we do. We make and fix things that others cannot." He stood up and went over to a box and produced a couple of hydration pouches and vacs of protein, "Here take this, you look like you could use them."

Kessler and Doc drank the water and wolfed down the contents of the vacs. The detective's hands shook as he squeezed the food supplement into his mouth, his tired and aching body ravenously craving every last drop of the tasteless synthetic paste. Once he was finished, he looked up to see Opek smiling at him and, looking at the empty pouches and vacs at his feet, wiped his mouth and spoke, feeling slightly embarrassed, "I didn't realise how hungry I was."

Opek continued to smile, "Our home is your home." He turned and walked over to his son, "Bendle, bring over the chem burner and a couple of blankets for our guests," then began moving around taking various items from the many makeshift shelves that littered the room's perimeter.

As the two Techs darted around in a flurry of movement, Kessler sat taking deep breaths, wheezing and coughing as his body took in the oxygen. Doc gasped and winced as he inspected the angry gash on his leg which wept blood onto the clear plastic floor. Soon Opek had finished laying out a seating area. In the centre of the room he placed a pot of water atop the chem burner and lit it with a magma stick, "Please, join us and have a drink. I have ale and hot cha?"

Kessler sat down and took a cup of ale and eagerly drank it down before asking for another, "That's good stuff."

"Yes, I managed to swipe a couple of barrels from the kitchens before we came down here. Epsom had them all well stocked."

"Epsom Energy?"

"Yes. They run Acheron, well, did run Acheron."

Through the dirt and grime Kessler's eyes glanced Epsom's lightning bolt symbol above his name tag, "You work for them?"

"All my life. The Epsom family have been good to us. Provided us with skills and tools, fed us and kept us safe. Isn't that right, son?

"Yes, pa." Bendle smiled and saluted by tapping his oversized hard hat before returning to cleaning his father's piston wrench.

Opek spoke with pride as he wiped his grimy name tag on his overalls. "I was sent down here a few years back to repair the generators and to help keep the furnaces running. There was so much work to be done that we ended up staying in Acheron. With the Council's hunger for energy there was always plenty of work to do."

"Working with plasma is a dangerous business." Kessler spoke as he feverishly gulped down Opek's booze.

"Yes, but essential if the city is to keep running, keep providing warmth and light to its citizens." Kessler nearly choked on his ale as Opek quoted the popular Council mantra. He had not had many dealings with the Techs of Dis. They were never allowed to have much interaction with citizens, but the servants of the Council were always in the background keeping everything running. They were known to be fiercely loyal to their corporate masters. Kessler looked at the beaming face of Opek and thought that he had never seen anybody smile so much. Opek's continued chatter brought his attention back to what the Tech was saying, "These pipes go far down below our feet where it finds the plasma that drives the turbines and gives us the vast amount of energy we need to power Dis. Unfortunately the heat cools over time making us dig deeper and deeper. Epsom does not look kindly on power failures so we are always digging, always searching for more plasma." He nodded and stirred the bubbling water, "You're right though, it's very dangerous, the machinery has to operate under vast amounts of pressure. There are often accidents, difficulties keeping the furnaces going. I remember, one day there was a terrible explosion. One of the thermal pipelines caught fire and so many were injured, so many killed by the blast." He again looked over towards his son for a few moments and eventually returned his focus back to Kessler who was staring at the flickering flame of the chem burner. "I'm sorry, I do talk a lot at the best of times."

The pot of water began to bubble loudly prompting Opek to sprinkle some powder into the liquid and immediately the spiced aroma of cha filled the room. Doc hobbled over into the light from where he was attending to his injury and sat down with a sigh, "Proper spiced cha, I never thought I would smell that beautiful scent again,"

"Epsom are a great believer in providing its employees with the very best. An appreciated worker appreciates great work." Opek poured the hot liquid into a cup and passed it to Doc. He did the same for himself and his son, "Bendle, your cha is ready."

"Tech, I do believe that my love for this delicious drink may just be as strong as your love for Epsom." Doc eagerly drank.

Moments passed with the four silently drinking, each breathing in the relaxing spiced fumes. After finishing another cup of ale, Kessler spoke, "Opek, what happened here?"

Finishing his drink, Opek took off his hard hat, put his hands through his thick grey hair and sighed, "Yes, there's no getting away from it, no forgetting what has happened." He filled his cup with more cha before continuing, "In the months that followed another explosion, this time in an exploratory passage, one of our deepest, strange men began to appear in town. It's very rare to see odd faces this deep in the city as only those licensed by Epsom or us Techs are allowed here, however these men were not citizens of Dis at all." He sighed again, "They were bigmen like you sirs but…" The Tech took another sip of cha, scrunched up his face and closed his eyes, his smile now gone.

"Go on, who were they?" Doc urged.

Kessler leaned forward towards the light, "Sorry that we're reminding you of these horrors. We've seen a few ourselves on our travels."

Again moments passed without a word until the quiet was broken by a loud wail and creaking that reverberated around the room.

"Nothing to worry about, it's just the sound of the pipes straining under the pressure. They are used to being alive with the buzz of energy from far below but are dead now. Apart from the odd energy cell I can scavenge, we are reduced to burning chem to keep us warm, and, of course, to keep the Seekers away, they so love the dark." Opek looked up from his drink and spoke, "I'm sorry for my weakness. Talk of what happened here hurts. To not here the buzz of the generators, the hiss of pistons and the chatter of machinery breaks my heart. You asked about what these bigmen were like. Well, I don't know if they were men at all. They hid in the shadows with their black eyes and pale faces, whispered words in bigmen's heads, tried to get them to do things for them."

"The Malebranche?" Doc had wrapped his hands around his hot drink and breathed in its vapours.

"Yes, I would later know to call them that. They began to appear soon after the explosion when the town was bustling with gossip and fear. Citizens and Techs had been disappearing. Nobody knew where they were going as, down here, there aren't many places to disappear to. They just seemed to vanish. These strange men whispered promises of salvation from the troubles ahead. They said they would offer us light in the darkness, warmth and protection. I tried not to listen to them. I said to them that Epsom provide me and my family with all these things but, still, the voices continued. Their solution, this promise of light and warmth, soon appeared. Take a hit of it and all will be ok, they told us. Most of the bigmen did and, I'm sorry to say some Techs too. I'd never known Techs to partake in chems but some took it, the rest, those who didn't, just disappeared." He took his son's hat off and ruffled his black hair affectionately. "Eventually, those taking it began to not show up for work. Important maintenance wasn't completed on the furnaces, the pistons finally stopped on the main generator as there was nobody to operate them. Acheron, despite all the dangers and setbacks, had never stopped running to my knowledge but that all changed when those strange bigmen began to appear." Opek put down his cup and continued, "Techs always turn up for work, sure there was the odd incident, I remember Gibbs had drank too much of his home brew and broke Tech Hector's fisson belt. He was so mad, but it was soon dealt with by the Watch, both soon friends again." Opek looked down at his drink, "All gone now, Hector was taken down below and Gibbs was soon chasing that light of theirs." Opek rubbed his eyes, "People down here were always focused on their work, keeping the energy flowing, that is what Epsom wanted and that is what we did. Now Acheron is quiet, the energy rages above us unharnessed. Soon it will all run dark. Heartbreaking." He started to sob quietly into his hands but quickly stopped when he saw that Bendle was looking at him. "People just left their posts. Good Techs, I've known all my life," he shook his head and sighed, "a good Tech never leaves his post, rule number one. Isn't that right son?"

"Yes, pa!"

Opek continued, "I've seen some terrible things while we have been hiding here, watched others do terrible things."

"Lux." Kessler sighed.

"That's what they call it. When the Seekers began to arrive, those not on Lux were all killed. It was all I could do to grab some supplies and take Bendle and hide down here in these tunnels. Nobody knows them better than I do."

"More news of people disappearing." Doc looked at Kessler who nodded.

"You've heard of this happening elsewhere?" Opek rubbed his hands near the flame.

"I first encountered their work up in District 1. Bodies of Dregs taking Lux were beginning to pile up in the skin labs. In D2 citizens had been going missing for months, whole sectors are now empty. I've seen citizens, Dregs, Mutes and even a priest all succumb to Lux. The Malebranche seem to be very persuasive indeed."

The flame of the chem burner began to lessen and Opek refilled it with more oil. The Ox-rich controlled atmosphere of the room was cold and the four leaned close to the warmth of the burner.

They each sat and stared into the dancing flames in silence. Kessler enjoyed the Tech's ale and eagerly drank down the frothy liquid. It had a thick, smoky, metallic taste that reminded him of the bitter, rancid Midtown air whose harsh conditions he was beginning to miss. This far down city, in this strange place, underground, surrounded by rock, plasma fields and raging electrical storms, he actually missed his rundown apartment in Midtown. He felt light-headed. The room was filled with a haze of smoke from the chem lamps and the heady spices of the cha. His body ached and his eyes stung and he felt the inevitable hunger begin to creep up on him. It slowly clawed its way up his insides, raking across his throat and coiling tightly around him. The itch behind his eyes was almost unbearable. He knew it would only get worse and drank another large gulp of brew trying to forget the horrors for now and looked up to see that

Opek's son had fallen asleep. He was now curled up in a thick blanket. Doc sat resting his head in his hands, the flame of the burner reflected in his spectacles as he slowly drank his cha.

Opek ended the quiet, "May I ask what you are doing down here? I've not seen anyone, much less a bigman from above the Rim, in a long time." He looked down at his small hands and shook his head, "Long time," he repeated forlornly.

"A friend of ours was taken from us by the Seekers and we have been told she was brought to Acheron. We've come to get her back."

Opek rubbed his beard in thought, "I've never heard of anyone returning from down below." The Tech paused for a moment before continuing, "You must love her very much to risk everything. I've never known anyone to be so brave as to walk amongst them like you two did up there. Hiding your scent behind their own. Very impressive indeed." He shook his head, "But once the Malebranche have you, you never come back. I'm sorry to be the bearer of bad news after you have travelled so far. The boy and I know more than anyone about the loss you feel, he lost his mother to them, she disappeared soon after the tunnel collapsed many months ago."

Kessler looked into Opek's eyes which shimmered with sadness despite his broad smile, "I'm sorry for your loss but the girl we're looking for is nothing to me like that. I'm a detective that she hired. My role in this is purely financial, I'm afraid."

"And doctor, how do you find yourself on this perilous journey?"

Doc had his eyes closed. His slender face a garish combination of reds, yellows and oranges from the monster's gore and dark purple bruising had spread across his cheeks and jaw line. His nose was also bloodied and broken, a far cry from his usual manicured, Hightown finish. Kessler looked at his friend and felt a harsh pang of guilt, "I forced him…" he muttered under his breath.

Doc spoke, interrupting Kessler, "I have known Kes for a long time, I'm just here to help out a friend." He looked at the detective, blinked and, with a bloodied hand, adjusted his now bent spectacles. He tried to smile but winced at the pain from his swollen face. He had lost a couple of teeth. It may have been the pain, tiredness or sheer relief to have escaped the Seeker's clutches but Kessler roared a hearty laugh. He could not remember the last time he had laughed so hard.

"You look ridiculous, Doc, but I'm glad you're here with me."

"Yes, well, I'm not, I assure you," he smiled, "besides you have not seen what you look like."

The laughter was infectious and Opek began to chuckle. "It's good to laugh. This causes for some of Acheron's finest spirits. It tastes slightly of machine oil but warms the heart! I've been saving it for a special occasion and I believe this must be it."

Kessler's laughter had developed into a cough. "Now that is the best idea I've heard in a while."

"And you doctor?"

"Not my usual tipple, but on this occasion I'll take you up on the offer."

Kessler held out his cup. Doc and Opek stopped laughing suddenly as both stared at the detective's shaking hand. "It's ok it will soon pass." Kessler dropped his cup and rubbed his hand self-consciously. Opek looked at Doc and then returned his attention to the detective but Kessler spoke before the Tech could, "I said it will soon pass," he picked up his cup and held it out, "now some of that spirit if you would?"

"I don't mean to pry but I don't need to see a shaking hand to tell me you are a user. I can see it in your eyes, Mr Kessler."

"Yes I did, I am. But I don't do Lux. That's different."

Opek spoke slowly as he poured the spirit into Kessler's cup, "But you are controlled by those that supply your chems and eventually a horrible death follows. Is Lux so much different than any other chem? Sure it is more powerful but the ending is the same. Death."

"Don't compare me to those things above us or the Chaff that chase the light. I'm different." Kessler was growing irritable, his mind racing, searching for examples to convince himself he was right, "I'm better than that."

"I apologise, I don't mean to offend. I've been down here for so long with only my son for company, I forget my manners. I know you are not like them. To come all this way to save someone is proof enough of that."

Kessler studied Bethany's cross which now hung around his neck, "Save the praise, Opek. I'm no saint." The potent drink was heavy in his stomach and he could feel it work its way through his system, its heady grip tightening around him. The smoky tendrils from the chem lamps flowed and pranced around the room, reminding him how tired he really was. "I've done some things in the past I am not proud of."

"No one is perfect in this world, Mr Kessler." The detective looked back down again at the cross and thought about Bethany. "That's an interesting necklace you are wearing." Opek leaned forward to examine it closer and Kessler took it from around his neck and held it up to the light.

"It was precious to Bethany, the girl who was taken from us. It belonged to her uncle. This cross represented her faith in a man who sacrificed everything so that we could live. I look forward to giving it back to her."

"Yes, I am familiar with the Christian faith from what I watch on the infogrammes." A serious look took hold of Opek's features, "The Council do not speak favourably of it and I have to admit I tend to agree. What can it offer us when compared to the Council? They feed us and keep us warm, make productive citizens of bigmen and keep us Techs happy with our machines." Opek looked around at his surroundings, "Well, most of the time." He chuckled to himself and took a drink.

"She would say that it offers us hope, hope that there is more to this world than the corporations and the Council, more to Dis than darkness, rain and lack of good air, more than just surviving every single day in this damned place."

Opek stared at Kessler, his big blue eyes and toothy smile appearing only to show kindness, "Life is what we make it, I suppose. Although, it's easy for me to say, I'm only a simple Tech and have only a few simple goals in life. Maintain the machines for Epsom and look after my family. That is all. I do not bother with matters outside of my job and family as most bigmen do not look kindly on us, are uncomfortable being in our company and think that because we're small we're not so important."

Kessler looked at the Tech and his sleeping son. He was right, they were looked at as servants to be used to service Dis, only there to help maintain the machines. Tools to do a job. Their small size was particularly useful for climbing down the millions of pipes and service ducts throughout the city. It was a dangerous job and many perished while serving their corporate masters. Kessler had never thought about how difficult their lives must be, never looked at their oil-stained smiling faces and thought of them as citizens. They were always just there to serve. "I'm sorry." Opek just smiled back. A sharp pain fired in Kessler's head making him wince in agony, reminding him of what he had to do, "Tell me about where they take the lost."

"Soon after the explosion and the tunnel collapsing, the furnaces stopped running. Governor Tillbrook ordered the construction of a council chamber, a place to meet and come together as a community, right over where the furnace room was. Everyone thought we were going to fix it, that's what we do after all, but the Governor was not interested. He wanted a place where we could be together through, as he put it, the difficult times. I heard that an Epsom official came down asking why we were not producing the energy, but I'm not sure what happened to him." Opek cleared his throat, "People became restless, we had no power, no light but Governor Tillbrook had the Watch make sure we followed his orders. Very soon the new council chamber was built but by then people began to disappear and that's when Lux started to be taken. Citizens stopped working and as the chem spread they all went to this new place. It's a large room at the centre of which is the old furnace and entrance to the Core Tunnel. That's where everyone goes."

"We need to get down there." Kessler looked over at Doc who had now curled up in the floor covered in one of Opek's plastic blankets. His eyes were heavy with tiredness and the effects of the brew. "We'll just rest here for a couple of hours if that's ok?"

"Of course. Stay as long as you need." Opek's glance returned to his son, "We really do appreciate the company."

Kessler lay down close to the chem lamp, the smoke drawing sleep ever closer, "You should come with us."

"I can't, I have my son to think about. Like I said, nobody returns once they disappear.

"Your supplies will not last long," sleep began to pull Kessler into unconsciousness, "Opek, what stops you from taking it? Embracing the light?"

"Why, faith, sir. Faith that Epsom will provide for us, faith that they will come and save us."

"Yes… Beth had faith."

"Well, maybe she still does, sir."

Kessler fell into a deep, troubled slumber.

·THE PLAN·

"*H*elp me, Kes. I can't breathe." *A familiar voice reached out to him from somewhere in the darkness. He raised his hands and pressed them against the cold stone that imprisoned him.*

"Hello? I can't get out."

"Kes, I'm all alone. It's dark." *The voice, Bethany's, cracked and wavered with fear.*

"Don't move. I'll come to you." *Kessler kicked the ceiling of his tomb hard but it would not budge.*

Bethany, somewhere in the distance, started sobbing, "Please don't take me there, please don't. I..." *Her pleading ended in a shrill scream which was cut off abruptly. Silence now filled the black void where her voice had been.*

"Beth!" *Kessler shouted,* "Beth, you ok?" *He punched kicked and yelled but could not free himself. The heavy choking, acrid smell of smoke began to fill his tomb and with it a scorching heat which boiled around him.* "Ahh!" *Kessler screamed himself hoarse,* "Help!" Somebody!"

He coughed and spluttered as the smoke filled his lungs, his body jerking manically as it frantically begged for air that was not there. The blunt wave of unconsciousness began to take hold of Kessler as the end approached and he began to drift away.

Bright light and the purest of air suddenly gripped him as the lid of his tomb was lifted away to reveal a light blue sky. A hand came into view with an open palm upon which rested a small sphere of bright light.

"Lux Ferre."

Kessler was thrown back into reality by the hammer blows of a thunderous headache. He raged aloud as bright light tried to invade his senses. He kicked out and hit something and this was followed by voices that added to the din.

"Easy, Kes. Opek, hand me over the medivent from my bag." The apparatus was placed over Kessler's face, the rush of medicated Ox relaxing his breathing. A sharp pain in his arm soon followed, "Just to help with the pain."

Kessler opened his eyes to see Doc, Opek and Bendle standing over him. "What you all looking at? Give me space to breathe." He wiped sweat from his brow with his sleeve.

"You were dreaming again, flailing your arms around like a mad man and you managed to open up the wound in your stomach." Doc spoke as he injected Kessler with more chems, "You haven't been using that Prinax like I told you to so it's become infected."

"Well it slipped my mind. I've been busy."

"Well, it is finished now. I took the last of it for my leg if that is ok with you."

"I heard her, Doc. Heard her crying for help." Kessler panted, his heart thundered in his chest.

"Who? Heard who?"

"Beth. She needed my help but I couldn't get to her." Kessler pushed Doc out of the way and barked at Opek, "These dreams, the Malebranche's voice you talk of, are they real? The images in my dreams, do they really happen?"

Doc pushed Kessler's weak hand away, "He is delirious."

"I've been told that they're more than dreams, you see what the Malebranche want you to see. Some tried to sleep as little as possible but it didn't matter in the end." Opek turned to Doc and spoke with concern, "He's in no state to travel anywhere."

"I know, but he will not listen." Doc returned to the far side of the room where he had been dismantling his rifle.

"You don't have these dreams?"

"No. Most Techs don't dream, it seems to effect bigmen more than us." Kessler looked at Doc who held his stare for a few moments before returning to his rifle.

The detective tried to find his voice through a dry and raw throat, "I just need some water."

Doc laughed but his face was serious, "You need more than water."

"Yes, but what I need is not here." Kessler shouted out suddenly in a rage that swept over him. He started to shake as waves of heat overcame him. He grabbed Doc's bag and started throwing its contents across the room, his hands a blur of movement, his body jerking in a series of convulsions.

Opek stuttered, "Doctor, what's wrong with him? Is there anything I can do?"

"No. It's withdrawal. He wants a hit of sim and we don't have any."

Kessler shouted, "Yes, maybe I missed one, maybe I put them in your bag instead of mine!"

"Kes, you know we don't have any."

"I don't believe you." He had a wild look about him. His shoulder-length hair was matted in sweat, a thick, tangled grey-speckled beard covered his face and saliva dripped freely from his mouth and onto the floor as he feverishly looked through Doc's medical supplies. "You just want them for yourself! Where are they?" He barked.

"He's gone mad." Opek shielded his son's eyes and held him close.

Kessler's hands went to his eyes, "This itch is never ending. I just want it to stop tormenting me!"

Doc leapt onto the raging, twitching detective and jabbed him with a syringe. Kessler slumped to the floor as the sedative took effect. Doc slumped against the wall, his chest heaving with the exertion. "That should calm him down."

*

Blurred images took a while to come into focus. From the haze, Kessler could hear Opek's unmistakable upbeat tones humming to a tune he did not recognise. Something or someone was standing above him. Bendle. "Water?" His mouth felt heavy. Whatever Doc had given him still lay thick in his veins.

"Pa, the bigman's awake! I think he wants some water."

"Great. Go get him a hydration pouch from the store, son."

Kessler, having been lying prone on the clear plastic floor, propped himself up against a wall and waited for the feeling to return to his legs. "Doc, you wait till I get my legs back and then it's my turn to knock you out."

"Now, Mr Kessler," Opek stopped packing ration packs into a satchel and turned to face him, "Doctor Galloway had your best interests at heart. You were only going to do yourself an injury."

"Humph." Kessler grunted, reached into his pocket and held out a cigar, "Hey Opek, give us a light?" The Tech approached him and, with his magma stick, showered the room in light for a few seconds. Kessler coughed as the smoke cleared and inspected the glowing embers, "Thanks."

Doc knelt beside him and inspected his bandages. "Much better." He batted away smoke and smiled, "Back to your usual self I see."

"Yea," Kessler looked sheepishly around him, "sorry about before, I have it under control now."

Doc leaned close and spoke in a low whisper, "It will get worse before it will get better. Without proper medical help, without the right drugs and monitoring, the withdrawal can kill you."

"Just patch me up, Doc, you know the routine."

Doc changed the subject as he injected a stimulant into the detective, "The dreams are stronger here. I couldn't get much sleep."

Kessler cleared his throat, "The less time spent down here the better." He spoke quietly to Doc and then raised his voice for Opek to hear, "We have spent too long here, we must be on our way. We can't thank you enough for your hospitality, Opek. It has been a while since we've experienced such kindness."

"I'm coming with you." Bendle came up the ladder from the store and his dad put his arm around him, "I've been up all night thinking over what we spoke about and you're right, we can't stay here. Our food will not last another month."

"Listen Opek, we had quite a lot of that brew of yours and, well, maybe its best that you stayed. Where we're going is no place for a kid."

"I'm old enough, sir." Bendle's voice had the high-pitch tones of a young child but spoke with confidence, "I may be small in stature but I'll be fourteen years old in a few weeks. I can look after myself." He held a large servo hammer aloft and hit it hard against the wall, "I'm not a kid anymore."

"Easy son." Opek patted the young Tech lovingly on his shoulder before returning his attention to Kessler, "I've thought it through and we'll go with you. I even have an idea on how we can escape up city, get us as far away from this place as possible."

Kessler looked over at Doc who had just finished cleaning his Lazarus rifle. He flicked the safety off and with a buzz the rifle was ready to fire, "Listen to him, it's our best hope, Kes."

"Ok. So what's the plan?"

Opek turned to Bendle, his smile even broader than usual, "Son, go get me one of those spare battery packs please."

"I thought they were for emergencies only?"

"This is an emergency. Please son, quickly." Opek pushed Bendle away and walked over to a blank monitor on the far wall. "These service tunnels run the length of Acheron and are all linked to the furnace room. We can reach it down that tunnel." Opek pointed towards one of the many shafts that led off from his room. "Look, see?"

Bendle had returned with the battery pack and Opek connected it to the console. In a whirl of light it brought up a 3D map showing the network of tunnels which ran throughout Acheron, at the centre of which the Core Tunnel could easily be seen. Opek typed in a command on the keyboard and out of the maze of passageways their route lit up with a buzz. "It should only take us a couple of hours to get there."

"Ok. Surely it can't be that easy." Kessler took a puff on his cigar.

"No it certainly will not be. I know that the tunnel on the other side of this airlock here," he pointed at the flickering map, "is full of Seekers, at least it was when we first escaped down here. It will be tricky getting through them. There's also no power and it's open to the rads so that means we'll have to suit up and take Ox with us. After that, in the furnace room itself and beyond into the Core Tunnel, I'm not sure what awaits us."

"Ok. So we go down this tunnel towards the Core, take a look around, find Bethany and escape. How do we get away from all this, how do we get back home?"

Doc was looking closely at the holo map, fiddling with his bent spectacles. "Damn these things, I should have got implants a long time ago."

"That's the interesting part." Opek looked very pleased with himself, "Just above the Core Tunnel is a Tech shaft that runs all the way up through Downtown to District 1. It's not operational as the power is out but with these energy cells I might be able to get it up and running."

"A Tech shaft?" Doc did not sound convinced.

"Tech Shaft Six. Epsom Energy built it because so many Techs were dying trying to keep the furnace running. They used the shaft to get us down as quickly as possible, replace those that had fallen. It will be a tight fit, it was never meant to be used by bigmen but we will manage. Somehow."

"Do you think we can actually do it?" Doc asked Kessler.

Opek spoke up. "It can be done but, he looked up at Doc's rifle and took a deep breath and shook his head, "Us Techs do not like using weaponry, we can run almost any engine, fix any machine or operate any computer, but using weapons, no. I'm afraid me and my son will be relying on you to protect us from the Seekers." He looked back to the map, "Finding your friend, Bethany, may be impossible, we do not know what is waiting for us down there. Our escape is also uncertain. Not only does Tech Shaft Six have no power but it may have been damaged in the explosion when the tunnel collapsed. I'm not sure what condition its in."

"Great. Let's suit up and get this over with." Doc moved to the entrance of the tunnel.

"Are you sure you still want to come?" Kessler spoke to Opek before joining Doc.

"Some chance of living is better than none at all." Opek reached down for his tool bag, slung it round his shoulder and picked up the piston wrench, "Come on son, make sure you stay close to us and stay within the light at all times."

·FALTERING LIGHT·

The shaft was lit with numerous lamps the light from which was dulled by their acrid smoke which clogged the tunnel's small space. Kessler led the group, all crawling, crouching low in single file. His free hand supported his weight as he leaned against the series of pipes and wiring that ran along the walls, the other held his Luther, ready to deal with whatever dangers lay ahead. The new bandages which Doc had applied to his wounds felt good and the stimulant delivered much needed energy to his aching limbs. Opek and his son followed, their two small bodies looking almost identical in their red Epsom heat suits, their swinging lamps and torches lighting the way. The only difference between the two was the large magma stick which Bendle carried in place of his father's piston wrench. Both moved down the tunnel with the same stride, both swinging their tool bag in unison. Years spent working together within the inner workings of Dis had created a bond between them, not just the close bond developed between father and son but a relationship forged over time between a master and his apprentice. Kessler had watched how the two worked together back in the room, had seen the respect which Opek had for his son, had seen the pride at which Bendle took in his work and his desire to please his father. Down amongst all the chems, through the thick haze of addiction and bad memories, Kessler felt the empty void. He had never had that in his life, something decent that was not corroded by this damned city, something not tainted by the filth which spewed out of its every pore. As he waited for the group to clamber up the tunnel, their scrambling footfalls sending creaks and groans up through the pipes, his thoughts turned to Macy. Somewhere, far, far above him, he hoped she was in hiding, away from the clutches of Little Chi, away from the dangers which he had brought upon them. He looked down and saw that his hand was clutching Bethany's cross, and wondered if she was still alive. He took a sip of water and tried to banish such thoughts from his mind, he didn't have time to dwell on such things, he had to remain sharp, get the job done. The two Techs had caught up with him and immediately began checking their equipment, Opek checking the power gauge on his spare energy cells, Bendle powering up his magma stick and rummaging through his tool bag. "Doc, you ok?" Kessler tried not to speak too loudly, aware of the danger around them.

Doc's shuffling form quickened its pace and eventually slumped by Bendle and rested on the floor, his breathing heavy, "Sorry, it is so hot down here I find it difficult to breathe and these damn suits are difficult to move in."

"I know. How's that leg of yours?" Kessler knelt by Doc.

"Painful but I'll live." He was sweating profusely. His heavily bandaged leg made walking difficult and he cradled it carefully as he sat on the tunnel's floor fumbling with his rifle and satchel which were both slung over his shoulder.

"Do you want me to carry your bag for you?" Kessler reached down to take it.

"I'm fine thank you." Doc pushed Kessler's hand away. "How far does this tunnel go on for, Opek?"

"It'll take us another thirty minutes before we get to the bulkhead and then, beyond that, about another hour to the furnace room."

"You look tired, Doc." Kessler's hoarse voice coughed words.

"So do you," Doc replied.

"Have some water and up your Ox if we need to." Kessler put his arm around him and leaned towards his friend, "Nearly finished Doc, the end's in sight." He smiled and gave him a friendly shove.

"That's what I'm afraid off," Doc smiled back, "I want to lay off the Ox until we need it, just in case."

The group continued their way up the tunnel and soon they reached the bulkhead. Opek immediately moved close and brought his wrench up to the opening mechanism, "With the power down we have to open this the old fashioned way. Make sure your vents and suits are secure."

Kessler placed a hand onto the airlock, "You said back at the room that beyond this door Seekers lie waiting for us?"

"Yes, unfortunately."

"Ok. Everyone turn on your torches. If the power is going to be out then there will be the darkness for those creature to appear in. Opek, you and Bendle, once you have opened that door, stay close between myself at the front and Doc who will bring up the rear. Ok?"

Both Opek and Bendle spoke in unison, "Yes sir!"

Opek already had his suit secured and was checking to make sure his son's was on correctly. He spoke slowly to him, "It will be dark, stay in the light." He adjusted the brightness of his son's lamp by twisting it clockwise and placed a finger under his chin. He raised Bendle's face up so that he was looking into the eyes of his father. Opek smiled and playfully tapped his son's visor before looking up at Kessler and Doc.

After a nod from the detective, Opek, with a heave and a puff of his cheeks, pulled down the wrench, turning the valve which hissed and whined and eventually, with a loud metallic clunk, the bulkhead disappeared into the walls of the tunnel. Immediately Kessler's ears popped and the group was hit with a torrent of hot air that brought with it the smell of death and decay. Their four beams of light pierced the darkness a few feet ahead of them, revealing the ravaged state of the tunnel. Oil dripped from torn pipes covering everything in its greasy slime. Shredded wires, capacitors, relays and insulation foam hung from the ceiling and lay scattered throughout the shaft. Everything had a heavy industrial, chemical stench to it.

"It's worse than I thought." Opek ran over a particularly large hole in the side of a conduit and shook his head with worry, "Oh my, this just isn't right. This will take a long time to fix, if it can be fixed at all."

Bendle put his arm around his father, smiling reassuringly, "Don't worry, pa. Us Techs can fix anything."

"You're right, son. Of course, you're right."

"Opek, I think we have more to worry about than the state of this tunnel." Doc scratched his head and looked at Kessler in exasperation.

"You don't understand, doctor. A lot of time, energy and lives went into creating the machines and the infrastructure that power the furnaces. Raw plasma is such an unforgiving resource, extremely difficult to find, nearly impossible to harness. Many Techs have fallen to bless Dis with the energy that everyone takes for granted. I know personally eighteen techs that died servicing these tunnels this past year. I hate to see their work desecrated, destroyed like this." He hugged Bendle as he inspected the wreckage, "Look son, this is the conduit that Tech Higgs built to carry the plasma overflow away from the Core Tunnel's generator. Do you remember the problems he had keeping the flow stable?"

"I do, pa but he did it in the end."

"Yes, he did. Look, there is his field dampener, he had to wait weeks to get that sent down from above." Opek shook his head, "A real shame."

Kessler interrupted, "Doc's right, Opek. We don't have time to stand around here, it's not safe."

Opek's gaze went from the torn conduit to Kessler. Behind his visor tears streamed down over his cheeks and into his beard, "Lead the way, Mr Kessler."

The group shuffled through what was left of the tunnel, piercing the thick shroud of darkness with their shaking light. Every so often something would brush up against Kessler's burly figure or catch on Doc's rifle making the two jump with a start. After a while the detective stopped and raised his hand for those behind him to follow suit.

"What is it Kes?"

"Can you smell it?"

"Yes." Doc replied from the rear of the group, "For a second there I thought we would get away without seeing them again.

Opek spoke, his upbeat tone in stark contrast to Doc's wavering stutter, "We're nearly there. In a few moments we'll come to a ventilation duct which looks out over the furnace room."

They continued crawling. The potent, sweet smell intensified with every step, and with it the barbed reality of impending danger. A dull noise began as a hum, a throb in their ears above the hiss and wheeze of their respirators and the metallic clunk of their footfalls on the tunnel floor. Very quickly the sound developed into a series of long drones that vibrated through every pipe, tube, wire and duct.

"What is that noise?" Doc shouted over the din.

"Seems to be coming from all directions. You can hear them, put your head close to the pipes and listen." Kessler looked ahead and then behind them where, beyond the groups light, the darkness lurked. "Ahead or behind us, it's hard to tell, I can't see anything."

Doc stammered as the noise increased to a clamour, "What else does this damned place have in store for us?" He pulled his hood tight over his head in an attempt to drown out the sound.

The group stood still, waving their torchlight around them

trying to keep the darkness at bay. The sickly-sweet stench had reached an unbearable intensity. Opek tapped Kessler on the shoulder, "What now, Mr Kessler?"

An ear-piercing, sustained scream stopped him replying. He staggered back as the screeching wail thundered through the tunnel, nearly tripping over the two Techs who sat on the floor, eyes shut against the terror, holding on to one another in sheer fright. Doc yelled as he waved his rifle manically at the darkness which threatened to devour their small juddering island of light.

"Make it stop!" Bendle cried, his small hands covering his ears.

The unmistakable, feral sound of the Seekers' barks and howls could now be heard over the booming clatter.

Doc whimpered, "Oh no."

Claws and fangs leapt from the shadows and penetrated their shaking light. Immediately the scorching burst of Kessler's Luther joined the cacophony with a barrage of plasma rounds, each blast banishing the darkness with brief pulses of sheer white light revealing glimpses of the horror unfolding around them. The crack of Doc's Lazarus rifle exploded behind Kessler as its razor sharp steel filament shells sliced through scales, skin and bone.

As the chaos raged a shrill yelp from behind alerted the detective to the flailing arms of the doctor as he lost his footing and fell to a tide of Seekers who swarmed over them. Opek swung his piston wrench wildly and Bendle's magma torch spat flames.

"Doctor!" Opek yelled.

"There are too many of them!" Kessler struggled to keep a grip of his carbine as Seekers grappled with his arm.

Bendle squealed as one of the beasts took hold of his foot. Opek lunged for him but in an instant he was gone, pulled into the frenzied horde. "Bendle!" Opek screamed as he threw himself at the monsters but was immediately blown back by a sudden explosion of heat. He tumbled into the detective who fell back into arms, legs, claws, an entanglement of bodies, as long tendrils of flames raced along the walls of the tunnel.

Opek's squeal came from underneath a pile of the vicious beasts, "The flames are catching the oil!"

Kessler wrestled with a claw which threatened to rake across his face, "Run, if you can!" His words were cut short by a calamitous roar as a searing fireball flashed across them. The detective closed his eyes as panicked squeals and screams were abruptly consumed by the explosive flames and he awaited the inevitable, waited for the fire to take him, waited for the light of the flames to release him from his pain.

*

"Remarkable really." Someone coughed, a hacking, wheezing sound and then continued, "I cannot believe it."

"Ugh…" Kessler moaned. His voice grating across a bone-dry throat.

"Doctor, Mr Kessler is awake." Opek's unmistakable high-pitched voice.

Kessler tried to open his eyes, "What… what…"

"Happened? I tell you what happened, old friend. We actually survived, a bit frazzled perhaps, but we survived. All thanks to Bendle and his magma stick."

"But the Seekers? There were so many."

"All gone, burnt to a crisp." Doc reached down and pulled Kessler's still smoking body to his feet.

Bendle stood by Opek who had his arms protectively round his son, "Pa is always telling me to keep my flames away from the machine oil. Very flammable." Bendle smiled through a blackened, tarnished helmet.

"The leaking oil which these tunnels are caked with is extremely flammable and these heat suits…" Doc coughed and took on more water, "they're flame proof, they shielded us from the inferno. Fascinating material."

Kessler tensed and tried to breathe. He looked around the tunnel and tried to piece together the reasons why he was still standing, still surviving. Darkness had returned and, with it, thick acrid smoke which clung to the dead air. Their torches and the Tech's lanterns tried unsuccessfully to carve their way through the dense fog, only allowing him to see a few inches ahead. However, emerging from the thick murk, the grotesque charred remains of the horde lay in smouldering piles all around them, clogging the tunnel's confined space with their smoking corpses. A familiar nervous rattle brought the detective's attention to his shaking left hand which he quickly held still with his right. He looked up to see the Doc, Opek and Bendle all staring at him. "So what now, Mr Kessler?" Opek still held his blood-soaked piston wrench in both his hands.

"Yes, what now, Kes?" Doc winced as he shuffled his weight away from his injured leg.

The three looked at the detective and waited for his instruction, waited for him to tell them what to do next, tell them that everything was going to be ok. After taking a moment to breathe some Ox he relaxed and smiled back at the burnt, charred group, "We get out of this damn tunnel."

·DANCE OF THE MACABRE·

As the group walked through the smoking remains of the Seekers a deep booming sound emerged from the darkness ahead of them. At first it began as a low, repetitive drone but quickly its volume increased.

"More monsters?" Doc stuttered.

"No. The sound is different." Kessler had stopped and held his hand out for the group to do the same.

"It sounds like…"

"Music," Opek finished Kessler's sentence for him.

Kessler led the group tentatively forward. Soon they arrived at the end of the tunnel and he peered down through a wire-mesh grate to the furnace room below. Bright lights flashed every few seconds bathing the area briefly in a strobe effect of cold white that seemed to pulse to a heavy, bass beat of music. Between each shock of light, the darkness revealed walls covered in graffiti which glowed yellows, reds and blues, all revealing the toxic phrase, the words that had brought Kessler so much grief, dread, pain and agony – 'Lux Ferre'. He stared out across the room at those words, almost lost in a trance as the music, the lights and the gaudy collage of colours all seemed to dance in unison, transfixing him and drawing the detective towards them. He leaned forward, pressing himself against the grating, as if he was trying to reach out and touch the vile words that had haunted his dreams. It came loose and fell to the floor below, Doc grabbed his heat suit and pulled him back into the tunnel. "Easy there, Kes," he shouted over the noise into Kessler's ear. Doc looked down, beyond the detective and into the room, "It's like some low city trance club." Below him was a sea of writhing bodies which gyrated, warped and twisted over one another as if in communal ecstasy, all moving as one to the rhythm of the music and the pulse of the lights. It was difficult to focus on the features of any one individual as the bodies were entwined together but gradually small details began to emerge and through the intermittent strobe lighting a flash of red, the same overalls worn by Opek and Bendle, a torn tunic, a cap with the Epsom logo and white boots, revealed themselves. All had grey, gaunt, burnt faces. Those without shades or optics revealed the now familiar black voids where the whites of their eyes should have been. Doc retreated back into the tunnel, "So many, seems like what's left of the town is down there. Look at their eyes, all high on Lux, and their skin, without heat suits they are rotting away. How can they still be alive?"

Kessler let out a low sigh and looked at Doc wide eyed, "Am I like them?"

"Like who?"

Kessler raised his voice over the din and spoke without averting his gaze away from the furnace room, "Am I like them, the Chaff? Beck said that only the good souls were taken, leaving the bad to get burned out on this junk. I wonder how bad mine really is." His hands went up to his helmet. All he wanted to do was to claw at his eyes. Anything to get rid of the itch.

"Kes, calm down. Look at me." Doc pulled the detective's hands away from his visor and stared into his bloodshot eyes, "Look at me," he repeated, "you are nothing like them. If you were you wouldn't be here. You have come all this way to save Beth and try and make a better life for you and Macy. You are different than them. And besides, I have not been taken and, as

313

you know, if souls do exist then I have a very fine and handsome one." Doc smiled through his visor.

Kessler nodded.

Doc coughed into his vent, the white, sporadic glare from the lights revealing the harsh angles of his broken, bloody nose and the deep purple swell of his eye, "I must look some sight." He had noticed Kessler staring at his face and smiled back with his cracked-tooth grin.

The detective returned the smile, "Nothing a couple of sessions in your skin lab wouldn't fix."

"I will send you the bill."

Kessler took another glance into the room and saw in its centre, the large, square metal box that he assumed to be the furnace block. It towered up through the sprawl of flailing hands, bodies and feet. An intricate network of pipes led from the block up to the ceiling above and from them hung the powerful torches from which the intense staccato barrage of light originated. Kessler looked at Bendle and then up to his father, "Any ideas?"

Opek shook his head. "Sorry sir. Your friend and our way back up city lie beyond those doors, right across the other side of the furnace room." Opek pointed to the other side of the room.

"There are too many of them, they'd swarm over us. We wouldn't make it." Kessler looked at the thousands of densely packed bodies and despaired. "We've seen citizens taken by Lux before and they are vicious."

All three stared down at the hundreds of Chaff who twisted and ground to the hammering beat. Soon the pitch of the tunes changed to an almighty whine and the strobe lighting, in a flash, blanketed the room in stark white light. Doc shouted over the constant scream, "What is happening?"

Liquid exploded from pipes hanging from the ceiling spraying all the Chaff below. The crowd began to roar as they looked up and, with mouths open, drank the deluge. Soon, the lights turned to darkness again as the music lowered to a deep, thumping rhythm and the strobe lighting resumed its rapid pulse. "They're feeding on Lux. That is why they come here." Opek sighed loudly, "Of course, that's it!"

"What?" Kessler and Doc spoke in unison.

Opek looked pleased with himself, "The Chaff, with their bodies full of this chem, are no danger to us. It's only when they crave more that you have to be wary. Bendle and I learnt that lesson quickly while hiding in the tunnels all this time. We should move now whilst their hunger is satisfied." Opek again pointed across the room.

"What? Just walk right through?" Doc did not sound convinced.

"Quickly, doctor. We don't have much time."

Doc looked at Kessler who shrugged his shoulders, "You heard him, let's go."

"This is crazy," Doc stammered.

"What part of the last few days has not been crazy?" Kessler braced himself to jump down.

Doc peered down at the hundreds of bodies dancing their grim trance, "True," Doc agreed, "well at least there does not appear to be any Seekers down there."

Kessler held his Luther before him and Doc quickly followed with his rifle, "No, but I'm not taking any chances." Kessler replaced the power cell in his carbine and, holding it aloft, after a brief pause with a look of pure, grim determination, he jumped down to the floor below with a thud, landing close to a group of Chaff who twitched and jolted to the music, their heads looking up with mouths open, completely oblivious to his presence. Doc landed awkwardly next to him but immediately sprung up with his rifle raised. He backed up to the wall and aimed his weapon at the hordes surrounding them.

Kessler looked up to see the dangling legs of Bendle

plummeting towards him. He had to react quickly, forcing his sim-starved muscles into action. He bit down hard on his vent as he lunged and caught the flailing Tech. Opek peered down and raised his thumb to confirm his son had landed ok before he quickly followed.

The group stood still, frozen in place as they stared into the throng. After a few moments Doc spoke, his voice nearly lost in the cacophony, "Maybe the Tech is right? Maybe they will not notice us?"

"Just stay close and follow me. Doc, I'll go first and you follow behind like back in the tunnel. Don't let Opek and Bendle out of your sight."

Kessler strode forward and the other three quickly followed his lead. A wall of limbs and bodies, clammy and drenched in sweat, immediately pressed up against them. Kessler grabbed the neck of one reveller, a round face with a small, pointed nose with large, spiked hair. Its pitch-black eyes seemed to only look inward at whatever was playing out in its mind. He threw it to the side. Doc kicked and punched his way through, often using his rifle to bludgeon any who threatened to bar his way. As Opek had said, the Chaff did not seem to notice them, instead their attention was locked into playing out the final act of their debauched play. Fists pumped the air, long, dirty nails clawed skin, faces tensed in silent screams.

It did not take long for them to become lost in the mayhem and wave after wave of gyrating bodies threatened to drown the group. Kessler found it hard to breathe as a hand caught hold of his suit and pulled at his helmet. He grabbed hold of it and twisted it hard away from him. Even over the wail of the music he heard the sickening crack of bone and snap of tendons. He turned to see a young women, or what was left of one, with deep sunken dark eyes and skin a sickening blue, grey colour. Her body was shrivelled, her dirty clothes tattered rags that hung from a bony frame. Her face had a tattoo along one side that ran down her neck which would have looked pretty once. Kessler let go of her now limp arm which, from a sickening jagged piece of shattered bone, flailed about wildly as she continued her automaton trance. He went to move forward but had lost his bearings. He twisted and turned until the reassuring sight of the furnace block came into view, the hundreds of pipes and wiring towering above him meaning that he had made it halfway across the room.

The blast of sound increased in volume and the beat became more rapid and, as if in reply to Kessler's brief moment of relief, the horde began to gyrate more aggressively as the tempo of the tunes became more manic. The detective was shoved to the ground as a wall of open-mouthed revellers crashed into him. He gasped for Ox as he was punched, kicked, elbowed and clawed. Bodies piled on top of him pressing down on his chest, sucking the breath from his lungs as the sheer blast of sound battered his senses into oblivion. He felt weak and helpless as the weight of the writhing bodies pinned him helplessly to the floor. Kessler roared as he tried to heave himself up one last time but to no avail, his voice immediately lost amongst the screeching music. Everything went dark as Chaff fell across his visor, blinding him. He frantically sucked on his vent for more Ox but it wasn't enough. His body craved the elation, the energy, the strength that sim would provide. He bit down harder on his vent but the Ox did nothing. He couldn't breathe.

Something twitched beside him, an arm, a head maybe? It moved and Kessler could again just make out the stuttering white of the strobe lights. An intense smell of burnt hair and flesh suddenly threatened to overpower him just as something got hold of him and pulled him back into the light.

Doc stood there with his smoking rifle in one hand and Opek and Bendle clutching onto the other, desperately trying not to let go as the tide threatened to take hold of them. Doc shook his head, his shout just audible over the noise, "We thought we lost you."

"I thought so too." Kessler held his chest and breathed deeply. Below his feet were the smouldering remains of a pile of Chaff, whose lifeless black eyes stared blankly back at them. Kessler turned to look around him and waited for an attack that never arrived, "They ignore us."

Opek spoke but his voice was consumed by the din.

Bendle lost hold of Doc and was beginning to be taken by the crowd when Kessler bent down and hauled him up onto his shoulders, "There you go little fella, you'll be safe up there." Straight away Bendle, from his lofty position, pointed the way forward.

Soon, after what felt like an age, the group emerged from the crowds. Kessler could see the large double doors which led down to the Core Tunnel and began to make for them when he realised that Opek and Doc were not following him. They stood staring at a raised platform to their left. Doc raised his rifle as if to shoot. The platform was the origin of the music which spewed out of speakers that towered above their heads. This close, the noise took on almost a physical presence as if each beat thudded into Kessler's body like a hammer blow. He returned and shouted, "What's wrong?"

Bendle yelled into the detective's ear, "Over there. That is Governor Tillbrook. I can tell by his clothes." He pointed at a figure atop the raised platform wearing very elaborate red robes who swayed slowly behind a large desk.

"He was a friend, I must see him," Opek shouted.

"Like you said, Opek, no one can be saved from this place. Let's continue to the Core Tunnel."

"You believe the girl can be saved." Opek looked up at Kessler, his wide eyes pools of innocence despite his advanced years. "I must see him."

Doc knelt down, clutching his Lazarus rifle in both hands, "It will only take a couple of minutes, Kes."

Kessler arrived at the top of the platform first and immediately shouted for Bendle to come no further. "Stay back, child. Like everything in this forsaken place, he's gone. It's no sight for a child."

Doc and Opek joined him and reeled back in horror at the sight before them. "Stay back son, wait for us at the bottom of the stairs." Opek raised his hand up, "Please son, stay where you are." Bendle crossed his hands and sat down with his back to the others, tapping his magma stick on the hard carbonised iron steps in frustration.

Kessler, Doc and Opek turned their attention to the Governor. The flowing red plastichem robes, their shiny surface reflecting the white glare of the strobe lights, were all that remained recognisable of the man this creature once was. His skin had been flayed from his body which was now encrusted in a red and black scab. Ears and nose were no more and only holes remained. His eyelids were gone so that his two eyes glared at them, rolling around in their cavernous sockets. His bald head, with its random tufts of wiry black hair, jerked back and forth as if jolted by an electric current. Skeletal hands quivered and shook over a console. Two huge chains emerged from his tattered robes and hung from the ceiling high above, preventing him from moving far.

Despite Opek knowing the Governor for many years, the creature showed no signs of familiarity with the Tech who stood still with an expression of abject horror.

"His eyes are not like the others." Doc stared in macabre fascination, "They are not the black of Lux." Kessler pulled him back just as Tillbrook's head turned towards them.

"Easy Doc, this is no time for your grim fancies."

"Release me. Please." The creature interrupted Kessler, his rasping voice could barely be heard above the noise. He moved towards them but immediately the chains pulled tight. He tried to scream but only a jagged wheeze escaped his lungs.

Kessler approached him with his Luther raised before him. "Why have they done this to you?"

"I failed them. The Light Bringer has abandoned me." He sobbed and smashed a bloody fist into the console making the music change to a deeper, grinding drone. "I can hear their voices, hear their words, they draw me towards the light." He turned to look deep into each of their eyes, "I can see it, my eyes are never closed to its beauty," he smirked to himself, "smell the sweetness," the bloody hole where his nose once was twitched and drew in the stagnant air, his head slowly rocking from side to side as he savoured the aroma. "I can taste it," a tongue emerged between raw, cracked lips and licked their bloody surface, "It's so good." He tapped his bald head with his fist, "Imagine the escape, the warmth, the light. But can I get to it?" He shook his head, "No." Pulling the chains in dejected acceptance they clinked tight. "They were kind enough to keep my eyes open so that I could forever watch others go to Him." His words were spat out of his mouth with venom. "I'm left here, alone, with only my pain!" He wailed.

"His mind has gone," Doc interrupted, "look what they have done to him, what pain he must have endured. Let's put him out of his misery and be done with it." Doc brought his rifle to bear.

Governor Tillbrook continued a conversation with someone, something, lost within the ether of his broken corrupted mind, "Release me, I did as you asked. I gathered them here, showed them your way. I know I should not have let her leave, I know this now, free me. I will bring Gwen to you. I promise!" He pulled at his chains, his back arcing in agony and he repeated his cackled wail, "Release me from these bonds!"

Opek spoke, his back turned towards the Governor, "I can bear it no more! His poor Gwen, his daughter." He turned to look at the creature but quickly looked away again, his eyes pressed closed in an attempt to shut out the sickening images of Tillbrook's tortured form. He took his bag down from his shoulder and rummaged briefly in it to find a cutting tool and powered it up. "They did this to him because he tried to save his daughter. He deserves to be free."

Opek moved towards him before Doc pulled him back, "He may have saved his daughter but he helped the Malebranche kidnap, helped them push Lux, allowed your beloved machines to stop working. You told us that yourself, Opek."

"Your friend is right to be wary of me." He pointed a finger at Opek and continued, "The torture, agony of Dis has worked its dark way through this broken body, making me do," he paused as if in thought, "terrible things."

Doc powered up his rifle, "It was not this city that made you betray your citizens who looked to you for leadership, relied on you to protect them. You did that yourself."

He wailed, "Please don't." The Governor's gaze turned from Doc's rifle to Kessler. "You know what escape feels like don't you? That search for a release from the torments of this life? When every waking second is time spent trying to get away from the darkness that surrounds us? You know this, you know what citizens would do to be free from the pain?" Governor Tillbrook bowed down close to the floor, his thin arms spread subserviently before him. His stare now returned to the barrel of Doc's rifle, "Good citizens, I have suffered enough in this life, in this damned city for too long. Break my bonds, release me so that I can have my escape."

"First, tell us what you can about where those taken by the Malebranche have gone. Are they down through the Core Tunnel?" Kessler raised his Luther and took aim.

Governor Tillbrook flinched at the sight of the weapon, stopped his fidgeting, and slowly began to nod to himself. "The Lost? Why, they are gone. What use have you for them?"

"The Malebranche have taken someone and we need to get her back."

The creature slowly nodded, "A deal then. Free me of my

321

bonds and I will tell you where to find them." He clinked his chains to emphasise his point.

Doc stepped forward to protest but Kessler held out his hand, urging him to be quiet. "Sure."

The Governor cackled, "Go down to the Core, just follow their screams. You cannot miss them. Unless the fire has taken them already that is." He laughed hysterically until the chains pulled tight and he squealed in pain.

"Don't play games with me or I'll leave you to preside over this horror show, monster." Kessler stepped forward and stared into the creature's wide, darting eyes.

Tillbrook went abruptly quiet and examined Kessler for a few moments, "If you truly mean to go down there you will find those that are left in cells above the plasma field."

"Who guards them? The Malebranche? More of these Seekers?"

"All but one of the Malebranche have long since left us to spread the light to the city above and you will not find Seekers this close to the plasma." He chuckled to himself, "There are no souls for them to seek down here. Minos on the other hand," Tillbrook continued to cackle to himself but quickly stifled his laughter after one glance at Kessler, "the Malebranche left him here to look after the Chosen, he will not be best pleased to see you try and take one of his flock."

"His Chosen?"

"Yes, those that are lost. Those needed to help open citizen's eyes."

Kessler powered up his Luther and took aim at a chain and pressed down on the trigger, with a flash the bond shattered. Kessler moved onto the next and, just before he could release another blast of plasma, an explosion of heat threw him across the platform into Doc, who collapsed onto the floor beneath him. An agonizing scream was followed by the bitter smell of burning flesh. Flames washed over Tillbrook and within seconds he was engulfed in a ferocious inferno.

322

Bendle stood close to his distraught father who was now, belatedly, trying to wrestle the smoking magma stick from his son's hands.

·FIGHT ABOVE THE FIRE·

With the hiss of unseen pistons and the loud, rapid thud of cogs quickly turning, the massive metal doors slammed shut and the great noise of the furnace room immediately left their ears. Two lines glowed red either side of the tunnel and produced a dull crimson light which added to the sense of dread in the pit of each of their stomachs as a fiercely hot wind brought with it ghostly howls and foreboding shrieks.

The four stood and stared down into the gloom, each of their minds plagued by the same horrors, each wondering what new evil lay waiting for them. Doc leant against the tunnel wall, his rifle pointing feebly into the vast red void ahead of them. Opek, with a blank expression, stared at his son who stood a small distance away from the group, looking down at his gloved hands.

Kessler's body ached and his mind was tormented by his all-consuming craving. He tensed his left, twitching hand, a constant reminder of what he needed and did not have. He closed his eyes and steadied his breathing in an attempt to control himself, try and delay the inevitable. "Move forward," he muttered, "focus on getting Bethany and getting out of here."

Opek spoke with a forced smile, "This tunnel is an amazing piece of engineering. These pipelines come up from the plasma field, an extremely hot sea of raw plasma from which we get the heat which powers the whole of Dis. It's a sight to behold. Do you know how difficult it is getting enough cadermite to forge the conductors necessary to handle such heat?"

Kessler forced his gaze from the darkness and took in the hundreds of pipes which lined the walls. The vast tunnel, whose ceiling towered far above their heads, had been carved straight out of the bedrock. Everything appeared to fluctuate in the fierce hot breeze that whistled its way from somewhere down in the depths below.

"This scorching wind brings with it the screams that Tillbrook mentioned," Doc's voice wavered as he spoke.

Opek continued, "When the furnace is fully operational it would be impossible for us to be here, even with these heat suits the temperatures are too great." He turned to Bendle who still sat away from them, his head resting in his hands as he stared down into the tunnel. "Isn't that right, son? A fine piece of engineering." Bendle did not respond but Opek continued regardless, "We have had to dig deeper and deeper as the plasma cooled and retreated, extending this tunnel further down into the ancient world." Opek's attention again returned to his son, "See the pipe work, son? It runs the length of the entire town and up to the highest reaches of Dis, a major feat in engineering." Bendle at last looked up at his father and gave a slight smile and nod. Opek turned back to Kessler and spoke quietly, "I fear that he may be losing his way. Young Techs are never allowed into the Core Tunnel, they would usually do anything to be able to glimpse all this engineering." The excitement on Opek's face while talking about the tunnel soon faded to be replaced with a sense of foreboding and dread, "I can't believe he took Governor Tillbrook's life. Techs should only be concerned with machinery, not meddling in bigman's stuff." The wind howled loudly making Opek swallow down hard, "I don't much fancy going down there, Mr Kessler."

Kessler looked over at Bendle then back to his father, "Opek listen, we'll be out of here soon." The Tech continued to stare at his son who, with an expressionless, cold set face, had carefully laid out his tools and had begun to clean them. The detective knew he had to get Opek's full attention if they were to get out alive, "You said that there was a Tech shaft somewhere round here? A way we could escape?"

Opek slowly turned around to face the detective, "Yes there is." He looked back again towards his son with concern.

Grabbing hold of him, Kessler spun the Tech around so that his visor and vent were nearly touching his own, "Opek," his grip tightened on the startled Tech, "you need to focus on the task at hand. Any, and I mean any, lack of concentration could mean the death of all of us," he looked deep into Opek's eyes, "and that includes your son." He let his barked words settle for a few moments before continuing, "Now, you said that the Tech shaft was a short distance from here?"

Opek nodded and rubbed his visor with his cloth, "Yes, it's just down there," he pointed down the tunnel, "let me show you." He walked passed Doc who was still staring into the darkness. "Come on Bendle, we must hurry." Bendle raised himself off the floor, gathered his tools up and slowly plodded along after his father.

The tunnel descended steadily downward and the deeper they travelled the hotter and stronger the wind became. Evidence of the explosion Opek had mentioned began to materialise; large boulders lay strewn across the tunnel floor and at various points cadermite girders and struts had been erected to support the roof. The heat and the difficult terrain did not seem to effect Opek and Bendle, their years working in the most dangerous conditions allowing them to move freely, but Kessler struggled and had to stop to take on water numerous times. "This damn heat's unbearable," he gasped.

Doc, his long, gaunt features shining with sweat in the red glow of the tunnel, checked Kessler's Ox levels and gave him the thumbs up, "Just take steady breaths."

"I know."

Opek's voice came echoing up through the tunnel, "Found it!"

Doc and Kessler soon caught up with the Techs who were a blur of movement. Their tools were laid out on the ground ready for use. Opek's short legs stuck out from an opening in a panel just above their heads and Bendle was sorting a bundle of frayed wires that hung down ominously from a large bank of circuit boards.

"It's much worse than I thought." Opek's muffled voice emerged from the panel where he was working, "Not only is there no power but the explosion has done a fine job on the capacitor.

"Ok, is that a problem?" Doc sighed.

"Yes, this is designed to get Techs down here as fast as possible, time is money to Epsom. It travels so fast that we need to ensure the shaft is clear of traffic before we use it. Only one pod can travel at a time. Without a capacitor we cannot power the pod or communicate with top side to clear the way for us."

"Right, I don't see any pod though." Kessler looked through the small circular entrance to the shaft.

"That's our other problem. If we can fix the capacitor and get power flowing again we'll have to get the nearest pod sent down to pick us up."

Kessler peered up to where an oil-covered helmet now looked down from where legs had been before, "Can it be done?"

"Yes, maybe. If there is anyone still working the Tech station on D1 we should be able to get a pod sent down but we have very limited power here, one, maybe two hours at most before my batteries run out of juice."

"How far to the plasma field?"

"About another fifteen minutes further down the tunnel."

Doc stepped closer to Kessler and whispered, "We will not have long if we are to make it back."

"I know." Kessler fell to his knees, any energy he had left seeming to evaporate in an instant. "It's no good. No one could survive down here. She's lost." Kessler shook as he spoke.

Doc knelt beside him. "Take it easy Kes. It's the withdrawal talking, you've been through a lot. I have nothing left to give you to mask the pain so you will have to just grit your teeth and get the job done."

"It's no good." Despite the heat of the tunnel Kessler shivered as a chill swept over him, "It's all for nothing."

"Mr Kessler, you're wrong. If it was not for meeting you and the doctor, Bendle and I would not have the chance to escape. You've given us hope."

"No." Kessler turned his back to the others and slumped against the wall.

"No, sir!" Opek spoke with a sudden intensity, "Have faith sir. We will fix this Tech shaft and you will find her. Now go on, soon we'll escape this place. Have faith," Opek urged.

"Faith," Kessler repeated. He raised his shaken, weak form up from the floor and spoke, "Doc and I will go down and look for Beth, we'll be back in one hour, maximum, with or without her," he gave Doc a sideways glance, "you two stay here and get this damn thing operational or else we're all done for."

Opek lowered himself down from where he was working, "Here, take this." He took something from Bendle's helmet and handed it to Kessler, "Its a short-ranged com. I would normally use it to keep tabs of Bendle when we're at work. It will allow me to keep you informed of our progress."

*

The journey down into the plasma field took the fifteen minutes Opek had said but to Kessler it felt much longer. The vast size of the tunnel soon closed in on them from all sides and the constant wailing which travelled up from the depths grew in intensity striking Kessler to the pit of his stomach with a fear that sapped what little energy he could muster. Together they travelled through the wall of searing heat and down through the thick crimson mist lost in their own tired, disturbed thoughts, their minds teetering on the brink as they continued down deeper and deeper.

The tunnel came to an abrupt end and immediately Kessler and Doc stumbled back as they were greeted with an awesome sight. They dropped to their knees as they took in the majestic spectacle through their protective visors. The floor was a great sea of white hot plasma. It churned, bubbled and careered in bright reds and yellows, thickly flowing in vast rivers across the cavern floor. Large flows of the liquid also burst out of the walls hundreds of feet above their heads and rained down flecks of light from above.

Kessler had never seen anything like it before. He smiled in awe, before all this began he had only ever travelled as far down as D2. It seemed like years ago, like another lifetime, when all he was used to was a world of plastisteel and carbonized iron, now he was surrounded by rock from the ancient world only heard about in stories and myths told to children. Now the destructive force of the Council was replaced by this ancient world's own natural power.

"Wonderful isn't it?" Doc croaked. He leaned against the tunnel's entrance and wiped his visor, "Who would have thought something so destructive, so chaotic, could be so beautiful."

"We've seen so many strange sights on this journey." Kessler peered into molten fire as it danced below him.

"Well, let us get this over with and live to tell the tale."

A large gust of the scorching gale enveloped the two. This close to the plasma field, the shrieks now became more clear. Amongst the wails, individual cries and sobs could be heard. Every so often the infernal wind would bring with it a snatched word or phrase of despair.

"Can you hear it?" Doc stood up and listened.

Kessler took out his view finder and Doc peered through his scope. Hanging from the cavern ceiling, hundreds of cages rocked from side to side in the wind. Each cell contained piles of scorched bodies, some lay prone while others hung limp between bars screaming into the inferno.

"They are alive," Doc gasped, "at least some of them are. They have been given some kind of primitive breathing apparatus by the looks of things but they don't appear to be wearing any suits, the rads will soon kill them. "

"Why have they been brought here? What good are they to anyone?" Kessler spoke with exasperation, his ears filled with cries from above.

"I do not know. I do not know anything anymore."

A loud horn blared out from across the cavern, sounding six times before going quiet. Doc again looked through his scope, "There is movement on the far side, I can just make it out through the fire."

Kessler adjusted the focus of his viewfinder and stared through the bubbling plasma towards a large outcrop of rocks upon which stood a metal structure which was joined to the platform high above them by a tube which swayed in the thermals. All around the building huge containers were stacked in tall columns; each one had the yellow sun symbol printed on its side. Small creatures scurried back and forth. They reminded Kessler of the Seekers with black scales and beast like faces, only these were smaller, tiny critters which frantically scampered around working levers, pushing buttons and carrying boxes. Within seconds thick black smoke billowed from large stacks, pistons hissed and lights flashed and, on a huge conveyor belt, hundreds of boxes, came pouring out of the building. "A factory producing Lux. The burning sun is all over the boxes." Kessler muttered

"All the way down here? I don't understand." The sounding

of the horn seemed to give a terrible energy to the wails of those caged as their shrieks and moans grew frantically louder.

"Will you be ok?" Doc spoke with concern as Kessler stopped peering through his viewfinder to see his friend staring at his shaking hand which rattled by his side.

Kessler stretched his fingers out for a few moments, cradling them in his other hand and spoke, "Like I said, let's get this over with." He made a fist and punched the ground.

Right on the edge of the tunnel there was a ladder that scaled up to a series of platforms above them. Doc slung his rifle over his shoulder and went first but after one look at the churning fire below stepped back and looked up at Kessler, his visor reflecting the orange and red flames of the plasma. "I'll be ok. Just need to take a breath."

"How's the leg?"

"Fine. Worry about yourself, I'll be ok."

Kessler put a hand reassuringly on Doc's shoulder, "I know, I'll be right behind you."

Doc took a long breath and with a shrug of his shoulders began climbing up to the platform above. Kessler followed, his own tired limbs struggling to pull his weight up each rung at a time.

At the ladder's summit, Doc stopped and peered down from the top, his visor and bespectacled face apearing above Kessler who coughed and groaned as he climbed up the swaying ladder. Doc reached out an arm and helped lift his large frame up and onto the metal grating.

Cages hung either side of the walkway swinging on chains that were secured to the ceiling far above their heads. The cells bobbled about in scorching gusts constantly hitting against the walkway. Kessler gripped the rail tightly as the platform lurched sideways after each clatter from the cells. He glanced down at the molten lake below and took a deep breath. He had already drawn his Luther and Doc followed with his Lazarus rifle, as

331

they looked down the long passageway and took in the sheer scale of the task that lay before them.

Against the dull orange glow from the fire far below and that which fell perilously from above, a constant low hum of despair and anguish came from the cells, waves of cries and moans where hope had long since been abandoned enveloped the pair. From the two cells closest to them bodies, all scorched and blackened, lay draped like rag dolls across the cell floor. Limp, lifeless limbs hung out between the rough-cut, jagged bars. Kessler stood rooted in place, transfixed by the sight. Doc leaned close, "Come on, let's see if Beth's here and then we can get out of this nightmare."

Kessler's stare remained fixed on the cages ahead of him, "I'm not sure if we'll ever wake up from it."

Doc put his arm around him and urged the detective forward, "We are nearly there, Kes."

The stench of human waste stung their nostrils. Grey lifeless eyes in red, burnt faces looking out over crude, ancient respirators became alert as soon as their presence was discovered. A shriek was quickly followed by a flurry of frantic hands which desperately reached out from the depths of the cages, all trying to grab hold of them. Doc stumbled back onto a cage on the opposite side and was immediately crowded by a mass of blackened, thin, bony arms which grabbed hold of the folds in his suit and pulled him hard against the cell. Kessler reached over and heaved the doctor towards the middle of the walkway.

"Quiet!" Kessler barked a whisper towards those caged. The desperate pleas for help were getting louder, it would not be long before whomever was guarding them would hear the commotion. He pulled Doc close and spoke, "There's so many of them. You take the left side and I the right, just call out Bethany's name."

"That is the plan? We will surely be discovered."

"Best get on with it then, quickly!" Kessler coughed and took a breath to steady himself.

The two split up and immediately began working their way up the walkway through pleading hands and manic cries for help. It appeared that the Malebranche did not discriminate who they took from the streets and homes of Dis. The rough, mutated faces of the lower districts, the delicate features of Hightown and the childlike Techs all were here, both young and old. All were desperate to be freed. "Bethany? Bethany Turner?" Kessler raised his voice above the prisoner's pleas.

"Help us! Please! I can pay!"

"I beg you citizen, I have children."

"For the love of the Council, free us." The mob pleaded back in a garbled mass of words. Ignoring them all, Kessler batted back the rush of hands to peer into each cage desperately searching for Bethany.

Doc placed his hand on Kessler and shouted, "It's no use she's not here!"

"Just keep looking!"

Kessler returned to searching his side of the walkway and just as he had shouted out Bethany's name once again into yet another cage his eyes met a familiar face. It had changed since he had last seen it. Red raw and scorched black from the fire, he had lost weight since their last meeting, his cheek bones sunk even deeper into his skull than before, the distinct sharp edges of bone appearing under his feverishly, glistening, blackened skin. His cap was gone, leaving a bald head with small beady ears, his distinctive grey uniform was barely recognisable. Ripped and shredded, his tunic hung limply from his emaciated frame. However, the distinctive cyberware remained. The red eye, its gyros and optics audibly twisting and turning as it focused and stared straight at him. Lieutenant Bane of the DPD sat a short distance away from the rest of his fellow detainees, his back propped up against the corner of the cage. One of his trouser legs had been rolled up to the knee revealing a dirty, bloody bandage that didn't quite cover a huge wound that festered across his calf muscle.

He coughed and spluttered, pain seeming to rattle his skeletal form, "You again, Bounty? Your garb is different, but I would recognise that carbine anywhere."

"Bane," Kessler's gaze lingered on the officer's broken form before pressing his face to the cell bars and speaking low, "I'm looking for a girl, Bethany Turner."

"You should be locked up. Breach of Protocols 16, 40 and 107. That holo suit was illegal tech and is going to bring you down, there's a warrant out for your arrest," he coughed as he struggled to speak, "not that it matters anymore."

"Listen, I don't have time for this, have you seen her? She's Christian, you may have noticed her praying to her god."

"It does not surprise me that a Getta like yourself be associating with illegal cults," he broke into another coughing fit, doubling over in pain, "you dishonour the name of whomever earned that Luther. It represents honour, principles too high for your breed."

Kessler gripped hold of the bars, pressed his face hard against them and continued, ignoring Bane's barbed words, "She's tall, long black hair, her skin is pale, a porcelain white. Green eyes. You would remember her if you'd seen her. She has a course, Upper Downtown, accent," he frantically tried to think of the words, "but it's softened with education? Please, have you seen her?" Kessler spoke in desperate rasps, looking down the walkway every few seconds expecting to be discovered at any minute.

Bane stared at him in silence for a few moments, the cage lit up briefly in a deep orange glow as a huge, thick stream of plasma fell from above casting shadows over the ghouls that weakly clambered about the cage trying to get his attention, "I have seen no girl of that description, she may be in one of the other cells or she may already be gone."

"Gone?" Kessler batted away hands as they clutched and grappled him, "What's happening here? Why are they keeping you in these cages?"

"Don't you know? Every time the horn sounds he takes four of us to that doorway up at the end of the walkway. They go in and never come out again." He spoke with no emotion, only a grim acceptance. "I have watched them down below, making that poison from that factory of theirs. Stacking their boxes high to be shipped up to the city above, creatures that have come from the depths to destroy our beloved Dis."

"I don't understand."

Bane forced a laugh, "You fool, they are using us, mere ingredients for their toxins." Bane dragged his body closer to Kessler, "Their chem, Lux, is a plague that will destroy the city. The Council has been trying to stop it for months but…" he turned his face away and coughed blood onto his sleeve, "we cannot. Dis is finished."

"Ingredients?"

"All I know is when the machine below stops, when Lux stops being produced, the horn sounds and down we go. Quick and easy. Soon black smoke bellows out of their chimneys and more chems are produced."

A shout from Doc further up the walkway alerted Kessler and he went to leave when Bane barked, "Wait!" He grabbed hold of a bar with his gloved hand, hauled himself up, grimacing in pain as his lame leg dragged dead behind him, "The city will fall to this scourge, millions of citizens will die, if not down here, then above us, to this Lux." His body shook with the effort to stay upright but his voice was steady with a clear intensity, "The Malebranche must be stopped, you must stop them." He looked down to Kessler's Luther which he still held, "Perhaps something of what that stands for has rubbed off on you. The beast that keeps us will be here soon to take more down. Kill him, stop him, free us."

"The man who earned this and what he stood for died many years ago. There is no room on Dis for a man like him, not anymore."

Kessler moved on to the next cage and Bane fell wearily to the cell floor, "You Gettas are all the same," he cursed.

Doc's voice sounded again, this time louder than before, "Kessler, quick, I've found her!" The detective bounded over to where he was waiting.

Bethany looked like any of the wasted, broken bodies that lay within the cells. Her long black hair was thick with dirt and grime and her delicate features now disappeared into a skeletal frame that threatened to break through stretched, worn, blackened skin. However, her deep green eyes still blazed with life. They looked up at Kessler, tears freely flowing over her respirator, as she held tightly onto Doc's arm. She wept, "Kes, I was alone…" words were forced between hacking sobs, "I kept praying for you but…"

"We do not have time for this, Kes." Doc, on his knees, reached through the cage with his free hand and put it around the sobbing girl. "Bethany," he turned her head so that she stared straight into his bespectacled eyes, "we have to leave this infernal place."

"It… it," her sobs raked her bony frame as the pain and despair freely flowed from her every pore, "holds all the horrors my uncle warned us about and more. The Devil keeps watch over us." Her words trailed off into a sobbing whisper.

"This creature, Minos is his name, is he near?"

"Lucifer, Satan, The Father of Lies. He watches us, goads us. He tells us terrible things. Do you know what they do to us?" Bethany peered wide eyed at both of them.

"It does not matter now, Bethany. We are going to get you out." Doc continued to comfort her and hold her close.

She continued to babble, barely coherent, "His words appear in our minds as he walks by and picks the sweetest of souls. He's a demon." She hacked a cough, "Our souls, what makes us human, they grind them down to feed them to us." She burst out in manic laughter, "They are picky though, they only seek out the best for that privilege." Her brief laughter returned to tired, exhausting sobs.

Words failed Kessler as Doc continued, "Bethany, it's going to be ok, we are going to get you out of here," he repeated and looked to Kessler urging him to say something as she broke down.

"Listen, Beth, remember back in the church when the fire nearly took us. I protected you then just like I'll do now. You can always depend on that." Kessler cleared his throat, "Doc and I are here for you, we'll get you out. Everything will be ok." Kessler reached into his suit and held out Bethany's cross, "Here I have something of yours. It saved me out there when I thought all was lost."

She took a few moments to steady her breathing and stared at the sparkling silver cross as it hung from Kessler's grasp. She placed it around her neck, wiped away a tear and spoke quietly, "Ok." She coughed up blood and shook with the effort.

Doc whispered to Kessler, "We need to get her out of here fast. She is sick from the rads, they're killing her."

The detective gripped the glistening, polished black bars, "These cages seem to be wrought out of the rock itself, stand back." He drew his Luther and took aim at the lock mechanism of the cell door. Bethany's fragile frame disappeared into a mass of stick thin limbs and grey rags as the occupants of the cage clambered to the far side of their prison. Doc took a step back just as Kessler sent a bolt of plasma crashing into the stone cell. The smoke cleared to reveal the gleaming surface of polished black stone, completely unscathed from the blast.

"I did not think it was going to be that easy." Doc sighed and readied his rifle.

"I've never seen anything like this, it didn't even make a dent." Kessler holstered the weapon and desperately pulled at the bars. He took out a knife and with it tried to jimmy the lock.

Bethany shouted words that wheezed from her dry throat, "He has the keys."

"Minos." Bane and Bethany's grim tales raced through Kessler's head.

"They hang from his waist on a chain. When he comes for us I can hear them clink as he walks."

At that moment, Kessler's ear-piece crackled to Opek's high pitch voice, "Mr Kessler, Tech Shaft Six is operational and they're sending down a pod. It'll be here in twenty minutes."

Kessler pressed his hand against his ear, "Ok, Opek. Good work."

"Well, we did what we could – don't have much power though so hurry."

"You just make sure the pod is waiting when we get there. Kessler out."

"Ok. What now?" Just as Doc finished speaking, the horn blasted another six deafening times, its bellow dampening out the wails of those caged, the howl of the searing wind and the broiling roar of the plasma. Bethany immediately stopped her desperate attempt to prise the door open and curled into the foetal position on the floor as a wave of cries and a manic terror washed over everyone.

"Oh God! We're too late!" Beth panicked, "He's coming!"

Kessler returned to trying to pick the lock and Doc peered down the passageway, his rifle ready. "Quickly, Kes!" Doc barked as the door at the end of the platform opened to reveal a small, hunchbacked old man. Despite his age, he moved quickly towards them stopping by a cell's door where he led out four who followed him in docile obedience. His slight, hunched form was nearly lost in the folds of a lavish purple robe that spilled onto the platform around him. His hands were outstretched, beckoning the four towards him.

Immediately Kessler dropped the knife and fell to his knees as he began to hear the words. They came to him in thundered screams which drove him to the floor in agony.

'*Lux Ferre is here. Come to me. Reach out for the light.*'

The words screeched between his ears, its barbs stabbing every nerve ending, a jagged bright white light exploding in his head. He opened his aching eyes briefly only to see Doc drop his rifle and fall to his knees. "What are you doing, Doc? Shoot him!" Kessler was not sure if the words had ever left his mouth as the cacophony of voices continued to fill his head and drown out everything else.

'Reach out for the light. Take it and all your pain will end.'

The words were warm and a temporary respite from the blaring pain. On all fours, Kessler tried to reach Doc's prone form but again was stopped by blinding agony. He looked up to see the man standing over him, his small frame now engulfed in brilliant, dazzling light.

Two black eyes, dark pin pricks in the white blaze, stared down at the detective and appeared to pause for a moment, examining him, before speaking words which appeared within his mind, 'Your soul is tarnished with the sins of this world. Take the light and all will be cleansed.'

"Are you the Light Bringer?"

A laugh, deep and powerful, resonated through Kessler's body, sending arcs of pain across his mind.

'No Chaff, but you will meet him soon.'

Minos dropped a large syringe onto the floor next to him and walked over to Doc and did the same. The light from his body faded as he returned to the end of the walkway to the four Chosen who stood, trance-like, waiting for him by the door.

Kessler screamed. His body weighed him down, each slight movement firing up a thousand nerve endings. He breathed heavily into his vent and tried to fight the hurt. He stared at the syringe and reached out for it. So much pain. He rested the large needle against his forearm and pressed down hard as it penetrated the thick material of his suit. Finally the escape he needed. Finally he could rest his tired mind. He could feel it begin to prick against his skin. Finally he could forget about all his suffering. Forget about Bethany. A voice called to him. Quiet. Only a whisper amongst a million shattered threads of thought. Words lost in the clamour. "Bethany?"

"Faith Kes, I believe in you."

"No I can't," he grunted through gritted teeth.

"Faith," Bethany urged.

Kessler pulled himself up and looked around him to see Doc sat on his knees, the syringe in his hand. "No!" Kessler yelled as Doc injected the poison into his outstretched arm. He grabbed his knife from the floor and staggered towards Doc, every sinew straining, his mind full of the poisonous words that hammered his psyche. Using all his strength he brought the knife to bear on Doc's arm and, in a fountain of blood, it was severed. Doc gave a brief scream before slumping to the ground unconscious. Kessler emptied his friend's bag out onto the walkway's metal grating and quickly found a roll of bandages and made a tourniquet above the weeping stump. He looked at the doctor's pale, sweat covered face, "I couldn't let you do it, old friend. I'll get you out of here, I promise."

Lying on the platform beside Doc, Kessler, his head now clear, could see far below, amongst the flames and the broiling inferno, the crates of Lux piled high. There was a thud from the end of the walkway where Kessler saw Minos pushing a body through an open door. The long chute shook as it descended and, to a series of excited squeals down below, the building lit up as the factory came to life. The creatures were suddenly full of energy and scurried around the conveyor belt which now began to churn out more of the chem.

Pulling himself up from the floor, Kessler staggered towards the small man who beckoned another of his Chosen towards him. He noticed, amongst the deep folds of his robe, the large set of keys hanging from his waist. The door's mechanism began to whirl as it opened again and Minos took a step forward. Using his last reserves of energy, he hauled himself towards the creature, took hold of the keys and kicked him through the open door and down the chute. Kessler watched Minos fall as, with a sudden jolt, his feet flew from under him as the creature's cape caught hold of his foot as it followed its owner down into the darkness and the fire below.

Kessler's feet flailed wildly, unable to get any grip on the smooth sides of the chute. One of his hands hung by his side gripping the heavy metal keys, the other clung desperately to the platform's edge. The Chosen came alive, screamed and ran away, their frantic footfalls making the walkway sway back and forth. Kessler's grip loosened. He had no energy left, his body was on fire, his muscles ached. The heavy heat suit pulled at him, his grip slipping even further. He could take no more as he was pulled down into the darkness.

Doc's gloved hand appeared from the platform above and held Kessler's firmly, "Where do you think you are going?" He hauled him back up, his slight frame struggling to lift Kessler's heavy bulk, his blood soaked stump lying limp by his side. He coughed and wheezed at the effort.

They both lay flat on the metal grating catching their breath, "Doc, your arm, I'm so sorry." Doc did not reply. His body shook and fell back into unconsciousness.

There was an almighty shriek from down below. Kessler peered over the platform's edge to see the distinctive robes of Minos far below moving amongst the tiny creatures. He howled again. "It's not possible that he could have survived that fall!" Kessler shouted in exasperation.

The door from which Minos had originally emerged, closed and an elevator began to descend. Still lying sprawled on the walkway, Kessler cursed. Taking aim with his Luther, he fired two rounds, quickly making the closed doors a smoking mass of twisted metal. Another blast quickly severed the elevator's cables. He picked up Doc's prone body, threw him over his shoulder and, wincing as his own body struggled to take on the extra weight, he made for Bethany's cell. The heavy ring of keys fumbled in Kessler's large hands as he tried frantically to find the correct one.

"Doctor!" Bethany eyes moved from Doc's unconscious form to Kessler as he fumbled with the keys, "Hurry up!"

"I know, I know!" Finally the correct key slid effortlessly into the lock and the cell door swung open. Immediately the detective was knocked to the floor as the desperate inhabitants poured out.

"We must save the others." Bethany stammered feebly and tried to help Kessler up.

"We have no time." A lash of flame flashed passed them scorching the air. Kessler glanced down below to see Minos, cape billowing in the wind, climbing up towards the platform. A large curling lick of flame extended from his hand. He shrieked again and fire exploded against the underside of the platform.

"He'll be upon us soon." Bethany winced as yet more flame crashed against one of the cages setting alight to those within. The smell of incinerated flesh clung to each wail of terror.

"I'm not leaving without the others," Bethany shouted.

Kessler did not have the time to discuss options and grabbed Bethany, "We run!" They moved quickly down the walkway, smoke billowing all round them as yet more flame screeched past them. As he passed Bane, who was pressed tight against the front of the cell by a wall of wide eyed screaming faces, Kessler threw him the keys. Bane caught them and began to say something, but his voice and the red glare of his optics were lost amongst the desperate yells of burning bodies and the manic cries of the caged.

"All those people!" Bethany sobbed as she ran.

"I threw them the keys, it's every citizen for themselves now."

They began making their way down the ladder. Bethany first and Kessler moving slowly behind her. Sweat poured from every part of his body as he struggled to keep hold of each rung and bear Doc's weight. More lances of fire shot towards them from the platform as an infernal cry bellowed from above. Minos had climbed back onto the walkway and was reigning an inferno down upon them. He seemed to have grown in stature since his fall, the hunchbacked man now seemed to stand tall, his billowing robes parting to reveal a muscular, dark frame. His eyes were red with rage and the white light, which had so nearly tempted Kessler into the dark, was now gone. Fire exploded just above his head violently rocking the ladder.

At last they reached the entrance to the Core Tunnel. Bethany checked Doc's Ox, "He's still breathing," and pressed her ear against his chest, "what do we do, Kes? Where do we go?"

"Home." Kessler adjusted the weight of Doc's limp form and began to move quickly up the tunnel. Bethany followed behind. He wheezed and heaved into his vent at the exertion as he staggered up the tunnel. He eventually fell to the floor panting for breath.

Bethany knelt beside him, put her arm around him and drew him close, "C'mon, Kes. You've come this far, don't let it all be for nothing." Her voice cackled through her respirator's filter. Without a word he struggled back to his knees and continued pushing himself onwards.

They arrived at Tech Shaft Six to be greeted by the grimy, grinning faces of Opek and Bendle, "You took your time, Mr Kessler!" Opek crawled out of the shaft but his humour changed as soon as he saw the state of Doc, "What happened?"

Kessler shoved past Bendle and heaved, with some difficulty, Doc's body through the shaft's entrance and onto the waiting platform, "We need to get out of here. Quick." He turned to Bethany, "Beth, meet Opek and his son." The two Techs stepped into the small circle of light shone from their lanterns, both with their oil-stained gloved hands extended in greeting, "Hello Miss Bethany, Mr Kessler and the doctor have told us much about you."

Bethany knelt down low and shook both their hands, "I can't thank you enough for helping us." Bendle blushed and looked away. "But we can't leave just yet."

"We can't?" Opek looked up at Kessler, confused.

"Kes," Those green eyes, which so often raged with the passion of her convictions, now seemed broken, dulled with despair, "Back when I was in the cage, you told me that everything was going to be ok but it won't will it? Not unless we stop this, all of this, now, while we can." Despite being caked in dirt, sweat and dried blood and even though her skin was burnt red raw from exposure to the rads, her innocent, fragile beauty still managed to shine brighter than ever before. Kessler realised he admired her more now than he had ever admired anyone else before. He had never met a girl like her.

"We can't. We need to get Doc up top to be patched up and besides, what can we do?" Kessler stepped closer to Bethany and banged his fist against his chest, "What can a banged out old junkie like me do to save an entire city? I'm no good, too old, I have nothing left to give."

"You came all this way, and don't tell me it was just for the cred, Kes. I know you."

"You think you know me but you don't."

"I know you, Kes," Bethany repeated, "This world won't be worth anything if we let them continue to spread their poison. Kes, you have seen what they're doing, they're throwing our souls into the grinder and using it to make Lux. Whether you believe in God, Council, yourself, whatever, this is evil and it must be stopped."

Kessler could not bear looking into her eyes anymore and turned away only to be greeted by the Techs' concerned faces. Opek had his arm around his son who spoke, looking for guidance, "So what now Mr Kessler?" The youngster looked up at the broken detective, shrugged his shoulders, smiled and waited.

He looked at the Tech shaft that offered escape but escape to what? How long would it be before Bendle and other kids like him succumbed to Lux? Kessler's voice cracked with emotion, "I can't. I don't have any sim left and my strength has left me long ago. I'm not the man I once was."

"You don't need any sim, Kes. I saw you up above by the cells, I saw a strength in you, the will, the faith, to save me and Doc." She pressed her hand to his chest, "All you require is right here. My uncle always told me that whatever happens to our body, our soul remains pure. You just need to find it again and believe in yourself."

"How can I destroy them? My weapon and Doc's rifle are all we have."

Kessler felt something tug on his suit and looked down to see Bendle beside him, arm outstretched holding up a small bag. "That should do the trick, Mr Kessler."

"I don't understand." He took the bag from the young Tech.

"Engineer's blast powder, we use it to get through this rock and, generally blow stuff up." Bendle smiled, "Here's the detonator, just keep it on the powder and press this button when you are a good distance away."

"Wait." Opek shook his head, "We don't have enough energy for any delay, my batteries will fail and we'll be stuck here."

"We can power down the relay for a few moments without losing connection, can't we pa? That should give us some time."

"Yes, but not much, maybe thirty-five minutes, forty maximum."

"Ok. If I hurry, that gives me just enough time to set the charges." Kessler could not believe what he was saying or what he was about to do.

Opek looked at his son, stroked his chin and smiled, "Yes, that should work but Mr Kessler after forty minutes we're going, we will not be able to wait for you."

Doc coughed and moaned, Bethany gripped Kessler and wheezed, "You must hurry."

With a nod of his head, Kessler turned on a display in his visor which began a count down from forty minutes and raced back down the tunnel towards the fire.

·THE DARKNESS OF LIGHT·

Kessler arrived at the end of the Core Tunnel and fell to the ground heaving for air, the canisters in his respirator flashing empty. He quickly grabbed more Ox and feverishly breathed in the new air. A quick check of his time revealed ten minutes had expired. With his viewfinder, he quickly caught sight of the factory across the plasma field, the only route to which was a small walkway dug into the wall of the vast cavern. With no time to lose he ran holding his Luther in one hand and Bendle's blast powder in the other, trying to ignore the insanity of what he was doing. "It's simple," he spoke aloud, trying to convince himself, "set the blast powder in the factory and run as fast as possible back up to safety. Simple." His respirator hissed and whirled as he breathed hard, struggling to get Ox into his tired lungs, the putrid sulphurous fumes from the plasma threatening to overcome him. A quick glance at the broiling, bubbling thick liquid a few feet to his left reminded him to watch his step.

As he approached the factory he realised that it was a much larger structure than he had first imagined. Kneeling behind an outcrop of rock, he looked for a way he could approach the building undetected. Smoke bellowed out of numerous stacks and steam hissed from stuttering pistons as it churned out its poison. Beyond the stacked boxes of Lux, Kessler could just make out the conveyor belt which moved at a steady pace surrounded by those small black scaled creatures he had observed from the other side of the plasma field. They stood at just over a foot high, each wearing gloves and an apron as they inspected the boxes in a flurry of movement and excitement.

The horn sounded its dreaded knell and the factory came to a juddering halt. The workers stood still each looking up at the platform above, waiting for their grim delivery. Kessler went to leave the cover of the rock but each time had to return. He cursed his cautiousness. He should have approached the factory under the cover of its smoke and noise while the creatures were distracted by their toils. Now, with production of Lux stopped, he had to wait.

It was not long before the screams of those caged above reached his ears and the chute began to shake as somebody, some good soul, plummeted down to its terrible end. The thin material of the chute stretched and pulled as it shook, a dull yellow light from within making it semi translucent and, much to Kessler's disgust, he saw the dark shadow of a body pass down into the main structure of the factory and in a few seconds boxes of Lux appeared as the conveyor belt began to move.

The production line was in full flow and with it the distraction Kessler needed. Using the smoke and steam that roared out of the stacks and vents as cover, he hunched down low and quickly made his move. The building itself had an outer shell constructed of cadermite that protected the inner workings from the intense heat of the plasma. Through a window, he could see hundreds of cogs turning rapidly below which was a vast array of transformers, breakers and switches. He doubted that the blast powder was that powerful and knocking out a small part of the machinery would not halt production for long, certainly not permanently. He took another panicked glance at his visor's display to confirm what he dreaded, only fifteen minutes remained until they left for the city above. Hardly enough time to make it back.

Another look through another window revealed cables leading from pulsing blue energy cells which hummed with power. Immediately Kessler knew that if the unstable plasma found within the energy cells came into contact with even a small blast then the combined explosion would be devastating. A quick search soon found a hatch a few feet to his right and he turned the handle and entered.

Kessler was greeted by a vast room that would be in complete darkness if it was not for the orange glow from the small windows and the numerous flashing lights covering the walls, consoles and panels that threw blue across various pieces of equipment. He knelt down underneath the power cells and unravelled the air tight sealed bag which contained the blast powder and rested the explosive charge by the energy cells. He held the remote detonator up to the bright, flashing blue light of a nearby panel and examined it briefly before turning it on.

Just as he had set the charge the flashing blue haze turned to a deep red and a high pitch whining noise began to squeal. Kessler spun round for fear of being discovered when a platform began to lower from the ceiling. He pointed his Luther at the rapidly descending floor, readying himself for the worst.

Through the red light, Kessler first saw the face, arms, a torso and then finally feet appear as it descended down into the depths of the room. It became immediately clear to Kessler that this person was of no threat to him. The rag-covered, emaciated body of what he could only assume was one of the Chosen hung, suspended, upside down, arms outstretched either side of his body. Hundreds of black wires had attached themselves to his chest, stomach and face and they fed into a large container that stood up right next to him. Kessler was transfixed by the gruesome image and nearly dropped his carbine to the floor as he stared at the face, mouth wide open, frozen in one last silent scream. His eyes, wide with terror stared out between a thick fringe that was soaked with dirt and sweat. Kessler could only imagine the horror of what he had gone through. He moved closer as the container began to bubble and fill with a white liquid. His gaze returned to the man and reeled back, falling to the floor, as his eyes moved. Kessler gasped as the body weakly struggled, pupils erratically darting everywhere in panic. He got back to his feet, "I'll get you out of this!" He frantically pulled at the wires which had embedded themselves deep within his body. Each tug seemed to give him more pain as his eyes widened further in shock until they eventually rolled into unconsciousness and finally death. In seconds, before Kessler's eyes, the body began to shrivel up until only the skeletal form remained, empty bags of leathery skin hung from bone. He could not bear another glance at the face of what was once a man.

"So this is how they make their poison," Kessler muttered to himself. He had never believed in the soul, never thought there was more to this life than this city and the pure instinct of survival. Bethany and Beck had both said that the Malebranche sought out good souls for their chem, only the best they said and he wondered what good in this fetid city this citizen, this person, had done.

In his desperation to get out he ran out of the hatch and right into one of the small creatures. Both fell to the floor. The tiny creature, with its black scaled skin and tiny red eyes, jumped back up to its feet quickly, hissed and spat at him with a long tongue which protruded from a red, fang-filled maw.

A buzz in his ear brought a message from Opek, "Mr Kessler, you there?"

"Yes Opek, go ahead." The creature, tilted its head slowly from side to side, focused on his every move.

"We really need to be going! We're running on empty."

"I'm coming now, just hold on Opek."

"Ok." With that the com was silent.

With a renewed urgency, Kessler left the strange creature

behind and ran for the tunnel. Pain, tiredness, sim, all were forgotten, replaced by the all consuming desire to escape this place.

When he was some distance away from the factory he stopped. Pushing the button on the detonator immediately produced a huge explosion that mushroomed up towards the cavern ceiling as the plasma in the energy cells ignited. The factory collapsed in on itself bringing the chute, which was already ablaze, crashing down from the platform above. He turned and resumed his race back to Opek and home.

For the first time in a long while Kessler began to believe that he may actually make it back home alive. He could now easily make out the entrance to the Core Tunnel just ahead. Another explosion thundered overhead bringing down with it a shower of debris as the platform and its cages crashed into the plasma.

A flash of flame burst in front of the detective throwing him to the ground. His knee hit hard off the rocky floor twisting awkwardly causing pain to shoot through his body. He yelled as he tried to stand, shifting his weight onto his good leg.

Out of the smoke from the blast emerged the huge form of Minos. His long flowing robes had mostly burnt away and the material that remained was charred and still smouldering. Dark black and red polished scales glinted in the light of the fire raging all around them. Gone was the old man, gone the brilliant white light and now all was replaced with gleaming scales and vicious barbs which covered his muscular form. He snarled, revealing long black fangs in a blood red mouth as he walked towards Kessler, toying with his fiery whip which snapped flames from its lash.

Kessler, yelled, "You can't make anymore of that filth. It's finished."

Minos smiled and hissed, his voice reverberating through Kessler's mind, "*You Chaff are so dramatic.*" He words mocked the detective, "*You think this world begins and ends with your pitiful existence.*" He snapped his whip causing flame and smoke to encircle them, "*Whatever occurs here will not stop the inevitable. You have heard the voice, yes? In your dreams you see it happen. This city is drenched in sin, you can see it everywhere, smell it,*" he sniffed the air, "*taste it, touch it. Delicious.*" He stood over Kessler and laughed, "*This will be home, the light is coming to this city. It is inevitable.*" The voice echoed in his head as explosions caused rocks to rain down from above as the cavern itself violently shook. Huge pieces of debris plunged into the broiling plasma causing splatters of the fiery liquid to fly through the air and drench the rock around them in flashes of sizzling smoke.

Minos stood over the detective who raised his Luther in defence before a quick snap brought down the flaming grip of the whip around his arm, throwing his carbine skidding away across the floor. Flames began to engulf the detective's arm as the creature stood over his prone body which teetered on the edge of the path and pressed a black, clawed foot down hard on Kessler's helmet, forcing him ever closer to the bubbling plasma. He flailed wildly as he desperately tried to throw the monster off balance however Minos had him pinned firmly to the ground. More flame caught his suit and Kessler screamed as the heat took hold. "No!" He bellowed hoarsely as Minos's deep blood-curdling laugh resounded throughout his mind.

Fire had danced its way across Kessler's body and he could feel the searing agony as his suit began to melt all the while Minos, with his clawed foot, pushed him down towards molten death. Another explosion rattled the cavern as a torrent of rubble crashed down upon them striking Minos and throwing the creature from him. Immediately Kessler rolled along the ground desperately trying to dampen the flames which were consuming him.

Smouldering, he picked up his weapon and glanced over to

where Minos lay buried beneath a large boulder. Kessler breathed a quick sigh of relief before quickly making his way up through the Core Tunnel, his busted knee and scorched, half melted heat suit forcing him to stagger and lean onto the tunnel's wall for support. Explosions were joined by screams and wails as some of the Chosen ran past, frantically scrambling their way up the tunnel.

A flash of light illuminated terrified faces and a horrifying roar, from somewhere behind them, bellowed bringing with it screams of fear. Kessler tried to quicken his pace but the sheer agony from his knee reduced him to a feeble shuffle. Another burst of light brought with it a streak of flame which caught hold of one of the Chosen just ahead of Kessler and in a blurr of movement the young lady was dragged back down the tunnel. The light disappeared instantly, quickly replaced by the dark red glow. 'Minos…' Kessler thought and he cursed himself for not killing him when he had the chance. Another flash and again a lance of flame screamed passed him as another fell to the flames in a series of gurgled screams.

At any moment Kessler knew that the monster would be upon him and he waited to feel the flaming lash of his whip. He clung to the tunnel's side as he desperately hobbled forwards, hoping, praying that each flash of burning light did not mean his end. However after a few moments of clambering forward, Opek's lantern came into view just as another roar thundered up the tunnel. Kessler gritted his teeth and he scrambled for the Tech shaft.

Reaching the shaft's entrance, he fell to his knees and began to sob, all his strength gone, his hopes dashed. There was nobody there, only darkness where the capsule should be. He slumped to the floor as tears streamed down over his respirator. Another feral scream as the tunnel lit up in fire to the sound of cries and wails which resigned Kessler to his fate, "Come and get me!" His voice cracked in his scorched dry throat, "I've nothing left." He pulled himself up and aimed his Luther down the tunnel towards the explosions of light and the angry howls of Minos who was getting ever closer.

"Don't give up now, Mr Kessler, we aren't home yet!" Opek's high-pitched voice and the screech of mechanical gears from the descending platform greeted the shocked detective who stared tearfully into the light of Opek's torch.

"You came back for me? I thought you'd gone." He scrambled onto the platform and fell, his knee giving in as the two Techs hauled his bulky frame into the small space.

"We heard the commotion down the tunnel and thought we'd hide further up the shaft but we must go now, the batteries are almost out!"

"Quick, he's right behind us!" Kessler squeezed himself into the cramped pod and held onto the unconscious forms of Doc and Bethany.

Opek dialled into a small console which projected a keypad, illuminating the interior in green light. "End of the line, D1. Downtown here we come!"

The capsule began to ascend when a deafening roar came from below followed by an explosion of flame which crashed against the underside of the capsule. The platform came to a juddering halt and lurched sideways. Opek gasped, his small hand holding onto the side of the pod as part of the floor gave way. Kessler grabbed hold of his arm as, below, the flaming face of Minos stared up at them, the long fiery tendrils of his whip curled tight around Opek's leg.

"I'm losing him!" Kessler struggled to keep his grip on Opek's oil-stained overalls as flames took hold of him. The capsule's motor whined and creaked with the strain as it tried to pull away.

The whip tightened as the pod began to buckle, "I love you son," and he was gone, his small body tumbling down into the darkness and the flames below.

Bendle screamed, "Pa!" He went to leap from the capsule

when Kessler grabbed him around his waist and hauled him kicking and screaming back away from the edge.

"It's no good Bendle, he's gone, he's gone!" Kessler held him tightly with one arm, the other cradling both Bethany and Doc as the pod picked up speed and ascended away from the chaos of the flaming light and towards the cold darkness of Dis.